"The frequent and chilling zombie encounters highlight both Campbell's competence in presenting horrific gore and his insistence that dedication to humanity is also the strongest definition of faith."

—*Publishers Weekly*

OMEGA DAYS

"A highly entertaining read with a style that grabbed me from the very first page . . . There are creepy echoes . . . of masters like King and Koontz . . . If you want highly entertaining, escapist zombie fiction with plenty of action, peopled by rich and interesting characters, you couldn't do better than *Omega Days*."

—*SFRevu*

"Nobody writes an urban battle scene quite like [Campbell] does. The pace of his storytelling will leave you breathless, and his characters are so real and so likeable you will jump up and cheer for them. *Omega Days* is, hands down, one of the shining stars of the zombie genre."

—Joe McKinney, Bram Stoker Award–winning author of *Plague of the Undead*

"Characters as diverse as a priest fallen from grace to a prisoner who finds his heart are all in this story of terror . . . Campbell is good with characters . . . It's stories like *Omega Days*, with a setting in a popular city that most people have heard about, that can take an average story and make it unique."

—Examiner.com

"An impressively convincing vision of a world suddenly gone insane . . . The maelstrom that Campbell creates is a somber portrayal of the human capacity for both selfishness and, more rarely, altruism. He effectively builds a mood of terror that sweeps the reader along in this powerful example of the zombie thriller genre at its best."

—*Publishers Weekly* (starred review)

Berkley Books by John L. Campbell

OMEGA DAYS

SHIP OF THE DEAD

DRIFTERS

DRIFTERS

AN OMEGA DAYS NOVEL

JOHN L. CAMPBELL

BERKLEY BOOKS, NEW YORK

THE BERKLEY PUBLISHING GROUP
Published by the Penguin Group
Penguin Group (USA) LLC
375 Hudson Street, New York, New York 10014

USA • Canada • UK • Ireland • Australia • New Zealand • India • South Africa • China

penguin.com

A Penguin Random House Company

This book is an original publication of The Berkley Publishing Group.

Library of Congress Cataloging-in-Publication Data

Campbell, John L. (Investigator)
Drifters / John L. Campbell. — Berkley trade paperback edition.
pages ; cm. — (An Omega Days novel ; 3)
ISBN 978-0-425-27265-7 (softcover)
1. Zombies—Fiction.   2. Survival—Fiction.   3. Virus diseases—Fiction.   I. Title.
PS3603.A47727D75 2015
813'.6—dc23
2014035727

PUBLISHING HISTORY
Berkley trade paperback edition / January 2015

PRINTED IN THE UNITED STATES OF AMERICA

10 9 8 7 6 5 4 3 2 1

Cover images: Omega symbol © Morphart Creation; Landscape © Alta Oosthuizen;
Helicopter © Ivan Cholakov; Texture © Sanexi; Zombie © Jeff Thrower—all Shutterstock.
Cover design by Diana Kolsky.
Interior text design by Laura K. Corless.
Title page art © iStockphoto.com/trigga.

There are precious few people we know who truly believe in us; they will stand by us no matter what we do or say, and will defend us against all foes, real or imagined. They love us, want the best for us, let us lean on them when we're not strong enough to stand on our own, and encourage us to be amazing when all the world says otherwise. They are the people upon whom we build a life. For me that is, and will always be, Linda. This book is for her, because of all that she is and because she shares the dream.

DEAD
OF JANUARY

ONE

In life she had been Sharon Douglas-Frye, thirty-three, mother of two. A music scholarship took her to the University of Illinois, where she met Joseph, a grad student with plans for starting a heavy equipment dealership in California. Marriage, house, kids, book club, Pilates.

She had been bitten while sitting at an outside table of a sidewalk café by a little boy wearing an Angry Birds shirt, a wild little thing with no mommy in sight. Not even a real bite, really, more of a nip. She cleaned and bandaged it at home. Joseph was away on business, no need to worry him.

Sharon died of fever in the master bedroom of her lovely Chico home.

She came back and ate her children; parts of them, at least.

Then she ate Joe when he got home from his trip. The kids helped her with Daddy. Since that day, Sharon had seen none of them and wouldn't have recognized them anyway.

Now, five months later, Sharon Douglas-Frye shuffled barefoot through a January hay field of brittle stubble, her feet black and torn, the meat worn off several toes. She wore the tatters of a floral-print nightgown that drooped off one shoulder, exposing an emaciated body with flattened breasts, jutting ribs, and skin the color of old wax. Her face was drawn and tight, decaying jaw muscles visible through holes in her flesh, teeth clicking incessantly. Her eyes were a cloudy blue shot through with black blood vessels.

The hay crackled beneath her feet and her arms flopped as she walked, following the sound of crows. That sound always meant food, either what the crow was eating or the crow itself, if it wasn't fast enough. The birds were usually too quick and clever to permit Sharon to catch them, however.

A few others of her kind slumped through the field around her. Sharon paid them no mind.

It was cool; the barest of breezes made her knotted hair rustle about her shoulders. She trudged directly through the skeletal remains of a cow, the bones gnawed clean, catching and ripping her nightgown on a thick, upward-curving rib. As she moved past, her left hand banged against the rib, and Sharon didn't notice when both her engagement and wedding rings at last rattled off her bony finger and dropped into the hay stubble.

The crows called, and Sharon kept moving.

To her right, a man who had once sold used cars moved through the field with jerking steps, still wearing the remains of a shirt and tie, his skin a mottled olive streaked with black, now split and hanging about him in loose, sour ribbons. Strands of a comb-over fluttered about a face so torn it revealed bone, and the car salesman was bent forward and to the side by a pair of fractured vertebrae, grinding against each other with every step.

The three coyotes that had been trailing the salesman for the past hour finally decided he posed no threat. They darted in and took him down at the knees, and the salesman groaned and flapped his arms as they devoured him.

Sharon didn't notice the coyotes. She heard crows.

A sharp, twisted piece of metal severed two toes on Sharon's left foot as she walked through the hay field. She stumbled, then got tangled in a swirl of burned electrical wiring. That made her fall down, and she crawled toward the sound of the crows for almost an hour before she managed to free herself of the wiring and could stand once more.

There were a lot of sharp things in this field, bent shapes and pieces of metal blackened by fire, scattered over a hundred yards. The hay stubble was brittle and ashy where it had been burned, snapping under her feet, and she could still smell the smoke from the fire. That usually meant food too. She fell again, this time tripping over a long, slender length of melted polymer, constructed in a honeycomb pattern. Sharon rose once more, walked on, and at last reached the place with the crows.

Half a dozen of the glossy black birds were perched on the fuselage of the Black Hawk helicopter, which lay on its side in the field. The tail boom was gone along with both turbines, and only the troop compartment and shattered cockpit remained, all of it scorched.

The crows shrieked in annoyance as Sharon stumbled to where the cockpit windscreen had been, a few melted fragments clinging to the edges of the frame. The body of a tall man was still strapped in the pilot's seat, slumped against his belts, his blackened skin picked away to reveal dripping, red meat. His flight helmet and head had been caved in when the cockpit hit the ground nose first, and so he was not moving.

Sharon moaned and reached inside, tugging at an arm, trying to bring it to her mouth, snapping her teeth. It didn't quite reach, and so she started to whine, pulling herself up through the frame and into the cockpit, tearing her own flesh on jagged aluminum and sharp

Plexiglas. Her feet left the ground as she wriggled through, at last stuffing the fingers of the pilot's dead hand into her mouth. Sharon chewed and grunted, and the crows watched.

Orlando Worthy was a biter.

The Chico police had long ago nicknamed him Orlando the Impaler. He had drifted into the Northern California city at age twenty-six, after receiving parole on a seven-year stretch for armed robbery (he slashed a female store detective's face with a fish-cleaning knife in front of a discount store) and had remained in Chico for the next twenty-two years.

In those two-plus decades Orlando had bitten nineteen people during meth transactions, bar fights, domestic disturbances, and just because. He bit another nine police officers and seventeen store detectives over the course of fifty-three arrests for petty theft. He bit a cocker spaniel when it barked at him in Bidwell Park. As payment for the biting, he had been hit with nightsticks, pepper spray, Tasers, a beanbag round from a less-than-lethal police shotgun, two kitchen knives, a tire iron, and countless punches and kicks.

By the time he turned forty-eight—the summer of the plague—Orlando already looked like a zombie, the meth wasting his body and aging his features. He was so distorted by the drug that a twenty-year montage of his booking photos had become one of the highest-viewed online features at Faces of Meth, a dramatic progression of decline that he bragged was his second claim to fame.

His first was boosting. Orlando Worthy had been a professional shoplifter for his entire life. Not professional in the sense that he was too good to get caught—he had been caught plenty of times, and his face was known by every cop, retailer, and security guard in Butte County—but in the fact that he did it for a living and was skilled in using the tools of the trade.

His bony hands could snap off security tags faster than an electronic detacher. When he couldn't break the tags, he used wire cutters, or stuffed the goods inside foil-lined bags to defeat the electronic pedestals at the front doors. If a garment was affixed with ink tags, he would just put it in the freezer overnight and snap them off harmlessly in the morning. For the big, cabled Alpha tags, the screamers, he would go in with a large drink from 7-Eleven, dip the sensor until it shorted out, and then clip it off with his cutters. Retailers called this *drowning tags*. A flat-head screwdriver could get him into locked electronics and jewelry cases, and threats of violence and biting stopped most store owners and at least two-thirds of store detectives from trying to apprehend him.

Some weren't intimidated, and Orlando had taken his share of beatings.

Orlando Worthy stole whatever he could sell, and that was most everything. There were always buyers for Polo shirts, fragrances, Timberland boots, and Under Armour. Anything Apple was a hot commodity, as well as electronic games and learning toys. Shrimp, condoms, batteries, leather jackets, women's shoes, Lego, and pocketbooks—everything had a market. He would steal powdered baby formula by the case and sell it to drug dealers who used it as a safe way to cut heroin, or to welfare moms who paid him twenty cents on the dollar. If a woman walked away from her purse at a grocery store, it was his. If someone left their car unlocked near him, they would return to find their GPS and any spare change missing.

Orlando liked to think of himself as the Prince of Thieves. He didn't understand the literary reference to the nickname *the Impaler*, and no one bothered to explain it to him.

In August of last year, Orlando scooted out of a store with seven pairs of snowy-white Nikes, aluminum foil wrapped tightly around the sensors to prevent the pedestals from sounding. He ducked behind the store, on high alert for signs of pursuit, relaxing only when he realized no one was coming. He was shaking, not just from the adrenaline; the pipe was calling. Not just calling, but *singing*.

A beefy kid in his twenties emerged from behind a Dumpster, a store detective Orlando knew well, and who knew the meth addict just as well.

"Oh, shit," Orlando said, bracing himself as the kid galloped in and tackled him. As they hit the pavement together, Orlando growled and bit the kid's arm.

The kid bit him back and damn near tore his right ear off.

Orlando shrieked and hammered at the store detective with his fists, squirming beneath his bulk and slipping free. The kid snarled, glassy-eyed with Orlando's blood smeared across his face, and the meth addict ran. He didn't care about Nikes anymore. The look on the kid's face held the promise of death beside a stinking Dumpster.

He made it seven blocks, stumbling along a sidewalk with both hands pressed to the dangling flap that had been his ear, blood streaking his neck and dampening his clothes. A police cruiser slid to the curb and the young officer inside immediately recognized Orlando. He leaped out of the cruiser and slammed Orlando to the ground, cuffing him. If Orlando Worthy was running and bleeding, he surmised, then he had been up to some illegal shit and that was probable cause enough. The young officer didn't want to hear his protests of innocence, cared nothing for the meth head's claims about a cannibalistic store detective. He took him to Enloe Medical Center.

Enloe folded within twelve hours.

When Orlando turned, he had a pressure bandage with heavy gauze wound around his head and was handcuffed to a bed rail in the emergency room. He tugged and rattled the cuff for five months before decay finally tightened his flesh enough to pull his hand free.

There was nothing left to eat in the hospital, so he wandered out. Eventually he heard crows, understood that it meant meat, and made his way to the sound. When he reached the debris of the wrecked Black Hawk, he saw that another of his kind was already dangling out the cockpit as it fed. Orlando Worthy crawled up and in beside her, moaning as he pushed her over a bit so he could also reach the meal in the flight suit.

Sharon didn't appear to mind the company.

They had both been dispatchers for Chico Emergency Services, Patty Phuong and Patty MacLaren. The first Patty was petite to the point of being childlike, the second a solid woman with red hair and a booming personality. Cops, firemen, and paramedics, without exception, called them Rice Patty and Patty Wagon. Neither woman took offense, and they even had coffee cups at their workstations bearing the nicknames.

Friends both on and off the clock, the two women no longer knew one another as they shuffled across the winter hay field, walking together by chance alone. Their uniforms hung in tatters and the flesh beneath was a speckled gray and maroon. Rice Patty had lost an eye and most of the flesh on one side of her face. Big Patty Wagon was missing her left arm at the shoulder, and her meaty body was peppered with blackened buckshot patterns.

The women began moaning as they neared the Black Hawk, spotting the figures already feeding there. Then their attention was drawn to the right as a pair of indignant crows, working at something on the ground, took flight in a flurry of black feathers. Rice Patty and Patty Wagon lurched over to see what the birds had been eating.

It was the lower torso of a woman, hips and legs only, with burned fatigues tucked into combat boots. The crash had pitched this bloody mass thirty feet away from the helicopter. The two Pattys dropped to all fours and began to feed, side by side.

.   .   .

Along the length of Mulberry Street in Chico, drifters wandered with arms dangling at their sides, shuffling through blown trash and dropped luggage and abandoned cars. They moved beneath darkened traffic signals and past houses and businesses with broken windows and kicked-in doors. Spray-painted signs, messages to family members about whether someone was alive and where they had gone, marred walls and pavement. A drifter locked in the backseat of a patrol car pressed its rotting face against the glass and pounded a fist with a steady rhythm. Black, crispy shapes moved through the skeletal remains of a burned movie theater, and things dressed in the baggy clothes and knit caps of hipsters walked stiffly along the paths of Chico State University.

Coyotes loped through the quiet streets. Sometimes they fed, sometimes they were fed upon.

A single rifle shot echoed through the bare limbs of winter trees, and a V of honking Canada geese passed high overhead. The wind blew newspapers and foam cups down boulevards of stopped vehicles, and whistled through the space left between a pair of municipal trucks parked nose to nose in an attempt to block a street. Drifters wearing summer clothes shuffled around the ends of the trucks and kept going with no particular destination in mind.

Along Vallombrosa Avenue, where it ran alongside Bidwell Park, crows perched on the wooden crosspieces of the tall, heavy crucifixes planted there, picking at the flesh of still-moving corpses lashed and nailed to the wood in a line that stretched for three blocks. Occasionally a crow would get careless and a head would snap over, teeth crunching down on bone and feathers. For the most part, the birds were clever enough to stay clear of the bite.

The wind ruffled the clothing and hair of the crucified, carrying their moans away.

TWO

August—Sacramento

It was two minutes past six when Dean West let himself into Premier Arms, deactivating the alarm and locking the doors behind him, switching on a few lights. Opening wasn't until nine, and Tony and Juan wouldn't be in until eight. The daycare offered early drop-off hours, which worked well as Leah was an early riser, and so Dean looked forward to a couple hours of solitude before the actual workday began. He was restoring an M-1 Garand, the standard-issue rifle of World War II GIs, and the quiet would allow him to give the old weapon the attention it deserved.

Dean was thirty-three and fit, hardened by his former military service, and maintained by five days a week at the gym, plus racquetball. He had to stay in shape to keep up with his wife, a fitness junkie. Not that he minded her dedication. Angie West was a MILF if ever there was one, though he caught a hard slap on the behind when he used the term. Just shy of six feet, handsome by any standards, Dean had tousled brown hair, dark eyes, and a scruff of whiskers on his angled face that Angie said made him look rugged and sexy. He suggested the sexy came from his biceps and washboard abs. She didn't disagree.

According to their every-other-day rotation, it was his wife's turn for drop-off at the daycare, but Angie was in Alameda today filming a segment with her uncle, Bud Franks. They were showing off the fifty-caliber Barrett. Flexibility, Angie and Dean agreed, was one of the keys to a successful marriage, and since she was traveling, he took up the slack. It would balance out later when it was his turn to be out of town, and he didn't mind, anyway. He was crazy about their two-year-old daughter, and even at her tender age, she knew she had her daddy completely wrapped around a tiny finger.

Thinking of being out of town, Dean reminded himself to check his calendar. He was pretty sure the producers of *Angie's Armory* were planning a shoot for next week involving a "Life at Home" segment, featuring scenes showing Dean and Angie around the house, having dinner, and playing with Leah. He'd have to get a haircut. They also wanted him to do a shirtless bit, but he hadn't yet decided if he would. Actually, Angie hadn't decided.

Premier Arms was a Franks family enterprise, but Dean and Angie ran it. Her dad was semiretired and contented himself with occasional shifts at the smaller shop he had up in Chico, only showing up here in Sacramento for an occasional business meeting or when filming required his attendance. Premier Arms was the "big" shop comprising converted warehouses nestled between Sacramento's industrial and commercial areas. It boasted a large store that served as the showroom; a public firing range; the machine shop where they fabricated, serviced, and restored weapons; some small offices; a receiving bay; and a pair of classrooms for gun safety courses. There were over forty full- and part-time employees, and they needed six or seven more now that the show had taken off, driving traffic and sales.

Dean walked through the silent showroom and into the back, setting down his coffee and switching on the shop's lights. At his regular worktable, the metalwork of the Garand rested in a pair of clamps. He turned on the iPod nearby, set it to a nineties playlist, and within minutes was lost in the detail work of professional gunsmithing.

"Dean!"

The yell made him jump, and Dean spun to see Juan Vega, one of his senior guys, standing at the end of the worktable. The digital clock on the shop wall read 7:01. He hadn't even noticed the hour go by. He switched off the iPod.

"I been calling you," said Juan, "and yelled at you three times."

Dean shrugged. "The music's on. What are you so worked up about?" He had meant it to be casual until he noticed that Juan *was* worked up. He looked pale and was sweating, and his eyes darted around too much and too fast. Then Dean noticed that Juan was wearing a big-frame automatic in a belt holster. "You okay, man?"

"Where you been?" Juan demanded, his voice higher than normal. "What are you doing here?"

Dean frowned. "What does it look like? Is Tony with you?"

Juan shook his head angrily and waved a hand. "No, why are you *here*?"

Now Dean got angry. "Because it's my place. You're not making sense. And why are you strapped?" He pointed to the pistol on Juan's hip.

The other man seemed not to hear him. "I tried calling. I didn't think anyone would be here, but I drove down just to check. I saw your truck outside. Tony isn't answering either. I'm going to pick up Marta and the kids." It all came out in a rush, and Juan was leaning a palm against the worktable as if he might fall down. Dean held up his hands.

"Slow down, buddy. Breathe or you're going to pass out."

Juan looked at him as if Dean were speaking another language. "You haven't heard the radio?"

Dean shook his head and pointed to the iPod.

"You don't know shit, do you?"

Dean shook his head again.

"It's fucking crazy out there," Juan said. "There's rioting, bodies in the streets, fires. . . . People are attacking each other, killing each other with their bare hands. I saw a police car on fire." Juan grabbed his friend's arm and gave him a shake. "Are you listening? I saw a helicopter fly over, and the guy in the door was firing his machine gun down into the street, looked like at a crowd of people." He wiped a shaking hand across his face.

Dean tilted his head. "Don't fuck with me, Juan. This better not be some gag you and the crew worked up, some punking bullshit."

The look on the other man's face told Dean it wasn't. Juan wasn't that good an actor.

"Tony doesn't answer his phone," Juan said again. "I'm going to get Marta at her office, and then we'll get the kids from her mother's. Where's Angie?"

"Oakland. She's with Bud and the film crew."

"You gotta get Leah, man," Juan urged, tugging on his friend and leading him out into the showroom. "You gotta get the fuck out of Dodge. People are gonna come here." He gestured at the locked cases of rifles and pistols. "They're gonna take all this. You can't be here when they do."

Before Dean could reply, Juan went around one of the counters and used his keys to unlock a rifle case and the cabinet beneath it, pulling down a pair of black clip-fed Mossberg twelve-gauges and stacking several boxes of shells on the glass. Dean said nothing, only pulled out his cell phone and dialed the daycare but only got the busy signal. He dialed Angie and it went straight to message. He texted her, *R U OK?*

Juan quickly loaded both shotguns and came from behind the counter, handing one to his boss along with two boxes of ammuni-

tion. "The radio was talking about a virus," he said, "probably ter-
rorism, some kind of biological attack. Another station said zombies—
fucking *zombies*, man. I saw some shit in the street on the way
over. . . ." He trailed off, looking at the door.

Dean snorted. "Zombies? Brother, if this is some kind of punk,
you are *so* fired."

Juan just nodded slowly, his eyes on the door. Then from outside
came a pair of pistol shots, close together, and both men jumped. A
third shot rang out.

"Does that sound like a punk?" Juan asked.

"Watch the door," said Dean, going behind the counter and
unlocking another cabinet, pulling out a Glock forty-caliber in a pad-
dle holster and clipping it to his belt. "Go get Marta. Call me when
you can."

Juan looked sharply at his friend. "You're not gonna try to stay
here, right?"

"Hell no, that's what insurance is for. It covers civil disorder, but
I don't know about zombies." Dean had said it to make his friend
smile, but it didn't work, and that scared him. "Let's go out together."

The two men moved to the front door and peeked outside. In the
lot was Juan's white Jeep parked next to Dean's black Suburban. Out
on the road that ran past Premier Arms, a tractor-trailer was stopped
in the far lane, the driver's door open, no sign of the trucker.

"When I was coming over here," Juan whispered, "I saw—" He
hissed and pointed. "There! What the fuck is that?"

A woman in a yellow tank top was walking past the Suburban,
her shirt covered in fresh blood, most of her face missing, head tilted
at an odd angle. She suddenly increased her pace, breaking into a
grotesque gallop as she moved to the left and out of sight. A moment
later there was another pistol shot, followed by a man's scream.

Juan crossed himself and muttered something Dean couldn't hear.

"Let's go," said Dean, racking his shotgun and pushing through the door. Once outside, Dean took the time to lower and lock the security gate—no sense making it easy for the bastards—before turning toward the parking lot. Juan was a few feet away, staring at a point just past the tractor-trailer. The woman in the tank top was on all fours in the road, kneeling next to a man in gray coveralls. They were ripping at the body of a man in a flannel shirt and work boots, still gripping a pistol. They were . . . eating him.

"Go," Dean said, pushing his friend. "Go get Marta."

Juan nodded and walked to his Jeep, moving like a sleepwalker, unable to take his eyes off the grisly scene. Dean jogged to the Suburban and fired it up but didn't pull out until Juan's Jeep finally started moving. In his rearview he could see the two figures devouring the third, and he didn't miss the fact that the sounds of the starting engines made them both look up. Moments later Juan was on the road, and Dean pulled out, heading in the opposite direction.

Sunrise Daycare was five miles away, almost an equal distance between Premier Arms and his and Angie's house. It was a good place, a safe place where the teachers and kids regularly drilled on crisis procedures. Leah would be okay.

The busy signal that greeted him every time he called seemed to argue the point.

She would be okay, he insisted. But it didn't prevent him from stomping the accelerator and rocketing into the commercial district.

Juan had been right. It was coming apart.

The black smoke of structure fires climbed over the roofs of buildings, and the air was full of sirens. There was traffic, even at this early hour, and it was moving fast, people blowing lights and cutting through corner gas stations, swerving around vehicles stopped in the street. An olive-drab helicopter swooped low over a strip mall, followed a moment later by a second and a third.

Dean watched the choppers pass from right to left and gripped the steering wheel tightly to keep his hands from trembling. He tried to control his breathing as he switched on the radio, punching in a local news channel.

"... *biological hazard, said Major Phillip Jeffries, U.S. Army physician and part of the Army's program on chemical and biological warfare. Dr. Jeffries stated that he was in regular contact with the governor's office, and that every effort was being made to coordinate military activity with civilian authorities.*

"*Repeating the most recent release of information from the California Department of Public Safety, 'The infection appears to be highly contagious, and contact with the infected is to be avoided. Those exposed to the virus may experience periods of rage and violence, and if avoidance is not possible, they are to be isolated and contained. Citizens are advised to remain in their homes and keep roadways clear for emergency vehicles.'*

"*From the State House, the governor has declared a state of emergency for all California counties and has activated National Guard units to maintain order. In a statement an hour ago, Governor Young said that all incidents of violence and looting will be dealt with swiftly and harshly.*

"*In Washington, the president . . ."*

Dean slammed on the brakes and cranked the wheel, putting the Suburban into a sideways slide as he raced toward an intersection where several cars and a postal truck had tangled. The tires stuttered and then stopped, and Dean let his breath out in a great *whoosh.*

A Sacramento motorcycle cop was walking around the wreckage, shooting people still trapped inside. A man with his face covered in blood. A little girl reaching out through a window.

"No!" Dean screamed as the cop's pistol went off, and he reached for the door handle and the pistol on his belt simultaneously. Before he could get out, however, another hand shot out from the wreckage and caught the motorcycle cop's ankle, jerking him off his feet. More hands gripped the man's legs and together dragged him screaming into the shadowy tangle of bent steel and broken glass.

Dean didn't wait to see more. He gunned the Suburban around the traffic accident and accelerated, knocking over the cop's motorcycle, a moment later flashing by a wailing ambulance headed in the other direction. A burning Applebee's went by on the right, with no fire trucks in sight. People ran out the front of a liquor store carrying cardboard boxes, chased by a man with a green apron and a baseball bat. The Suburban went faster, Dean trying to keep an eye on the road as he tried his cell phone again. Now there was simply a *No Service* message.

As he approached the turn for Leah's daycare, a minivan swerved at him and blared its horn, scraping down the Suburban's left side before rocking back into its lane and disappearing behind him. His brain had a second to recognize the driver as one of the regular drop-off moms from the daycare, though he couldn't remember her name. She had a daughter with a lot of freckles. In that instant, he saw blood on her face, and she was screaming.

Dean's heart was pounding now as he made the turn and headed down the long, curving drive to Sunrise Daycare. At the far end of the road was a low, stucco-sided building with finger-paint masterpieces taped to the windows and a fenced playground off to one side. The parking lot and driveway were packed with vehicles, many stopped at odd angles, many more with their doors standing open, completely blocking the path.

Dean wheeled up over the curb and tore across the lawn. They could bill him for the landscaping.

He stopped thirty feet from the entrance, the big SUV's nose buried in a long hedge, and jumped out expecting to see mommies and daddies streaming out through the front doors, their little ones in their arms.

But there was no one.

Dean left the shotgun in the car and pulled his shirt down over the pistol as he moved across the lawn. A handgun at a daycare, no matter who you were or what was going on, would result in an immediate call to the police. After what he had seen at the intersection, he had no wish to encounter Sacramento's finest.

Then he saw why the lot was empty. The glass front doors to Sunrise Daycare were closed, and packed with adults on the other side, staring wide-eyed at the sidewalk beyond, some covering their mouths. The cement walk just in front of the doors was splashed with blood, the body of a woman in a charcoal business suit lying facedown to one side, unmoving. Closer to the doors, another woman was crouched on all fours, just like the one he had seen earlier, biting and ripping at something small, something with a pink top and matching pink sneakers. . . .

"Oh, God," Dean gasped, stopping.

The woman lifted her head, eyes glassy, face a red smear, and she snarled. He recognized her, Miss Daniels, one of the preschool teachers. The woman snapped her teeth several times and went back at the little body.

Dean's Glock .40 cleared leather as he stepped to her and pulled the trigger. A sharp crack, red and gray exploding out the other side of her head, the tinkle of a brass shell hitting the sidewalk.

There was rapid pounding at the glass doors and Dean looked up to see the cluster of parents frantically pointing behind him. He turned to see the woman in the business suit, Veronica something, mother to the little one in pink, standing and lurching unsteadily toward him. Her throat was a torn, red void, and her eyes had that same glassy quality.

"Veronica . . ." Dean started, but the woman made a sound that was half growl, half gurgle, and lunged.

Dean shot her in the chest. She stumbled and kept coming.

He raised his Glock ten inches and fired a round, stopping her.

It was like opening the flood valves of a dam. The front doors burst open and parents flowed out carrying crying children. They moved past Dean and ran into the parking lot.

"Watch out for that one," one mother said as she passed, pointing at the little girl in pink. Then she was gone, the lot quickly turning into a mass of gunned engines and horns. Dean looked past the hopelessly blocked lot and saw half a dozen people stumbling in from the street, probably parents who had seen that they couldn't get their cars in. They moved like people who had just been through a prolonged artillery barrage.

Dean went into the lobby, no longer worried about the pistol in his hand, where he met Miss Pottermeyer, the center's director. She held up her hands. "She's fine. Leah's with Miss Pam, playing with a few other kids. We haven't been able to reach all the parents yet. I'll go get her."

While the woman was gone, Dean looked out at the still-snarled parking lot. There were fewer honking horns now. Then he looked at the two women he had killed.

Infection? Biological attack? Zombies?

He ejected the partially used magazine from the Glock and pulled his spare clip from its slot next to the holster, looking at his hands. They were steady. Thank God for that. He loaded the full magazine and looked at the bodies again. No hyperventilation, no racing heart. Again, good. He'd worry about how he felt about them later; he needed his game face right now. And they weren't his first, were they? Or the first women.

Miss Pottermeyer returned with Leah, blond, blue-eyed, and two (two and a half, he corrected himself), wearing little white shorts and a powder-blue top with a kitten on it. Her sneakers had kittens on them as well.

"Daddy!" She ran to Dean, and he swept her up in his left arm, holstering the Glock with the other hand.

"Outside . . . I . . ." He looked at the center's director and shook his head.

The woman held up a hand. "Dean, you did what needed doing. No one could leave while she was out there. And I can't even think of her as Miss Daniels after what she—she was a monster, and that's all."

Dean shook his head. "But the other ones." He remembered the dead girl's name was Kayla but realized he had never met her mom, except to say "hi" in passing. "How did they . . . ?" He trailed off again.

"They come back," Miss Pottermeyer simply said. "They're not people anymore." Her voice was flat, her face without expression, as if a hard shell had closed over her emotions. It was a survival technique, and used especially by those with responsibility for others. He had seen it many times and had done it himself, in a place of sand and high temperatures.

Miss Pottermeyer took a step toward him and lowered her voice. "Monsters, Dean. Don't you forget that, and don't you hesitate. You've seen what they do, and they don't differentiate between adults and children."

They were the words of a combat leader, and the fact that they were delivered by a preschool administrator made it all the more surreal. Still he nodded.

"Is Angie okay?" Pottermeyer asked.

"I don't know. I can't get in touch with her."

The woman reached out and ran her fingers up Leah's back, making the little girl giggle. "You need to get her far away from here," she said, her voice still low.

Dean nodded. "The family has a crisis plan. We're going north, to the ranch. Angie will know to meet us there. What about you?"

The woman gave him a sad smile. "There are still four little ones here waiting for their parents and 911 just goes to a recording. I can't leave while they're here."

"Then we'll put everyone in the Suburban—" Dean started.

Pottermeyer cut him off. "Their parents might be on the way now. I can't take them anywhere." She squeezed Dean's arm and forced a smile. "I called my husband when the phones were still working. He's coming with the Explorer, and I told him to bring his pistol. If the parents haven't arrived by the time he gets here, maybe Miss Pam and I will put the kids in the truck and we'll all leave together."

"Where's Mama?" Leah asked, squirming in Dean's arms.

"She's working, sweetie."

"Why is she working?"

Dean smiled at their old routine. "Why do Mommy and Daddy go to work?"

"To make that money," Leah said.

Miss Pottermeyer reached out and took Leah from Dean's arms, surprising him. She turned so that the little girl was facing the other direction. "The door," the woman said.

Dean turned to see Kayla, the little girl who had been torn apart on the sidewalk, standing and bumping against the glass, smearing it red. Her eyes were milky and dead. It was an impossible sight, the little corpse pressing her face against the glass, biting at it. The damage to her body was extreme. She shouldn't be standing, shouldn't be moving.

Watch out for that one, the fleeing parent had said.

Dean didn't think he could shoot a little girl, no matter what she had become. Miss Pottermeyer saved him from the decision. "Come with me to the fire exit," she said, crossing the room. Dean followed her down a hallway with brightly colored doors and bulletin boards covered in construction-paper creations and panda faces made from paper plates. They passed a classroom with a viewing window, where he saw a young black woman on her knees singing a song with four preschoolers. Miss Pam looked up and smiled.

Dean stopped in the hallway. "I'm staying with you until your husband gets here."

"No," Pottermeyer said.

"I have a shotgun in the truck. Let me—"

"No," she repeated, this time in her teacher's no-nonsense, now-hear-this voice. "Richard is on his way. We'll stay locked inside until he gets here. We both have kids to watch out for; go get yours to a safe place." She gave Leah a kiss on the ear, getting a giggle in return, then stood on her toes and kissed Dean on the cheek. "God bless."

A moment later the fire door was clicking shut behind him, and Dean was trotting across the grass toward the Suburban, the Glock once more in his hand. A few of the cars seemed to have managed their way out of the lot, but most remained where they had been. There was no more honking, in fact no more movement. A few of the open car doors were now streaked red, and there was broken glass strewn across the asphalt. Low growling came from within the jam of cars.

Dean quickly buckled Leah into her seat, handing her a stuffed Cookie Monster with a rattle inside to keep her busy. She let it drop to the floor at once, declaring it a baby toy. Then the big SUV's tires were carving furrows in the lawn as Dean backed up, turned toward the main road, and headed for home.

First there had been no traffic, and then suddenly he was sitting still, cars and trucks backed up from the intersection ahead, horns unable to drown out the unmistakable rattle of automatic weapons. Dean saw a squad of infantrymen in full combat gear running along the sidewalk to his right, toward the gunfire.

He felt a tremble at the corner of his eye, his mouth going dry.
Not now.

People had begun to get out of their cars to see what the holdup was, despite the shooting. *Idiots,* Dean thought, and threw the Suburban into reverse, crunching into the grille of a BMW and hurling it backward. With this new space he was able to wheel out in a hard U-turn, ignoring the shouted curses and horns, scraping the front fender across the brick face of a pizza joint and then shooting back the way he had come, away from the intersection.

"Daddy, you crashed," said the voice from the backseat.

"Just a little, honey."

"Did you hurt the car?"

"Nope, we're fine."

"Juice!" Leah yelled.

"When we get home, honey."

"Juice! Juice!"

He was driving up a tree-lined road and had to swerve right and stop on the shoulder to get out of the way of an oncoming line of vehicles, all moving at high speed. Three desert camo Humvees roared past him in the other direction, followed by a sheriff's deputy with flashing lights. All three military vehicles had men in the turrets, two behind mounted fifty-calibers, the third behind an automatic grenade launcher. Overhead, pacing their movements, a Black Hawk in desert colors flew so low it made the trees shake.

Without warning, the beat of the rotor blades suddenly hurled Dean into his past. He felt the desert heat, and heard the cries of men who now only existed as ghosts.

King-Six, King-Six, we are fully engaged.

Call in the goddamn fire mission!

Get third squad moving on the right flank—

Requesting medevac, coordinates to follow.

Dennis is hit! Oh, Christ . . .
Negative, King-Six, we cannot—
Dean? My legs, man . . . I can't find them. . . .

The convoy and helicopter were gone, and Dean blinked, shaking off the ghosts. Not real, not anymore. He pulled back into the street and put his foot down, urging the big SUV on. It was bullshit, he didn't have *it*. Eight years in, three combat tours completed, and all of it was almost five years behind him now. Lots of guys had come home with it, but not him. It wasn't creeping up on him now, despite the . . . moments . . . he had experienced over the last six months. Post-traumatic stress was something other guys had to deal with. Dean had coped just fine with what he'd seen. It had been horrible, yes, and there were bad memories, of course. But that was all they were.

"Mama!" came a shout from the backseat.

"We'll see Mama soon, sweetie."

The Suburban turned into Sierra Oaks Vista, Sacramento's most upscale residential neighborhood, a sleepy place of large, estatelike homes with lush landscaping and meandering roads. It was tough to buy here because houses rarely came on the market, and before even being able to schedule a showing, potential buyers had to prove they could qualify for the million-dollar-plus loans. He and Angie had been fortunate not only with the timing but to have found a place they fell in love with and could also afford. The schools were first-rate and the neighborhood was safe. He made a series of turns to reach the house.

Over five thousand square feet, the sprawling two-story sat well back from the street across manicured lawns shaded by mature trees. A four-foot stone wall ringed the property, more for aesthetics than security (it was only four feet, after all), and a pair of iron gates closed the paver-stone driveway off from the street. Dean pressed one of six buttons on a remote clipped to his sun visor, and the gates swung in.

The Suburban shot up the curved drive as Dean depressed another button, opening one of the five-car garage's roll-up doors. He turned to back in and saw a woman walk through the driveway gates before they could close.

She was walking with sort of a stiff-legged lurch.

Bobby and Angel Levine had the house next door. They were a couple close to his and Angie's age, with a little boy about six months older than Leah. They were nice people and there had been playdates, barbecues, and drinks by the pool. Pulled into the shadows of the garage now, Dean shut off the engine and watched Angel shuffle up his driveway. She had always been an attractive woman, with long black hair, longer legs, who jogged and was religious about yoga, committed to maintaining her figure, much like his own wife.

Angel was dead now. She had to be. No one could live with their torso ripped open like that, internal organs dangling and bouncing against their thighs. It was a sight Dean knew he'd see later in dreams.

"Potty, Daddy!" Leah called. "Gotta go!"

Dean shut the garage door. He was fairly certain the rest of the house was locked; it usually was before he went to work, so Angel Levine would have to wait. He got Leah inside and to her potty chair in time, then carried her to the family room and turned on Nick Jr. He wanted the news, but he had priorities, and keeping his toddler amused so he could carry out his tasks was at the top of the list. Leah clapped when she saw Dora. Dean was just happy there was still a cable signal.

"Daddy will be right back." Dean touched his daughter's head and then looked out the windows, searching for Angel. He didn't see her, but it wasn't the best angle. She could be near the garage door, or moving around back. He made a quick tour of the doors and windows on this floor, making sure they were locked and look-ing constantly for his neighbor. There was no sign of Angel. As he took the stairs two at a time he tried Angie again but had no signal.

In one of the hall closets, filling most of the space at the bottom, was the family go-bag. It was made of bright orange nylon and packed with clothes, first-aid supplies, a little food and water, flash-lights, spare cell phone batteries, and a wad of cash. The bag was a discipline he and his wife had adopted in the face of the many natu-ral disasters and terror attacks that had plagued the world in recent years, one that made sense. They had basic supplies they could take in a hurry and a plan for where they would go, even if they were separated and out of contact. It was simple, but he knew most peo-ple didn't even have that.

However, as he pulled out the bag he realized it hadn't been updated since Leah was younger. It held diapers, wipes, powdered formula, and onesies she hadn't fit into in over a year. Leah had given up the bottle twelve months ago and was now potty trained. Almost. He cursed the reality show for making their lives so busy they neglected the details, then shook his head. *Blame yourself, buddy,* he thought. *The History channel's not responsible for your family.*

Dean dumped the baby items and grabbed clothes from Leah's room, remembering to snatch Wawas off her bed. The much-gnawed, soft little walrus was the center of Leah's world, and failing to bring along the stuffed animal would launch its own sort of apocalypse.

He left the go-bag in the upstairs hall and went into his walk-in closet, tapping in the code for one of two gun safes. From a shelf above the hanging clothes he retrieved a heavy black nylon bag with *PRE-MIER ARMS* printed on the side. His selections went into the bag.

A Smith & Wesson .45 automatic with shoulder holster.

One box of rounds.

A clip-fed, twelve-gauge auto shotgun—like the one in the truck—with fold-out stock.

Four boxes of shells.

An AR-15, illegally converted to full-auto capability.

Ten magazines, loaded, in a nylon bandolier.

A Browning .380 auto with ankle holster.

Two boxes of shells for his Glock.

An Ingram MAC-10 machine pistol with suppressor in a custom leather shoulder rig.

Eight loaded thirty-round magazines.

Two boxes of forty-five-caliber rounds for the Ingram.

When the world ends with zombies, it doesn't suck to own a gun store. It sounded like one of those snarky greeting cards people posted on Facebook. The black gun bag weighed a ton as he heaved it and the orange go-bag downstairs and through the house to the garage. He glanced at Leah as he went by. She was sitting criss-cross-applesauce on the floor. Dean could hear Miss Pottermeyer's voice admonish him, "We don't say Indian-style anymore, Mr. West." On the TV, Dora and Boots were trying to find their way to the snowy mountain.

Both bags went into the back of the Suburban, along with a five-gallon container of fuel he kept for the riding mower, and a propane camp stove. He raided the kitchen pantry, sweeping canned goods into a pair of canvas totes, then added them, along with a three-quarters-full case of bottled water, to the rear of the SUV. He looked around the garage, grabbing an axe, a short-handled shovel, and a blue plastic tarp. He hadn't used any of his lawn or house tools since the show went nuclear and he could afford a landscaping service.

Dean was intensely aware of the time, felt it pressing down on him as minutes slipped away. He knew a few things about crisis in an urban setting, and one of the first things he had been taught was that those who didn't get out immediately usually never got out at all. He had seen it and lived it overseas, and had taught it, along with other skills, during his days at Fort Lewis. Specifically at the fort's Urban Warfare School, where soldiers were introduced to a close-combat, high-stress environment, one in which death waited at every doorway, window, and corner. They were lessons the school's graduates dared not forget.

"Sweetie, time to go," he called, walking quickly back through the house.

Leah wasn't in front of the TV.

Dean's heart tried to crawl up his throat for a full second before he saw her. She was standing at one of the windows.

"Miss Angel," Leah said, pressing her nose to the glass and waving.

Dean felt like he was moving in slow motion as he went for Leah, knowing what would happen, seeing the dead arms crash through the glass and drag his little girl to her death. But they didn't. He reached her and saw that Angel Levine was indeed outside the window, but held back by three feet of tight, trimmed hedge, grasping hands reaching but falling short. Mercifully, the bloody damage to her torso was out of sight beneath the top of the hedge.

"We'll talk to her later," he said, forcing his voice not to waver.

Leah laughed and waved. "She's funny."

"We need to go for a ride, baby."

"*Not* a baby."

"No, a big girl. We'll get a juice box for the car, okay?"

"Want Dora." She huffed and crossed her little arms. Dear Lord, she looked like her mother. Dean pulled the stuffed walrus from his back pocket and wiggled it. "Look who I have."

Leah squealed, "Wawas!" and grabbed for the animal. Dean held it low but out of reach, walking fast through the house, making it a game as Leah laughed and chased him to the garage. There he swept her up, snapped her into the car seat, and handed her Wawas.

"Shit," he said as he slammed the door, and went back into the house, every second ticking like rumbles of thunder. How long had he been here? It felt like hours. He returned with the potty seat they kept in the downstairs bathroom, along with a box of wipes and a half-full package of juice boxes. He made one more trip inside, scrawling a note to Angie and pinning it to the front of the fridge with a magnet. *Gone to the ranch.*

Behind the wheel at last, Dean stared at the closed garage door. Was Angel Levine on the other side? Was she dangerous? Maybe to the first, of course to the second. He wasn't going to shoot a neighbor in the head in front of his daughter. What would he do . . . run her over?

He opened the garage, then clicked open the gates at the end of the drive.

Nothing moved.

He gassed it, going too fast down the drive, catching a peripheral glimpse of a figure staggering toward them across the lawn before he reached the street. Other than the absence of joggers, people getting their papers, and cars pulling out for the drive to work, Sierra Oaks Vista was as quiet as any other weekday morning. Only now, Dean wondered at what was moving behind those stately walls and curtained windows.

Within minutes he was clear of the neighborhood. Now all he had to do was escape Sacramento and make it the hundred miles to Chico.

Several blocks away, a gas station went up in a loud *WHUMP*, a red-and-black plume mushrooming into the clear morning sky. To his right, a police helicopter was hovering low over a parking lot while a SWAT officer hung out one door, firing his rifle. In the street ahead of him, bloody and mangled bodies dragged their feet as they moved in search of prey.

So many choices. Dean West gritted his teeth and got moving.

THREE

Halsey awoke to a cold cabin. He had been dreaming about the stables again, but in this dream, the stables were filled with the rich smells of hay and horses, and the mare named Starlight was still in her stall, belly heavy with the foal she would drop soon. It was peaceful, a good dream.

He sat on the edge of the bed for several minutes, waking up and waiting to see if he was hungover, deciding he wasn't. His face was scratchy, needed a razor, and he wondered—as he did every morning—why he bothered shaving anymore. He would, though, just as he had every day of his fifty years since he was sixteen. A dull ache materialized behind his eyes. Maybe he would need some Advil after all.

Starlight. It was the horses that had drawn them, perhaps the smell, perhaps the lure of flesh trapped helplessly in their stalls. Halsey had been out when it happened, had returned to the ranch to find the horses slaughtered, Starlight and her colt partially devoured, dead things shuffling around the cabin and outbuildings. He had shot them all down, and then he'd cried, a fifty-year-old man on his knees in the packed dirt, sobbing like a child.

He didn't go into the stables anymore.

Halsey shuffled into the main room of the cabin, wool socks whispering on the hardwood floor. He was tall and slender, with ropy, muscled arms, and his short hair was bristly, the color of iron. He switched on the generator, tucked into a separate locked shed against the outside of the cabin and wired into the house, then set a kettle on the hot plate. He sat at the kitchen table and picked up an Elmore Leonard novel, starting from the page he had folded at the corner, waiting for the whistle.

The cabin was small, simple, and clean with a bedroom, a bathroom, an eat-in kitchen, and a tiny living room. There had been a flat-screen TV mounted over the fireplace, but Halsey had taken it down and left it out in the weather behind the stables. He had never watched it much anyway. In its place hung a large map of Butte County, covered in circles and notations from a red felt-tip pen. The cabin's furniture was crafted from heavy wood, sturdy and comfortable, the décor a simple western theme. Like him, a simple, single man steadily moving out of his prime.

When the coffee was ready he fried up a skillet of canned hash, longing as he often did for eggs and milk. He couldn't keep the animals that supplied those things, however. Their presence attracted the dead.

Halsey shaved and washed up with a rag and a basin of water, then dressed in jeans, boots, and a thermal shirt, pulling on a brown Carhartt jacket and an old John Deere cap. He went to the window beside the front door—all of them were covered in sturdy, barred wooden shutters—and slid open a peep slot like he was a doorman at a Prohibition speakeasy.

A pair of DTs—Halsey's shortening of *Dead Things*, since the word *zombie* just felt like kid's stuff—was out there, a man shuffling past Halsey's dusty Ford pickup, a woman in what had once been a suit but was now gray rags standing in place, swaying side to side and staring at the cabin. Halsey peered at her.

"I'll be damned," he said. "You've come a long way, Dolores."

That was the problem with living in the sticks. You knew the folks you shot. Dolores was the branch manager at the bank Halsey had used up in Paradise, five or six miles from here. The gray-black skin of her bare feet was filthy and torn. In life she had been a pleasant sort. Halsey had liked her the way a man likes people he meets only once in a while, those who remember that other folks matter just as much as themselves.

The ranch hand strapped on a tooled leather gun belt with .44 rounds pushed through the loops all the way around, a big Colt six-shooter hanging low on the right side, the walnut grips worn smooth and dark. He selected a .22 rifle from the rack beside the bedroom door and headed up a ladder made of wood that was newer than the rest of the cabin. Where the ladder met the roof, he unbolted a stout wooden hatch and kept climbing another eight feet before emerging on a covered platform with waist-high walls all around. It looked a bit like a park ranger's tower, and rose above the cabin's peak. From up here he could see all the way around his house, and out among the outbuildings; the stables, the smokehouse, the storage shed, and the garage. There was also a commanding view of the valley. Halsey had built the tower himself and knew it was solid.

Misting rain was coming out of the gray January sky, and it couldn't have been more than forty degrees. People forgot that parts of California could actually get cold, especially this close to the Sierra Nevada. In Halsey's experience, most folks thought California was made up of Los Angeles and San Francisco, somehow squished together. He expected that was the way people thought about New York too, just one big city, an endless Times Square. Not that there were many people left to think about such things, he reasoned. He took a pair of binoculars from a hook and scanned the area, rotating in a slow circle, looking close in, and then farther out during a second turn.

A short distance from the house was the square of earth he had turned and fenced off in the fall, intending a vegetable garden in the spring, the seeds and tools waiting in the shed nearby. A yellow backhoe was parked beside it, covered in a blue tarp. Two hundred yards beyond was the mass grave he had dug for the DTs, with that very backhoe. To the west and south, the gently rolling hills wore their winter brown and were studded with clusters of small pines.

Out past the stables was the airstrip, a long, paved stretch with a bright orange wind sock hanging limp in the morning mist. At the far end was a blackened snarl of metal, struts and wings and tails jutting out at all angles from where the small FedEx prop job had literally merged with Carson Pepper's private jet in a sudden and horrific fireball that Halsey had witnessed. It had been bad. What emerged from the flames had been worse, and Halsey had been forced to deal with it.

Carson Pepper had been Halsey's employer for decades, a multi-millionaire who had made his fortune in high-end cowboy boots. Halsey had maintained the ranch for him, and their relationship had been more like friends than business. It had hurt to put the man down.

The cabin and outbuildings, the actual *ranch* part of Carson Pepper's Broken Arrow Ranch, rested in a depression in the valley floor, hidden from view by a long ridge that sloped up toward the big house and crested. A dirt road curved up and around the hill to connect the working buildings to the main property, and a service road headed out to the Skyway, allowing Halsey to come and go with horses and equipment without the need to use the big house's long, brick-paved drive that extended to the highway and ended at gates flanked by stone pillars, each topped with a carriage light.

From his tower, Halsey could see black skeletal beams marking the remains of the main house's roof. It had been a spectacular home, with vaulted ceilings and walls of glass, six thousand square feet of luxury boasting seven suites, marble tubs and granite countertops, five fireplaces, a wine cellar, an indoor pool, and a home theater that could accommodate sixteen guests. A palace.

Halsey had burned it down himself.

Satisfied that all was clear, Halsey unslung the .22 and sighted on the dead man below. He waited until the DT moved away from his pickup—didn't want to put a hole in the Ford if he missed—then squeezed off a single round to the side of the man's head. The DT collapsed, the report of the small-caliber rifle little more than a *POP* that wouldn't travel far. The heavier rifles made a sound that carried for miles, so he used them sparingly, mostly for hunting. Or emergencies.

Dolores, still swaying in the yard below, looked up at the shot.

"Sorry for this," Halsey said, putting her down with a single round.

Then it was time for chores.

Halsey got his Polaris Ranger—an oversized quad called a side-by-side with a bench seat and steering wheel instead of motorcycle-style handlebars, a roll cage and a short pickup bed in the back—out of the garage. It looked a bit military, much like a small Jeep, and he liked it for its durability and power. It wasn't particularly quiet, but it could go where his pickup could not and get him back out in a hurry if the sound drew the wrong kind of attention. Halsey wrapped the two DTs in tarps and used the Ranger to drive them out to the grave, bringing along a bag of lime and giving them a coating that would not only accelerate decomposition but keep away animals and others of their kind.

He spent an hour splitting wood and carrying it inside, and then did his laundry in an oval-shaped stainless steel trough set beneath a hand pump, once a watering hole for the ranch's horses. An old-fashioned washboard that had once hung on the cabin wall as western décor was now back in service, and he scrubbed with powdered detergent before hanging his wet clothes on a drying rack inside the cabin. His usual outdoor clotheslines were pointless in this weather. The house had a septic tank, so he had avoided having to build an outhouse, which pleased him beyond description. He could just imagine sitting in a little wooden hut with his pants around his knees when a hungry DT came calling. More time was spent in the smokehouse preparing the last batch of venison he had brought in, and then he did some minor maintenance on the generator before topping off its tank.

His chores finished, Halsey loaded the side-by-side with hunting gear, a lever-action Winchester .30-.30 and a scoped .30-06. He also added some empty bags in the event he came across anything worth scrounging, a five-gallon fuel container, and a pair of canteens. His .22 went into the rifle rack at the back of the roll cage.

His days were routine, and he went at even the small tasks with discipline and structure, always the same. *Unplanned is undone,* his daddy used to say.

Inside, he packed a small lunch and made sure the cabin was buttoned up tight, triple-checking to see that the generator was shut down and locking the door before he left. The Ranger grumbled away minutes later, headed down a dirt quad trail that snaked into the hills to the west.

Halsey could have gone out to the Skyway, the four-lane road running through the valley that connected the ten miles between Chico and Paradise. There were certainly deer out there, but there were other things as well, dangerous things, and not all of them dead. The trails were better.

This trail cut through the hills and pine on a meandering route, crossing several streams and fire roads. The Ranger motored past three different houses, all summer homes for people from Southern California, all checked off in red on the map over his fireplace. Halsey had already scavenged anything of value. Someone in one of the houses had been a reader, and the ranch hand had scored an entire bookcase of popular paperbacks. Reading was, and had always been, Halsey's favorite leisure activity. Now the houses just stood as vacant reminders of the people who had once thought of them as escapes from the pressures of their everyday lives.

After an hour of driving—he saw not a single DT, though he knew they were out there—Halsey came to a particular stand of pines and shut the Ranger down, shouldering his pack, the .22, and the scoped .30-06. He walked into the trees for a bit and checked on the salt lick he had set on the pine needles. There were tracks and fresh spoor, so he retreated twenty yards until he found his lawn chair leaning against a tree. He settled down to wait, the heavier rifle across his knees, a nice sight line on the salt lick.

It was quiet. It had always been quiet here, of course, but now there was no rumble of jets in the sky, no distant hum of cars on the Skyway or a lonely trucker's horn. The sky still misted rain, and it dripped on him through the pine needles, but he didn't mind. Hunting was part of his work, and work needed doing, regardless of Mother Nature's mood. Halsey had time.

An hour passed, the only sound the brushing of pines against one another as a breeze passed through and the drip of moisture from the mist. There was no crunch of needles signaling a cautious doe approaching the salt lick. There might be nothing today, but that was how it often went. Halsey ate his lunch: a foil packet of tuna mix, some chips, and a bottle of iced tea. He missed bread, missed having a real sandwich, and reminded himself to look for a bread maker the next time he was searching houses.

A distant *BOOM* carried over the hills and through the trees. Halsey slung his rifle and walked out of the pines, looking west. It took a couple of minutes but he spotted a finger of black smoke rising above the hilltops into the gray sky. He estimated south Chico.

Halsey collected his gear and walked back to the Ranger.

B y the time Halsey settled into an observation point, the wreckage was no longer smoking. He had left the side-by-side on the other side of the ridge and walked the last hundred yards up a deer path, picking a spot near several trees where he could put his back to the hillside, therefore presenting no silhouette, and have a good view of the south end of Chico spreading out before him.

Through his binoculars he could see what was left of the chopper and instantly recognized it as a Black Hawk. Anyone who had ever turned on the news knew what they looked like, but Halsey had seen plenty of them in person. Like many young men in America, he had served a single four-year tour in the Army, almost thirty years ago now. It had been a time when the United States hadn't really been involved in anything more than small brushfire actions around the world, and in any event, Halsey hadn't been a grunt. He was trained as a heavy equipment operator. He had never been in combat, and other than during basic training, he had only fired a rifle during mandatory, annual qualifications. He'd spent his entire four-year hitch driving bulldozers at Fort Campbell, Kentucky.

But he recognized a Black Hawk, and if anyone had walked away from that one it would have been a miracle. He saw no one in uniform around the downed aircraft, but a number of DTs were approaching it from different angles. As he watched, one of them, a woman, wriggled into the cockpit through the smashed windscreen. Another one joined her minutes later.

He looked for what might have brought it down, seeing nothing but the empty southern end of the city, its streets populated only with the walking dead. Maybe it had been mechanical failure.

A hollow, thumping noise caused him to put his binoculars on the south. A dark shape appeared from behind a hill and moved slowly over the Black Hawk's wreckage.

"I'll be damned," Halsey said.

It left the downed bird behind and came straight toward him, moving slowly as it followed the highway that would lead to Paradise. In moments it was gone, its sound echoing among the hills.

Halsey ran for the path that would take him to the side-by-side. He would have to cut across to the Skyway. Driving the main road wasn't his first choice, but if he had any hope of catching up, or at least seeing where it went, he would have to risk it.

The ranch hand's boots pounded the earth as he ran faster than he had in twenty years.

FOUR

January 11—South Chico

Vladimir Yurish banked right and angled the Black Hawk over what Angie West declared was the south end of Chico, California. He had cautioned her that landmarks looked different from the air, and sitting to his right in her cockpit seat, Angie had quickly agreed. Now she was navigating from a road map, opened across her knees.

"We're looking for the Skyway," she said into her radio headset, peering out and down through the windows. "It's a good-sized highway running east into the hills." Vladimir acknowledged and slowed the bird so she could get her bearings. He held at a constant three hundred feet.

Another voice spoke over the intercom. "We've got wreckage down there," Skye Dennison called. "Looks like another Black Hawk." Skye was dressed in black fatigues and combat gear, a knit cap pulled down over her freshly shaved head. She was clipped into the safety harness near the starboard M240 door gun, leaning out through the opening, and the rush of wind and the beating of blades threatened to drown her out.

Vladimir strained to look down through the port windows, but the angle was off, preventing him from seeing the fuselage. He could clearly see the debris field, however, twisted metal scattered across blackened earth. Something had gone down.

"Survivors?" the pilot asked.

A pause. "No," said Skye, "looks like only drifters."

Angie could see better out her side. "It looks burned. Hard to say how old it is."

Vlad nodded. It could have crashed months ago or mere hours. They burned fast, and the smoke would have cleared quickly. He followed the course Angie called, lining the bird up with a four-lane strip of road leading into the eastern hills. The Russian left the wreckage behind.

Back in the troop compartment, Bill "Carney" Carnes was clipped into his own harness at the left door. He watched the burned and broken bird fade behind them, then looked out at Chico. From up here it was large and spread out, though it was really just a small Northern California city nudged up against the base of the mountains on one side, an expanse of rich farmland stretching out on the other. The center of town appeared to be a grid of tree-lined streets, whereas the south end looked more commercial. There were big parking lots for retailers and small industry, sprawling apartment complexes, and residential areas with curving streets.

No cars moved along the avenues, but he could make out the small shapes of people. What had been people. Now they were just lifeless, dangerous, rotten shells.

It was a little more than two hours since their helicopter lifted off from the USS *Nimitz*, their home now, purchased with the blood of their friends. Father Xavier had stood on the flight deck and waved as they departed. Time had become a strange and intangible thing for Carney now. Could that have only been this morning?

It was not so very long ago, he admitted, that he and TC Cochoran had been cellmates at San Quentin, both locked away for what would probably be the rest of their lives. The plague had granted them their freedom, releasing them into a violent and nightmarish world of the walking dead. He thought about their odyssey in the stolen riot vehicle, the horrors they had seen, and the things they had done to survive. Perhaps strangest of all to Carney was that with all the killing since their escape, he—a convicted murderer— had not taken a single human life. He had killed only the dead.

The same could not be said for TC, who up until his final moments had played the role life intended for him: mad-dog killer. Even though in the end he had tried to rape Skye and kill Carney, doing enough damage to them both to leave behind a wake of pain and scars, Carney caught himself missing his cellmate sometimes. He would never say it aloud, of course, and he was glad that Skye had put a bullet through the man's brain, but in many ways TC had been like a brother. The closest thing to a brother Carney had ever had.

An odyssey indeed, one in which he had chosen to join with and protect others instead of looking out for himself, had stormed an aircraft carrier when any sane person would have run the other way. He had friends now, people who cared about him. And the most unbelievable part of it all was that he felt the same way.

And of course there was the girl.

Carney looked across the troop compartment at Skye, now sitting with her legs hanging out the door and one arm wrapped around the machine gun mount. He couldn't see her face but knew it would be all business, her normal look. There was another side to her, though, a softer side that could still smile, and one that she had permitted Carney to see.

They had been together for a couple of months now, a casual thing with no expectations, nothing that would get in the way of serious business such as this. So he had assumed. But without warning or discussion, Carney had invited himself aboard the Black Hawk just before it left the flight deck. He told himself it was to add some firepower to the mission, but that didn't ring true to him. The ex-con didn't want to admit what he really suspected, that he had come along in order to protect Skye.

He frowned, imagining her reaction if he even suggested she couldn't take care of herself.

Carney watched the winter landscape passing below and shook his head. He was mooning over a girl, acting like a lovesick kid. He hadn't realized he was so soft.

The Black Hawk thumped up the valley, pine-covered hills extending to both sides, the snowcapped Sierra Nevada invisible behind the mist. Beads of moisture raced off the windscreen.

"It's about five more miles," Angie said from the co-pilot's seat.

"Then we are nearly there," said Vladimir.

Angie stared out at the gray ribbon of asphalt winding up the valley, leaning forward in her harness and touching the blue teething ring hanging around her neck by a chain. Almost there. After all this time they were almost there. She didn't notice the ache in her right shoulder, where TC Cochoran's bullet had punched through, didn't notice the throb in her right arm, the bones still knitting together after TC had fractured both the radius and ulna. There was only what lay ahead.

Leah, two years old and away from Mommy for five months.

Dean, her husband, her rock, keeping Leah from harm.

This was the story she had told herself since the outbreak, that Dean and Leah had fled to the family ranch and were now riding out the crisis in safety with her mom and dad. In minutes they would all be reunited. Angie hadn't yet told her companions that she would be staying, that they would return to *Nimitz* without her. She silently urged the helicopter to go faster.

"I think we're coming up on the turn," she said, pointing. "Up on the left. Slow down and get a little lower."

Vladimir eased back on his airspeed and let the bird sink to one hundred feet, the wind from his blades thrashing the tops of pine trees. The four-lane Skyway wasn't completely choked with vehicles like the silent graveyards of cars and trucks they had seen during their flight from San Francisco, but it wasn't empty, either. An abandoned logging truck a quarter mile ahead blocked two lanes, pickups and SUVs sat on the shoulders with their doors open, and almost directly beneath the chopper was what had to have been a fatal accident involving an office supply truck and a lime-green VW. Several figures wandered past automobiles, a few even reaching up toward the sky as they stumbled in the direction of the Black Hawk, but these were not survivors.

Angie was now able to make out the ranch's mailbox, mounted alongside a dirt road that peeled off the Skyway and headed north into the trees. The box was bright red, and attached to a wagon wheel.

"That's the road," Angie said, her heart pounding faster. "The ranch is two miles in. We're almost there."

Vlad climbed to avoid clipping treetops with the blades and moved slowly up a new, much narrower valley. The dirt road moved in and out of view beneath the pines. In the troop compartment, Skye and Carney looked at each other and nodded, tightening their gear and readying their personal weapons. Their friend was expecting a tearful reunion while they were preparing for the worst.

Skye crouched behind the M240 door gun. During the flight, Vladimir had given instructions over the intercom on the weapon's use and reloading. He had even cruised low over some roads and fields where corpses moved, giving his two gunners some practice.

Trigger time, he called it. Skye was impressed with the firepower, the door gun chattering, vibrating in her hands as brass streamed out of the ejection port like water from a faucet, falling out and away in the downdraft. The M240 tore hell out of anything it touched: abandoned cars, asphalt, earth, the undead. Bullet impact threw the corpses to the ground, blew them open, and chopped off limbs, but head shots were rare, accidental, and she growled in frustration. Carney fared no better.

Vladimir had told them it was to be expected, reminding them that the weapon was designed for living targets, where a single touch of one of its deadly rounds could exterminate life. It was not a surgeon's tool, it was more like a bulldozer. Now, as the Black Hawk slowly followed the road below, Skye and Carney leaned their mounted weapons out and down.

Groundhog-7 covered the two miles in short order, and then the trees came to an end, the road moving into open ground as the valley widened to either side until it reached pine-spotted hills. The brown valley floor rolled gently as the road followed a small stream.

Angie wore a tense smile as she strained against her harness, the house coming into view. Then the smile faltered. And fell.

"No," she whispered. "No, no . . ." Her voice was climbing. "No!" Her hands balled into fists and tears blurred her vision. "No!" she screamed.

The Franks ranch was fenced, a sturdy line of high chain link marching into the trees, but the gate that closed off the property at the tree line was open. Not open, but knocked down and driven across. The house where Angie had grown up, a large, two-story log home with a wraparound porch, was a rectangle of ashes and charred timbers, a blackened, river-stone fireplace rising at each end. The stables, the barns, and all of the outbuildings had been similarly burned down. Her father's pickup was black, resting on melted tires, and in what had been the front yard, something was planted in the earth, a post of some kind. A dozen drifters roamed through the destruction, turning toward the sound of the approaching helicopter.

"No," Angie gasped, slumping back into the co-pilot's seat.

A small earth mound rose at the back of what had been the house, a heavy steel door set in the side of the small hill at an angle. It was standing open. As the helicopter thumped in for a landing, everyone aboard could see that the ground all around the ranch was torn by tire tracks.

Dean's Suburban was parked near the bunker entrance, charred and shredded by gunfire.

"Gunners," Vladimir called over the intercom, "clear the area."

Using the M240s, Carney and Skye chopped up every drifter within a hundred yards, burning through ammo until the bodies were not only down, but no longer moving. Any other time, there would be cries to conserve the ammunition, but the gunners at both doors were committed to getting their friend safely on the ground. Rage played a part as well, a reptilian urge to destroy the things they had all come to hate so much. As the Black Hawk's wheels touched down, Skye and Carney unsnapped their harnesses and jogged out from under the turning blades, using their rifles to finish off anything that had survived the airborne fire.

Angie climbed out the side door and walked slowly toward the postlike object stuck in the earth in front of the house. Her fists trembled at her sides, and tears streamed down her cheeks.

The post was actually a crucifix made from wooden beams, and there was a zombie tied to it. The creature gnashed its teeth, wiggling in its bonds, and let out a long, low moan. Crows had been picking at its face, but it was still recognizable.

It was Angie's father.

FIVE

Skye retrieved Angie's Galil assault rifle from the chopper and pressed it into the crying woman's hands, then held her by the back of the neck and pressed their foreheads together. "I'm so sorry, Ang."

Angie's body shook with sobs.

Skye's hand tightened. "We'll find who did this," she whispered fiercely. "We'll kill every last one of them."

Angie shook her head slowly. "Why would someone . . . ?"

Skye closed her eyes. "I don't know."

Behind them, Carney walked a slow circle around the Black Hawk, out beyond the turning blades. The M14 was at his shoulder, and his blue eyes were narrowed, looking out. It was a survival habit he had developed in prison, a necessary skill in the cell blocks that served him well in this new world. When there was a commotion, something drawing everyone's attention, that was the time to look in the other direction. Death's favorite tactic was ambush from behind.

The former inmate popped several drifters walking through the fields around the burned ranch. The gunfire made Angie jerk away from Skye. "Don't! He could be out there!" She grabbed Skye's combat harness in one fist. "Did you kill him?" she demanded, her eyes darting and wild. "Dean could be out there! Did you and Carney kill him with the door guns?"

Skye stepped back. "We only shot dead things, Angie."

The other woman held on to the harness, sobbing.

"I'll help you look for them," Skye said, softly.

The brown grass was pressed flat in every direction as Vladimir kept the Black Hawk's blades turning, just in case they needed a quick exit, and Carney remained close on security while the two women walked together, examining bodies. Angie couldn't look at what had become of her father, groaning and struggling up on his cross, and she wasn't prepared to deal with him. Skye didn't know what Angie's husband looked like, so she stayed close to her friend. There wouldn't be any trouble identifying a murdered little girl, however.

Half an hour and a full circuit of the grounds revealed only dead drifters, most of them fresh kills from the door guns, and none of them Dean or Leah. There was also no sign of Angie's mom, Lenore, even among the cinders and fallen timbers of the house. They looked inside the small, original fallout shelter her grandfather had built, which Lenore now used as a potato cellar, but it was empty of both the living and the dead. Then they approached the entrance to the main bunker.

"Why is it open?" Angie moaned. "It should be sealed, they should be locked inside."

Skye didn't have an answer, and she knew Angie hadn't really been talking to her.

The door yawned wide and debris was littered on the ground around it: some batteries, a can of string beans, a gray sweater, and a gas mask with a cracked eyepiece. The ground outside was pocked with craters, and there were at least a hundred shell casings, the empty brass of an assault rifle scattered across the torn earth. A set of narrow concrete steps descended like a throat into the darkness, and both women switched on flashlights. Angie went down first.

Daddy is on a cross, he's on a cross, they killed him and he's on a cross. Her boots scraped on the concrete steps. *He's on a cross and he's like them, like them, he's dead, oh, God, my daddy is dead!* She felt like screaming.

To say the bunker was made out of concrete was misleading. It was actually a series of eight-foot segments made from connected corrugated steel pipe, sealed in reinforced concrete and covered in earth, resting fifteen feet belowground. It was designed to be bomb resistant. The main entrance was the outer steel door, four inches thick, that was supposed to cover a long flight of steps leading to a second, inner door, this one as solid as a bank vault and ringed with a rubber gasket to make it gasproof when it was closed. The inner door, however, also stood open.

The design was simple: a long central tube with a raised floor, two chambers opening off each of the left and right sides. There were dedicated areas for supply storage; a bunk room; the well pump and water storage; a generator and air-handling room; a chamber to handle waste, complete with sinks and showers; and the armory. The bunker had not burned, but it was immediately apparent that it had been completely looted. The flashlight beams threw a cold, blue-white light on the central chamber, revealing empty shelves and pallets where supplies had once been.

Why are the doors open? Angie screamed silently. They should have been sealed up tight in here. No one could have reached them.

A scrabbling, chittering noise came from the well chamber, and the two women advanced, rifles ready as they peered inside with their lights. Some of the blue plastic barrels holding the water supply were still in here, and the motorized pump that serviced the well still looked intact. A dark shape moved low against the floor, peering out from behind the pump motor with yellow eyes that caught and reflected their lights. The baby raccoon darted back out of sight.

The women stepped back into the central corridor.

The string of overhead lights running the length of the tube remained, but every fuel container had been taken. Pallets that had once held cases of dried goods, clothing, medical supplies, batteries, and flares now stood empty. No longer were there neat rows of toiletries and gas masks, flashlights and hand tools, spare radios and maps. A few clean air filters leaned against the wall by the air handler, but the portable battery-powered TVs and the sophisticated ham radio set were missing.

The armory was bare. Empty weapon racks were bolted to the walls; vacant pallets sat on the floor. Whoever had been here had taken every rifle, every handgun, every last bullet.

Skye hadn't even bothered to look. She knew it would be empty, and in fact the armory was probably what had drawn the raid in the first place. Instead she conducted a more thorough examination of the two chambers toward the rear of the bunker, the pump room and the waste/toilet facilities. In here, behind the big unit that ground and pumped waste out of the bunker, presumably into a septic system, Skye found a small, circular steel hatch mounted in the wall. It had a wheel in the center—just like the hatches on the *Nimitz*—and a pair of deadbolts.

"Ang, come in here," she called. "What's this?"

Angie entered the room, knowing at once what her friend was looking at. "It goes to a tunnel," she said, "an escape tube, sort of. You have to crawl on your hands and knees." She squatted and pulled it open, a puff of cold air rushing into the room. A flashlight beam showed that it was dry and very long. The light was swallowed by the darkness. "It travels for half a mile, and lets out inside the far tree line."

"It was unlocked," Skye said. "It only locks from the inside, right?"

Angie frowned and nodded.

"I want to check it out. Is that okay with you?"

Another nod. "I'll be okay. Don't get lost, and be careful."

Skye said she would and disappeared into the tunnel, flashlight and rifle muzzle leading the way.

Angie watched her go for a minute, and then went to the bunk room. She stood in the doorway, hand on the frame, her breathing rapid. Sporadic rifle shots came from outside, muffled by the still-turning rotor blades. *Carney cleaning up the dead,* she thought to herself. At last she entered.

There would only have been her parents, Dean, and Leah. They would have wanted to stay close together, and her mom would have wanted Leah sleeping where Grandma could watch over her.

Why are the bunker doors open? Why?

Angie passed the flashlight over a room that had been lived in. Four bunks had tangled bedding, as if the occupants had gotten up in a hurry. She inspected the sheets for blood, found none. Then the beam fell upon a small blue blanket covered in puffy white clouds, balled up in a corner of a bottom bunk. Angie let out a sob and fell to her knees, clutching the blanket to her chest, burying her face in the fabric and breathing in the faint scent of her daughter. Then she began to cry.

Skye crawled. The tube was also made from ribbed steel, high enough to pass through on all fours, but she'd had to leave her pack behind. She didn't want to try to push or drag the pack and handle the flashlight and her weapons all at the same time. Her hard plastic knee pads banged and scraped at the metal—crawling in just jeans would have really hurt the knees, she thought—and her flashlight beam wobbled across the metal walls. A half mile. There was no sense of direction or distance down here, so she couldn't tell how far she had gone. It felt like forever.

The beam of light swept over an object in the tunnel about thirty feet away and then quickly centered back on it. It was the top of a head, strands of thinning hair clinging to it, gray in the light and lying facedown.

It reeked.

And then it moved.

The drifter's head snapped up, yellow eyes and teeth gleaming in the flashlight beam, and it let out a snarl. Then it scrambled to its hands and knees and began quickly crawling toward her.

Skye's M4 was equipped with a suppressor, something she had taken from the pile of gear left on the *Nimitz* by the dead Navy SEALs, but so was the pistol under her arm. She chose the rifle, dropping prone and sighting on the snarling thing, squeezing off a round. It clipped the top of the thing's head, digging out a chunk of rotten gray meat and making a *spang* sound in the tunnel beyond, but the drifter kept coming. She took a breath, held it a half second, and then blew it out slowly, squeezing.

The 5.56-millimeter round punched a hole next to one of its eyes and blew out the back. The creature flopped limply onto its face.

Even with the suppressor, in this tight metal space the shots had been loud, and she shook her head to clear it before crawling forward. By the time she reached the corpse she had her knife in hand, and she plunged the blade through what turned out to be a soft, giving skull, just to be safe. Up close, the corpse was pungent, flesh starting to slough off its hands. It had been a man, maybe in his seventies and dressed in overalls. Not Dean, she was sure of that.

Skye bit her bottom lip and crawled over it, her knees and one gloved hand sinking into the fermented rot with a squishing sound. She hurried and was quickly past, crawling faster to get away from the smell, knowing it was now clinging to her. Then she realized it might not have been down here alone, and she slowed her crawl to let the flashlight probe ahead.

After what seemed like an hour, a crescent of light appeared in the distance, the far hatch, partially open. She still needed the flashlight, but in short order she could see that nothing else had crawled into the escape tunnel. When she reached the end, she found another wheeled hatch, again capable of being locked down from within, the exterior a smooth steel face painted brown and green to blend with the forest. She pushed it open and saw pine trees all around, a carpet of brown needles underneath.

In the light spilling through the opening she saw something on the curving, ribbed steel wall to her right. It was a single word, spray-painted in black. She reached for her Hydra radio to tell Angie what she had found, ask her what it meant, and realized the radio was back with her pack.

"Damn," she muttered, crawling out into the forest and straightening, stretching her back for a moment and breathing untainted air. The forest was quiet around her.

Then she started crawling back.

When Angie finally emerged from the bunker her eyes were red and puffy, and she was holding her daughter's blanket close. Vladimir had since shut down the Black Hawk's engines to conserve fuel. Angie saw that the Russian and Carney were using entrenching tools to dig a hole in the front yard, a figure wrapped in a green poncho on the ground nearby.

The crucifix had been pulled down and was now empty.

Angie began to cry again, torn between running at them, demanding to know which one of them had shot her dad, and just curling up on the ground to weep for the people she had lost. Instead she simply stood near the helicopter and watched them finish digging, then carefully lower the wrapped figure into the earth before covering it quickly. When the dirt was tamped, the men looked at each other, then at Angie.

Skye came out of the bunker then, walking to them and taking it all in. Telling her friend about the word on the tunnel wall could wait.

The pilot, towering over Angie, put an arm around the woman and lowered his head. "I do not have the words. I am sorry." Carney just looked at the sky.

Angie nodded, hugged the Russian, then did the same to the former inmate. She looked down at the fresh dirt for a long moment. "I wish Xavier were here. He'd make it better. At least he'd know what to say." She wiped at a tear and blew the dirt a kiss. "Bye, Daddy."

They gathered at the helicopter, looking around at the devastation, the burned buildings and Dean's shattered Suburban. No one knew what to say, where to start, but they all shared Angie's hurt. And then a voice called to them from the road leading into the ranch, making them spin and raise their weapons.

A man was on the road less than a hundred yards away, standing next to a side-by-side green quad. He was simply dressed and wore a John Deere ball cap, a rifle slung over one shoulder. He raised a hand.

"Angie West! Don't shoot, I'm coming in."

Halsey squatted with his arms resting on his knees, as if he were about to draw a picture in the dirt. He spat tobacco and looked up with a weathered face at those gathered around him.

"It was over by the time I got here," he said. "I was hunting, and it sounded like a damn war up here. I came through the pines on foot." The ranch hand gestured back at the trees and spat again. "I'd been up here a week earlier, just to check on everyone. Dean was here with your folks, Angie, and Leah was just as right as rain." He smiled. "Pretty little thing. Your folks asked if I'd had any trouble over at the Broken Arrow, wanted me to pack my gear and bunk with them. Course I told them I was just fine at my place." He looked at the dirt. "If I'd taken them up on the offer, if I'd been here, then maybe . . ."

Angie was sitting in the door frame of the Black Hawk, looking at the ranch hand, a man just a few years younger than her father and a man Angie had known her entire life. Halsey worked for Carson Pepper and was the caretaker and general handyman for the Broken Arrow Ranch, but he had often come over to help her dad with jobs around the Franks spread.

"It's not your fault," she said. "I'm glad you're still alive."

The cowboy nodded, still staring at the dirt, and then looked up. "Same here."

"What happened?" Carney prodded.

Halsey looked at him. "Everything was burning. The house, the barns, Dean's truck. They were emptying out the bunker, and your daddy was . . . already up there."

Angie fought back tears. The family bunker hadn't been the big secret they had all thought. The TV notoriety, the publicity had obviously seen to that, and it had drawn looters.

"Dean and your daddy must have put up a hell of a fight," Halsey continued, "'cause there were bodies on the ground, and plenty of 'em. It just wasn't enough. Too many of them. And they had an armored vehicle, something from the National Guard, most likely."

Angie didn't speak for a moment, and when she did her voice was low and had a different tone. "Who were they?"

Halsey shrugged. "Can't say. Even with the binoculars I couldn't recognize any of them at that distance. Some locals, I expect. The rest looked like biker trash." The ranch hand looked at the woman whose childhood home had been reduced to ashes. "I wanted to cut your daddy down, Angie, to see him off proper. I feel real bad about not doing it. But by the time the trash left, the dead were up and walking. I was gonna risk it even at that, but then the Stampede came out of the trees."

The others looked at the man, eyebrows raised, and he spat.

"I can't help thinking of them in terms of animals," Halsey said.

"A life spent on a ranch and all. When I see 'em walking alone or in pairs, I see them as strays, and they're easy to handle. I call it a pack if it's less than a dozen, and if you're holding the high ground with a good field of fire, they're manageable too. Crowds of twenty or thirty, that's a herd, and you're best to steer clear, especially if you're alone." He squinted, his eyes seeming to disappear into leathery creases. "But there's a bigger group out there, wandering the forest." He waved at the trees and hills again. "Got to be a thousand or more, all staying close and moving together, damned if I know why. When they pass through, it looks like something out of that Kevin Costner movie, the one with him and the Indians, hunting buffalo. The Stampede leaves a crushed-down path in its wake. And that's what come out of the trees that day." He spit again. "I headed out right away, and I haven't been back until today." He shook his head. "But I'm still awful sorry about your daddy."

Angie let out a shaky breath. "He's resting now, Halsey. What made you come back now?"

"I saw your chopper," Halsey replied. "Made it out to the Skyway just in time to see you bank over this way. There's nothing out here except your daddy's ranch." He told them he had no idea Angie was on board. He had only wanted to know what all the helicopter activity was about and that maybe it was a sign that things were getting under control. Then he told them about seeing the Black Hawk wreckage shortly before their arrival. He hadn't gotten close to it and could offer no suggestion as to who they might have been.

"What about Dean and Leah?" Angie asked. "We didn't find their bodies. Are they . . . ? Did they . . . ?"

The ranch hand shook his head. "I was watching, and if those sons of bitches had taken them when they left, I'd have seen it. Maybe they got away." He didn't add that maybe Dean and their daughter rose from the dead and just wandered off. Halsey was a direct man, but that didn't mean a person had to deliver unnecessary cruelties.

"What about my mom?" Angie said. "Did you see her?"

The cowboy's eyes cut away and he said nothing, only spat tobacco.

"Halsey, did you see her?"

He sighed. "After." Then he looked up at the woman. "Your mama's dead, Angie, but she came back." Halsey thought again about unnecessary cruelty, and weighed it against a young woman's right to know what had happened to her mother. "They took her. That trash put a collar on her and chained that woman into the bed of a pickup truck, like they'd caught a mountain lion or some damn thing, and they took her."

Angie closed her eyes as her body shook. Carney put an arm around her and pulled her close.

"When did all this happen?" Skye demanded.

Halsey took a moment and squinted up at the misting, slate-colored sky. "Oh, I'd say two, three weeks after all this started. Call it the first week of September."

Skye looked at her friend. "I found something at the far end of the tunnel, Ang. A single word spray-painted on the wall." She told them what she had seen, and Angie became animated, hugging Skye fiercely, new tears in her eyes, but smiling now.

"They're alive," she breathed.

The others simply nodded, none of them prepared to throw cold water on their friend's sudden relief by reminding her that had been more than four months ago. A lot could have happened in that time.

Angie planted her fists on her hips. "I'm going after them."

Skye looked at her friend. "You know I'm in. No matter what we find."

Carney nodded, a thin, unpleasant smile on his face. "And we need to kill some motherfuckers."

Angie squeezed their shoulders, mouthing a silent *Thank you* at each.

Vladimir clapped his hands. "Yes! We will find Angie's family, and there will be killing of the motherfuckers. I like this!" He pointed at the Black Hawk. "That, however, is going to be a problem."

When they looked at him, Vlad shook his head and spat out something in Russian, folding his arms. When he spoke, it was as if to children. "Tell me, is there anything left in this world that draws more attention than a working helicopter?"

"How about an aircraft carrier?" muttered Skye.

The Russian wagged a finger. "You are most amusing. The answer is *nyet*. It calls to the dead like a bell for the dinner, and it will alert the men you seek long before you find them."

Halsey stood up from his crouch. "He's right. They're most likely headed this way already. The dead, I mean, maybe the biker trash too, 'cause there's no telling who saw you fly in here. Pray to God it doesn't attract the Stampede."

Angie nodded and looked at the Russian. "You'll need to stay with the bird, you know that."

"Being the only pilot here, I have come to that conclusion," Vladimir said, not unkindly. It made the woman smile, despite the fact that it was the last thing she felt like doing. "You have your radios," he said, "and when you call for an extraction, I will come." There was no bravado in his voice, and the others knew that this tall, homely man who had spoken so simply would keep his word. Even if Vladimir Yurish had to fly into the fires of hell, he would come when called because it was his mission. And he would probably have a sarcastic remark for the devil when he got there.

"Staying here's no good," said Halsey. "You can park that thing at my place, if you like. It's out of sight, and we can see anything coming from a good distance off." The cowboy smiled, his face seamed with lines. "Hope you don't mind simple chow. Don't have any caviar, I'm afraid."

The Russian thanked him and shook the cowboy's hand. "An adult beverage, perhaps?"

Halsey grinned and winked. "Now *that* I can deliver."

The ranch hand gave up his Polaris Ranger, and Angie, Skye, and Carney unloaded their gear from the Black Hawk and piled it in the short rear bed. They would use back trails and fire roads, entering Chico—where Angie was convinced Dean had gone—without being detected. Hopefully. Halsey would ride with Vladimir and guide him into the Broken Arrow Ranch from the air.

And then the Black Hawk was airborne, slipping over the tops of the pines and out of sight. Angie knew the terrain, so she drove as Carney rode shotgun and Skye settled into the back among the gear, facing backward with her rifle between her knees. The Barrett fifty-caliber, still in its hard plastic case, was so long that it stuck out the back.

As the Ranger churned along a dirt road, heading for the shadows of the tree line, a blue teething ring bounced around Angie's neck on its chain.

SIX

January 11—South of the Skyway

Halsey suggested the landing zone, and after circling the ranch, Vlad agreed and set the Black Hawk down about halfway between the mass grave and the cabin. It had been a short flight, taking them past the charred ruins of a mansion and over a hill before reaching Halsey's place. There was only one walking corpse in view, out across the fields about half a mile, slowly making its way in.

Vladimir grabbed his bag of personal gear but left the rest of the supplies—spare ammo, extra weapons, and food—strapped to the deck of the troop compartment. Together the two men walked slowly toward the cabin.

"What is this place?" Vladimir asked. "The large house that burned?"

Halsey spat tobacco. "Pepper's Broken Arrow Ranch. Carson Pepper's place, one of his places, anyway. He has several. One for every million in the bank, I expect."

Vlad didn't know who Carson Pepper was. The look on his face said as much.

"Pepper Boots," Halsey said as an answer to the unspoken question. "Kinda like Tony Lamas, only lots more expensive. Cowboy boots of the stars, Pepper used to say." The ranch hand stopped and lifted a boot. "Wearing a pair right now, only they're a little beat-up. Pepper used to give me a new pair every year for Christmas. I could never afford to buy them myself, they cost over a thousand dollars, and I wouldn't spend that kind of money on boots anyway. I gave 'em away as presents. I'll get four, five years out of a pair, and hell, they're not even broke in for two."

The pilot nodded. To him they were boots and he had still never heard of the brand, but then his taste in footwear leaned more toward comfort and utility. He looked over his shoulder toward where he had seen the moving corpse in the field, but his view was blocked by a long, low building. The cowboy beside him seemed not to notice or care where the creature was.

Halsey ambled slowly toward the cabin. "The Broken Arrow was Pepper's California ranch. He has—had—others in Montana and Wyoming. He had a lot of money, no denying that, but he was a down-to-earth fella. I liked him." He spat again. "It felt bad, shootin' him like that."

The Russian raised an eyebrow.

The ranch hand pointed out at the airstrip, where the small FedEx plane had merged with the private jet. "Pepper must have decided to ride out the plague right here at the Broken Arrow. He'd called and said he was flying in from Los Angeles. He's still in that jet over there, though I had to put him down. He was trapped in the wreckage, burned up but still moving."

Vladimir looked at the crash, his pilot's eye doing a quick assessment. "The jet landed, and turned to taxi back in," he said. "The cargo plane attempted to land. . . ." He clapped his hands together.

Halsey nodded. "It's like you saw it happen. Burned like holy hell too. Nothing I could do but watch. And shoot down the FedEx pilot when he came walking out, all on fire."

Now it was the Russian's turn to nod. Aviation fuel burned extremely hot, and the cowboy wouldn't have been able to get anywhere near it. He thought about the FedEx pilot, attempting to land on an obstructed runway. *Idiot. Or desperate beyond reason. Who knew what his crew members had turned into?* Vladimir had some experience with that.

They were standing in the hard-packed dirt yard in front of the cabin now, and the pilot gestured up the nearby hill. "It was not the aircraft fire that burned the big house, though."

"Nope," Halsey said, resettling the straps of the two rifles on his shoulder. "Lit the fire on that myself after what happened at the Franks place. A place like that attracts folks, and even after I burned it down, there's been a couple of times when trucks started up the main driveway to have a look. They turned right around when they saw what was left, though, and you can't see my place because of the hill." The ranch hand jerked a thumb back at the Black Hawk. "Same reason no one's gonna see your bird."

Vladimir thanked him and looked around at the barn and the stables, asking about animals. Halsey explained why there were none. He didn't go into detail about what had happened at the stables.

"I can offer you a damned comfortable couch, Vladimir," Halsey said, "someplace to lay your head without worrying about something biting you in your sleep. The food comes out of cans, mostly, but I've smoked some venison. You don't strike me as a man who needs a lot of luxury."

The Russian grinned. "I assure you, I do not."

"I'd be obliged if you could help out a bit," the cowboy said. "Ranch work never seems to be finished, and you're younger than me. Hell, twenty years younger, looks like. You afraid to chop wood or maybe mend some fences?"

"It is the least I can do to repay your hospitality."

Halsey shook his hand firmly. "That's all for tomorrow." He

looked at the sky. "It's getting late; we best be getting inside. I'll throw together some supper, and we'll get you that adult beverage."

Vlad was about to thank him again, then noticed a hard look drop over the other man's face. He was at once afraid he had said or done something to offend his host. Then Halsey moved past him, unslinging the smaller of the two rifles. The corpse they had seen earlier was coming around the corner of the barn, jerking toward them and increasing its pace, glaring with unblinking, filmy yellow eyes. It let out a moan.

Halsey put a .22 round through its forehead.

"And of course there's this chore," Halsey said, heading for the motionless figure, "and I don't think it will ever be done."

A fire was crackling in the small living room, and Vladimir was seated at the kitchen table while Halsey cleared the plates. The low hum of the generator came through the wall, and the door and all the shuttered windows were bolted tight. A kerosene lantern glowed on the table beside a saucer Halsey had produced to serve as an ashtray for the Russian. Vlad blew smoke at the beamed ceiling.

"You have been here since this all began?" the pilot asked. "Living alone?"

"I've been living alone since I got out of the service," Halsey said from the sink. "Had some lady friends over the years, none who wanted to settle for a beat-up ranch hand. I'm not complaining."

"It is lonely out here, is it not?"

"I'm used to it. And I've got my books."

Vladimir had already seen a pair of full bookcases, with more paperbacks stacked in piles near them.

"How about you?" Halsey asked. "Any family?" Then he cleared his throat. "I'm sorry, that's probably the wrong thing to say."

"Not at all," the Russian said. "I had a family. They were gone before all this."

The ranch hand returned to the table with a bottle of amber liquid and a pair of glasses, taking a seat. "Well then I'm sorry, but at the same time it seems a blessing."

Vladimir agreed. That was exactly how he saw it.

Halsey pushed a glass at his guest and twisted the top off the bottle. "I don't have any vodka. Never acquired the taste. This will have to do."

"It will be fine. I do not care for vodka either."

The ranch hand stopped before he could pour. "You're bullshitting me."

A homely grin. "Yes, I know, a Russian who does not drink vodka. Unthinkable. So I will also tell you that I am inept at chess, I do not care for snow or opera, and I cannot dance. I am indeed a very poor excuse for a Russian."

Halsey smiled and poured. "I imagine the boys in your squadron had their fun with you."

They touched glasses. "Look at me, my friend," Vladimir said. "People have been having fun with me all my life. But they are all gone now, the friends along with the tormentors."

The ranch hand lifted his glass. "To those who are gone, good and bad alike."

They drank throughout the evening, finishing the partial bottle only to have Halsey produce a new one from a kitchen cabinet. Vladimir explained how a serving flight officer from the Russian Federation had managed to be in California when the world ended. His native country had purchased a number of Black Hawks from the United States and had sent Vlad and several others to America to learn to be flight instructors. When the plague hit, and spun quickly out of control, Vladimir had been pressed into service, flying rescue missions out of a California naval air station.

Halsey talked a bit about ranch life and taking care of Carson Pepper's spread, but he seemed more interested in listening to the

Russian. As the liquor warmed his insides and loosened his tongue, Vlad spoke more about his experiences around NAS Lemoore, the large group back in the Bay Area, and the USS *Nimitz*. He also told Halsey about Sophia and little Ben. The other man smiled and told the pilot he was lucky to have people who cared about him, and that they were safe. Then he explained the map over the fireplace, pointing out places he had explored and looted. The Russian pointed at the small town just to the east.

"Paradise? It sounds nice."

Halsey spit tobacco into a mason jar. "Not anymore. Used to be nice enough, I guess, just a little town, nothing special. Had a bit of a rough element there, though, more trailer parks than churches." He tapped the map. "There's a bad bunch up there, vagrants and alcoholics and disability cheats, all come together like a pack of wild dogs. I call 'em Paradise Trash. Ran into them a couple months back when I was scavenging, had to put one down. They'll kill you for your shoes, that bunch. Nothing like the ones that burned out the Franks place, but bad enough." Halsey dropped into an armchair. Vlad took the couch. "Don't it figure that so many good folks have died," Halsey said, "and garbage like that just keeps on surviving? It's not right."

"That is a very old story, my friend," the Russian said, draining his glass and leaning his head back, closing his eyes.

Halsey looked at the fire. "I suppose it is."

The pilot was snoring minutes later. Halsey watched the flames dance for a while and then faded out to the sound of something scratching at the cabin door. It was a noise with which he had grown comfortable.

SEVEN

January 11—East Chico

Russo and Lassiter looked up at what sounded like a long crackle of distant thunder. A light mist still fell from the pewter sky, but there was no storm. Not one of nature's, anyway. After a fifteen-second pause it came again, sharp cracks in short succession, the echo rolling over the dead city. They went back to work, continuing south on Forest Avenue, walking side by side down the center of the road. They were glad they weren't involved in the not-thunder.

Well, at least Russo was. He suspected Lassiter would rather be there than here. Five years older than Russo, Lassiter was a cop wannabe with a severe crew cut—people called them buffs, right?—who for whatever reason had been repeatedly denied entrance into any number of law enforcement agencies and ended up as an armored-car driver. The man wore body armor and a harness of magazines for the AK-47 he carried, and tucked his fatigue pants into the top of his combat boots like he was in the Army.

The younger man would have laughed at him, but he was afraid Lassiter might gun him down in the street.

"We're getting a little far from the truck," Russo said.

"Don't worry about it," came the reply.

Russo was scruffy and in need of a shave, but good-looking under the stubble. Twenty years old, he wore an L.L.Bean jacket and, underneath that, a black T-shirt with the image of a reaching corpse over the words *Zombie Apocalypse? It's About Time!* He had a knit cap and a striped scarf, a large backpack and hiking boots. If not for the shotgun and the pistol on his hip, he would have looked like any other Chico State student, which was what he had been before the world went sideways. He lit a cigarette as he walked.

It earned him a sharp look from Lassiter. "They can smell that."

The younger man grinned. He had straight teeth, turning an ivory shade despite his youth. Russo had smoked since he was thirteen. "C'mon, with all that racket over there?" He waved in the direction of the not-thunder. "You're worried smoke is going to attract them? How about the two Happy Meals walking down the middle of the fucking road?"

Lassiter made a sour face. Russo thought that was the right word for most everything about his partner.

The former armored-car driver looked away. "Just remember to keep checking our six."

Russo raised an eyebrow. "Our six? Do you mean behind us?"

"You know I do, asshole."

Of course Russo knew what he meant. In the months they had been paired, he had grown accustomed to the wannabe tough-guy's mixture of police and military slang. The guy just begged to be made fun of, and even though Russo suspected screwing with the man could be unhealthy, sometimes it was just too hard to resist. The trick was to mock him without actually laughing. Besides, Russo was bored.

"Copy that," he said, deepening his voice.

Lassiter grunted.

"Roger and ten-four. Wilco. Good copy."

"Fuck you," said Lassiter, walking faster to get in front of the other man. Russo snapped a flat-handed, British salute at the man's back and whispered, "Okey-dokey, kilo-victor."

They were moving through a commercial district made up of retail stores, chain restaurants, small hotels, and strip malls. In many places windows had been covered with plywood, most of them pasted with yellow and black biohazard warnings. Russo knew the message by heart.

AVOID CONTACT—REPORT ALL EXPOSURE

The street had its share of abandoned cars and overturned bicycles, but not as many as there would be in the major cities, Russo thought. He tried to imagine what it would have been like in the bigger cities like New York, Dallas, Philadelphia, millions of people packed into what would quickly amount to killing jars. He thought about Chicago right about now, a frigid January wind coming in off Lake Michigan, snow on the ground, and frost-covered corpses moving slowly through those urban canyons. Russo shook off a chill.

The two men walked around a Chico Municipal dump truck that had been painted black, now sitting cockeyed in the road. They peered up and in at the stacks of body bags arranged in rows in the bed. One was moving.

Just beyond the truck, in the parking lot of a multiscreen movie theater, they saw a trio of wild dogs harrying a corpse in a hospital gown, lunging in and nipping, darting out when the zombie turned as another leaped in to bite at its gray legs. The dogs would eventually win, Russo knew, but they were just as likely to be a meal themselves tomorrow if they ran into a pack of skinnies.

That was Lassiter's word for them. He said it was what the Army had called them. To Russo, it sounded a little racist.

"We're too far from the truck," Russo repeated. "We should go back for it."

"That truck was a piece of shit. I'm looking for a new truck," Lassiter said.

The younger man shook his head. "Uh-uh, that's not what we were told to do."

Lassiter stopped and looked back at his partner. "Then walk back to the truck. But I have the keys, and I'm going this way." He continued in the direction he had been heading.

This was stupid. Lassiter's confidence was nothing but ignorant bravado. If they ran into a sizable pack or got cornered, they would be dead meat on foot. "No one said anything about a new truck. You're going to get us both in trouble."

"You're going to get us in trouble, boo-fucking-hoo," Lassiter called back in a falsetto. "Why don't you man up?" He kept walking.

Russo watched him go, looked around at the deserted stores and parking lots, then hurried after his partner. "You're a dick," he muttered.

Lassiter ignored him.

As they continued down Forest, they came upon a man hanging from some overhead power lines, his body dangling ten feet in the air. The man snarled and snapped at them from above, twisting in the air, and the two men in the street stopped to stare. The corpse wore the green flight suit and patches of an Air Force pilot, and he was hanging from his own parachute lines, the shroud tangled in the wires above.

"This fits with what we saw at the edge of Bidwell Park," said Lassiter. Months ago, during one of their many scouting runs, they had encountered the wreckage of a fighter jet that had plowed into the trees near the west end of the giant park.

Russo took out his pocket camcorder and filmed the snarling pilot.

"That's sick," said Lassiter. "No one is ever going to see your stupid movie."

The younger man ignored him. Before the plague he had been a film student at Chico State, about to begin his junior year. What the other man said might be true, no one would ever see his work, but that wasn't stopping Russo from putting together a kick-ass documentary. He already had several sketch pads of notes and storyboard drawings, but the film footage was the real prize. His only difficulty had been keeping his camcorder powered. There were several generators back where he, Lassiter, and the others lived, and scavenging crews went out regularly to collect fuel from Chico's many gas stations and abandoned cars. The toughest part—the most *frightening* part—was sneaking his camcorder battery in for charging. It certainly wouldn't be seen as a priority, and he was more than a little worried about what would happen if he was caught. Not enough to keep him from doing it, however.

The documentary was a priority for *him*. For after the plague. There *had* to be an after, right? This was history, happening all around him, and future generations would want it chronicled.

A rattle of chain link on their right got their attention. A dead teenage boy had his fingers hooked in the fence of a car rental lot, staring and moaning at them. This was why they should have the truck, Russo thought. It started with one, and then more came to the sound, and soon they were running for their lives instead of just driving away. Sometimes the truck's engine attracted more attention than two men walking, but in addition to scouting—their destination wasn't far now—they were supposed to scavenge as they went, and they needed the cargo space. Russo had his own opinion about the intelligence of sending out only two-man teams, but he wasn't about to argue with the one who sent them. The not-thunder was a perfect example of why.

A dead woman in only bra and panties, her many bite wounds turned black and green, joined the teenager at the chain link. Russo caught up with his partner and tucked his camcorder away. He had plenty of footage of corpses shaking fences.

They passed a Burger King with abandoned cars still lined up at the drive-through, windows smeared red. At a spa in a strip mall, someone had bagged a zombie—Russo refused to think of them as skinnies—with a shot to the head. A woman in a white terry cloth robe was slumped beneath a rusty splatter on the wall of the spa above her head, another motionless corpse lying half in and half out of the front doors, also in a robe, wearing one slipper. At the neighboring dentist's office, an old man still wearing a blue paper bib thudded against the inside of the glass door, cloudy eyes staring out at them.

Russo shook the empty satchel hanging over one shoulder. "We don't have shit to show for this run, man. We're not going to come back with anything if we keep walking past places."

Lassiter jerked his head. "You want to see if the dentist has some shit? Maybe some Oxy samples?"

The film student looked at the old man behind the streaked glass. Somewhere in there would be the dentist, an assistant or two, other patients . . . "No," he said.

Lassiter laughed. "Didn't think so. Besides, we're about to score, big time."

Russo had an opinion about that too, but he kept it to himself.

They came upon a minivan sticking out of the front window of a dry cleaner, its sides covered in long, dark streaks. A small Asian woman was pinned beneath one of the rear tires, arms reaching and fingers clawing endlessly at the asphalt, the flesh worn away to chipped bone. Russo stopped to film it, and this time Lassiter didn't give him a hard time, only stood and stared. After a minute, Russo put the recorder away again and they moved on. Neither even considered putting the thing out of its misery.

The two men took a right onto Notre Dame Boulevard, passing first a bridal shop with a smashed and empty display window, a fluttering white veil caught on a shard of glass. Russo stopped and pointed.

"They've been here!" Color came into his face. "I've seen that bride mannequin, and so have you."

Lassiter shrugged.

"Look," Russo insisted, "they've already *been* here!" He pointed toward the parking lot of a Raley's supermarket. The grocery store had been looted, debris scattered across the lot. Parked on the lot closest to them was a Greyhound bus with the word *EVACUATION* stenciled on both sides in white, the interior windows streaked with gore and the slap marks of bloody hands. Off to the right a flatbed Army tractor-trailer was parked with the rear ramp down, the flatbed empty. It was big enough to have carried a bulldozer.

"Why would they send us down here if they'd already checked it out?" Russo demanded, his voice rising in volume. "Are they trying to get us killed?" He was close to shouting now.

Lassiter suddenly grabbed the younger man by his scarf and yanked him close, lifting him onto his toes. The armored-car driver was stronger than he appeared. "No, *you* are, dickhead. You're fucking yelling."

Russo blinked and looked around. Corpses that had been drifting aimlessly through the lot or in and out of the grocery store were all facing their direction now, and moving as one.

"Good job, dick," Lassiter snarled. "I should fucking feed you to them." He gave Russo a shake and pushed him away, the other man stumbling backward. Lassiter turned and started to jog away from him.

Russo stared at the dead, at his partner's back, and choked down a sob. Why did the world have to go and shit on him like this? He missed his friends, missed the Internet and Facebook, missed regular showers and being able to just switch on a light when you walked into a room. Food that didn't come from a can, being able to speak your mind and not risk getting shot for it, coming and going as he pleased *without getting fucking eaten!* Now he did sob, a brief, semisuppressed gurgle of a noise. Lassiter was a first-rate bag of shit, but now he was getting farther away, and being alone out here was worse than all the rest. Russo had to run to catch up with him. The armored-car driver didn't say anything when the younger man reached him, only smirked.

Lassiter stood in the road and stared, ignoring the muttering of his partner beside him. Maybe Russo had been right. Maybe they shouldn't have left the other truck behind. He would never give the little punk the satisfaction of agreeing with him, though. As to being sent out here to die? They were valuable, at least he was, and wouldn't just be thrown away. Someone had a good reason for sending them out here, and that was enough for him.

Their orders had been to scout Pro-King Range, a large gun store and indoor shooting range at the south end of town. And there it was on the other side of the Skyway, burned to the ground. A lone, charred skinny shuffled through the ashes. Lassiter wasn't even going to bother crossing the road. There wouldn't be anything left of value in those ruins.

"So we scouted it, and now we know," he said aloud.

"You don't think they saw this when they were down here?" Russo said, his voice a whine that grated at Lassiter.

"They wouldn't have sent us if they did." The older man looked at the light running out of the cloudy sky. "Time to head back." He headed down the westbound lanes of the Skyway.

Russo pointed back the way they had come. "The truck's that way."

"And you got the skinnies all stirred up back there, didn't you?"

Lassiter called over his shoulder. "We'll get up onto ninety-nine and head north."

The film student jogged up beside him. "There's going to be lots of cars up there, lots of zombies."

Lassiter shrugged. "You can try getting back through the neighborhoods if you want to. Good luck. I'm taking the freeway."

Russo didn't reply, just followed, wishing all manner of hateful things on a man he knew he didn't have the guts to stand up to.

Within a quarter mile they came to a point where Route 99 crossed the Skyway at a slight angle, with the expected on- and off-ramps. They walked up one ramp, passing only one empty car against the guardrail, and soon they were forty feet above the dead city. As Russo had predicted, there were cars, SUVs, a few buses and motor homes, some tractor-trailers, but not as many as either man expected. A highway patrol car with all its doors and trunk standing open had been stripped of anything useful, and a Frito-Lay truck had been emptied as well. A handful of bodies lay rotting on the asphalt, so decomposed it was impossible to tell if they had died during the chaos of the outbreak or had turned and been put down later. Every motionless corpse was approached with care, however, for fear it would begin to stir. Both men had seen that before. Not all skinnies were up and moving; some just seemed to run out of gas and go dormant, waiting for stimuli. Lassiter had long ago given up trying to figure them out.

Below the highway on their left stood a four-story Courtyard Marriott. Several of the upper windows looked as if they had been broken out from the inside, and something white hung limp from the rooftop, the misting rain plastering it to the side of the hotel. It was a king-sized bedsheet, and on it in black spray paint someone had written *HELP*.

Lassiter stopped and held up a fist. Russo almost ran into it before he remembered that was the signal to stop. "Look at that," the armored-car driver whispered in a reverent tone. Ahead of them, close to the inner guardrail, was a black, jacked-up Ford F-250 pickup. The owner had tweaked it, adding customized black rims, tinted windows, and chrome push bars. Its mud flaps bore the familiar silhouette often seen on eighteen-wheelers of a curvy, sitting woman cast in chrome. A sticker in the back window showed a devious-looking boy pissing on a Chevy emblem.

"That's what I'm talking about," Lassiter said, his face spreading into a wide grin. He trotted toward the pickup with Russo tagging along behind.

"There's no way it's going to run," the younger man said, taking the time to check around the surrounding vehicles for zombies. He didn't find any. Ahead of him, the big Ford's engine roared to life, making him jump. There was a burst of radio static, then silence, and then the thunder of Metallica erupted from the truck's sound system.

Lassiter's laughter rose over the rumbling bass. "You bet your ass!" he shouted.

Russo opened the passenger door and was about to climb up and in when the former armored-car driver suddenly pointed out the windshield. "No shit," Lassiter said, "it's my lucky day."

She was three, maybe close to four, and she wore tattered gray shorts with little gray-and-white sneakers. Her once-white top bore the image of a happy cartoon panda. A bite had taken a large chunk of meat out of one cheek, and another bite on her forearm had exposed bone. The little dead girl stumbled at them, bumping into cars, leaning slightly forward with her chin raised, arms flopping at her sides.

Lassiter was out of the driver's side in an instant. "Looks like we're not going back empty-handed after all," he said, and took off at a run, heading straight for the girl. He straight-armed the preschooler like he was carrying a football in for the big win, knocking her down. In a second he had her facedown on the pavement, pinning her with a knee in her back and shrugging out of his backpack. He quickly dug out a short wooden dowel and forced it past her snapping teeth, then wound duct tape around her head to hold it in place. Next, he taped her wrists together behind her back and leaped up to a standing position, throwing one hand in the air.

"She's tied!" he yelled.

"I never get used to seeing you do that," Russo said, his tone somewhere between awe and revulsion as he pulled the camcorder from his L.L.Bean jacket.

"Keep an eye on the street," Lassiter said, fixing a leather dog collar around the struggling corpse's neck and pulling a pair of chains from his pack, clipping them to the collar. As he hefted her over his shoulder like a fifty-pound bag of dry dog food, he looked into Russo's camera. "I'm getting faster at this," he said, grinning, and then waved. "Hi, Mom."

Russo shook his head, laughing in spite of himself. "You're an asshole."

Lassiter tossed the little girl into the bed of his new pickup and hooked one chain to each side, holding her in the center. She stood and lunged but was jerked back short. "Maybe there's another—" Lassiter started, but then Russo barked, "Shut up! Get down!" and ran in a crouch to hide behind the truck.

The former armored-car driver looked up at a new sound, a distant thumping, and immediately saw the dark helicopter coming in from the south. He ducked down beside Russo and then walked in a crouch to the front of his truck, peeking around the bumper.

The Black Hawk—he knew what it was at once—came in low and then slowed when it reached the wreckage of the other chopper, the one Corrigan and his boys had brought down earlier. It paused for only a moment before banking and heading east into the hills, following the Skyway. The two men waited until it not only was out of sight but could no longer be heard.

Lassiter looked at his partner. "We need to tell them."

Russo nodded, looking fearful and sick. A moment later they were in the Ford, Metallica switched off, the truck weaving its way up the highway toward the center of town.

EIGHT

Little Emer Briggs stood in the cold, misting rain, peering around the tail end of a garbage truck. It was parked at an angle on Vallombrosa Avenue, about seventy-five yards from the post office.

"Offer the terms," said Little Emer.

The young man beside him, a kid named Fraley who had once worked at a cell phone kiosk in the mall, swallowed hard. His knuckles were white around the assault rifle he was holding.

"They could just shoot me," the kid said.

Little Emer smiled at him. It was a beautiful smile and he was a handsome man. It was that smile that had helped him bed women and put his enemies at ease just before he struck. Six-foot-four, muscled, with a closely shaved head and several days' facial stubble, he wore boots, jeans, and a leather biker's jacket. On the back was a patch bearing the image of crossed Bowie knives, the word *Skinners* on the rocker above, and *Spokane* on the rocker below. On the front near his heart was a one-percent patch, proudly announcing his out-law status.

Briggs put an arm around Fraley's shoulder. "It's just talking. They're in no position to bargain. We'll back you up, so don't take any shit." Again the smile.

Fraley looked up the street and took several quick breaths, bob-bing his head, then started walking, holding aloft a strip of white cloth tied to the muzzle of his rifle. A biker named Braga with long frizzy hair and an acne-scarred face stepped up beside Briggs.

"Fifty yards," said Braga.

"He'll go the distance," Little Emer said, watching the young man walk slowly toward the post office.

Braga smiled. "That's a bet. That diamond pinkie ring you found the other day?"

Little Emer nodded and tapped an emerald-and-titanium ring on the other biker's finger. "That's mine when you lose."

"You got it," said Braga, and they turned to watch.

Fraley made it up the street, to right in front of the post office, and Braga cursed, handing over the ring as Little Emer laughed. There was conversation up there that neither man could hear from this far away, and then the kid began to gesture angrily with his rifle.

"Mistake," Little Emer said.

Someone inside the post office shot Fraley in the head a second later.

Braga cursed again. "Why couldn't they have done that while he was still walking in?"

Little Emer Briggs chuckled and admired his new emerald ring, then held out a hand. A third biker, a man called Titan who wore a black goatee, handed over a two-way radio. The biker leader keyed the mic. "Send in Baby."

The post office had been a problem for months. Little Emer had known there was another band of survivors out here but hadn't been able to find their camp. When he at last located them, well fortified inside this concrete building, the two scouts responsible for this area had paid for their lack of observation skills with their lives.

At first Little Emer had encouraged them to join his own group. When they refused, he tried threatening instead, and when that hadn't worked, ground troops had been sent in. The post office people repelled the attack, costing Emer valuable bodies. Fuel and ammo expenditure ceased to matter as rage instantly replaced reason, and so today, after taking two days to regroup, the biker had come back in force. Never one to shy away from extremes, Little Emer had brought along Baby. He didn't use it often, and its commander frequently complained of maintenance difficulties, of using up heavy ammunition that couldn't be replaced. But Little Emer got what he wanted, and he now wished he had simply skipped negotiations with the post office people and used Baby first.

From farther up the street came the harsh rumble of a big diesel engine coming to life. Baby came into view a moment later, emerging from a side street and racing up the avenue, closing fast on the post office.

Olive and tan, still bearing its National Guard markings, the M2 Bradley infantry fighting vehicle was twenty-seven tons of steel capable of moving at forty miles per hour. As it drew near, bullets fired from inside the building began sparking off its aluminum armor. Designed to transport infantry across a hostile battlefield, while providing fire to suppress enemy troops and armored vehicles, the M2 was an older design, this particular unit manufactured in 1986. Its age had meant it went to a Guard unit, but there was nothing mechanically wrong with the vehicle.

The twenty-five-millimeter chain gun in its turret could fire two hundred rounds per minute and was capable of shredding both light and medium-armored vehicles. The concrete front of Chico's post office was no match for its firepower.

A rapid, metallic thudding sound split the air as a torrent of white fire spat from the main barrel, spitting a mixture of armor-piercing and high-explosive incendiary rounds. The front of the post office, its solid front doors and high, barred windows, disintegrated in a cloud of flying metal and concrete dust.

"I *love* that bitch," Braga yelled from behind the garbage truck, covering his ears with his hands.

Still firing, the M2 pivoted in the street, its tracks chewing into the asphalt. The thudding sound continued as the vehicle rumbled closer to its target. At close range, the auto-cannon tore the front off the building, and most of the roof collapsed in on the interior. Then the twenty-five-millimeter stopped, and the 7.62-millimeter machine gun built into the turret beside the main gun chattered to life, sweeping back and forth across the structure as the Bradley's turret swung left, right, and left again.

Little Emer permitted the assault to go on for a full minute before calling, "Cease fire," through the walkie-talkie. The firing stopped at once, leaving echoes rolling down Vallombrosa before being replaced by silence. What had been the post office was now a ruined shell, something from news coverage during the war in Bosnia. Baby grumbled in the street outside.

"Let's go," said the biker leader, and moments later five Harleys, followed by a pair of pickup trucks filled with armed men and women, rolled up the avenue to stop in front of the crumbled structure. Briggs's people leaped from the trucks and entered the building.

"Any bets on survivors?" Little Emer asked, arms folded.

On the bike beside him, Braga shook his head. "I'd say no, after all that, but you've been lucky. No bet, man."

Briggs chuckled.

The bikers sat astride their rides while the others secured the ruins. There were five of them, including Stark, who had once planned to be a professional wrestler before choosing this life, and an older man named Reed Cornish, whom everyone called Red Hen. They wore Skinners jackets like their brethren. Titan lit a joint and passed it around.

The shooters who had gone inside emerged with five corpses: two cops, a man in camouflage, and two women. The bodies were quickly gagged with duct tape and had their hands zip-tied behind their backs. A middle-aged man who had once been a restaurant manager came out with a small, squirming burlap sack over his shoulder, depositing it in the truck with the bound corpses.

Three survivors were brought out as well: an older man, a teenage boy, and a strong-looking young man in his midthirties with trails of blood streaming from his ruptured eardrums. They were lined up in front of the bikers, too dazed and shocked to do anything but stand and stare.

"He goes with us," Little Emer said, pointing at the wounded young man. He was taken away at once. The biker leader looked at the other two and held out a fist. He popped a thumb up, then rotated his hand so that it pointed down. The men beside him laughed.

A pair of heavy wooden crucifixes was pulled from the second pickup, and the two survivors were pushed toward them. The rest of Briggs's people began toting supplies out of the shattered post office: food, bottled water, medical supplies, weapons, and ammo.

Little Emer took the walkie-talkie again. "Corrigan," he said, "put Baby to bed and get yourself a beer. You've been a busy man."

"Copy," came the reply.

The biker grinned at the handheld radio. *Blowing out a nest of uncooperative survivors and shooting down a helicopter in one day. The man had been very busy indeed.* In the early days they had all been busy, not just surviving but establishing a safe haven. Once that was completed, however, life had quickly settled into a routine of gathering supplies—a task conducted by others—and looking for stray refugees that could be forced into service or slavery. It was quiet, even boring at times, and Little Emer relished these infrequent chances for action.

The nailing of hands and feet had begun, and Little Emer Briggs wasn't interested in staying around for the screams. The motorcycles gunned down Vallombrosa, back toward the center of town.

S aint Miguel sat a block off the Esplanade on Ninth Avenue, north of the university and Enloe Medical Center. The line of Harleys rolled past Chico's main hospital, the riders looking over at the parking lot jammed with cars, at ambulances sitting at odd angles with their rear doors standing open, at the fluttering yellow police tape strung between sandbag barricades. Drifters in soiled hospital gowns, Army uniforms, and summer clothes wandered the lot. The hospital had been gutted by fire, and a Life Flight helicopter stuck out of a fourth-floor wall, buried in the side of the building up to its tail.

They passed two other churches but not the one they wanted. The Presbyterian church was barely standing, a burned-out shell. At the Mormon church, someone had bolted plywood over every door and window, reinforced with two-by-fours, and then spray-painted *LIVING DEAD* across the wood.

Only a handful of corpses moved along the Esplanade, and the bikes avoided them easily. Soon, the bell steeple of Saint Miguel came into view over the rooftops of what had been a quiet, established middle-class neighborhood of neat houses. Then the rest of the church appeared, positioned at the corner of a large lot.

Rome, Little Emer thought upon seeing it. And he was Caesar. He liked the idea of being *warlord* better, though.

Chico's oldest Catholic church had celebrated its 150th anniversary more than a decade ago, but regular maintenance had allowed it to weather the passing time gracefully. Built of stone and heavy timber, faced with dark almond stucco and capped with red tiles, Saint Miguel looked like the Spanish mission it had once been. Narrow, arching windows looked down at the street, formidable double oak doors studded with iron bolts guarded the front, and the airy steeple commanded a long view in all directions.

In addition to the church itself, the grounds included a small school with daycare and playground facilities, along with a youth center boasting a gymnasium and small indoor pool. A baseball field sat behind the gym, and the entire grounds occupied nearly half a city block.

Improvements had been made since the outbreak.

Every house on the same block that was not part of Saint Miguel had been burned and bulldozed flat. The perimeter was now lined with steel shipping containers brought in from the rail yards and shoved in tight together to create a defensive wall. It had taken weeks, but there had been more than enough equipment in Chico's rail and truck yards—forklifts and flatbeds—to accomplish the impressive task. Afterward, the trucks had been abandoned on side streets, and those not already run dry were siphoned for their last drops of fuel. The constant talk and worry over fuel use bored Little Emer, but in this case, he could proudly declare that it had been worth it. The wall kept out the dead.

Wide openings had been left on each side at both Ninth and Tenth Avenues, then protected by gates made out of steel cut from other containers. Riflemen were positioned in the bell tower, and armed men and women patrolled the top of the container wall, picking off the dead that wandered up to thump against the steel.

Then there were the dog runs. The warlord was especially proud of these, mostly because they had been his idea.

At three of the four intersections around the fortress Emer Briggs called Rome, steel cables had been strung across the street. Drifters in collars clipped to the cables by chains formed curtains of the dead, able to shuffle back and forth along the length of steel without straying too far, the rasp of sliding metal clips and dragging feet joined together. Little Emer reasoned that anyone—any *living* person—who wanted to enter the intersection would be forced to face the dead. He hadn't encountered any enemies or refugees at his walls, so he assumed it worked.

The Harleys approached via the only road without a dog run, motoring up to a gate that rolled open to greet them and closed as soon as they were inside. Little Emer and his biker brothers drove through a parking lot and backed into a curb beside the church. At the far end of the lot, the M2 Bradley was backing into its own shelter, a high aluminum canopy intended to cover motor homes. A trio of men in Army uniforms emerged from the armored vehicle, threw a wave, and walked into the nearby school.

No one else waved at the bikers, not the handful of people at the gate or on the wall, not the riflemen in the tower, and not the woman trundling a wheelbarrow of human waste from the church out toward the baseball diamond. They all made a point of finding somewhere else to look.

Saint Miguel's main chapel was warm as the men entered, a fire burning in a large, freestanding iron bowl in the center of the room, smoke climbing into the high, arching beams before drifting out a hole in the stained glass. The pews had been removed, making room for the pallets of goods and supplies lining the walls. A mannequin in a bridal gown stood near a pallet of canned goods, her face painted to look like an overdone prostitute. Muted light from the stained glass combined with the fire to cast deep shadows, and motorcycle boots echoed across the marble floor. Where the altar had been now rested a heavy Gothic chair of intricately carved dark wood, pilfered from the Regents Hall at the university. A pair of human skulls had been wired to the uprights at the top of the chair.

Little Emer climbed three marble steps and dropped into his royal seat. The other bikers settled on the steps as Titan produced a six-pack of warm beer and Red Hen lit a pair of fat joints. Their weapons—a collection of assault rifles, sawed-off shotguns, hand-guns, and axes—littered the steps around them.

They bullshitted about nothing in particular for almost half an hour before a pair of dirty men in need of shaves walked in, marching the captive from the post office between them. His hands were bound and the blood from his ears had dried. They stood him at the foot of the marble steps and then backed out of the room. The man stared at the big biker in the throne and lifted his chin.

"What's your name?" the biker leader asked. When he cocked his head, showing the blood running down his neck, Emer laughed and yelled the question.

When he spoke it was in a too-loud voice. "Oliver Fields."

"What did you do before the plague, Oliver?"

"I was an office manager at a lumberyard."

Emer looked him over. He was dirty, like most people these days, but he could tell the man had at least made an attempt to take care of himself. He had a solid build. Otherwise, he was a plain-looking man in his thirties.

"Did you have family at the post office?" Emer yelled.

He shook his head.

"What to do with you?" he murmured, making the man squint and lean his head in. He drummed his fingers on the arm of the throne, and then in a loud voice said, "What will it be? Fighting, fetching, or feeding?"

The men on the steps chuckled. Oliver Fields drew back a step.

Briggs spoke loud enough for him to hear through damaged

ears. "You're a big boy, strong. I could give you a weapon and put you on the wall, but I don't think I want you armed after what happened at the post office. And you passed up your chance to join us."

Oliver looked at the floor.

"I could put you to work, have you cook and clean and empty the shitters." Little Emer smiled that beautiful smile. "And then there's feeding. We could leash you to the dog runs afterward."

"I vote for feeding," said Red Hen.

"Me too!" Stark yelled.

The man's head snapped up, his eyes narrow. "Touch me and I'll break your necks."

The bikers exploded with laughter. Braga tossed his shoulder-length hair and made a sharp snapping sound with his teeth.

Little Emer looked past him for a moment and then held up a hand. "Oliver, hold that thought." He motioned to the two men who had entered the far end of the chapel. Lassiter and Russo approached the throne, rifles slung. Both nodded, almost a bow, as they stopped before the pack of bikers and the big man on the skull-tipped throne.

"You made it back," said Little Emer. On the steps, Titan shook his head. He had bet that they wouldn't, and would have to pay up.

"We saw a helicopter," Lassiter announced. "Not the one you shot down. Another one." Russo was nodding beside him, and the two men explained where they had been and what they had seen.

Briggs's good humor slid off his face, replaced by a frown and brooding forehead. He waved the two men out without further conversation. The biker leader looked at his men, who exchanged glances. *A second helicopter. What did it mean?* Little Emer decided he would have to talk to his daddy.

The warlord looked back at the man standing at the foot of the altar steps, and his eyes hardened. "Break my neck, right?" The corner of his mouth lifted. "Oh, you're definitely fucked." He glanced at his men. "Let's get Oliver started on his new career."

Stark and Braga seized him at once, and the man began to thrash and fight. Red Hen punched the man in the head until he went limp, and then the bikers dragged him out of the chapel.

Little Emer Briggs followed with his hands in his pockets, thinking about helicopters and his father. He sighed, hoping that a little fun with a new captive would improve his mood. It usually did.

NINE

A dirt road made a rough rectangle around the Franks ranch, passing mostly through high pines on the left and right and a seven-foot fence topped with coiled razor wire fifteen feet off the right side of the road. Ed Franks, driving an old pickup truck, had more than a decade ago contracted with an outfit out of Sacramento that specialized in the design and installation of correctional facility fencing, assuring his fence was taut and strong.

The truck moved slowly, and Dean West was sitting with an arm cocked out the passenger window, sunlight dropping in individual beams on the road ahead through gaps in the pines. It was hot, and he waved at the occasional mosquito, watching the fencing slide by. He was looking for weak points where a tree might have fallen against it, or, God forbid, caused a breach. So far the perimeter looked intact.

Ed Franks was in his sixties, having fathered Angie later in life. He kept his gray hair short, framing a handsome and weathered face with light blue eyes. Ed chewed gum to replace the nicotine urges of a habit given up more than twenty years ago. Most of the time being an older father didn't bother him. Now, however, when the world had turned upside-down and demanded both strength and stamina, he cursed his advancing years.

"Lenore is going to ask you to do something," Ed said to his son-in-law.

"Name it," Dean said, not taking his eyes off the woods.

"You can say no. You should say no. It's my responsibility."

The younger man looked over at him. "What's wrong, Pop?"

Ed Franks stopped the truck and threw it in park, looking out the driver's-side window and sighing. "I told myself I wasn't going to say anything. Told myself I was going to tell Lenore not to say anything, either."

Dean just looked out the windshield and waited.

"Getting old is no fun at all," Ed said, spitting his gum into the trees. "A man has this sense of who he is, what he can do, and that never really goes away. But our bodies have other ideas. They don't give a damn about who you *think* you are."

"Pop, you're sixty-six. Nowhere near an old man."

"Ha. Tell that to my back at the end of the day, or my knees in the morning. Tell it to my bladder, getting me up three times a night to take a leak." Ed flexed his rough, lined hands on the steering wheel. "In my heart I'm still twenty-five," he said, "but the rest of me is pushing seventy."

Dean shook his head. "Most men would kill to be as fit as you are, Pop. I'm half your age, and you could still kick my ass."

Ed Franks laughed. "I do believe I said as much to you at your wedding reception."

"Yeah, with your brother Bud standing right beside you nodding."

"Well," said Ed, "Johnnie Walker was doing most of the talking that night, if I recall."

Dean laughed and gave his shoulder a shove. "You were a scary old man."

Ed smiled. "And you're the best thing that ever happened to my daughter. You're a good son. And she'll be coming soon."

They were quiet for a while, the not-uncomfortable silence that falls when men who care about each other admit it.

The older man finally cleared his throat. "So Lenore is worried about Harris MacDonald and his family."

Harris was one of Ed Franks's oldest friends, semiretired as well, who often worked in the gun shop in town. *Work* wasn't the right word; *hung out and shot the shit with Ed* was more accurate, but Ed loved the man like another brother. When it all fell apart, they had kept in touch with a CB radio, Harris MacDonald refusing the invitation to bring his family out to the ranch, telling Ed he was hunkered down at home with plenty of supplies and weapons. Harris had kept them updated on happenings in Chico for the first couple of weeks, and then suddenly there was nothing, not a single word on the radio, and no response to calls. It was three weeks now since the outbreak.

"Lenore wants him here, dragged if necessary," Ed said. "When I told her I'd go, she crossed her arms and looked at me the way she does."

Dean nodded. He had been on the receiving end of those crossed arms before.

"She told me right to my face that I was too damned old," Ed said, "that it's work for a younger man."

"She's right, Pop."

"Goddammit, I know she's right, and I know it's pride that's got me so mad about it." Ed unwrapped another piece of gum and chewed it angrily. "Lenore keeps saying it's only ten miles from here to town. I tell her that's a dangerous ten miles, and you've got Leah to worry about, not some old fart in Chico. After what you two went through to get here . . ." His voice trailed off and he looked at his lap. "It's not right to ask," Ed said, then looked up and into his son-in-law's face. "But I guess I'm asking."

On the trip to Chico, Dean had seen it all coming rapidly apart. County workers had been erecting roadside signs that warned of contagion, and sheriff's deputies were telling people not to attempt entering the little towns north of Sacramento. National Guard roadblocks forced him onto side roads or to turn around completely, causing him to backtrack to find another way north. He had seen parties of men in hunter orange patrolling the roadsides and seen the dead as well on those same roads. They were the worst, shuffling corpses that had once been people with lives and hopes, now predatory cannibals gnashing and thumping at vehicles as they went past, taking down those foolish enough to be out on foot. Dean had seen plenty of that too.

Leah needed two potty stops, spent time playing with Wawas, sang some songs, demanded animal crackers once, and had grown crabby another time before finally dropping off to sleep in the car seat. Dean hadn't been able to keep her from seeing the dead beyond the Suburban's windows—there were so many of them, and it seemed more every hour—and she had begun calling them Icky Men.

Once they got beyond Sacramento, there had been only one real scare, and it was during the second potty break, just south of Oroville. Dean had pulled to the shoulder and set Leah's potty chair up close to the Suburban, standing a few feet away with the combat shotgun in his arms while his daughter did her business. They both saw the creature at the same time.

"Icky Man," Leah said, pointing at a teenager stumbling out of the trees and onto the shoulder thirty feet away. The boy's skin was ashy, his lips a dark purple, and he was missing an arm. The teen-ager lurched toward them at once.

"All done, honey?" Dean said, moving slightly to put himself fully between his daughter and the corpse, bringing the shotgun up slowly. He did not want to squeeze off a round this close to his daughter. The sound from his handheld howitzer would traumatize her. "Ready to go?"

"Gotta poop," she said.

Dean took a sharp breath and sighted on the teenager. "Are you sure?"

Leah was humming. The corpse was close enough for Dean to hear it grunting, sneakers scraping at the pebbles on the shoulder. He wasn't going to have a choice, and his trigger finger tensed.

"No, all done," said Leah, changing her mind and hopping off the little seat, pulling up her tights. Dean immediately slung the shotgun and swept her into the car seat, hands moving fast to click her harness belts closed.

"Potty," Leah said, pointing at the ground outside. Then she pointed past him. "Icky Man."

Dean spun, slamming the Suburban's rear door closed with one hip, his right hand falling to the butt of the forty-caliber and clear-ing leather in a single, fluid motion, bringing the pistol up. He touched the barrel to the lunging thing's brow and blew its brains out the back of its head.

A moment later he was in the driver's seat, starting the engine. From the backseat Leah said, "Did you shoot the boom-boom?"

"I sure did, honey. Was it too loud?" He had hoped the single shot had been somewhat muffled through the glass.

"It's okay," she said.

Dean dropped the gearshift into drive.

"Daddy, potty chair!"

He braked, sighed, and got out.

. . .

Now, sitting on this quiet dirt road beside his father-in-law, Dean smiled at the Potty Zombie episode, not at what he had done, but at the resilience of children. There had been no more incidents after that, and he had gotten them to Chico safely. Though the world was falling down, here on the ranch they were untouched. But now Ed Franks wanted him to go back out there to look for a family friend who might or might not still be alive.

"I'll go this afternoon," Dean said.

Ed shook his head. "Tomorrow morning will be just fine. I want to finish checking this fence. I'm . . ." He choked for a second. "Thank you."

Dean smiled and patted the old man's knee. "Don't worry, Pop. If old Mac is out there, I'll bring him back."

When Dean stepped onto the porch in the morning, Leah was sitting with her grandmother, playing with a stack of plastic blocks, her stuffed walrus within easy reach. She had settled in well at the ranch, and its remote location had been a blessing. The dead made it as far as the fence in the woods and remained there until Dean or Ed came by to clear them off. Leah had seen none of it.

Their only visitor had been Halsey, the caretaker over at the Pepper place and one of Ed's friends, who had come by once to check on them. Ed had long ago given him the code to the heavy Maglock-secured gate on the ranch road. Lenore tried to insist Halsey come bunk with them, but he had politely refused. He was a man who looked after himself, and Dean liked him.

Sitting on the floor of the porch with her granddaughter, Lenore Franks looked up at Dean and smiled, her eyes showing gratitude and worry. Even at sixty she was a striking woman. Ed Franks pulled the

Suburban around front and loaded it with a spare fuel can and a couple of plastic jugs of water, placing Dean's combat shotgun in its dashboard mount.

Thank you, Lenore mouthed, and Dean gave her a smile and a kiss on the forehead. Then he picked Leah up and gave her a loud kiss on the cheek and a hug.

"Daddy!" Leah yelled, squirming and laughing. "You're scratchy."

Dean ran a hand across his whiskers and smiled. "Daddy has to go out for a little while," he said, setting her back down next to her blocks. "Be good for Grandma and Pop-Pop. I'll be back soon."

"'Kay, Daddy." She grabbed Wawas and used the stuffed animal to knock down a stack of blocks.

At the Suburban, Ed said, "Keep the radio on channel eight, and stay in touch. If Mac's not at home, he might be at the Silver Dollar."

From Harris MacDonald's frequent updates they had learned that the authorities in Chico had been unsuccessful in containing the steady spread of the walking dead and had set up a safe refugee camp at the Silver Dollar Fairgrounds. MacDonald said there was a National Guard presence in Chico, and together with the police department they had managed to at least keep that area secured, confident things would turn around quickly.

But that was a week ago, and there had been only silence since.

After Dean climbed in, Ed Franks slammed the driver's door and leaned on the window. "If it's too bad . . . if you can't . . ." He shook his head angrily. "Just come back to us, no matter what you find."

Dean said he would.

If the silence of the CB channels had been the first sign that something had gone wrong, the Skyway was the second. Cars and trucks were stopped along its length, some crumpled together in accidents, all of them silent and still. At one point Dean saw that a fire truck had run off the road and down the embankment, its grille twisted around a pine tree. The emergency vehicle was covered in strapped-down luggage, fuel cans, and sleeping bags, transformed into an evacuation vehicle.

The Suburban idled past a rusting Taurus station wagon with a figure still belted into the front seat. A fat black crow exploded out the open window in a storm of feathers, making Dean jump and jerk the wheel. The decaying corpse in the station wagon's driver's seat rolled its head to the left and looked out with a pair of holes where its eyes had been, jaw working soundlessly.

The warm morning air was scented with pine but, like a cheap odor spray, failed to mask the greasy aroma of spoiling flesh underneath. The scent drifted out of the cars and in through his windows, and Dean was soon forced to buzz them up and turn on the air conditioner. It helped, but only a little.

The smell of rot wasn't only coming from the cars. It wafted off the corpses walking slowly along both the inbound and outbound lanes. Figures dressed in shorts and T-shirts dragged themselves across the pavement, weaving among the stopped cars and trucks. Their graying flesh was marred by rips or pocked with buckshot, eyes milky orbs in slack, gray faces. There were children among the dead, and this made Dean shudder.

His right hand trembled, but he made a tight fist until the tremor went away.

He had seen the corpses, of course, in Sacramento and during the journey to Chico, but he wasn't used to them yet. He had come across them standing at the fence in the woods, cold fingers gripping the chain link until a thrust with a pointed metal bar pierced their brain and made them fall off. Dean had heard the reports on the CB while it still worked, from old Mac and on other channels, had heard that their numbers were increasing as the plague spun out of control.

Anyone that dies comes back, the voices on the radio had said. *Destroy the brain. Bites spread the disease. The big cities are lost; the smaller ones are barely hanging on. The government is working on a cure.*

And then nothing.

Dean navigated the black Suburban down the Skyway, nudging the dead aside with the big SUV's front bumper, not wanting to risk damaging the vehicle while he was out here alone. The inbound lanes held fewer cars and corpses than the outbound, and for a two-mile stretch there was only unobstructed road on his side of the highway. Then he reached the short bridge that crossed Butte Creek, just outside Chico's outskirts.

It was a woman—had been—and the tatters of a flowered sundress hung in flaps around its neck, split completely up the seams. Now its swollen breasts rested atop an even more swollen belly, bulging arms and bloated legs making it look like a balloon in some hellish Macy's Parade. Piggish eyes peered out from folds of flesh in its face.

It was green and looked ready to pop.

The creature had somehow dropped into a sitting position and become wedged between the front fender of an abandoned car and the bridge's guardrail. It slowly kicked its bloated legs and waved its arms, unable to free itself or stand. Dean drove by slowly and carefully, sensing that if he nudged the abandoned car it would squeeze the dead woman. He could only imagine what would happen next.

The bloated green corpse behind him now, he checked in with Ed and Lenore on the CB, telling them what he was seeing, but not about the green woman. He was told to be careful and get back quickly.

Dean's questions about what had happened to Chico were answered first by the complete absence of moving vehicles on its streets. The city's fate was next apparent in the form of boarded-over

windows, biohazard warnings, and abandoned roadblocks. The sight
of a coyote loping alone and in daylight down the Skyway, completely
without fear, told him more than a radio broadcast. The occasional
wandering corpse seemed almost like a sideshow compared to the
boldness of the coyote.

The Suburban passed beneath the Route 99 overpass, where
someone had spray-painted *END TIMES* on the concrete. He continued as the road became Park Avenue, the Silver Dollar Fairgrounds appearing on his right.

He did not see that less than a mile behind him, a column of
trucks, SUVs, and motorcycles, followed by a boxy military vehicle,
rolled out from Notre Dame Boulevard. They turned onto the Skyway and headed into the canyon.

Dean slowed, unable to take his eyes off the fairgrounds, the
place Harris MacDonald had reported was a safe zone for refugees.

When the fair wasn't in town, the Silver Dollar was a local speed-
way, an oval track with spectator stands, all within a high fence.
There was no racing now. Instead, the track was crowded with camp-
ers and motor homes, cars, trucks, and military six-by-sixes. There
were ambulances, fire trucks, and a trio of delivery vans from a local
party rental shop. The grassy infield was filled with tents of all
shapes: Army field tents, nylon camping tents, canvas Red Cross
structures, and white canopies from the party rental trucks, once
used for barbecues and weddings, now converted to refugee shelters.

The fence had collapsed in a dozen places. The dead wandered
the fairgrounds freely.

Dean's voice caught only once when he reported the scene to Ed
and Lenore, announcing that he was on his way to the MacDonald
house. Again, he was told to be careful.

Harris MacDonald and his family lived just north of the fairgrounds, in a quiet neighborhood not far from the Sierra Nevada
Brewing Company. In fact, the old man could see the plant's high,

stainless steel towers from his front yard. Dean accelerated and left the fairgrounds behind, traveling the final distance in minutes through empty streets.

He saw all he needed to from the curbside. The bricks of the middle-class home were pocked with gunfire, windows smashed and part of the roof torn away as if by a giant's crowbar. Bulldozer-like tracks scarred the once-pampered lawn, and what remained of the front door stood open.

Harris MacDonald had been crucified in his own yard, his corpse left to rot, the black spot of a bullet hole in his forehead visible even from the street. Dean looked at the house. He knew that searching for surviving family members would be futile, so he reversed direction toward the Skyway and headed back the way he had come.

He had just cleared the 99 overpass again when the CB burst to life with Lenore's voice. ". . . Dean, Dean . . . oh, God!"

Dean snatched up the handset. "Lenore, come in! Talk to me!"

There was a pause, a brief crackle, and then an open mic. In the background he heard a sound with which he was intimately familiar, the chatter of an automatic weapon. Then he heard his daughter scream.

"Lenore, come in!" he screamed into the radio. "Ed! What's happening?"

There was no reply.

Dean dropped the hammer on the Suburban and shot up the Skyway into the canyon.

The chain of events that led to what happened at the Franks ranch would have been difficult to predict, but it almost certainly began with Angie West. Angie had always thought the family bunker—so well stocked with supplies and arms—was a secret. Its existence, however, was revealed two years earlier to the wrong people by her own loose tongue.

It had been at a cocktail-fueled, after-hours get together with several of the producers for *Angie's Armory*. When asked about the private lives of people so involved in firearms and combat shooting, Angie had dazzled the producers with tales of the bunker and the stockpile of arms within, winking and saying that her family was ready for anything. One producer suggested the family qualified as *preppers*, and a segment on the ranch and the bunker would make for captivating television.

No, Angie had said, they weren't preppers, and the bunker was just between them. Tipsy from wine, the young woman had smiled and held a finger to her lips. By the following morning she had completely forgotten about the conversation.

The producers didn't. There was discussion in the studio offices all that week, without any of the Frankses or Wests present. Should they push, get Angie to go along with a bunker segment? How much of a sweetener could they offer to get her cooperation? Was the value of bullying her for the segment worth making their star unhappy? In the end, a senior studio executive weighed in and ruled that Angie's wishes would be respected, and the subject was tabled.

A junior producer had been present for the talks, and he complained to his assistant that Angie West was being unreasonable. Imagine, an underground bunker packed with automatic weapons. Fans would eat it up! The producer's assistant repeated the conversation to her roommate, who in turn shared it with her cousin, a rabid fan of *Angie's Armory* who never missed an episode, a man named Terry Lassiter who worked as an armored-car driver up in Chico.

When the plague hit and that same Terry Lassiter fell in with some dangerous people, the story of the weapons cache was repeated. Plans were set in motion.

. . .

D ean's Suburban roared back across the bridge over Butte Creek, and he scarcely noticed that the car that had pinned the bloated green zombie was now crushed against the guardrail. He went by too fast to see that the pavement was green and wet, a burst corpse trapped and flopping beneath the car.

But he saw other vehicles on the Skyway that had been crushed, flipped over, or rammed out of the way. Corpses had been run down and torn apart, a few still twitching and trying to rise, and he saw places in the pavement where something heavy with tracks had pivoted and gouged the asphalt. Former staff sergeant Dean West recognized the passage of an armored vehicle when he saw it.

Those same tracks turned off the Skyway and onto the dirt road leading to the Franks ranch.

Trees flashed by, the heavy SUV bouncing and swaying along the dirt road, threatening to slide off the edge. Dean kept the accelerator down, gripping the wheel with both hands and fighting for control. Through the open windows he could hear the ripple of distant gunfire, and then the unmistakable triple boom of an auto-fed heavy weapon.

Suddenly the trees parted and there was the gate, knocked flat now, the metal piping bent and twisted from being driven over by something incredibly heavy. A mud-splattered Jeep was pulled off the road near the gate, a man with a baseball cap and a rifle standing nearby. He jumped at the roaring engine suddenly coming toward him out of the trees.

Dean ticked the wheel and put the right side of the grille into the man at fifty miles per hour. Blood exploded across the hood and windshield, the shattered body momentarily airborne before crumpling to the earth. The Suburban didn't slow.

There was smoke ahead, and as the SUV crested a rise in the dirt road, Dean saw flames and chaos. Every building was burning.

Pickups and motorcycles tore across the lawns, circling like Indians in an old western, riders and passengers firing wildly on the move. Another handful of men took cover behind a bullet-riddled yellow Hummer, firing around the ends or over the hood. An M2 Bradley infantry fighting vehicle threw turf into the air behind it as it sideswiped and collapsed a burning outbuilding, then pivoted to charge around the rear of the main house.

Dean spotted Ed Franks then, the older man keeping a low silhouette in the open doorway of the bunker, firing an assault rifle in quick bursts. One of the men hiding behind the Hummer grabbed at his throat and fell.

The Suburban chewed up the ground as Dean left the road and tore across the grass, clipping a motorcycle and sending its broken rider spinning through the air. The distinctive cracks of an AK-47 came from his right, and a line of rounds stitched down the Suburban's side, one of them punching a hole in the fuel can back in the cargo space. The reek of gasoline filled the SUV at once.

At the bunker entrance, Ed Franks was firing, turning slightly, firing, adjusting again. Another man fell behind the Hummer, and the windshield of a moving pickup disintegrated, showered with red, the vehicle slowing instantly. Dean's Suburban was fifty feet from the bunker's entrance when the M2's twenty-five-millimeter chain gun opened up. The bunker's concrete entrance, its steel door, and Ed Franks vanished behind a storm of high-explosive incendiary rounds. Earth and cement erupted in a cloud, and Dean stomped the brakes, cutting hard left to avoid driving into the heavy weapon's fire. One shell, however, found the mark and blew away the SUV's right front tire and fender, wrenching the vehicle hard to the side as metal fragments tore through the engine.

Dean bailed out the driver's door. There wasn't time to retrieve the combat shotgun, but he jerked the MAC-10 from its custom holster and ran in a crouch through a cloud of smoke and concrete dust. A figure appeared on his right, a howling man wearing police body armor and carrying a rifle. Dean swept a burst of forty-five-caliber fire across the man's face and put him down. He fired a second burst at a figure running behind the first, and that man hit the ground, dead or alive Dean couldn't tell. Then he was at the bunker opening, jumping through and onto the stairs, dragging Ed Franks's limp body down after him. Bullets chopped at the opening above, and the thunder of the M2's big diesel drew closer.

Ed was gone, he knew it in an instant. At the bottom of the stairs lay Lenore, facedown, her back peppered with shrapnel from the twenty-five-millimeter, blood pooling on the cement floor. Leah lay beneath the lifeless body, her grandmother's arms wrapped protectively around her.

Leah was crying.

"Daddy's here, baby," Dean said, choking on the words. He shoved the MAC-10 into its holster and pulled his daughter free. Holding her stuffed walrus to her face, Leah began to shriek and kick, and he held her tight, pinning her to his chest. The small body shuddered, and the screaming stopped, but not the tears.

"Daddy's here," Dean kept repeating, hurrying through the bunker to the sleeping chamber. The four of them had been spending their nights down here, buttoned up against the darkness. Daytime had seemed safe enough, so they used the house when it was light, able to see anything approaching before it got there. They had been expecting the dead, and Dean cursed himself for being a fool. Ed Franks must have seen the bandits coming and quickly hustled his wife and granddaughter down to the bunker before making his stand.

Dean grabbed the bright orange go-bag from the spot on the floor where he had dropped it three weeks ago and threw the nylon strap over his neck. He checked the bunker's main chamber before emerging, saw that it was clear, and hustled for the armory door, holding Leah close.

Voices behind him, the scrape of boots on the stairs, and then the clatter of something metallic hitting the floor. There was a *whoosh* and a hiss as smoke began filling the main chamber.

No time for the armory. Dean slipped into the rear chamber and found the exit hatch, snatching a can of black spray paint off the top of the generator before crawling through the opening, Leah under one arm. Using his fingertips, he pulled the hatch as far closed as he could, then turned and began a fast crawl through the darkness, keeping his head low. The go-bag dragged behind him, and Leah fussed and cried under his other arm, calling for her mommy.

"Hush, baby, we're okay," Dean whispered. "We'll see Mommy soon."

The distance felt endless in the absolute dark, and despite his best efforts Dean cracked the top of his head twice on the low tunnel ceiling. He felt that at any moment, dead hands would reach for him out of the black ahead, or the hatch behind would open and the tunnel would be sprayed with gunfire. He crawled faster.

Then he banged his head against metal once more, cursing until he realized he had crawled right into the hatch at the far end of the tunnel. He turned the wheel and broke the rubber seal with a soft hiss, pushing outward as daylight fell on them. Leah let out a soft sigh between her sobs.

Quiet woods waited just beyond the tunnel opening, green and fragrant, whirring with insects and dappled with sun and shadow. Dean scanned the trees as long as he dared, then shook the can of spray paint. "Daddy has to leave Mommy a note," he told his daughter, then scrawled a single word on the tunnel wall. He knew— hoped—Angie would know what he meant. If she ever saw it.

LEWIS

Dean scooped Leah into his arms and ran into the forest. Behind him, the Franks ranch burned.

TEN

A single candle rested on the coffee table, the little house's curtains drawn to prevent the light from being seen outside. Skye and Carney sat together on a sofa, and Angie was perched on the edge of an armchair across from them.

"Dean enlisted the day after 9/11," Angie said. "That was long before we met." She was staring into the candle's steady yellow flame. "He did three tours in Iraq by the time he was twenty-five, and then they sent him to Fort Lewis, Washington."

Skye sat close to Carney, warm against his muscled body. The former inmate's arm was draped around her shoulder.

"That was where the Army trained him to be an urban warfare instructor," Angie said. "Dean always said he was glad to have the chance to teach what he had learned. He said urban warfare wasn't like regular Army."

They were drinking instant coffee, the remains of their meal on the nearby kitchen table. Outside the temperature had dipped below freezing, and they had been fortunate to find this little house—someone's summer place—down a short gravel drive off Stilson Canyon Road. Searching half a dozen similar places between here and the ranch had uncovered no signs of Dean's passage, and no other survivors. They had found only drifters, which Skye quickly put down with her silenced M4.

Carney sipped coffee from a mug bearing a football team logo. "Is that related to what he left on the tunnel wall? Lewis?"

Angie nodded. "The urban warfare center at Fort Lewis. I think he was letting me know he was going into the city instead of the wilderness."

"Why would he go there?" Skye asked. "That's probably where the raiders came from, and there would be a lot more drifters." She gestured with her coffee mug, chipped with a faded purple flower on one side. "Why not a place like this? Or even stay out in the woods? With his training, he could make it."

Angie smiled at her friend. "He's got a little girl with him. He can't keep her out in the woods."

Skye nodded.

"And a place like this is no good," Angie said. "If he's on the run, he'd have no place to go if he was discovered. A city has more places to hide, more resources." She said it with a certainty she didn't feel. It was all conjecture, and the simple truth was that she just didn't know. Maybe Dean had looped around and gone up to Paradise. She didn't think so, couldn't say why, but it was a possibility. They might be looking for him in the wrong place.

Angie set her own cup down on the table. "I'll take first watch. You two try to get some sleep; we'll move at first light." She picked up her rifle from where it leaned against the chair and moved to a spot at the front of the house, where she could look out a window and see the driveway's approach. The Polaris side-by-side sat quietly in the moonlight.

Skye took Carney's hand and led him into the back bedroom. They didn't speak, and made love quietly. Afterward she rested her head and one hand on his broad chest, listening to his breathing as he slept.

Part of her felt guilty for the intimacy so close to where her friend stood a lonely watch, tormented by fears for a missing family. The other part, and, she admitted, the stronger part, cared only for getting lost in this man's embrace, in his powerful arms and in those blue eyes that burned into her with such deep emotion.

What is this? Skye wondered. It felt like nothing she had experienced before. The sight of him made her heart beat faster, and even in tense and dangerous moments, his presence reassured her, made her feel safe. Was this love? Or liability? A cynical voice, born during her time alone in Berkeley and Oakland, argued that this relationship with Bill Carnes was a distraction, that allowing herself to love would only lead to heartbreak.

And how did he feel about her? Carney didn't say much, wasn't a man to express many feelings, although he had opened up to her about his past, and she knew what kind of courage that had taken. Was she simply something to help pass the time and satisfy his needs? She didn't think so, and Carney's eyes said something else.

She sighed against him, listening to the steady thump of his heart, feeling herself begin to drift off. She'd turned a year older, she realized, the random thought coming to her in that fuzzy way things do on the edge of sleep. Her birthday had been in the fall, and she hadn't thought about it until now. *Happy birthday to me.*

With this in her head, she slept.

Skye awoke sometime in the night to find herself alone in the bed, the blankets cold beside her. She pulled on a shirt and padded to the bedroom door, peering out.

Angie was asleep on the sofa, rifle propped nearby. Carney sat in a chair by the front window, his back to the bedroom and his M14 across his knees. He was having a cigarette in the darkness, the window open an inch to let the smoke out.

Skye closed the bedroom door and knocked out two hundred crunches followed by fifty diamond push-ups, trying not to think about the warm bed and her desire to crawl back in. And have company under the covers. When she was finished, she dressed, pulled on her boots and combat gear, and collected her weapons. Then she slipped out to join her man in his watch at the window.

Carney heard her approach, soft as it was, and smiled in the darkness. He would be happy for the company.

He had been thinking about what they had found here. It wasn't so very different from Oakland, only less populated. Still a place of shattered life and emptiness. Still a realm of the dead. Could Angie's husband and daughter be alive out here? He didn't think so and hadn't believed it during the months Angie had spoken of her family while they recovered aboard the *Nimitz*. When he climbed onto the helicopter it had only been for Skye, and to support a new friend. Faith in finding a man and a child who had survived all this destruction was a dream, and Carney was not a dreamer.

The pain Angie felt over her child was not lost on the ex-con, however, and he found himself thinking often of his own lost little one, Rhea. The similarity in names didn't go without notice, either. Lost children; it was something he and Angie shared, two parents unable to save their little girls. Carney had used a baseball bat to focus his rage on the two people who had killed his daughter. Angie's rage was focused on the world as a whole, and the former inmate knew where that led. Angie would burn herself out and accomplish nothing.

He wanted to believe they were out there, safe and alive.

In his heart he knew they weren't. And yet he would say nothing, would stand by her side until she came to that realization on her own, then try to be there to pick up the pieces. He let out a soft, cynical huff as Skye's hand trailed across his shoulders. Maybe he *was* changing.

They investigated half a dozen more houses along Stilson Canyon Road before ten o'clock, finding only the dead or homes untouched since the outbreak. There was no sign of Dean having come this way, and no more messages like the one in the tunnel. Angie said it didn't mean anything, and her two companions remained silent on the matter.

By the time they reached the outskirts of Chico, a point where the forest dropped behind and the road became a paved stretch descending out of the hills and into a residential neighborhood, the sun had brought the temperature up to a tolerable forty-two degrees. It was here that they decided to abandon the Polaris Ranger and go ahead on foot. The side-by-side was noisy and would attract too much attention. They parked it among some trees, gathered their gear, and set out. Angie hung the fifty-caliber Barrett and its bandolier of rounds across her back, leaving the hard plastic case behind.

By agreement, Skye walked point, machete in hand. Angie followed with the younger woman's silenced M4, and Carney walked last with the heavier-caliber M14, constantly checking behind them. They kept to the sidewalk when possible, as there was no way of knowing who or what might be watching, and it made little sense to offer themselves up as better targets walking down the center of the street.

Before leaving the Polaris behind, Carney had checked in with Vlad by way of the two-way Hydra radio, the signal strong and clear. The Russian reported that all was well with Halsey and the ranch, and that he would be standing by.

Up here close to the hills and forest, the houses were larger, the neighborhood affluent. Down many driveways, boats and motor homes were tucked away and covered against the winter weather. But affluence had been no protection against the plague. Garages stood empty, front doors hung open, and lawns were littered with personal items as people fled in a hurry. In a few upper-floor windows of these beautiful homes, pale, rotting faces stared out, hands pawing at the glass.

A small dog skittered across the street in front of them, pursued by the corpse of a woman in cutoff jeans and a tank top, galloping stiff-legged after her prey. When the dead woman saw the three people in the street, she altered course and limped toward Skye.

Skye took the creature out with an overhand swing of the machete, burying the blade in its head up to the bridge of its nose.

Angie looked at the spot between two houses where the little dog—a terrier maybe—had disappeared. That it was still alive was a marvel to her. The small domestic breeds wouldn't survive long in this dangerous new world, and most had likely died trapped in their homes or devoured by their owners. Those that made it out would have to forage and hunt, and face not only the hungry dead, but other predators thriving in the apocalypse, like coyotes and, eventually, wolves. She silently wished the terrier luck and returned her attention to the street.

Some of the houses they passed were tightly shuttered or boarded up, with black-and-yellow biohazard warnings stapled to their doors. Others had spray-painted messages scrawled across their stucco walls.

GONE TO OROVILLE
JOHN, MEET US AT REFUGEE CENTER
AMY, THE KIDS ARE WITH ME

As they walked, Angie felt a deep sadness settling over her. Had any of these messages been seen by their intended readers? She somehow doubted it. Both the writers and those they were trying to contact were probably now rank and file in the legions of the dead.

But not her daughter, and not Dean.

He and Leah were out here somewhere, and she would find them.

As blocks passed, affluence gave way to middle-class and blue-collar neighborhoods. The cars in driveways and along the curb were older, in worse shape than in the better neighborhood, and the houses and lawns were smaller. The spray-painted messages continued, however.

MEET US AT THE HIGH SCHOOL, JACK
MOM, DAD IS DEAD. STAY AWAY FROM HIM
CHRISSIE, I'M BIT. I LOVE YOU

Angie swallowed hard at that last one, then told herself that wasn't the case with Dean. He wouldn't let that happen. She wished she could believe it.

Skye used her machete to dispatch a pair of drifters that came at them across a brown lawn on the left. One of them was rustling along in an olive-green biohazard suit, rotting behind the Plexiglas face shield. She had no sooner dropped the pair than Carney called, "On the right." Skye turned and moved toward a young man in a light-green grocery apron, who was followed by a decaying thing in a tattered state trooper uniform. They were too close together to risk engaging one and not the other up close, so she pulled her silenced automatic and put them down, one bullet each.

Angie continued to search for a message from Dean, something he could leave that only she would understand. Though she didn't want to, every time they saw movement—drifters on their street or blocks away down a side avenue—she stopped to examine them with binoculars. She was looking for the dead versions of Dean and Leah, and praying she wouldn't see them.

They came to an intersection with a wine shop on one corner and a run-down ice cream parlor on the other, a seedy place with *TONY B.* spray-painted across its front window. Snarling came from within the ice cream parlor, and then a pair of shapes tumbled out the door. Weapons snapped up, but it was only a pair of mongrel dogs, fighting over a rotting, severed leg still wearing a Nike on its foot.

PUFFT, PUFFT. Angie put down both dogs with Skye's M4.

The street continued for another block and ended at the entrance to a trailer park. *Twin Pines* was stenciled on a rusting metal archway stretching over the drive, with lines of angled trailers marching down both sides of the road beyond. The few cars in sight were beat-up and smeared with rust-colored bloodstains, windshields spider-webbed with fractures. The trailers rusted on cinder-block foundations, their cheap tin skirts missing panels or dangling on old bolts. Laundry still hung on lines between them, and patchy dirt yards held plastic toys and more than a couple of engine blocks. The scent of death drifted from open trailer doors.

"Let's move through here quickly," said Carney from the rear. "This is pretty close quarters, and it doesn't look like the kind of place your husband would choose as defensible."

Angie agreed, and they picked up the pace. Skye sheathed her machete in favor of her pistol, and the other two kept rifle stocks to shoulders. They were far enough into the park now to see that the roads were set up like a pair of plus signs, one atop the other, two streets crossing the main avenue. Slow-moving figures on the side streets began to turn toward the trio, and other shapes began to appear from between the trailers. In moments, every dead thing in the trailer park was headed their way.

Fifty yards ahead, Skye saw that their street would lead them through another metal arch, out of the park and back into a neighborhood. She began moving faster, her pistol raised in a two-handed grip. Then Carney's M14 went off to their rear, shattering the still morning.

"Holy *shit!*" Carney exclaimed, firing twice more.

Angie and Skye spun to see a woman lumbering past an old Suzuki Samurai vehicle that was so rusted a good wind would blow it to pieces. The woman wore a yellow floral-print housecoat seemingly the size of a ship sail, her bare feet torn to the bone, swollen gray calves as thick as saplings. Her mouse-brown hair hung limp across a wide face, and glassy yellow eyes stared out from behind the strands. She looked to be four hundred pounds plus, and not from the green bloating they had all seen. There was a fresh bullet hole in one cheek, and another two had torn away much of her thick neck.

The woman made a meaty noise in her throat and waddled into the road, chubby fingers clutching at the air in front of her. Carney fired two more rounds, hitting her in neck fat and punching into the same cheek, both without effect. Angie fired as well, clipping off an ear.

"For Christ's sake, kill her already!" Skye yelled, laughing.

Carney did. He finally put a 7.62-millimeter round between her eyes, blowing a cloud of black and maroon out the back of her head. The woman's mouth dropped open with a wheeze, and then she fell face-first onto the road with a heavy thud.

"Holy shit," Carney repeated, letting out a shaky laugh. "She scared the crap out of me."

Skye was still laughing, even as the trailer park's dead closed in. "How the hell could you miss a target like that?"

Carney was about to give her a smart comeback when a man in his forties, carrying a long-handled shovel, bolted out of a trailer just ahead of them. He was also carrying a toddler and ran for the far entrance to the trailer park.

"Don't let him get away!" Angie cried. "We need to talk to him!"

She began using the M4 to clear out the drifters that were closing on their little group.

"I got him," Skye called, sprinting after the man, with Carney chasing close behind. Skye was only a few yards away when the man dropped the toddler, screamed, and swung the shovel at Skye's face. Startled by the attack, she didn't react in time. The blade connected with flesh in a flat, dull thud, but it was Carney who took the blow across his shoulder as he leaped between the two of them and went immediately to his knees. Skye saw the look of surprise on the man's face just before she broke his nose with a furious punch, laying him out flat. The toddler was screeching as she kicked the shovel away and crouched beside Carney. Angie ran up and leveled her rifle muzzle at the shovel man's bloody face.

The man paid no attention to the rifle and crawled to the child, a boy of two, calling, "Drew, Drew, it's okay." He pulled the child to his chest and looked at Angie, crying and hugging the boy tightly, tears mixing with blood.

"Please," he begged, "don't take my little boy."

ELEVEN

The grow was located in a long, narrow greenhouse behind the Saint Miguel School. A flatbed work truck loaded with coils of irrigation hose and bags of potting soil sat outside. From within the greenhouse, muted by glass walls, flowed a harmonious blend of guitars, an early Eagles tune.

The January sky was overcast and drizzling again, raindrops chasing one another down the sloped greenhouse roof. Little Emer Briggs followed a sidewalk between the church and the school, rain streaming down his closely shaved head and muscled neck, pattering against his leather biker's jacket. A large-frame automatic rode on one hip, an eighteen-inch hunting knife on the other, and an Uzi dangled from a strap on his shoulder. The chains on his motorcycle boots jangled with every step.

Little Emer saw the man sitting in a lawn chair out in the rain beside the greenhouse door, oblivious to the weather, smoking a joint in a cupped hand to keep it dry. He was thin and muscled, in his late forties, wearing a loose button-up shirt, baggy pants, and dark sunglasses. He wore a .45 in a shoulder holster. Little Emer had known Andrew Wahrman since he was a boy, and the man never seemed to change, never aged, and never—in Emer's memory—took off those damned sunglasses. Wahrman was his daddy's grower and had been for decades.

"What's up, pothead?" Little Emer said, stopping and towering over the slender, older man.

Wahrman smiled without showing teeth and looked up, raindrops dancing on his sunglasses. "Quality control testing," Wahrman said, offering the joint.

Little Emer took a hit and handed it back, blowing the smoke out through his nose. "New crop?" the biker leader asked.

"Nah, just simple herb."

The biker looked at the man sitting so relaxed in the rain. Andrew Wahrman rarely left his grow. Not so long ago he had worked acres at a time in the California back country, living out of tents and trailers, tending his plants and stringing trip wires for Claymore mines to keep out thieves and federal drug agents. Despite a lengthy list of arrests, Wahrman had managed to do only county or light state time, and he had never rolled on anyone, not distributors or benefactors, not even mules. His cultivation skill was legendary.

There was another legend about the man, one that belied his easygoing, pothead appearance. It was said that once upon a time he caught a DEA agent in his grow up near the Oregon border, shot him in the head, then chopped him up and buried him in the soil beneath his plants. That particular crop had been packaged and marketed under the name *Fed Food*.

"Your daddy's in the back," Wahrman said, staring at his own toes as he wiggled them in his sandals, taking another hit. Little Emer went inside.

The interior of the greenhouse felt almost as damp as the morning outside, the humidity from the warm plants steaming up the glass. It was pleasant and fragrant in here, and Emer palmed rainwater off his face as he made his way down the space between long tables of soil. The crop at this end of the building was young, the plants only a few inches high. They grew progressively taller the farther back one went, transitioning from tables to pots and then to large buckets on the floor, some towering more than seven feet high and reinforced with long wooden stakes.

The Eagles were singing about Winslow, Arizona, but it wasn't quite loud enough to drown out the metallic clipping noises coming from behind a high wall of dark green cannabis. Emer found his father perched on a stool at a worktable, clipping heavy buds off a stalk and placing them in a plastic bin.

At fifty-six, "Big" Emer Briggs—the nickname a mere result of being the older of two men sharing the same name—was twice his son's age and half his size. Balding in front, he wore a scraggly gray ponytail in back and a goatee that was almost completely silver—or would have been silver if it weren't an ivory shade from the nicotine. The man's eyes were sunken in dark hollows, the skin of his face drawn close to the bone as advanced lung cancer steadily consumed him. He looked worn down, old beyond his years, and extremely ill. A lit cigarette dangled from his lips.

When those dark eyes flicked up at his son's approach, though, there was not even a hint of frailty. Within those eyes was a cunning, an intelligence blended with a talent for violence and an even greater talent for evading a long-overdue accounting for his crimes. The tip of the cigarette flared, and the voice that followed was like a hard wind over a gravel road. "You had another one in the playpen last night, didn't you?"

Little Emer grinned and nodded.

The older man clipped off a bud. "Old farts like me go to bed early. Fucking screaming kept me awake." He shook his head. "You're a sick one, Junior."

His father was the only one who dared call him Junior. "We broke the post office yesterday," Little Emer said.

Snip went the shears. "Do you want a medal?"

A smirk. "I gave them a chance to swear allegiance," Little Emer said, "but they chose to defy me."

"Allegiance? Defy you?" Big Emer looked up. "You still playing at that Roman emperor shit?" The older man had only a slightly higher level of education than his son, but it was enough to know that the younger Briggs had it all muddled. Romans in a Catholic church? Medieval warlords and skull-tipped thrones? What was next, cowboys and pirates?

The son pulled a stool up to the opposite side of the worktable and shook a cigarette out of his old man's pack.

"Get your own fucking smokes," Big Emer growled, snatching the pack away and lighting a fresh one from the lit butt in his other hand. He was no longer picky about his brands, and there was no shortage of them in the many convenience, grocery, and retail stores. It was just the principle.

The younger man chuckled and lit his own smoke, waving it back and forth. "I just put six minutes back on your life, old man."

"Like I fucking care." *Snip* went the shears.

"And why not a Roman emperor?" Little Emer asked, leaning his elbows on the worktable. "I've got the army, the fortress city, hell, I've even got a gladiator pit." He laughed. "And didn't the Romans crucify their enemies?"

"Get your history straight," said the old man. "The Romans crucified criminals."

"Wrong. The Roman emperors crucified whoever the fuck they wanted. Friends, rivals, enemies, even family members."

Big Emer stared at his son through a haze of smoke. "Gladiator pit," he muttered. "That abomination you call a *playpen*." He pointed the shears. "You're living a fantasy. God knows how you got the size and not the brains. Fucking imbecile, you and your idiot friends." He went back to harvesting his buds.

The warlord regarded his father with eyes as flat and lifeless as a shark's. These were minor insults and no longer even left a mark. Little Emer wasn't playing. Yes, he knew he wasn't a real Roman, and what he had done in Chico was microscopic compared to what his heroes had accomplished. He had discovered them in prison, demanding his cellmates read to him about ancient Rome and specifically its rulers. They were men who took what they wanted, did as they pleased, and made no apologies. Men without remorse. The subject more than fascinated him, and he bore the names of his favorites as tattoos across his broad back.

There was *Maximinus Thrax*, who had ruled through fear and conquest, murdering dozens of friends and advisors. *Diocletian* murdered more than three thousand Christians by crucifixion and beheading and was known as the Caesar who popularized throwing Christians to lions. *Nero* executed his own mother and blamed the Great Fire of Rome on the Christians, using them as living human torches to light his gardens.

Little Emer thought he would like to see how that would work.

Caracalla was the master of repaying an insult. When he heard he had been mocked in a play in Egypt, he sailed his legions to Alexandria, burned the city to the ground, and slaughtered its inhabitants. Twenty thousand died for that little barb. The emperor *Commodus* ordered that all cripples, hunchbacks, and undesirables in the city be rounded up and placed in the Coliseum, where they were forced to hack one another to death with cleavers.

These were the men he admired, for their audacity, for their strength and willingness to live as they pleased without regard for the outraged cries of others. But great as they were, none inspired Little Emer as much as the Roman emperor *Caligula*. Here was a man who proclaimed himself a god, and who murdered anyone who had ever wronged him in life, or even disagreed with him. He made his favorite horse a high priest, had sex with his sisters on banquet tables crowded with guests, murdered entire families for a perceived slight, and publicly cannibalized the testicles of live enemies who had personally wronged him. His crowning move, in Little Emer's opinion, came at the Circus Maximus. When the dungeons had been emptied of criminals and none were left for Caligula's favorite event, the lions, he ordered his soldiers to force the first five rows of spectators down onto the sand, where they were promptly devoured for the emperor's amusement.

Little Emer pictured feeding his father to lions. Then he shrugged and said, "Everyone needs a little fun."

"You need to think about being smart instead of having fun," the old man said, jabbing the shears through the cigarette smoke. "Like the way you burn through fuel, especially with that goddamned tank running all over the place. Do you even know how much diesel you have stored up? Or how much is left in Chico? Smarten up."

"I *am* smart," the biker leader said, but the confidence was running out of his voice.

A snort. "Right. Spell *cat*, dumbass. I'll give you a hint, it doesn't start with *T*."

Little Emer flinched at that. His dyslexia was a very sensitive spot, and an easy target his father knew well. Big Emer alone could bring it up without fear of maiming or death. Others hadn't been so fortunate.

"No one asked you, cancer cluster."

Big Emer began to laugh, and it immediately turned into a savage, back-breaking coughing spasm. Bloody spittle hit the cement floor around the older man's stool, and a full minute passed before the coughing tapered off to a rattle. Big Emer steadied himself with a hand on the table as he wiped a rag at his mouth and nose. It came away bright red.

"That's the best you can do?" he asked, his voice barely a whisper.

Little Emer didn't respond, only sat and smoked his cigarette, staring at the old man in front of him. There had been a time when his father's mere presence in a room loosened his bladder, a time when Daddy's hand brought pain and humiliation that only abated when one felony conviction or another made him the state's problem for a while. Little Emer had grown up swearing he would kill his daddy one day, but that day had never seemed to come, even when the old man was weak and sitting defenseless right in front of him.

The elder Briggs lit another cigarette and squinted at his son with runny eyes. They held a look that whispered, *Any time you think you're man enough, little boy.* Little Emer Briggs, a rock-hard biker lord who had put twelve people in the ground *before* the plague, felt his father looking into him and had to stiffen to keep from trembling. When he was a child, his father's presence had sometimes caused him to urinate without warning, a fact that still made him burn with shame.

The old man gave him a knowing smile of yellow teeth and returned to his clipping.

"I need to talk to you," Little Emer said in a small voice, angry at becoming that little boy who said the wrong thing and was backhanded across the kitchen for it.

"We're talking," said his father.

"Some of the boys," Little Emer said, and then his voice cracked. He started again. "You heard we shot down a helicopter yesterday."

The old man nodded. "I heard that nutcase Corrigan and his fucking tank shot one down. I don't know about *we*."

"Right. He shot it down on the south end of town. He said he was rolling through the area and saw it coming in."

"Anyone check to see who or what was inside?"

Little Emer nodded at his daddy. "Yeah, as soon as the fires were out. Corrigan said it looked like a pilot and a door gunner, could have been a woman. Both were in uniform. The dead started coming in not long after, so everyone split."

"And this helicopter," Big Emer said, inspecting a particularly heavy bud and placing it gently in the plastic bin, "what was it doing?"

"Landing," said the biker. "It looked like it was landing."

The older man snorted. "So naturally your stupid buddies blew the shit out of it."

"I . . . We didn't . . ." Little Emer flushed as he fumbled. "They might have found us."

Big Emer pointed the shears again. "What, they might have discovered your pathetic little empire and ruined all the fun?"

The biker's face reddened further as he furiously crushed out his cigarette, his hand shaking just enough to earn one of those yellow grins from his old man. "They might have compromised us," Little Emer finished.

His father's eyebrows rose. "Ooh, a fifty-cent word. Care to spell that, Junior? I'll spot you the C."

"Fuck you!" Little Emer shouted, standing up fast and knocking over his stool, his large hands turning into fists. "It was my decision."

Big Emer shrugged and snipped a bud. "And now it's over," he said, his voice soft, no longer taunting.

The younger man stood there, unsure of what to say or do, and then the rage just drained out of him. He knew his father knew it would. He righted the stool and sat at the worktable again, reaching for another of his old man's smokes. This time Big Emer didn't protest, and even leaned across the table to light it for his son.

"You're a big dummy," his father said, his voice a rasp, "but I love you."

Little Emer closed his eyes and nodded.

The elder Briggs regarded his only son for a long moment. Brawn, a spark of cleverness, and an absolute willingness to visit death and destruction upon his fellow man had kept the boy alive so far, but Briggs wondered how long that could last. Certainly longer if he listened to his old man, as he had done fairly consistently throughout his adult life.

Little Emer and his Skinners motorcycle club had been the distribution arm of Briggs's marijuana business for some time, with a small but lucrative sideline in illegal weapons. Of course they also dabbled in meth and white slavery, but it was the weed that kept them flush and, as it turned out, the weed that saved their lives when the world went tits up.

Briggs senior and Andrew Wahrman had been running a sizable indoor grow at a warehouse near the train tracks on the west side of Chico. In mid-August, Little Emer and his Skinners rolled into town after a successful distribution run to Seattle and Spokane. Not only did they return for more grass, they brought with them a cache of military-grade automatic weapons, which they intended to sell in Sacramento. Fate put them all together when the plague struck: violent, well-armed men used to working together. It was a combination that allowed them to keep the dead at bay while they gathered the supplies they needed, keeping their distance from military and civilian authorities who were losing more and more control over Chico every day.

But then his son had gotten this conquering warlord shit in his head, going out and taking from others, forcing people to join his "army" with the threat of death, slaughtering any who opposed him. Big Emer wondered how much of it was real, and how much was just for kicks. Not that it mattered, the results were the same: a lot of dead and frightened people, a lot of shattered lives. Big Emer was no humanitarian, but he had always believed violence should not only serve self, but have a bigger point. Beating his son throughout the boy's childhood had made Little Emer strong, for example. He didn't see much of a point in any of this, however.

Not that it was his place to stop the boy. The cancer would take him soon, and then none of this bullshit would matter anymore. Yet he had spoken the truth; for all the flaws he *did* love his son, and he worried what would happen to his boy once Daddy wasn't around for counsel and advice.

Little Emer looked at his father. "Some of the boys saw another helicopter yesterday. A second one, military just like the first."

The older man set down his shears and crushed his smoke.

"They said it hesitated over the wreckage," Little Emer continued, "then flew up the canyon toward Paradise."

Big Emer traced a nicotine-yellow finger over the curved blades of the shears. "Two helicopters in one day," he said. "We haven't seen *one* helicopter in months. That," he said, reaching for another cigarette, "is a fucking problem."

Little Emer nodded. "What do you think I should do?"

His father smoked and thought for a bit, then leaned in and told him.

TWELVE

"Please," said the man on the ground, "please, don't."

"No one's taking your kid," Angie said. "Stand up."

Behind her, Skye knelt beside Carney, who was on his hands and knees. The body armor and his own muscle mass had absorbed most of the blow. "Hey," Skye said, "you think you're some kind of Secret Service agent, jumping in the way like that?"

Carney stood. "Yeah, that was stupid. I should have let the shovel take your head off."

Skye squeezed him. "You okay?"

The ex-con nodded, then eyed the corpses coming at them from all points. "We need to move," he said.

The boy the man was holding was bawling, and then there had been the echoing reports of Carney's M14. "We made a lot of noise," Skye said to Angie, "and this is about to get worse."

Angie prodded the man, who stood and wiped the blood from his broken nose. He didn't let go of the boy. "You're coming with us, so keep up," Angie said. She trotted ahead with Skye's rifle to her shoulder, pausing to fire, sweeping a slow arc left to right, dropping the dead. The man hesitated but got moving when Skye gestured with her silenced pistol. Once Angie had cleared a path, the little group moved out of the trailer park and back into the neighborhood. Behind them, a crowd of drifters numbering thirty or more followed slowly.

Angie led them right at an intersection, left at the next, then another left, putting distance between them and the trailing crowd. The M4 and Skye's pistol coughed as they engaged anything that moved in their path, both having to change magazines twice. Carney's M14 was silent, and Skye kept the newcomer moving. His little boy had quieted down and now bobbed in his father's arms, staring back the way they had come.

The neighborhood they traveled through was middle class, streets lined with small, neat brick houses that looked much like their neighbors. After several blocks they came upon an intersection where a UPS truck had crushed a red Mini Cooper against a telephone pole. Just beyond, at the far corner, a gas station had burned flat and taken half a block of homes and small businesses in each direction with it. A black and flaking corpse, little more than charcoal, shuffled blindly through the ash.

Angie took them right again and midway up the block detoured up a driveway, rifle at the ready. The drive curved behind a small brick house to a detached garage and a tiny yard with a swing set. To Angie's delight the garage door was open, and there were no cars inside. She led them in, and Carney took watch at the opening.

"Who are you?" Angie asked. The man was taking a lawn chair off a hook on the wall, settling his boy into it. The newcomer had no pack, no supplies, and both he and the boy were filthy. A raw sore bloomed on the man's cheek, another on his neck. Skye handed him a canteen, then went to work on the toddler's grubby face with a baby wipe. The little boy didn't flinch or complain, simply sat with his hands in his lap, staring through Skye as if she weren't there.

"My name's James Garfield," the man said. When Angie cocked her head, he nodded. "That's right, my parents named me after the twentieth U.S. president, assassinated after only two hundred days in office. God knows why." He took a drink, the canteen shaking in his hand. "I was a mortgage broker. That's my son, Drew."

"What are you doing out here?" Angie demanded, taking in his bedraggled condition and suspicious about his lack of weapons or supplies. "How have you survived?"

Garfield wiped at his nose and winced—it was starting to bleed again—and retrieved an oily rag from a workbench, pressing it gingerly to his face. "We've been hiding in a trailer for a week," he said. "There was food in there. We would have stayed but you stirred them up through the entire park." His eyes were beginning to bruise from the broken nose. "We were with a group for a while before that."

"What happened?" Angie asked. 'Why did you leave?"

"Because one of them got bitten, and the others were arguing about whether to kill him. I got scared."

"So you ran with a little boy and no way to defend yourself," Angie said, shaking her head.

"I'm not—I'm not confrontational." His eyes grew wet.

Angie ignored it. "I'm looking for some people," Angie said. "Maybe you've run across them in the past months. The man is Dean West, thirty-three, dark hair, ex-military. He's got a little girl with him, about your son's age."

Garfield shook his head.

"Are you sure?" Angie's volume went up, and she took a step toward the man. He took three steps back.

"I'm sure. No one like that."

Angie took a deep breath. "What about the others in your group?"

"You mean do they know him?" Garfield shrugged. "It never

came up. People came and went, I don't know who they met out there. Maybe."

Angie paced the garage, arms crossed. Skye produced a granola bar from her pack and offered it to Drew, who didn't respond. When she pressed it into his hands, he began to take bites, chewing slowly and still staring.

"Why did you beg us not to take him?" Angie asked, stopping her pacing and pointing at the little boy. Garfield moved to his son's side and rested a hand on the back of his neck.

"Because that's what they do."

"Drifters, you mean?" she said.

"I don't know what a drifter is. You mean the dead people?"

She clamped her lips and took another deep breath, nodding.

"No," the man said. "I mean, yes, but the dead take everyone. I'm talking about the people on motorcycles and their friends. They kill people."

Angie flashed to her family ranch in ashes, her undead father nailed to a cross.

"They find people hiding and kill them, take everything they have. I've seen it."

"What about the children?" Angie asked tightly.

"They take them," Garfield said, and now tears rolled down his cheeks and he wrapped his arms around his boy. Drew chewed the granola bar and seemed not to notice.

Angie turned to her two friends, lines of despair etched in her face. Skye shook her head, and Carney's expression was as unreadable as a stone. Angie looked back at Garfield. "Where is your group?"

"It's been a week," he said, "they might not even be—"

"Where *were* they?" Angie demanded, striding at him across the garage.

The man held up his hands and ducked his head. "At the elementary school! Little Chico Creek!"

Angie shouldered Skye's M4. "Take us there."

Garfield shook his head violently. "No, one of them is bitten, and Sorkin is crazy. I'm not going back there."

Angie's voice dropped to a whisper. "Oh, yes you are." The look in her eyes ended any further argument from James Garfield.

I t was seven blocks to the elementary school, Garfield pointing the way and regularly demanding assurances that Angie and her friends wouldn't let anything happen to his son. He never stopped talking, but he also never apologized for hitting Carney with the shovel.

He and his family—wife, fourteen-year-old daughter Kim, and two-year-old Drew—had reported to the refugee camp out at the Silver Dollar Fairgrounds, dutifully obeying the instructions of the authorities. They had been given cots under a white canopy, some Red Cross toiletries and bedding, and promises that they would be safe.

"There were soldiers there," Garfield said, "and high fences. Even Army doctors. Someone said they were going to inoculate us against whatever was changing people."

Angie, walking beside him, listened without taking her eyes or her rifle off the street.

Garfield told them how one day, two weeks after the outbreak, his wife and daughter had gone to get their family's daily water ration while he stayed at the cots with Drew. "The dead were always at the fences," he said, "shaking them. But they couldn't get in." His voice grew soft then. "But they did. The fences collapsed, and people were screaming, they were dying and we . . . we just ran." He was quiet for a long time and then said, "I thought for a while that they might be alive. Then a couple of months ago I saw Kim in the street. She was changed."

Angie stayed silent, not wanting to upset her guide more than he was already.

The silenced pistol and the M4 went off with regularity as they traveled the seven blocks, Angie stopping to aim, Skye trotting up to the dead and executing them at close range. The drifters came in every form: men and women, old and young, dressed in summer clothes or uniforms for jobs they had been at when their lives ended. All were rotten and gray.

The drizzling rain continued with no promise of stopping, bringing a steady, wet chill. Garfield steered them up Amanda Way, where an apartment complex stood opposite the school. An overturned grounds maintenance cart rested in some bushes against one of the apartment buildings, and it seemed that nearly every door bore the now-familiar black-and-yellow biohazard warning. Nothing moved along the complex sidewalks or behind apartment windows, and except for the patter of cold rain, there was only silence. They took shelter under a tree near the street.

"That's it," said Garfield, pointing. "We mostly came and went through a door in the back, by the cafeteria kitchen. The National Guard tried to set up a base in the rear parking lot. We were living off their supplies."

"How many of you were in there?" Angie asked, looking at the school.

"Other than us, there were five adults, no other kids. One of them is older, a retired cop."

"Are they armed?"

Garfield nodded. "The old man, Sorkin is his name. He has a rifle. It's the kind the soldiers carried. His daughter Hannah has a pistol. I think that's it."

Angie examined the elementary school, a one-story structure with a roof covered in solar panels. From here it was hard to judge the size of the building. She could see part of a parking lot to one side, and the nose of an Army six-by-six, but couldn't tell what else might be set up back there. Part of a playground was in view, and a large soccer field stretched out behind the building. There were a lot of windows, and getting close without being seen would be difficult.

"Do they post watches?" Angie asked.

Garfield suddenly looked afraid. "Why, are you going to hurt them?"

"No," Angie said, "I'm not going to hurt them. But I also don't want to get shot on my way in."

The man looked at her for a moment, holding his little boy close and trying to shield him from the rain. "We locked the place up as best we could," he said. "I always tried to stay away from the windows."

Skye joined them under the tree. "Who was bitten?" she asked, pulling off her knit cap and snugging it down over the little boy's head. He didn't react.

"A man named Deacon. He sold farm machinery."

Neither woman could tell if Garfield was scared to go back in because he was afraid of his old group, or of the man who had been bitten and, by now, turned. It occurred to Skye to think it odd how everyone she had met since the outbreak, upon introduction, seemed intent on announcing what they had done before it all. Mortgage broker, farm machinery salesman, writer and hippie and real estate salesman. Probably just unable to let go, she thought. Her former life felt as if it were a century ago. Now she just thought of herself as a shooter.

"Deacon was out at the National Guard trucks getting supplies," Garfield said, "and when he came back he was cursing and bloody. Something bit him on the elbow and broke the skin."

"Who wanted to kill him?" Skye asked.

"The old man and his daughter."

Angie looked at her friend and said, "Then those two will be the biggest threat." Skye nodded in agreement. To Garfield, Angie said, "Will they let you back in?"

"I don't know. I guess so. They didn't kick us out or anything, we just left."

"Then you'll make the introductions," said Angie.

Garfield shook his head. "I don't want any part of this. Please just let us go."

Skye rested a hand on his shoulder and stared at him. "We need you. You can keep people from being unnecessarily hurt."

Garfield looked at the gray-skinned young woman dressed in black tactical gear, and his lower lip began to quiver. Carney spat on the ground to show what he thought of Garfield. The man wouldn't last five minutes in the joint.

"Listen to me," Angie said, softening her voice. "We're not going to let anything happen to you or your boy. We have questions, and the people you were with might have answers. After we talk, you can do whatever you want."

James Garfield sucked in a deep breath and nodded, and then they were off, trotting across the street in a line, Angie in the lead. They moved toward the back parking lot, watching the school's windows as well as the area all around them.

Angie saw no school buses, no swarms of dead grade-schoolers, and for that she was grateful. Then she reminded herself that it had been five months, and even if school had been in session, the kids who had turned would have wandered away by now. They moved past an exterior wall with *Little Chico Creek Cheetahs* painted on it with the image of a running, spotted cat, the vision of crowds of dead, shuffling children still poking at Angie's imagination. In the parking lot behind the school, as Garfield had said, was the National Guard base.

It wasn't really a base, Angie quickly realized, more of a hastily erected command post, and incomplete at that. Someone had set up a square of sandbags to form a helicopter pad, but there was no chopper. At the corners of the command center someone had stacked sandbags for gun emplacements, with no weapons in evidence, and a square green tent was set up behind three six-by-six trucks parked in a row. Next to the tent was a boxy, tracked vehicle bristling with antennae, and a cluster of green fifty-five-gallon drums not far away. At the back of one of the trucks was a pile of debris, mostly plastic packaging and rain-soaked cardboard boxes that Skye immediately recognized as MRE packaging, the military Meals, Ready-to-Eat her fallen Guardsmen friends had introduced her to back in Berkeley.

Rain drummed on the tent and the flat metal roof of the antenna vehicle. There were no drifters here, but a wet crow perched on one of the antennae, watching them with black eyes.

Garfield pointed to a metal door in the back wall of the school, next to a group of Dumpsters. They started toward it. Angie was still twenty feet away when the door opened slightly and a rifle muzzle poked out.

"Stop there or you're dead," called a voice from inside.

Angie didn't like having guns pointed at her and nearly cut loose with a burst of automatic fire, but the impulse left before she could pull the trigger. She'd get no answers if she did. Instead she froze, as did the others behind her.

"Drop your packs and weapons," said the voice, "and get the hell out of here."

No one moved, except for Skye, who poked Garfield with her pistol. He stumbled forward. "Is that you, Sorkin?" he called, his voice wavering. "It's James Garfield."

"You sell us out to those animals?" the voice yelled. "I'll kill you where you stand."

"No!" Garfield didn't seem to realize that he had lifted his son to block his view of the rifle. "These people found me out there. They're looking for someone."

"We're not here to hurt anyone," Angie said. "We just want to talk."

There was a long silence from the doorway. Finally the voice called, "Put your weapons down and move away. We'll send someone out to collect them. Then you can come in."

"Fuck that," Carney muttered.

"Amen," said Skye.

Angie set the M4 on the wet asphalt, shrugged out of the Barrett, and dropped her sidearm and knife. "Just me then," she said.

"No," Skye said sharply.

Angie grabbed hold of Garfield's sleeve and pulled him along as she started toward the door.

"Angie, no!" Skye reached for her, but Angie pulled away. As she neared the door, it swung open to reveal a man in his late sixties, with silver hair and whiskers, wearing a checked shirt. The muzzle of his M16 was pointed at Angie's chest.

"Nice and slow, so there's no mistakes," the old man said.

Angie nodded, arms at her sides and palms up as she entered, Garfield and his little boy right behind. The metal door slammed closed, leaving Carney and Skye alone in the rain.

Skye retrieved her M4 and slung it across her back, scrambling up onto a Dumpster. "Watch the door," she said, then jumped straight up, catching hold of the edge of the roof. She did a smooth pull-up and swung over the lip onto gravel-covered tar. Below, Carney collected Angie's weapons and set them on another Dumpster, then turned to stand guard.

There was simply no way Angie could be allowed to be alone in there, Skye thought. There were too many unknowns, and she didn't trust this Garfield character. He didn't seem malicious, far from it, but he also didn't seem to be capable of making good decisions. How he was still alive was a mystery. Had he now unknowingly led her friend into a trap? Skye knew Angie was desperate for information, she got that, but desperation could lead to bad decision making as well. Skye had no intention of letting her stay in there without backup.

She found herself in a rain-soaked world of air-conditioning units, rows of solar panels and electrical boxes. From up here she could determine that the elementary school was made up of four quads set in a giant square, each with its own courtyard. She moved on the balls of her feet across the gravel, rifle up. Not even a quarter of the way across the roof, a Hispanic man in coveralls with the name *Jesus* on a patch over his pocket lurched from behind a bank of solar panels. His skin was the color and consistency of dough, and much of the flesh around his mouth hung in tatters.

Skye instantly put a round from the silenced M4 through his eye.

As she neared the first courtyard, she dropped prone and eased up to the edge. Below she could see trees, cement pathways, and a few benches. Long, continuous rows of windows looked out into the courtyard, many with grade school art taped to the glass. A pair of corpses, both women in advanced stages of decay, lay motionless on the paths.

Skye circled, spotting two doors, one beneath where she had initially looked down and another in the opposite wall. She was betting those inside wouldn't bother locking the doors to the interior courtyards, but the two corpses down there changed the dynamic. Were they really dead? Or were they like many she had seen, dormant and still, waiting for stimuli? If so, those doors would be locked. And if she did drop down to find that they were, she would have no way to return to the roof on her own. She moved on.

The next courtyard was similar, trees and paths, but this one was occupied by a trio of drifters, and they were moving. Locked doors, definitely. She continued her search, wanting to call Angie on the handheld Hydra but fearing that a sudden radio transmission would startle Angie's captors into shooting.

The dead maintenance man gave her an idea, and Skye went searching for a door or hatch that would give roof access from below. The man had to have gotten up here somehow. It didn't take long to find a metal square set in the roof at the northeast corner. She tugged at it.

Locked.

Cursing, Skye went back to inspecting the courtyards. The third one looked like the other two, but it was clear of corpses, moving or otherwise. She did a slow walk around it, rifle muzzle always pointed at the windows, ready to return fire. Nothing moved. As before, there would be no way back up once she was down. Mindful of how long Angie had been gone, she moved to a corner and did a dead hang before dropping the last five feet to winter grass. In an instant she tucked behind a tree.

No one fired at her, and no alarm was raised. There was only the rain dripping through the branches.

M4 to her shoulder, Skye headed to one of the courtyard doors.

Angie sat on the bench seat of a lunch table in a long, tidy cafeteria with posters on the walls warning against drugs, gangs, and bullying, and promoting healthy eating and exercise. Windows lined one wall. The other people in the room stared at Angie as if she had come from another planet. There were four of them. Sorkin, the ex-cop in his sixties, sat on a rolling office chair a few yards away holding an M16 that he kept pointed at Angie's belly. A woman in her early forties stood next to the man, a pistol on her hip.

For ten minutes, Sorkin peppered her with questions. Where did you come from? How did you get here? How many more are in your party? Are you with the bikers?

Angie was careful with her responses and said nothing about the helicopter. "We're here looking for my husband and little girl. We're not with the people you're afraid of."

"What makes you think you know what we're afraid of?" Sorkin demanded.

Angie looked at them all, and decided she knew quite a bit about them, actually. They were emaciated and dirty, covered in sores from lack of washing, and they smelled bad. All but old Sorkin had a haunted look, eyes constantly flicking to the windows and doors, cocking their heads to listen for noises that weren't there. Underlying their fear was a sense of hopelessness. They were just going through the motions of surviving. Except for Sorkin. There was still fire in those aged eyes.

"James told us you were here," Angie said.

Sorkin swung the rifle barrel toward Garfield, who ducked and let out a cry. "Turned rat, huh, Garfield?" Sorkin said.

"It wasn't like that," said Angie, holding up her hands. "We needed to ask some questions, that's all. We can trade for information. Supplies and weapons."

The two others in the room, a man and a woman, began rummaging through Angie's pack. She had already learned from Garfield during their walk here that the man's name was Dylan, a photographer and backpacker in his fifties. The woman was Abbie, a Red Cross volunteer who had been out at the refugee center when it fell to the dead. The two of them made happy noises as they found food, toiletries, and a box of nine-millimeter rounds.

"Trade?" Sorkin said. "Looks like I can just take what I want, can't I?"

Angie kept her voice even, wanting to tell them that Skye and Carney might have a different perspective. Instead she said, "You could, but you're not like that, are you? Not like the bikers." She looked at the old man. "Some people we know had some trouble with them too. They killed my parents, burned down our ranch." She fought against wanting to tear up at the thought of her crucified father, and Halsey's depiction of her dead mother chained in the back of a pickup.

Sorkin only snorted.

"James told us one of you was bitten," Angie said.

The woman standing beside the old man, whom the others had called Hannah—*this must be his daughter,* Angie thought—nodded. "Mr. Deacon. He was bitten on the arm."

"You don't need to tell her a damn thing," Sorkin growled, but Hannah quieted him with a hand on his shoulder.

"He was feverish for a long time," the woman said, "and there was some disagreement about what to do with him." She looked at Garfield and his little boy. "That was why you left, wasn't it?"

Garfield nodded and looked at the floor.

"In the end I took care of him," said Hannah.

Angie looked at the woman, at a face drawn not so much by years as grief. She wondered whom Hannah had lost. "James told us some of you might have had contact with others," she said. "I'm looking for a man named Dean West. There's a little girl with him."

Hannah and Abbie both shook their heads, and Sorkin glared. Dylan, the photographer, looked at Angie and said, "Her name's Leah."

Angie leaped to her feet, causing Sorkin to roll back in his chair and lift his rifle. "You just sit still, missy," he barked.

"No," said Skye, pressing the cold circle of the M4's silencer against Sorkin's neck. "You sit still." She had found the courtyard door open and slipped through the hallways on the toes of her boots, following the voices. Waiting quietly beyond a door frame, she had listened as the conversation grew increasingly heated, then decided it had gone on long enough. Now she was standing behind and to one side of Sorkin, and with her other hand she slipped Hannah's pistol out of its holster and shoved it in her belt. "Slowly give me the rifle," she said.

The old man muttered and cursed, handing over the weapon.

"Garfield," said Skye, "go back to that door and let Carney in."

The man nodded vigorously and hurried down the hall with Drew in his arms.

Angie moved close to the photographer. His hair was too long for a fifty-year-old, and the blue eyes in his wind-weathered face failed to conceal a deep sadness. "What do you know about Dean and Leah?" Angie said, her heart racing.

The sad-eyed man shook his head. "I'm sorry. They're dead."

ORPHANS

THIRTEEN

October—East Chico

Waging urban and guerrilla warfare is nearly impossible with a two-year-old around.

Regardless of one's level of skill, stalking prey, setting ambushes, and conducting silent reconnaissance all take a backseat to the truly important things: providing shelter, finding food and clothing, keeping her clean, keeping her occupied.

Keeping her quiet.

Dean's escape from the ranch and their two-day overland trek through the woods had become a blurry odyssey marked by fear and frustration. Leah had to be carried, and even at Dean's high level of fitness, she began to wear him out and prevented any real speed. Eventually he discarded anything in the go-bag that wasn't an absolute necessity, burying it in the woods. He cut a pair of holes in the bottom for Leah's legs, using the nylon strap to support her back, transforming the bag into a child carrier of sorts. It was awkward and uncomfortable, but it let them move faster and allowed him to keep his hands free.

Were the killers from the ranch tracking him? He had to assume they were, and with Leah present, he couldn't risk taking the time to leave any nasty surprises for his pursuers. He kept moving.

They spent that first night in a hollow surrounded by pines, Leah sleeping wrapped in a sweater from the go-bag and whining about the dirty ground and mosquitoes. Dean comforted her and was relieved when she finally dropped off. At least it wasn't cold, as the temperatures were still in the seventies. Dean did not sleep. Every rustle of wind or cracking twig could be a pursuing biker or, worse, the walking dead.

The go-bag had only two small bottles of water and some kid-sized cans of mini raviolis, which Leah didn't want. She wanted chicken nuggets. She wanted to watch Dora, wanted her grandma and her toys. She asked about her mommy.

Dean got them moving early, using his field skills to keep them on a westerly heading toward Chico, just over ten miles away. Ten miles overland and through woods, however, was not like traveling ten miles down a highway. It was slow going, and they were not alone. The first indication that the dead were in the forest with them came early in the morning, and it was Leah who spotted them.

"Daddy, Icky Man," she said, riding in the bag on his back and pointing to the right. Dean turned to see the corpse of a middle-aged man lurching through the trees, followed by a dead grade-schooler. The MAC-10 cleared its shoulder holster, the tube-shaped suppressor muffling the machine pistol's flash and sound.

KAFF-KAFF. Throat and forehead. The man went down. With a snarl the grade-schooler galloped at them, sneakered feet rushing over pine needles.

KAFF, neck, *KAFF,* neck again. *KAFF,* eye. The body went face-down.

"Bad boy!" Leah yelled, wagging a little finger at the dead body.

"That's right, honey," said Dean. "Look for more. You're such a good girl."

"I *am* good."

Dean grinned and moved on. Among the hundreds of things he worried about was the psychological impact of all this on his daughter. She had already seen death, moving and not, and had been there when her grandmother died shielding Leah's body with her own. Kids were adaptable, he knew this, but how much more would she see? What would happen if and when Dean had to go hand-to-hand with one of these things? It was sure to be messy, and Leah, watching it all over his shoulder? She could end up catatonic. It wasn't as if he could set her down while Daddy ran off to fight zombies. For better or worse, this little girl wasn't leaving his back.

By midday he found Deer Creek Highway and followed it while still keeping to the woods. Moving this way, father and daughter finally made it to the eastern edge of Chico.

The house was small, set back from the street with a one-car attached garage. Like many California homes, it had no basement. Dean selected it for its location, off a main street at the end of a cul-de-sac, and for the scattered toys in the front yard. He also noticed the pickup in the driveway, not for the vehicle itself, but for the 49ers flag in the rear window. He reasoned that football fans liked their game-day feasts, and that might translate into a well-stocked pantry. Fortunately there had been no dead people inside, and the presence of toys meant the house would be Leah-friendly. He was only partially right in his assumptions.

A boy of four had lived here, so he was able to keep Leah clothed, although she made a face and declared it to be "boy stuff." There were toys and books, however, and that seemed to balance things out.

Dean spent a lot of his time helping Leah with her letters and numbers, coloring, playing with blocks, and continuing her potty training. Since the toilet didn't flush, he used a saw from the garage to cut a hole in a child-sized plastic chair, then put a plastic bin lined with a trash bag beneath it, thinking it looked an awful lot like a cat box. Their waste went into the garage. Leah didn't like it and said so. She wanted her potty chair and asked her daddy to go get it. Eventually she adapted.

In the attic space, Dean found a proper backpack-style child carrier mounted in an aluminum frame, along with a disassembled crib and outgrown baby clothes in plastic totes. No potty chair, however.

He was wrong about the food. If the prior owners had been tailgaters or game-day partiers, they had done it elsewhere with friends. With the freezer and fridge off-limits, Dean and Leah were left with a small amount of canned and dry goods. Apparently, the previous residents had needed to go grocery shopping. The houses next door might provide more food, but it was a risk Dean would face only when his own pantry was bare.

On the shelf of the master bedroom closet he found a padded, zippered case holding a scoped .30-06 deer rifle and a box of forty rounds. There was a small safe for a handgun, but it was open and empty.

Dean hung blankets over every window, barricaded the doors, and settled in. They would be able to stay as long as the bottled water and soda, canned punch, and water in the toilet tanks—certainly not the bowls—lasted. Dean remained vigilant, watching for and seeing no signs of the bikers. The dead wandered down the cul-de-sac on occasion but left the house undisturbed.

It was a peace that would last just shy of four weeks.

. . .

*F*lak jacket, helmet, weapons and ammo. Full-battle rattle under a withering Iraqi sun, and 120 degrees. Staff Sergeant Dean West, 14th Stryker Mounted Cavalry, stood beside the idling, multiwheeled armored vehicle and watched the asphalt shimmer and melt. The sun threw a dazzle on his blue-and-green wraparound sunglasses as he gripped the M4 that hung on a strap across his chest, a gloved finger resting beside the trigger.

"King-Two, King-Six," called a voice in his headset radio. "There's a dirt road two klicks ahead of your position. Recon the road and the village five miles out."

"Any word on Wilson's Stryker?" he asked. The third vehicle in their unit had experienced mechanical difficulties on the highway several kilometers back, and command had ordered West and his remaining two Strykers to proceed without it. They had been waiting at this checkpoint for half an hour.

"King-Two, recovery vehicle is on site, all are returning to base. Proceed with recon."

Great, Dean thought. They would continue the mission at two-thirds strength. The area was supposedly secure, this was a routine patrol, but the term secure *was* an intangible thing out here in the sand.

"King-Two copies," he said, signaling to the men around him. They piled back into the Stryker, and Dean radioed the second vehicle behind them with the new orders.

To call it a road was an attempt at humor. Little more than a goat path, the twin ruts to which they had been directed cut away from the highway at an angle and vanished into the featureless, brown Iraqi desert. The two Strykers, maintaining good distance between them, kicked up a cloud of dust that could be seen for miles.

"*Another fucking village,*" griped a corporal seated on a troop compartment bench across from Dean. "*Did they tell you what we're supposed to be looking for, Staff Sergeant?*"

Dean looked at the corporal, a kid named Dennis from a small Montana town. He was reliable, a good piece of gear, and bitching was the favorite pastime of solders worldwide. "*Negative, Corporal,*" Dean said. "*Another opportunity to spread American goodwill, I'm sure. You got someplace better to be?*"

The young soldier nodded and proceeded to describe the exact place involving a part of a woman's anatomy.

"*None of that where we're going,*" Dean said.

"*None of that in this whole fucking country,*" the kid griped.

Dean leaned his helmet back against the vibrations of the armored hull and closed his eyes. "*Embrace the suck,*" he said. At once the words were echoed by the other men in the compartment: "*Embrace the suck.*" Most aspects of military life sucked, and getting used to it was really the only option.

"*Copy that,*" the corporal said, following his sergeant's lead and closing his eyes.

The two armored vehicles had just come within sight of the village when the right front tire of Dean's Stryker hit the IED. The blast from the improvised explosive device tore through the armor, killing the vehicle's driver and gunner instantly and shearing off the Stryker commander's legs. A storm of shrapnel and fire blew through the troop compartment.

Behind them, the second Stryker stopped and began to spin its turret to the right, just as a pair of men popped up from the desert with rocket-propelled grenade launchers and fired. The RPG warheads smoked through the hot air in seconds, hitting the vehicle broadside, blowing it open.

Dean couldn't hear anything. His first conscious impressions were the stink of roasted human flesh and the sight of the headless soldier *still seated beside the young corporal. Dennis, the kid from Montana, was on his feet and hauling Dean out of the vehicle by his combat harness, dragging him down the Stryker's open rear ramp. Dean tripped over something, realized it was a leg, then saw the corporal screaming something at him, yet couldn't hear a sound. There was smoke, figures moving, another body on the ground in desert camo bright with blood. The corporal lowered Dean and leaned him against the side of the vehicle, raising his rifle and disappearing. To his left, Dean saw that the second Stryker was ablaze and boiling black smoke into the sky. No one had escaped the fire.*

Muzzle flashes sparked in the desert on Dean's side, and he saw puffs of dirt kicking up around him, felt the vibrations through his back as rounds smacked the Stryker's side. He raised his own weapon and began to return fire from his sitting position, trying to put three-round bursts on the flashes that seemed to double and waver before him.

There was a roaring in his ears now, like listening to a large conch shell, and the sounds of the world flooded back quickly.

"Get third squad moving on the right flank!"

"Third squad is gone!"

"There! Put fire on that position. It's another RPG!"

Dean wasn't having any effect shooting into the desert, and he climbed to his feet, rounds still hitting around him. "Comms!" he yelled. "Call in the goddamn fire mission!"

". . . requesting medevac, coordinates to follow," a soldier yelled into his radio, at the same time trying to fire at shapes darting across the sand.

Dean was certain he was wounded, didn't know how bad, but knew that if he didn't turn this fight around right now it wouldn't matter. Of the eight who had been in the troop compartment, five were still up. Suddenly there was an RPG blast close enough to knock Dean to the ground, sand and shrapnel lashing the side of the Stryker.

"Dean," a thin voice called, "my legs, man . . . I can't find them."

He thought it sounded like Dennis, but he couldn't be sure. Two of his men were dead on the ground, and a third was down and twitching, bleeding out fast.

"Dennis is hit!" another man screamed. "Oh, Christ, over there! Kill that fucker!"

Automatic weapon fire rattled around them. Still no one had emerged from the second Stryker. They were alone. Dean shouted for his remaining men to cover both sides of the road, then began pouring fire into the desert.

A 5.56-millimeter, M203 grenades, an M249 squad automatic weapon: Everything that could deliver death was unloaded on the robe-clad attackers swarming in on both sides to complete their ambush. Figures fell to the ground, shell casings arced through the air, and cries of "Changing mags!" and "I'm hit!" were lost in the roar of gunfire.

The radio operator was still up; Dean could hear his voice, trying to keep steady. "King-Six, King-Six, we are fully engaged, requesting immediate air support at previous coordinates." A pause. "Negative, King-Six, we cannot hold."

The two soldiers on the left flank died a moment later as an insurgent got close and chopped them up with an AK-47. Dean's radio operator was hit in the neck and sagged to the ground, his blood soaking into the sand. A bullet tore open Dean's right calf, and he went to one knee. Several more slammed into his body armor, and one clipped his helmet, knocking him down. Blood ran into his eyes.

The only soldier left in his command, a nineteen-year-old named Wickham, ran toward his sergeant holding a trauma bandage. Bullets kicked up dirt and pebbles around him and he grunted, sliding face-first to the ground, unmoving. Three running shapes appeared on the left, and Dean's thumb flicked his M4 to full auto before he swept fire across them, throwing them back and to the ground. He lay on the

*ground, changing magazines and trying to crawl to Wickham, then
saw the spreading red stain in the sand around the boy's head. A bullet hit inches from his face, cutting his cheek with fragments of stone.
He could hear them now, shrieking in their fast, harsh language,
heard sandals thudding on the ground. Dean saw movement, tried to
raise his rifle.*

*The angry hum of auto-cannons tore the desert air in half, fol-
lowed by the deep-throated impact of rockets and the thump of rotor
blades. Bodies spun through the air or came apart in storms of blood
and bone as an Apache gunship, looking like a giant prehistoric
insect, roared overhead, blotting out the sun for just an instant. More
choppers followed, the beat of their blades overwhelmed by the thunder of weapons.*

*Staff Sergeant Dean West blinked at the blood in his eyes, then
slipped away into cold, dark pain.*

Dean crouched at the front window of the small house, staring out
through a slit in the blanket he had hung. The memory, so
intense he could smell the blood of his friends and feel the hot grit
of the sand, had come unbidden and quickly overwhelmed him.
Now his hands trembled and he bit the insides of his cheeks so hard
they bled.

Not now. Not now.

It had been months since he'd had an episode, and none so far
could compare with this. He was paralyzed, trapped in a shaking
body over which he had no control, sweating, breathing hard, fighting to hold down the moan trying to claw its way out of his throat.

Beyond the window, the cul-de-sac was filling with the walking
dead.

For weeks the street had been empty, undisturbed except for the
odd corpse. Now, only a day before Dean was preparing to relocate,

to find a new location that would replace their now-exhausted supply of food and water, they had come. Hundreds strong, a steady tide of walking decay was making its way into the circle at the end of the street, spreading out and stumbling across lawns and up driveways, pressing against houses and hammering at doors and windows. A dozen or more shuffled up the driveway to Dean and Leah's house, heads tipped back and turning left and right, scenting the air.

Dean gnawed at his cheeks. *It's our trash, the bagged waste in the garage, oh, God, they can smell it, oh, God.*

"Daddy, I want Dora," Leah said, standing in the living room behind him wearing a kid-sized football jersey that hung on her like a dress. She was dirty, they both were, and it was so hard to keep her clean when the water had to be saved for drinking. Dean trembled, stared at the corpses sniffing in the driveway. He couldn't reply.

"Daddy." Leah's voice was low and petulant. It had been one of those days when nothing made her happy or kept her occupied for long. "Daddy," she demanded, "want Dora. Want *Dora!*"

The driveway corpses stopped scenting and as a group turned their dead eyes on the front of the house.

Dean squeezed his eyes shut and tried to steady his breathing, wishing for some of the meds the VA gave to guys who'd had trouble after they came back from overseas, then instantly changing his mind. Some of those meds turned you into a living version of what was massing outside.

"We have to go," he choked out, and forced himself to look away from the window and at his daughter.

She stomped a foot. *"Want Dora!"*

Dean flinched at the noise and shushed her, praying his heartbeat would slow. *It wasn't right. He had made it out of there, done three tours and made it home alive. He had seen the horrors and returned intact. He did* not *bring that war home with him.*

The panic attack, brewing right on the edges of his self-control, disagreed. Dean knew he couldn't let it all the way in, couldn't allow it to have its way.

"We're going bye-bye," he told his daughter, and she cocked her head at the strange tone in Daddy's voice. "I need to put you in our fun backpack, okay, sweetie?"

She stomped her foot again. "Don't wanna."

Dean crawled across the floor on his hands and knees, arms still shaking. "We need to play the quiet game, and I need you to be my big girl."

"No." Leah ran back to the bedroom they shared. A moment later her voice shrieked down the hall. "Wawas!"

Dean bolted for the bedroom just as something heavy slammed against the front door. Leah was standing in the room, fists clenched, looking around frantically. "Wawas!" she cried, and then the tears started. The stuffed walrus was on the floor, mostly hidden by a Dr. Seuss book, and Dean snatched it up, pressing it into his daughter's hands. She snatched it and turned away, pressing it to her face, still crying.

There was a steady thumping from out front, the sounds of fists. Moans rose behind them.

"It's okay, baby," Dean said, pulling her to his chest and shushing softly in her ear. He felt *it*, what some combat survivors referred to as the *Fear Animal*, retreat inside him, frightened off for the moment by the power of a man's need to protect his daughter. He blinked and gritted his teeth. After all these years, all his denials, it turned out that the Fear Animal had indeed hitched a ride back from the Middle East. He had secretly suspected it was true for a long time, but now, admitting it and thinking of the implications, he felt a new hammer blow of fear. His denial and refusal to seek treatment of any kind now left him exposed, unprepared . . . and weak. How was he supposed to deal with this? *Could* he deal with this without help? How was he going to protect Leah if this was an example of how bad it could be, freezing up when he needed to act? And could it get even worse? He feared it would. In that moment, Dean knew only two things for sure: he hated the Fear Animal, and he wanted to kill it.

"We're gonna go bye-bye," he said in a forced, happy voice. "We can look for Dora too."

"Find Dora?" Leah asked, pulling away, her round, red cheeks wet with tears.

Dean smiled. "Yes. We're going to get in the pack and go for a walk, but we have to stay really, really quiet. Can you do that?"

She nodded.

He squeezed her again, then got them moving. Dean had prepared long ago for the time when the supplies would run out. The papoose pack was on the kitchen table next to a new, well-stocked go-bag. The deer rifle and the MAC-10 rested beside them, and the Glock never left his hip. Dean pulled on the machine pistol in its shoulder holster; settled Leah, the rifle, and the gear on his back; then moved to the back kitchen door, watching through a slit in the blanket.

Nothing moved in the backyard yet, and Dean didn't hesitate. In a flash he was out and running for the gate in the fence at the opposite side of the yard.

The surge, as Dean came to call it, forced them completely out of the neighborhood. He wondered at it, wondered why the dead would suddenly go from completely absent to present en masse. The best he could come up with was their trash. Perhaps there were uniquely human scents that the dead were particularly dialed into, and it gave him pause as he realized he had most certainly underestimated the acuity of their senses.

The two of them stayed on the move for close to a week, creeping between houses, scavenging what they could, never staying any-place for more than a day. Dean looked for food, water, and toilet-ries. He found no weaponry other than a hunting knife, which he immediately threaded onto his belt near the Glock. Mostly they hid. There was no other choice, as the residential neighborhoods seemed to be filled with the walking dead, as were many of the houses.

There were close calls. Once, Dean forced a door open only to have the corpse of a woman fling itself at the wood from the inside and slam it back at him, reaching a gray arm through the opening. Her aggression saved them from walking in on her.

Many times, the dead saw them and pursued, slow but relentless, sniffing after them even when visual contact was lost. Turning to fight wasn't an option, not with Leah on his back, and so he ran. The ugly panic attacks kept their distance for now, but Dean felt them circling, looking for an opening.

In time they came upon an apartment complex, a sprawling col-lection of three-level buildings with open breezeways and concrete stairs between them, surrounded by lawns gone shaggy and brown.

"Time to go apartment hunting," Dean murmured, scratching at his beard and eyeing the closest building from a position across the street.

"Home, Daddy?"

"Soon, baby. Daddy is going to find us a new home."

She gave him a kiss on his right ear. "I love you, Daddy. Is Mommy home?"

"Not yet, honey. We'll see Mommy soon." He reached back and stroked the side of her face. "We're going to have to make some loud noises. Daddy might kick some doors, but don't be scared."

"You mad?" she asked.

"No, sweetie."

"Not supposed to kick. It's bad."

"I'll only do it a little. There might be Icky Men."

"And bad boys," she said, nodding seriously.

"Maybe. But we won't be scared, right?"

She said she wouldn't, and even giggled each time her daddy kicked open an apartment door. Dean moved through swiftly, clearing rooms with the MAC-10 extended at arm's length. There were zombies in some of the apartments, and Dean shot them the moment they appeared.

Leah began giggling at that too, and that was both startling and unsettling for Dean. Part of him was relieved she saw it as a game, the part of him that needed her calm so he could search for the things they needed. The other part, the parent in him, felt a heaviness in his heart at the horrors to which the little girl was growing numb.

As he moved room to room he wondered if, instead of raiding, might they not set up here in a more permanent way? Something on the top floor with a good field of vision? Dean knew there was likely only drywall, insulation, and aluminum studs between the apartments. He could chop several escape routes or even break through walls to explore without having to go outside.

They were standing on a concrete landing outside a door with 3C attached to it in brass characters, when a voice spoke from the stairs to the landing below. "She's beautiful."

Dean pivoted and pointed the muzzle of the MAC-10 at the man's face, index finger sinking pressure down onto the trigger. The man was in his early fifties, with lots of hair and sad blue eyes. Dressed in jeans, boots, and a soft blue work shirt, he carried a bulging canvas laundry bag. There was a hatchet in a sheath on his hip, and a professional-grade camera on a strap around his neck.

The man blinked. "Please don't."

Dean didn't squeeze but didn't move the machine pistol away.

"Don't kill him," a woman's voice said softly to Dean's left. He spun, pointing the weapon at a blond woman in her thirties, standing in the open doorway of apartment 3D.

"We live here," said the man on the stairs. "Me and Shana."

The woman nodded. "Please . . . come inside."

Dean looked at them both, tracking the muzzle of the MAC-10 back and forth between them. A foul, black little voice inside him urged Dean to kill them both quickly and take their place and their supplies, to be ruthless in order to survive.

But the man who was a daddy to the wide-eyed, almost three-year-old watching it unfold could not do that. Dean lowered his weapon, and soon got to know Dylan Stern and Shana DiMarco.

I was backpacking when the plague hit," Dylan explained, sitting on a small sofa across from Dean and Leah. Shana had already provided bottled water and conjured up a juice box for Leah. She also offered a box of diaper wipes so father and daughter could clean themselves.

Dean thanked her and kept the MAC-10 in his lap, muzzle angled in their direction, finger resting beside the trigger.

Dylan noticed but said nothing. "I lived in the hills as long as I could," he said, "until I ran out of food. Then I had to come down." He was a professional photographer, he explained, paying the bills with portraits and weddings and graduations, but his real love was photographing the outdoors.

The man looked at Leah, who was sipping happily at her juice, sitting close to her daddy with Wawas tucked under one arm. Dylan said, "On the stairs when I said she was beautiful, that probably sounded creepy. It just came out; I do a lot of kids' portraits. I didn't mean anything by it, so thank you for not killing me." He gave a nervous, embarrassed laugh.

Shana sat beside him and put a paper plate of chocolate chip cookies on the coffee table, along with an open can of tuna and a fork. "She is beautiful," the woman said, smiling at Leah. "We haven't seen a little girl in a long time. Not one who wasn't . . ."

Dylan put an arm around her.

After a few moments, Shana told Dean that she had been the manager of a wine shop here in Chico. When the city ordered all nonessential businesses closed, she had chosen to stay in her home instead of report to the refugee center out at the fairgrounds.

"It's good you did," said Dean. "It was overrun."

Shana glanced at Dylan and put her head on his shoulder. "We thought something like that must have happened. It's been so quiet for a long time, no loudspeakers or helicopters, nothing in the street but *them*."

"We were both out wandering," Dylan said. "The dead keep you moving. We ran into each other in this complex, looking for supplies like you were. We've been here for a month now."

Dean let Leah have a cookie, and she gobbled down four before he had to ask Shana to take the plate away. Leah wasn't happy about that, but then the woman returned with a faded Raggedy Ann doll.

"I found it in one of the closets," she said. "It's pretty beaten up."

Leah squealed and reached with little grabbing hands, hugging the doll close. After some prodding by her father she said, "Thank you," and knelt on the carpet, where Raggedy Ann was soon engaged in a conversation with a stuffed walrus.

Dylan smiled as he looked at the little girl. "They get used to situations. Thank God."

"That's what worries me," said Dean, then looked back at his hosts. They seemed harmless enough. Was he prepared to trust them? "You had your camera with you," Dean said. "What do you take pictures of these days?"

The older man smiled and offered the digital camera. "It still has juice. I have a solar charger, and it comes in handy when I'm out in the woods for a week at a time. I photograph the same thing I did before: nature. There's lots of shots of Shana in there too, a few of the vacant city, but they're terribly sad. I won't photograph the dead," he said, frowning. "That's not nature. They're abominations. I delete any picture they show up in, no matter how good I think it is."

"You can stay," Shana said, then glanced at Dylan, who nodded. "We'll share what we have."

"Why would you do that?" Dean asked.

Dylan's sad eyes drooped just the slightest. "Because the world's become ugly enough without us being ugly to each other."

Dean told himself he didn't dare trust them, couldn't risk exposing Leah to strangers, but in the end he did.

By the end of October, Dylan and Shana were friends. Dean told them what he and Leah had gone through in Sacramento, and at the ranch. He told them about Angie. They said they were sure she was alive. Leah took to Shana, who, though she'd had no children of her own, seemed to happily assume the role of surrogate mother. Dean watched closely and was finally convinced that she was a genuine, caring person. He knew there probably weren't too many of them left.

Dean eventually grew comfortable enough to leave Leah in their care so he could go on short scavenging and scouting missions without being weighed down by a toddler. It was from one of these missions that he returned freshly bitten.

FOURTEEN

January—East Chico

Dylan looked at Angie and shook his head. "He told us it was a dog bite, even showed us the wound. I couldn't tell the difference, but I believed him."

Silence filled the elementary school cafeteria. Without thinking, Skye reached out a hand to Carney, and he took it with a gentle squeeze.

Angie tried to say something, but the words wouldn't come. Dylan filled the gap. "We didn't have any way to treat it, not really, only first aid. It got infected and Dean got feverish."

Tears welled in Angie's eyes, and she wiped at them angrily, determined to hear the rest, no matter how terrible.

"I never saw anyone turn," Dylan said, "because I was in the woods for the worst of it. Shana had, though, and she said there was a fever before it happened. She was scared. I still believed it was a dog, but she wasn't sure. We decided to go out to look for antibiotics."

"Both of you?" Angie asked. "You left Leah with him after he'd been bitten?"

The photographer nodded. "Shana refused to be alone with him, just in case it hadn't been a dog, but she didn't want to go out by herself, either." He sighed. "I offered to bring Leah with us, but Dean wouldn't have it."

Angie wanted to scream at him. How could he have left a little girl alone with someone who had been bitten? Her hands turned to fists to keep them from shaking. "What happened?"

"Shana and I started searching apartments on the other side of the complex, places we hadn't been." He gave her a sad smile. "She insisted we not go too far away from them." Then he swallowed hard. "She was the one who found the antibiotics, a Z-pack in a nightstand drawer. There were still four tablets left in it, and she was so happy she was laughing." He closed his eyes. "They got us in the breezeway outside the apartment, just came tumbling out through the door across the way. She never had a chance, and all I could do was run."

Angie saw the words behind Dylan's sad eyes, the ones he used on himself. *Coward. Failure.* Her fists relaxed, and she let out a long breath.

"There were a lot of them in the complex then," Dylan said, "coming out of apartments and in from the parking lot. I don't know, maybe we made too much noise, stirred them up."

"What about Dean?" Skye prompted.

Dylan looked at the young woman in black. "I was hiding and running; I didn't want to lead them back to our place. I spent the night in an apartment, and in the morning it looked clear enough to move." His voice took on a bitter tone. "The dead weren't gone, they just shifted over to the other side of the complex. Our side."

The photographer looked back at Angie. "I got close enough to see that the dead were all over the place, and I could see them up there, walking in and out of our apartment. I locked it when we left, but they must have broken in." He put his head down. "I'm sorry."

"Did you see them?" Angie asked, her voice breaking. "Were they turned?"

Dylan was shaking his head. "I had to keep moving. I didn't see them, but the apartment door—"

"They might still be alive," Angie interrupted, looking at Carney and Skye. Her friends nodded slowly.

"Not likely," said Sorkin, "and that part about the dog was just a story. All the dogs are dead."

"We've seen dogs," Skye said.

Sorkin acted like he hadn't heard her. "The dogs are dead and so's your family. The faster you get used to it, the better off you'll be, missy."

Angie looked at the old man and bit her lip, turning away. Skye gave the old man a sharp prod with her rifle barrel, saying, "You're an asshole."

"They could be alive," Angie said, looking at Carney. "They could have gotten out."

Carney looked back with hard blue eyes. "And we won't stop looking until we find them," he said. Then he looked at the people who had taken shelter in the school. "So, your friend who was bitten. He went through the fever, right? How did that look compared to what Dean went through?" This he directed at the photographer.

Before he could answer, Hannah cut a hard look at the other two. "Abbie and Dylan tried to take care of him. He shouldn't have been in here with us."

"That's right," said Sorkin, "we should have shot him as soon as he got bit."

Abbie pointed at the old man. "We can't just shoot people. We can't."

Sorkin raised his voice. "You're goddamned wrong about that, missy! He nearly killed us all when he turned."

"But you took care of that, didn't you?" Dylan said to Hannah.

"I had to," she said, raising her own voice. "You weren't going to do it. You wanted him in here."

"It was the right thing to do," said Abbie, starting to cry.

Standing across the room, James Garfield looked from one face to the other as his lower lip trembled. He hugged Drew more tightly. The child didn't notice, only stared at a wall.

"He was bit," Sorkin yelled. "He turned and she shot him, and I'd do it to any of you!"

Against his own practices, Carney's attention was on the argument, and he didn't see Garfield cradle his son's head against his chest and hurry out of the room down the hallway to the kitchen. "Quiet down," the former inmate told the room. His voice carried, and the arguing stopped. "All that's over now," he said, seeing their faces, a group divided. "This isn't helping, and neither is all the noise." He had their attention, and that was important. "We need to make a plan, figure out our next move."

"Our *move*," said Sorkin, "was to hide in here nice and quiet, and it was working just fine until you people showed up."

Carney gave him those hard blue eyes. "And now things have changed. There's strength in numbers." His time with Father Xavier and the others had taught him that lesson.

There was a thump behind them, and everyone turned toward the long row of windows. A pair of corpses had their faces pressed against the glass, and one of them slammed a fist into it hard enough to make it rattle in the frame. Both were moaning, and behind them, others of their kind were making their way across the grass, heading toward the window. The street beyond was filling with drifters.

"Not again," Abbie sobbed.

"We need to—" Carney started, but at that moment a trio of galloping corpses burst into the room from the hallway Garfield had taken and slammed into Carney.

James Garfield ran across the parking lot at the back of the school. Behind him, the kitchen door swung slowly closed but didn't latch. The man and his boy fled onto the soccer field, drawing the attention of a dozen drifters who immediately turned to follow.

At the school, a ghoul in paint-spattered jeans walked from behind a Dumpster, sniffed the air, and pulled open the back door. Before it could close behind him, two more drifters followed, and then a group of the dead moving through the parking lot headed in that direction.

Garfield held tight to his son as he ran across the brown grass, a low whine escaping his throat. Lurching, crooked figures angled in at him from the right and left, and when he risked a look back, he saw the crowd of dead people in pursuit.

"We'll be okay, we'll be okay," he chanted, puffing hard, heading for the low fence at the back of the soccer field and the row of houses beyond. "We'll be okay, we'll be okay."

Drew bounced in his arms, looking at the sky.

Skye yelled Carney's name, and the big man twisted just as a drifter in paint-spattered jeans hit him, reaching and snapping. Carney raised his rifle like a bar and held the creature back for a second, but then the other two struck and they all went down in a pile, Carney on the bottom.

The sound of dragging feet and an echo of moans came from the hallway.

Skye fired three times, hitting two of Carney's drifters in the head, then leaped to drag the bodies clear. Carney was barely holding the last creature's jaws away from his face by forcing the rifle into the thing's neck. Angie ran to the hallway entrance and began firing the Galil. There were screams and panicked cries in the cafeteria behind her.

"Get that," Sorkin said to his daughter, pointing at an assault rifle on the floor where someone had dropped it. Hannah did, and in a moment the old man was once again armed. Sorkin glared at Abbie and Dylan. "Piss on you," he spat before moving quickly through the cafeteria and down another hall, Hannah following without a look back.

"Lift its head!" Skye yelled, and Carney pushed as if he were doing a bench press in the San Quentin yard. The creature's head came up with a growl, and Skye put a bullet in it, gore blowing out the other side. Carney hurled the corpse to the side and got to his feet.

"The door's open," Angie shouted between cracks of the Galil. "They're pouring in!" She was dropping bodies in the hallway, but not enough. More were pressing forward. After several more rounds her trigger clicked and she shouted, "Changing mags," and stepped back. Carney stepped in and fired, the M14 deafening.

Now the cafeteria's windows were lined with the snarling dead, all of them slamming their fists. The glass began to fracture in a dozen places.

Angie was reloaded. "We can't stay here," she said, taking Carney's place at the hallway so he could switch to a full magazine. The sound of falling glass came from the far end of the cafeteria, where a pair of corpses was climbing through a broken window.

"The roof," said Skye.

"No," Angie yelled, "we do *not* want to get trapped on a roof."

"We'll be able to check all sides," Skye yelled back. "They can't be everywhere. We'll find a gap and get out. It's a short drop." The young woman pointed to Dylan and Abbie. "I found a roof hatch when I was up there. Do you know where the ladder is?"

Dylan shook his head, but Abbie nodded. "Sorkin made us go around and lock all the doors. I closed that one."

"Is it padlocked?"

Abbie said, "No, it's just closed with a latch. I didn't have a padlock." She looked at the rear of the cafeteria. The corpses were on their feet now, moving between the tables as others scrambled up and through the broken window. "But there's one of those things on the roof," she said, her voice shaking. "A janitor, I think."

"Not anymore," said Skye. "Show me the ladder. Angie, we're moving!"

Abbie, the former Red Cross volunteer, started toward the hallway Sorkin and Hannah had taken, then froze when a pair of zombies snarled and headed in her direction, bumping against tables. Skye shouldered Abbie aside and shot both creatures. "Show me!" she demanded again.

Abbie got moving, Dylan taking her by the arm. Angie fired several more times, and then she and Carney followed. The little group moved down a short hall lined with cubbies and coat hooks, crayon pictures on construction paper rustling in their breeze as they hustled through. Abbie turned left at an intersection, passing closed classroom doors, and stopped at one marked *STAFF ONLY*. Sorkin and Hannah might have come this way, but there was no sign of them.

"The hatch is at the top of a metal ladder," Abbie said, clinging to Dylan, "inside that room."

Skye opened the door, ready to kill anything inside. It was empty except for janitorial supplies and a metal ladder bolted to one wall. Skye slung her rifle and climbed, unlatching the flat metal hatch and pushing it up on hydraulic arms, popping it open. The gray light of January and a drizzling rain came in as Skye scrambled out onto the roof, disappeared, and then returned to the opening.

"All clear. Everyone up, right now."

Dylan spoke softly and urged Abbie up the ladder, climbing

close behind her. Angie came next, and Carney closed the door to the janitor's closet before following.

The roof was as Skye had left it, air-conditioning units and solar panels over wet gravel. She got her bearings, then led the group across the roof in a direction opposite the open rear door. Moans floated up from the school grounds, and they could see hundreds of the walking dead in the streets, shuffling in from intersections, hobbling across lawns.

"Hold them here," Skye said, leaving Abbie and Dylan with her companions as she trotted away to scout the school's perimeter. Almost at once, the picture looked grim. It seemed the dead were on all sides, spread out and scattered, but thickening into a dense crowd as they neared the walls of the school.

"Plan B," she muttered, taking the Hydra radio from her belt and keying the mic. "Come to my position. We're going to have to blast a hole." Then she knelt, settled the rifle against her shoulder, and scanned for an area she deemed the least populated. She fired, and bodies jerked and fell. Ten rounds, twenty, thirty, then a magazine change. She continued firing, shapes falling as puffs of gray and pink filled Skye's rifle optics, bodies spinning around or into each other, and in a smooth motion she was changing mags again, her mouth set in a grim line.

Die, she thought. *Stay down.*

A lane of sorts began to appear in the street, a long area that crossed from the school to the buildings on the other side, where only motionless bodies lay. The rest of the group appeared behind her, but Skye didn't look back, her rifle barrel twitching like an automaton now, left, left, right, left again, spent brass flying from the ejection port, the muzzle speaking over and over with its muted *PUFFT.*

"How will we get down?" Abbie wanted to know.

"You'll hang by your arms and drop," said Carney. "You'll be okay," he added when he saw the doubtful look on the woman's face, not adding that they would be lucky not to break an ankle. Angie lined them up and explained how they would lower themselves from the roof and drop to the lawn below.

PUFFT, PUFFT. Two more bodies fell.

Across the street stood a low brick building that looked like a medical practice and a large Victorian home that had been converted to legal offices. Several cars sat in the small parking lot between the buildings, and an electrician's van was parked lengthwise against the medical offices. A crowd of twenty or more drifters was surging out of the parking lot and into Skye's freshly cleared lane. One by one they appeared in the M4's optics; the weapon would kick, and a drifter would fall.

A woman in pajamas.

A teenager in cutoffs.

A man in a shirt and tie.

A girl in a bathing suit.

Ghastly faces appeared and disappeared, eyes glazed, flesh sagging or missing from rot or old bites, complexions of gray and green. And then the sight fell on a drifter with a bald head, bare-chested with taut skin defining every muscle, clearly dead from a savaged and open throat. It was impossible to identify its former race, because now it looked like nothing Skye had ever seen. Its skin was glossy, unnaturally smooth. Most startling of all was its dark, cherry-colored skin. It reminded Skye of something she had once seen online, the body of a person who had died from carbon monoxide poisoning. That person's skin had been nearly this shade, although blotchy. This thing appeared unblemished.

It wasn't following the other dead things, either, simply standing near the back of the electrician's van with one hand resting on the metal side. The creature's teeth were bared, and it stared directly up at Skye from across the street, then licked its lips with a coal-black tongue.

Her breath caught and she moved her eye from the sight for a second, blinking. She had never seen one of them do that before. Then she centered the sight's luminescent green chevrons on the thing's forehead, tensed her finger—

—and the creature stepped out of sight behind the van.

"Did you see that?" she shouted to the others.

Angie dropped to one knee beside her, rifle raised. "See what?"

Skye pointed. "There was a drifter out there, and it was looking at me. It moved behind that van just before I fired. Like it *knew*."

Angie used her binoculars but saw nothing but the same type of drifters they had seen for months, moaning and walking stiffly to fill the lane Skye had cleared. "I don't see it."

"It's behind that van. It's red, smooth, and kind of shiny. It was looking at me and it moved out of the way. They don't do that!" Skye made a growling sound and fired at the new drifters in her lane until her magazine was dry. The glossy red drifter did not reappear.

The dead frightened her, always had, though she had learned to control her fear. This new . . . creature . . . was even more terrifying. It was self-aware, that much was clear, and it could think. One of her literature teachers in high school had used a word once that resonated with her: *hobgoblin*. He said it was a creature that originated from Celtic mythology, but he told them the term had been used to describe other things as well. "Hobgoblin," he had said, standing in front of the chalkboard, "something frightening, dangerous, and hard to get rid of."

Hobgoblin, she thought. *That's what it was*. And then another word occurred to her. *Mutation*.

"This might not work," Angie said, watching as drifters immediately replaced those that fell. "It's not much of an opening, and the activity is drawing in even more."

But someone thought the gap was worth the risk. Below them, a fire exit banged open as Sorkin and Hannah bolted out of it. They ran across the lawn and into the street, into the lane choked with fallen bodies, Hannah in the lead. They dodged around reaching arms, the old man carrying the assault rifle and keeping up with the younger woman.

Hannah had almost made it all the way across when she cut too close to a reaching creature in khakis and a red shirt. It caught hold of her waistband, and though her forward movement jerked it off its feet, it also brought Hannah to the ground. Two more drifters galloped in as the first clawed a better hold on the struggling woman.

Hannah screamed. Sorkin ran past without stopping.

"Son of a bitch," Skye hissed, putting her rifle sights on the old man's back. But then she shifted right, trying to line up on the head of one of the thrashing figures atop Hannah. It was too late. Beside her, Angie saw Sorkin dodge more reaching arms and then run into the small parking lot and around the back of the electrician's van.

There was a horrible scream, quickly cut short.

Below, Skye's exit lane was full of the dead once more as drifters moved in to participate in the feeding frenzy where Hannah had gone down. Skye cursed and looked for another way out.

Then everything stopped.

Every *thing* stopped.

Every drifter in view came to a complete halt and slowly shuffled in place until they were all facing the same direction: southwest. Those feeding on Hannah climbed to their feet and did the same, and all the corpses tipped their heads back in the same instant. They were silent, standing motionless in the drizzling rain.

The survivors on the roof stared at one another with unspoken questions, but it was Angie, in a sharp voice, who said, "Don't ask, just take advantage. Everyone off the roof."

One by one they sat on the edge, turned, and hung from the lip, legs dangling before they dropped. Abbie made a small whimpering noise but did as she was told, and within a minute all five of them were on the ground without injury.

Skye took the lead again, and the others followed in a running line as they crossed the street, weapons raised, winding through the stationary dead. Nothing moved or reached, nothing moaned.

The young woman stayed well to the side as she took them past the electrician's van, her M4 switched to full auto and ready to shred the glossy red drifter as soon as she saw it. The pavement, the rear doors of the van, and the medical office wall were covered in what looked like paint cans' worth of red. Sorkin's assault rifle lay in a pool of it, and what remained of the man was difficult to identify. He had been torn to pieces. Separated limbs rested yards away from the savaged torso, as if ripped off and thrown, and the head was missing.

Abbie screamed and pointed. At the rear entrance to the medical offices stood a row of white metal boxes for lab pickup and drop-off. Sorkin's head sat upon one of them, eyes gouged out and mouth open in a frozen scream.

The head couldn't have landed there, in an upright position, by chance. It had been intentionally placed.

Of the glossy red zombie there was no sign, but Skye came to a halt and sighted, turning in a slow circle. Angie gave her a hard bump. "We need to keep moving," the woman said, taking the lead with her raised Galil. The others followed, but Skye stood there a moment longer, staring at the head as a shudder raced up her back.

When Sorkin's lips peeled back from his teeth and his tongue began moving inside the decapitated head, Skye caught up to the others.

The earth began to tremble seconds later.

Across town from the elementary school, at an intersection outside Saint Miguel and its fortress walls of shipping containers, a line of drifters stood in the late-afternoon drizzle. Each was collared and leashed to a long cable spanning the street, a dog run for the dead. There were twenty-two corpses forming a gruesome curtain, but a twenty-third leash, at the end of the line opposite the church, led to a row of hedges and out of sight.

In the shadows behind the hedge, a drifter lay curled on the ground in a fetal position. In life the drifter had been Anne Marie O'Donnell, twenty-four, with long red hair and a fair, almost pale complexion. She had once been a parishioner of Saint Miguel, before she was bitten by her own mother in mid-August.

Nearly twenty-four hours ago, Anne O'Donnell's tongue turned as black as soot, and she shuffled away from the others to crawl behind this bush.

Now her skin was a glossy crimson that had pulled taut to accentuate bones and muscle. Her body shook as if having a seizure, and a low, wheezing croak issued from her throat. No one noticed her absence from the dog run, and no one discovered her quivering body behind the hedge. Anne O'Donnell's corpse did not react to the tremor that shook Chico.

By nightfall, the body's trembling slowed and then stopped. The corpse stood and stared in amazement at its hands for a moment, slowly flexing its fingers, head cocked. It scented the air and looked across at the lights of Saint Miguel, at the wall and the sentries. A hunger pulled at its insides, along with a curious but pleasant, violent urge. The creature let out a low moan that came out more like a growl.

The newly born creature reached up and unbuckled its collar, letting it fall, staring again at its hands before breathing in the night. There was another out there, another like itself. It eyed the sentries once more, wanting to destroy and feed upon them, but sensed danger. Instead it turned and ran into the night, as fast as any human.

FIFTEEN

Russo and Lassiter sat in the cab of Lassiter's new Ford F-250, watching the column roll by on Deer Creek Highway, making the turn south onto Forest. There were three pickups packed with armed people, led by a pair of bikers wearing their Skinners colors. At the tail end was the Bradley, the armored vehicle rumbling down the center of the road and Corrigan riding high in the open hatch, one hand resting on a mounted machine gun. The prey they were hunting would require the heavy firepower.

Scott Corrigan, an Army deserter with a nasty scar down the side of his face and cold eyes, glanced over at the two men in the truck with a look Russo thought said he would enjoy rolling over them with the tracks of his Bradley.

Lassiter kissed Corrigan's ass whenever possible. Russo thought it smarter to avoid the man altogether.

"It's not fair," said Lassiter, watching the column move out of sight. "We're the ones who saw the damned helicopter. We should have been able to go look for it with the others."

Russo said nothing, just watched the rain trickle down the windshield. He had no wish to go on a raid. He didn't want to be here with this loser day after day, collecting supplies to better stock Briggs's fortress, risking his life for toilet paper and bottles of Advil. Russo had actually hoped that spotting and reporting the helicopter might earn them a reward, a chance to stay behind the walls for a while. He had been wrong.

His partner, Russo knew, loved being out here. He couldn't stop talking about how he had participated in the raid on that TV star's ranch, the place with the bunker packed with weapons. Russo had never seen the show himself, it wasn't to his taste, but a day didn't go by that Lassiter wasn't boasting about how he first heard of the place and reported it to Briggs, boasting of his bravery when he captured the female zombie out there and chained her into a truck bed.

Lassiter was drinking a warm Dr Pepper and munching on a Pop-Tart. Russo had a V8 and a bag of trail mix, which his partner called *bark*. The former armored-car driver had chosen a delightful spot for their picnic. On the left side of the road was a wide grassy stretch that had once featured saplings and a bike path. At some point during Chico's final days, officials had ordered the excavation of a long trench, tearing up the trees and obliterating the path.

Now little yellow hazmat flags poked from the earth around the excavation, and the trench itself was half-filled with decomposing corpses. The bodies were coated with white powder that clumped in the rain, and they gave off a punishing fragrance of lime and decay that burned the nose and eyes.

More gruesome than the pit, Russo thought, was the trail of clumping white lime that led away from it, across what remained of the grass and into the road. He tried to imagine what kind of chemical-burned nightmare that escapee would look like, and couldn't.

It was disgusting, all of it, but Lassiter disgusted him the most.

Sitting beside the former armored-car driver in the truck cab, Russo wondered if he could get away with killing Lassiter. He had never killed anyone, not anyone alive, anyway, but taking out Lassiter seemed like it would be easy. The man thought Russo was a spineless punk. He would never see it coming. Russo could shoot him in the heart, let him turn, then shoot him in the head. He could make up any story he wanted, something simple about Lassiter getting careless and getting bitten.

He smiled.

Russo had been fantasizing about murdering Lassiter a lot lately. Maybe it was time to put thoughts into action. Could he pull the trigger? He decided he could.

"What are you grinning about?" said Lassiter, sitting behind the steering wheel and staring at his partner.

Russo jumped, as if caught doing something he shouldn't. "Nothing," he said. "Just . . . nothing."

Lassiter glared at him, the contempt on his face unconcealed. "We gotta check the east side," he said. The man kept a suspicious eye on his partner as he drove up Deer Creek Highway, and Russo could only stare out the side window, his nerve broken. God, he hated all this. He didn't even feel like doing any filming for his kick-ass documentary, and the lime pit would have been compelling footage.

The Ford rolled ahead for a time, the roadway noticeably empty of the walking dead. When Russo commented on it, Lassiter just shrugged and said, "They're busy someplace else."

They stopped at the intersection where Notre Dame Avenue cut south from Deer Creek, Lassiter letting the engine idle. The two men looked at houses with drawn curtains, little rows of businesses with *CLOSED* signs hanging in windows and doors. Today they were specifically searching for painkillers, at the command of Little Emer Briggs. Where to begin?

Muffled gunfire reached them over the idling engine. Lassiter was out on the pavement a moment later, standing beside the hood, and Russo got out as well. The gunfire was distant, coming from the south, and it was steady, measured shots one after the other, muffled as if inside a building.

"The column?" Russo suggested.

Lassiter shook his head. "They're farther south by now. This is something else." The man listened to the shooting for another moment and then pointed. "Down there. That's where it's coming from."

Russo looked down the avenue and saw nothing.

"Come on," said Lassiter, breaking into a trot and heading for the sound of gunfire.

Kill him now! Russo shouted inside. *Shoot him in the back! Do something!* But he didn't, and suddenly knew he couldn't, no matter how much he told himself otherwise. If he wanted to get away from Lassiter and the madness of Chico, he would have to run. There was no particular destination in mind, and right now it was only away from here. He would have to pick the right moment, but this wasn't it.

He trotted after his partner.

James Garfield eased Drew to the ground over the low fence. The boy stood and stared forward. Garfield looked back to see a dozen corpses heading for him across the soccer field, and behind them, a stream of the dead poured into the school through the door he had left open. Gunfire came from inside.

It was just too much, he thought, climbing over the fence and collecting his son once more. The fighting, the arguing, crazy, angry Sorkin. That was why he had run in the first place. Garfield was no apocalyptic warrior and he knew it. He was a mortgage broker who had never even been in a schoolyard scuffle, a Democrat who voted for green initiatives and wished for stronger anti-gun laws. Did it make him less of a man that he didn't like to follow sports or go to the gym? He had lost his family and now had to take care of his frightened little boy until the government could find and rescue them. He had believed in their power, and now it was his turn to be supported.

But it was taking so long!

The thought of keeping the two of them safe and fed and quiet for more weeks and months was exhausting. Still, he picked up Drew as he hurried through a backyard and down a driveway past a small house.

He would just have to do it, he told himself, find a quiet place to hide and wait. Help would arrive soon, from people who didn't wave guns and act crazy and scare people. He neared the street. The government had a plan for something like this, didn't they? Of course they did. Someone would come.

The racking sound of a shotgun brought Garfield to a stumbling halt.

R usso had the twelve-gauge pointed at the man's chest, and Lassiter moved in fast, patting the man down for weapons. "Where you going in such a hurry?" he demanded.

Garfield, eyes wet and red, could only shake his head.

Russo gestured with his shotgun. "What's wrong with that kid?"

Garfield turned the boy away from the gun. "Nothing's wrong with him. He's just scared, that's all."

"Set him down," Lassiter said.

"No."

Lassiter rammed the muzzle of his AK-47 hard into one of Garfield's eyes, making him scream and grab at his face, losing his grip on Drew. Lassiter jerked the boy away from the man and then slammed the butt of the assault rifle into Garfield's stomach. The man gasped and fell, and as soon as he hit the ground, Lassiter was astride him with the zip ties, securing his hands behind his back and slapping duct tape over his mouth. He glanced back to where the man had come from, no longer hearing gunfire.

"Let's get him in the truck." Lassiter gripped his captive by the arm and started hauling him back up the street.

Russo looked at the vacant-eyed child staring through him, hesitated, then took hold of one of the boy's hands, hanging limp at his sides. Drew didn't protest, and allowed himself to be led after his father.

SIXTEEN

January 12—Halsey's Cabin

Vladimir wore a poncho with the hood up against the rain, the Hydra radio on one hip. It never left him. Halsey was beside him, water dripping from the brim of his John Deere cap. They stood on the muddy road that led to Halsey's cabin and outbuildings.

"I'm thinking I'll leave the road as it is," said Halsey, gesturing, "sink poles for a gate and start digging off to either side."

"You wish for a moat," the Russian said, envisioning what the cowboy described.

Halsey spat tobacco. "Yep, only not with water and crocodiles and such." He laughed. "Just a nice, wide trench, maybe ten feet deep. He turned in a slow circle. "All the way around, leaving the buildings on the inside."

The Russian kicked a toe at the muddy road. "Leaving this the only way in, blocked by a gate."

"That's what I'm thinking."

"And your machine can do this?"

Halsey smiled and looked over to the front-end loader, draped with a blue tarp. "She can do it. Might take a while, but I'd sure sleep better at night. Just let the dead fall into the moat."

The theory sounded reasonable to Vladimir. He put his hands in his pockets. "A man who does such a thing is planning to stay where he is."

Halsey shrugged. "Where else would I go? This is home, has been for a long time. If I can keep the DTs out, I could plant without anything getting into the crops, and I'd be able to have animals again. It wouldn't matter if their smell and noise attracted the dead."

"You have thought much about this."

Another shrug. "Got plenty of time to think."

Vladimir smiled. He liked this man, simple and direct, someone who said what he believed or did not bother to speak. It was a trait Vlad admired. "You could come with us," the pilot said. "You could be with other people again, and be most welcome."

Halsey spat. "Don't know if I'd care much for life on a ship. Too closed in. I might think it was hard to breathe."

Vladimir looked around at the rolling hills and open sky, smelled the clean aroma of the backcountry, and then looked at a man who had made it home. Part of him longed to do the same, to remain in a place where life was simple and quiet. The feeling lasted for only a moment. He had responsibilities, people to look after and others who wanted him home. He was a pilot, perhaps one of the last, and because of that he had an obligation that superseded his sudden fantasy of life on a farm. He chuckled at the thought of wearing overalls and milking cows. Air Lieutenant Vladimir Yurish, flight instructor and combat pilot, turned farm boy. *Nyet*, his was a different path, one of speed and physics and adrenaline.

The Russian looked at his new friend. "Your moat is a fine idea. I wish to help. When shall we begin?"

The ground began to tremble beneath them then, a vibration

that traveled up through their boots and intensified, threatening to throw them off their feet. A few loose shingles on the abandoned stables rattled off the roof, and then the movement ceased. The men looked at each other for a moment.

Halsey grinned at Vladimir's startled expression. "That was a baby. Either a little one underneath us, or a shock wave from something a little bigger somewhere else. You've never felt one?"

The Russian scowled. He had been in California for a while but had never experienced a tremor he could identify as earthquake activity. "We do not have these things up there," he said, pointing at the sky.

That made Halsey laugh. "Hell, I'd rather do some bumping around down here than be up there. If something goes wrong, it's a long way to fall."

Vladimir nodded solemnly. "You have a point, my friend. Now, about your moat?"

Halsey gave the mud a kick. "It's warm enough that the ground's not frozen, and the rain will soften things up a bit. Got plenty of diesel." He looked at the sky. "Light's gonna be gone soon. How about we start in the morning?"

Vladimir clapped his hands together. "Excellent. Then we shall have this evening to enjoy another adult beverage."

Halsey smiled. "I think I can take care of that."

At the Franks ranch, when Halsey had told Angie and the others about the Stampede, the mass of over a thousand corpses moving through the woods as a single group, he had been only partially correct. There was a group that size, but it wasn't the only one.

Paradise, California, the small mountain town ten miles east of Carson's Broken Arrow Ranch, had been emptying of the dead for days, thousands of corpses, all moving slowly south through the rugged terrain. The temperature had dropped, turning the light rain into wet snow. The corpse of a boy in swim trunks stumbled through the undergrowth, a crest of white on his shoulders and head where no body heat would melt it away. A minute behind him, a man in a plaid shirt, also coated in snow, limped in the path the boy's dragging feet made in the snow. Others followed: a man in a hospital gown, a construction worker, a housewife, and a truck driver. There were old people and more children, all dusted white, the color bleached from their flesh, eyes a milky gray.

The dead moved quietly through the woods, not moaning, the only sound the crack of branches beneath their feet. A few strayed from the horde, and others tumbled into ravines where they struggled and thrashed, but the rest kept moving west.

West, toward a small cluster of buildings with a helicopter parked at its edge.

SEVENTEEN

January 12—East Chico, near the Skyway

The column had nearly reached the bridge over Butte Creek when the shaking started. Standing in the commander's hatch of the Bradley, twenty-seven tons of armored vehicle rumbling beneath him, Corrigan didn't notice until he saw the line of vehicles ahead come to a stop, the bikers fighting to keep their rides upright.

"Driver, stop," he ordered into the intercom mic, and Marx, one of the two soldiers who had deserted with him, brought the armored fighting vehicle to a halt. At once, the vibrations traveled up through the tracks and hull. It reminded Corrigan of a coin-operated vibrating bed in a cheap motel.

For those on the ground it was a different story. The two bikers jumped clear of their Harleys just as the motorcycles were thrown to the pavement, and the bikers staggered for a moment before they fell down as well. One of the pickups stuttered to the right for several yards as its occupants bailed out, and a yellow *Bridge Ahead* sign on the shoulder shimmied violently before sagging over at a forty-five-degree angle.

Then came a tremendous cracking and a jagged black line raced across the pavement, widening, splitting both the inbound and outbound lanes. With a roar and a jolt that threw everyone on the road off their feet and even made the Bradley bounce, the road separated, the pavement on the far side of the crack dropping more than a foot before the shaking ceased.

Cries of alarm and awe rose from the road as people got to their feet and approached the crack, a fissure roughly six inches wide. The two bikers cursed as they righted their Harleys and examined damage done to paint jobs and chrome.

"Stand by," Corrigan said, hanging his radio headset over the mounted machine gun and climbing down, a stubby-barreled assault rifle hung over one shoulder. His fatigues were bloused into combat boots, and his shirt still bore a patch reading *U.S. Army*, but he had long discarded any insignia of rank. He didn't need stripes to show that he was in charge. The Army deserter walked past the pickups and stopped at the crack in the earth. He squatted and examined the two new levels of roadway.

The armed men and women from the trucks gave the man a wide berth. No one liked the way he looked at people, like a rattlesnake sizing up a small desert rodent. Little Emer Briggs might be a dictator not to be argued with, might be unpredictable and ruthless, might even be a bit crazed, but he had managed to create a sanctuary from the dead. These people who carried out his missions, manned the walls, and did the dirty work for the biker lord and his cronies may not have cared for Little Emer, but they were grateful. Having to sacrifice their humanity in bits and pieces to keep earning that sanctuary—sometimes *big* bits and pieces—was the price one paid for survival. Best not to think about the murder, to pretend the playpen didn't exist. Better to do as they were told and keep on living.

Corrigan was another matter. His sneer, his cold mannerisms and absolute contempt for human life had made him hated among Saint Miguel's survivors. Little Emer made people uncomfortable, but Corrigan was terrifying, and utterly without mercy. He had once barked for a teenage boy to bring him an empty fuel can from a supply shed near the parish school. The boy hadn't heard him, and Corrigan didn't repeat the demand. The Army deserter and his two men seized the boy and stretched him out under the Bradley's tracks, then fired up the engine and eased the vehicle forward an inch at a time, breaking bones and grinding flesh at an agonizing rate, while the boy wailed and screamed for mercy. There was none, and the killing took nearly five full minutes before the teenager was a red smear on the church parking lot.

Most of the Saint Miguel survivors wanted to make him dead. No one had the courage to try, and they all assumed that Corrigan alone could operate the Bradley. The security the armored vehicle provided was reason enough to let the man live.

Braga, the biker with the long frizzy hair, walked up beside the squatting ex-soldier. "We can make it over that," the biker said, "no problem."

Corrigan ignored him and stepped down to the lower pavement, walking toward the bridge. Behind him, Braga muttered, "Asshole."

Twenty yards took Corrigan to the concrete span across Butte Creek. The crushed remains of a car was pushed against the guard-rail on one side, put there when the Bradley had first come this way months back for the raid on the ranch and bunker. A wheezing moan came from the other side, and when Corrigan investigated he found a zombie pinned between steel and concrete, a green-and-black thing that looked like a deflated balloon. The creature made a croaking sound, fingers clawing feebly at the asphalt. Corrigan turned away and slowly walked the length of the bridge, eyes searching.

He spotted the fractures, lines that zigzagged across the cement, and the entire structure seemed to be tilted to the left. The tilt could have been an optical illusion, but Corrigan didn't think so. He walked back to where the others were waiting.

"I'm not taking the Bradley across that," he announced.

Titan, a biker who had once cut a man's ear off in a bar because the guy made a poorly considered joke about being a fed, snorted. "The hell you say. Emer told us to go up the canyon."

Corrigan glared, and the biker looked into that visage of scar tissue and hate and took a step back. "So go," the deserter said. "The bridge should hold the bikes and the trucks. I'm just not taking armor across it."

Braga joined them, drawing himself up to full height. "Not cool, bro."

"I'm not your bro."

The long-haired biker shrugged. "The man said you had to come with us for support."

Corrigan looked at him now. "I heard what he said."

Another shrug. "So you gotta come with us."

"I don't *gotta* do anything," Corrigan said. "You go ahead and look for your helicopter. I'll wait here until you get back. If you get in trouble, call me."

"What, and *then* you'll cross the bridge?" Titan asked.

Corrigan shook his head slowly. "No. But then I'll know to tell Briggs that you didn't make it."

Braga spit. "Ah, this is bullshit, man. You're a pussy, scared of a little bridge." He and Titan glared at the man for a long moment, showing their teeth, but Corrigan didn't rise to the bait, simply stood with an arm draped over his assault weapon. All at once the bikers were unsure of what to do next. They were long accustomed to bullying and threatening to get what they wanted, and were ill-equipped when it didn't work.

Braga gave an evil little smile. "No problem, bro, but you're going to have to tell the man why you didn't back us up."

"Yeah," said Titan, "unhealthy choice."

Corrigan looked back without expression. The urge to put a full-auto burst into these two was powerful, and his index finger even crept into the assault rifle's trigger well. But not yet. When he made his move it would be at a time and place of his choosing, not provoked into a gunfight on an open road where he was heavily outnumbered. These two would die, he would see to it personally, but not today.

"Good luck finding the chopper," he said, turning and walking back to the Bradley. *And good luck thinking they won't have security in place to blow your asses away after they saw what happened to the first bird.* Behind him the bikers cursed for a moment, and then they were yelling for the others to get back in the pickups. Within minutes the Harleys and the other vehicles eased down over the split in the road one by one, crossed the bridge, and disappeared up the Skyway into the canyon.

Corrigan leaned against the Bradley's sloping front armor and lit a cigarette. Marx and Lenowski, the gunner, joined him. Marx spit in the direction the raiders had gone. "Scumbags," he said.

"How much longer we gonna put up with their shit, Boss?" Lenowski asked.

"I'll let you know," Corrigan said, then simply smoked and said nothing more. After a minute the other two returned to the vehicle.

Black Hawks. They were much on Corrigan's mind.

When the military in Chico folded, and Corrigan and his men chose to fend for themselves instead of protecting the refugees out at the fairgrounds, he hadn't been sure how it would all turn out. The authorities might have regained control, and as a deserter he would be screwed. The authorities, however, were the ones who drew the short straw, and they were eaten along with the rest. It quickly became clear that there would be no return to the way things had been, and Corrigan realized that he and his men were truly free to do as they pleased.

Hooking up with Briggs had been simply taking advantage of an opportunity, a means to securing a safe place to rest and stockpile supplies. The biker leader appreciated Corrigan's military knowledge and ruthlessness, and so the deserter had allowed Briggs to use his men and the Bradley to build his ridiculous little empire, even nodding with pretend interest when the bigger man spouted his prison yard philosophy about conquest and his love affair with dead Roman Caesars.

Little Emer Briggs was violent and childlike, but he had a clever side too, and Corrigan reminded himself to not underestimate the man. Corrigan's days of taking orders were over, however, especially from a pack of fuckups like these bikers. When the time came, the ex-soldier planned to unleash a brand of hell on them that would have given any Roman emperor a hard-on.

A zombie appeared on the far side of the bridge, dragging a crooked foot as it shuffled slowly across. It wore a gray work shirt with a name patch Corrigan couldn't read at this distance. He flicked his cigarette butt into the road and watched the dead man move closer.

Helicopters. It was troubling. Two days ago he had picked up some brief radio chatter on a military frequency, a Black Hawk pilot talking to someone on the ground in South Chico. He and his men had taken the Bradley out to investigate, shielding the armored vehicle out of sight from the air by parking it beneath a gas station canopy. Once concealed, they watched the skies over the fields south of the city.

Within a half hour, a Black Hawk appeared, banking and descending quickly. Someone on the ground popped green smoke, signaling a safe landing zone, and the chopper angled toward it. They should have popped red smoke, Corrigan thought, remembering the moment with a smile. When he closed his eyes he could see it settling toward earth, could hear the beat of its blades, and he recalled with vivid clarity the single thought that had hit him like electricity.

They've come back to take charge, and I'll be shot for desertion.

His reaction was as impulsive as the thought, he knew that now. Using the machine gun mounted beside the hatch, Corrigan had poured an entire belt of 7.62-millimeter into the bird from a hundred yards away, raking it from cockpit to tail.

It crashed and burned. No one emerged from the wreckage, and their inspection of the site was cursory at best. Solution achieved: no military attempt to bring Corrigan to justice. Looking back, he realized he had been stupid. He should have waited until the Black Hawk landed, let whoever was on the ground get on board, then shoot it down as it was lifting off. That meant there were still military personnel with boots on the ground around here somewhere. He had not mentioned this fact to Briggs or his people.

Now here was a second Black Hawk, following right behind the first. It couldn't be coincidence, felt more like reconnaissance, and Corrigan realized his days in Chico were numbered. The deserter watched the zombie cross the bridge and approach the point where the roadway was freshly buckled by the quake. The creature bumped against the raised portion for a moment, then climbed up over it.

A second Black Hawk. Maybe the bikers and their screwup militia would find it and take it out. Corrigan doubted it. In fact, the more he thought about it, the more convinced he was that not only was the Army returning to the area, they were specifically coming for him. Coming to punish him for shooting down the first bird, to hang him for abandoning his post and his oath.

He put his assault rifle to his shoulder and squeezed off a three-round burst, making the approaching zombie jerk as the rounds stitched across its chest. A second burst shredded meat from its neck and shoulder. It kept coming. The assault rifle barked again, slugs punching through face and brain. It collapsed to the road.

Corrigan lit another cigarette and looked up the canyon, then at the sky. He would have to be ready.

Titan's and Braga's Harleys led the three trucks up the Skyway, snow-dusted pines on either side creating shadows where anything could be hiding. Neither biker cared for being out front, but it was necessary they show some leadership, at least for now. If shooting started, the men and women in the trucks could do the fighting and dying while the bikers took cover. *Until the action starts, put on a good show, then cover your ass.* This was one of Little Emer's principles of war, and so far it had been effective.

Before leaving Chico they had planned their search using a folding road map. It looked as if there were few places the Black Hawk could have landed—if it had landed at all—since most of the terrain was heavily wooded. There were a couple of ranches, like the one they had raided and another one yet to be explored, a place called the Broken Arrow. Both would have enough clear space to set down a bird, so both would have to be checked. Of course the Black Hawk could have gone to Paradise, or even kept flying into the Sierra Nevada, but they had no orders to check anywhere beyond the canyon, and besides, it would be dark soon.

Before investigating the ranches, however, there was a location that demanded exploration, and it could be done relatively quickly.

The two Harleys slowed, Braga waving and pointing with one arm to signal the trucks behind them. As a group they turned off the Skyway and onto a paved road, passing a sign for the Tuscan Ridge Golf Club. There was plenty of room to land a helicopter on a golf course.

EIGHTEEN

November—Southeast Chico

The cooler season forced Dean to layer a T-shirt under a black, long-sleeved turtleneck sweater, the rig for his MAC-10 across his shoulders, the Glock on his hip. He wore dark jeans and boots and had found a pair of black leather gloves. Scavenged scissors and a battery-powered trimmer had brought his hair back to a semblance of order and turned the beard into masculine stubble.

He was lying on the flat roof of a gas 'n' grocery, the hunting rifle on the gravel beside him as he peered through binoculars. Leah was safe back at the apartment with Dylan and Shana, and Dean was able to settle back into the comfortable role of scouting and reconnaissance. He munched on a granola bar looted from the store below.

A little over a block away, a minivan, a station wagon, and a jacked-up black Ford F-250 sat in the parking lot of a Target, close to the entrance. A man with a military look and an AK-47 stood in the truck bed keeping watch while half a dozen men and women repeatedly entered the store and emerged with shopping carts full of goods, loading them into the vehicles. Occasionally the man in the back of the pickup would raise his AK and fire several shots, dropping a dead thing as it walked toward the activity. Twice, muffled shots came from within the store itself.

Skeletons in summer clothes lay on the pavement in places, motionless beside empty, overturned carts or burned cars. A line of crows perched on the edge of the store's roof, watching intently.

Dean hadn't been looking for them intentionally; they had simply shown up. The longer he watched them, the more he recognized those on the ground and certainly the man in the truck bed as some of the people who had torn his family and his safe haven apart. These people, looking like innocent survivors trying to make it in a world come apart, were the enemy. Tangos.

They would all be easy kills for the scoped rifle lying beside him, but this was not a hunting trip. Dean needed to know what was out here. The raiders were obviously based somewhere inside Chico, but he had no way to follow them to find where that might be.

He ached to bring the fight to their door, to give them a final, terrifying taste of what a professional urban killer could do to their untrained ranks. But he could not. Leah needed a daddy to look after her, and that was a priority he accepted without regret.

Briefly, Dean considered leaving some booby traps for the raiders to find on one of their scavenging runs, but he immediately discarded the idea. Traps would maim and kill some of them, but not all, and would only serve to warn the others that there was a serious threat in their territory. They would scour the city to root out that threat, and soon no place would be safe for him and his daughter.

No, he thought, *better to be a ghost. Exist on their fringe and wait for Angie.*

A voice in his head whispered, *She's dead.*

Dean slammed the door on that voice at once. It was the thing he had brought back from the Middle East, a black-hearted creature living within him that preached hopelessness and despair, surrender and suicide. It made him tremble when he needed to be strong, and weakness was its religion. The Fear Animal. He refused to hear it, and this time was successful. He didn't always win that battle.

Angie would come. That was Dean's voice.

He watched the raiders until they packed up and drove away to the west, and then he went back down the ladder into the store's stock room.

The creature was on him in an instant.

Snarling, it lunged from behind a pallet of windshield washer fluid, a fast, dark shape in the gloom. Dean threw up his hands reflexively and it bit deep, jaws crushing down on his right hand, teeth piercing leather and breaking skin. Dean cried out as the thing growled and shook its head, clamped down tight.

The knife was in his other hand in an instant, and Dean hurled himself onto the dirty, mange-afflicted German shepherd. They went to the floor together, the big dog releasing the hand and twisting its powerful neck to snap at Dean's face. Dean drove the knife deep into its chest behind the foreleg, burying it to the hilt. The shepherd yelped, shuddered, and lay still. Dean gave the knife a good twist before pulling it out.

He pulled off the torn leather glove, wincing, and inspected the damage. The bite was deep, but the glove had prevented the shaking and teeth from ripping the flesh apart. He flexed his fingers and made a fist. No nerve damage. Dean found a wall-mounted soap dispenser in the store's restroom and used water from the toilet tank to clean out the wound, then searched for something to use as a wrap. The store had been heavily looted, but he found a chamois in the car care section. It would do for now.

Checking the street for movement, living or dead, he headed back to the apartment.

. . .

How do we know it was a dog?" Shana whispered to Dylan, the two of them in the apartment's small kitchen while Dean sat on the living room sofa, cleaning the bite with rubbing alcohol. "How do we *know*?"

"Because he said so," Dylan replied. "Why would he lie?"

Shana raised an eyebrow. "Because *that's* something a person would lie about."

"He's not lying. He would tell us if it was a zombie," Dylan said. "He's that kind of man."

Shana stood with her arms tightly crossed and glanced into the living room. Leah was playing on the floor not far from her daddy, engaged in a game of blocks and giggles with Raggedy Ann and Wawas.

"Maybe it was a dog," Shana said softly, biting her bottom lip. "But if it wasn't, what will we do?"

"We'll keep an eye on him. Dean won't be offended and we'll treat the wound as best we can." He shrugged. "What else can we do?"

Shana nodded, not taking her eyes off Dean West.

The bite wound became infected, and it brought on a fever. Dean was stretched out on the couch, wrapped in a blanket, sweating and alternating between being too hot and not being able to stay warm.

Dylan zippered his jacket and pulled on an empty nylon backpack, the hatchet in its case hanging from his belt. "I won't be long," he said, and Dean nodded, closing his eyes.

"I'm going with you," Shana said, emerging from the bedroom wearing a jacket and carrying both a butcher knife and Leah's papoose pack.

"What is this?" Dylan asked. "You need to stay to look after them. I'll be back soon."

"No." Her tone was sharp, and she dropped her voice to a whisper, stepping close. "Maybe that fever is from a dog bite, but zombie bites cause fevers too. I'm not staying alone with him like that, and I won't let Leah stay, either. He could kill her." Those last words were delivered in a hiss.

Dylan looked at Leah, who was sitting in a recliner with a coloring book and crayons her daddy had brought back from one of his scouting missions. The photographer knelt beside the couch, resting a palm on Dean's forehead for a moment and then handing the man a water bottle from the coffee table. Dean looked pale, and heat radiated off his skin.

"You need to keep drinking," Dylan said, "and try to sleep. We're going out to find antibiotics and whatever other first-aid supplies we can."

Dean looked at him and blinked.

"Do you understand? Shana is coming with me. We'll be back soon."

Dean swallowed the water and nodded.

"We're going to take Leah with us. Just so you can rest."

"No." Dean's voice was cracked, and his eyes held a fever glaze.

"She'll be safe with us," Dylan said. "You can sleep without worrying about her."

"She stays," Dean said, and the muzzle of his Glock peeked beneath the edge of the blanket, inches from Dylan's chest. "She stays with me," Dean said, his voice a whisper. "Do you understand?"

Dylan glanced back at Shana, who nodded and slipped out of the papoose carrier. The photographer bobbed his head. "I have the key, and we'll lock the door behind us. We won't take long. Please rest." He turned to Leah. "We'll be back soon, honey. Let Daddy sleep, okay?"

"'Kay," she said without looking up from her drawing, one fist clamped on a blue crayon, the tip of her tongue sticking out the corner of her mouth.

Dean's eyes were closing even as the lock clicked home.

D addy. Daddy." Leah stood beside the couch, shaking Dean's arm.
"Daddy. Icky Man."

Dean opened his eyes. They ached, and his mouth and throat
were dry, his head heavy and hard to lift off the pillow. He reached
for the bottle of water and found it empty. "What is it, honey?" he
said thickly. What time was it? The apartment was gloomy with
shadows, a last bit of gray light coming in through the front window. He could make out his daughter's shape. She had gone back to
the recliner to stand on the seat, leaning over the back and pointing
out the window.

"Icky Man," she said. "I want juice."

Dean threw off the blanket and sat on the edge of the sofa, putting his head in his hands. Heat radiated into his palms, and a headache throbbed behind his eyes. His entire body hurt.

"Juice, Daddy!"

Dean held up a hand. "Okay, sweetie. Can we use quiet voices?"

"Juice, Daddy," Leah called in a whisper. "Juice, *please*."

"Nice manners," Dean said, forcing himself to stand. "Good girl."

Leah smiled in the darkness and went back to looking out the
window. Dean walked slowly to the kitchen and flicked on the light
switch, frowned, flicked it several more times, and then stopped and
shook his head. He retrieved a foil juice packet and punched a straw
into it. Where were Dylan and Shana? He vaguely remembered
them saying something about going out. Had they left Leah here
with Dean passed out on the couch? Why would they— Then he
remembered pointing his pistol at Dylan. They had wanted to take
Leah. With that memory he retrieved the Glock from where it had

slipped down between the couch cushions and reseated it in his holster. Bending over made his head thunder, and he had to resist the urge to collapse back onto the couch.

"Here you go," he said, handing over the juice. "What are you looking at?"

Leah took a long sip. "Ickies."

Dean squinted into the winter twilight, the apartment's living room window giving him a view of a short lawn leading to a sidewalk and then a parking lot. The dead were everywhere, slow-moving shadows passing between cars, walking across the lawn. Dozens. Hundreds. And they were heading toward this row of buildings. It was another surge.

Dean's heart raced as he took Leah from the chair, setting her on the floor. "Time to be super, super quiet, okay, baby?"

"Not a baby."

He took a deep breath. "No, you're a big girl. Can you be quiet?"

She nodded.

"Play quietly with Wawas, okay?"

"And with Raga Ann," she said, running to her two stuffed toys.

Dean looked outside again. It was nearly dark, had to be after five o'clock. Where were Dylan and Shana? They should have been back before the sun went down. The dead kept coming, staggering into the parking lot from some place beyond, heading this way. Would they try to get into the apartments? Maybe, if they smelled prey inside. Dean knew they would. How would he hold them off, and for how long? No help would be coming. He did a quick mental inventory of his ammunition, the math difficult to process in his heavy head. It told him he could hold for about fifteen minutes at the most.

Could he barricade the door, keep the two of them inside and wait for the surge to pass? But if even one of them caught a scent, or heard a sound—and a two-year-old could stay quiet only so long— the others would follow. He imagined dozens of dead people crammed onto the concrete landing outside, hammering at the apartment door while more choked the stairwell. Their only way out would be blocked, and there was no way he would risk a three-story drop from a window with a toddler. Even if they kept the dead out, they would starve to death in here, or die from lack of water.

Dean got moving, trying to toughen himself against his aching body and head, to ignore the fiery throb in his bitten hand. He grabbed the papoose carrier off the floor where Shana had dropped it and collected their go-bag, now always kept properly loaded and ready. Then he filled canteens with water from plastic jugs and pulled on his MAC-10 harness. He loaded a second nylon bag, this one with a long shoulder strap, packing it with extra clothes for Leah, the rubbing alcohol and gauze, her coloring book and crayons. He bribed her with a chocolate chip granola bar so he could pack up Wawas and Raggedy Ann without a fight.

"We're going out for a while," Dean said, setting the papoose carrier down so Leah could climb in.

Still gripping the granola bar, she ran past him, into the hall. "Potty!" she yelled back. Her daddy had brought back an actual potty chair with an image of Dora and Boots on the seat, and Leah cherished it.

Dean's eyes shot to the door. "Okay, honey," he whispered. "Quick, quick."

Leah returned a minute later and let her daddy put her coat on, a padded pink thing with a fur-trimmed hood and a bunny on the chest, smiling when he called her a "good girl." Then she scrambled into the papoose pack, an experienced pro. Dean hoisted the weight and settled it on his back, slinging the two nylon bags and the hunting rifle over his shoulders.

He had humped more weight than this in Iraq, and in triple-digit temperatures, but never in such a weakened state with a raging fever. This felt like three hundred pounds, and sweat broke out on his forehead. He closed his eyes for a moment as the headache beat at his eyes from behind, holding onto the door frame as a wave of dizziness washed over him. For just a moment he heard the hiss of an RPG round slashing through hot air, heard a boy from Montana screaming as he crawled across the sand, looking for his legs.

A tiny hand caressed his right cheek, and a small head pressed against the back of his own. "Love you, Daddy," said a soft voice in the darkness. Dean opened his eyes. No desert, only a dark living room and his daughter's warm breath on his neck.

His eyes narrowed and he bared his teeth. "Hoo-ah," he whispered, reaching back and gently squeezing the little girl's fingers. He looked at his bandaged left hand. It was steady. From the front hall closet he retrieved an aluminum baseball bat he had discovered earlier in their stay. He paused, hand on the doorknob, then flicked the lock and stepped onto the landing, bat raised. There was nothing out here, and the stairs down to the next landing were clear. The moans of the dead floated into the breezeway.

"We might have to run a little, okay?" Dean said.

Leah clapped her hands. She loved the bouncing.

"We still need to be super quiet. If you see an Icky Man, just close your eyes."

Her hands pressed against his cheeks from behind. "Will they get us, Daddy?"

"Never," he breathed, and they descended.

The second-floor landing was clear, and then they reached the first-floor breezeway that cut through the building. To their left, nearly filling the opening that would lead to the parking lot, was a three- or four-hundred-pound silhouette on tree trunk legs. Its pants had burst at the seams, and its button-up shirt had popped open to reveal a massive, distended belly.

Even in the poor light Dean knew it would be green, its dead flesh marbled with black streaks, ponderous and sloshing. One of the *wet ones*, as he had come to call them. The creature made a thick gargling sound, as if the slime that swelled its body filled its throat as well, causing the neck to bloat. The sound came again, and it started toward them.

Dean moved away to the right and was about to exit the breezeway when a dark shape lunged from the bushes beyond the opening. Dean swung the bat and was rewarded with a metallic *thunk* as it rocked the zombie's head to the side, causing it to stumble and fall. He didn't stay to make the kill. He started running.

Dean headed down the sidewalk that ran the length of the building where their apartment was, seeing two dozen staggering shapes moving toward them across a grassy commons. Another figure appeared on the sidewalk, arms reaching, and Dean hit it on the run with an overhand strike, driving its head like a railroad spike, staving in its skull. He was past before it buckled to the ground.

The exertion of running with all this weight and swinging the bat made white spots swim in his vision. He felt his balance slipping.

"Potty, Daddy," Leah said, her voice a hush in his ear.

"You already went potty," he whispered back, stopping at the corner of the building and leaning against it with one hand, breathing hard and looking for movement. Then he dashed into another breezeway.

"Potty chair," Leah said. "Potty *chair*." She patted a hand on his shoulder for emphasis.

"Daddy will get you a new one," he gasped, and then they were out of the breezeway and into another parking lot. More ghouls moved among the vehicles, many changing direction as they turned his way. Dean kept running as the white spots began to fire off like paparazzi flashbulbs. The headache slammed the back of his eyes, and he felt like vomiting.

On his back, Leah said no more about the potty chair. She balled her hands into fists and pressed them to her eyes so she wouldn't see the Icky Men.

Moans pierced the evening, feet scraping on pavement as dead things turned, and Dean ran. He took them across a road, down a sidewalk, turned at a corner, and ran for two more blocks before turning again. Five times he had to swing the bat to clear their path, knocking the dead aside but not killing them.

One creature caught hold of the papoose pack nylon, snarling and reaching for the small pink-clad figure within. Leah screamed, and that time Dean did stop to make the kill, grunting and hammering the bat into the creature's head until the skull disintegrated, growling like an animal as he crushed the hated thing.

He didn't know where he was taking them as they ran by houses and stores with boarded-over windows, past a neighborhood bank with its front doors standing open and twenty-dollar bills scattered in the entrance like dead leaves. He rounded a corner and startled a coyote that was feeding on a limbless torso with a moaning, gnashing head, making the animal yip loudly and skitter into the falling night.

Dean didn't know their direction or how far they had gone, but finally he staggered to a halt and wrapped his arms around a lamppost to keep himself from falling, pressing his forehead against the cool metal.

Leah's hand touched the side of his face. "Daddy's hot," she said.

"I . . . know," he gasped. "Super quiet . . . okay?"

"Super quiet, Daddy."

He stayed that way for a couple of minutes, then stood, still holding on, and looked around, his gaze stopping on a nondescript building across the street, brick with a glass front door and blinds in the windows. He crossed, and once up close he saw a shingle next to the door: *J. M. SHAPIRO, D.D.S.* Dean tried the door, found it

locked, and after a quick glance at the street used the bat to smash
out the lower panel of glass. Fifteen minutes inside with a flashlight
found him what he needed: foil sample packets of antibiotics.

He filled his pockets with samples, aspirin, and a handful of
gauze pads. A three-month-old bottle of Snapple—*God, it tastes like
ass!*—helped him swallow three antibiotic tablets and two aspirin.
There was little else of interest here, though he also pocketed some
toothpaste and a couple of toothbrushes, a pink one for Leah. Soon
he was back on the street, moving at a brisk walk as night came on.

The antibiotics worked and beat the infection. Subsequent cleaning, antiseptic, and a poorly executed stitching job with needle
and thread turned a life-threatening dog bite into just an ugly scar.

Home turned out to be a tiny house with a detached garage
tucked behind a small neighborhood convenience store and deli. A
high board fence concealed the house's presence from the street, and
although the store was fairly well looted, Dean discovered that the
owner used the detached garage as a stockroom, and that had been
missed. He found water and soft drinks, canned and dry goods, toiletries, and even some toys for Leah. For himself there were maps,
batteries, a few paperbacks, and several cases of warm beer, to which
he treated himself on occasion. In a dusty box on a high shelf in the
store he found a freestanding plastic and aluminum adult toilet seat
for the disabled. After some coaxing and, to his daughter's delight,
permission to use her crayons on the white plastic to personalize the
chair, Leah pronounced it acceptable. Dean was sure to bag their
waste tightly and pitch it far over the fence into another yard.

Sometimes it surprised him how so much of what they did
revolved around the potty. He and Angie even called it that when
speaking to each other, and she once remarked that she hadn't gone to
the "bathroom" since becoming a mother. One time on set between

takes, Dean had announced to the director that he needed a quick potty break, and the crew had broken up laughing. The life of a parent, he supposed.

Dean and Leah lived quietly, and nothing came knocking. There was no sign of Dylan or Shana. On occasion they heard distant gunfire, and several times drifters came sniffing around the yard. Dean would have liked to dispatch them swiftly and silently with his knife, but then he would have had to deal with the bodies. Instead he had waited quietly until they wandered away. He left the house only for water collection, waste disposal, or resupply from the garage, and only when Leah was napping behind locked doors.

Once, however, after plotting their location on a map, he waited until Leah was asleep and left the house with a can of black spray paint, risking a two-block journey to a house he had seen with a large white wall facing the street. His idea had been to leave Angie another clue, maybe point her toward their hiding place, but after five minutes of internal argument, he left with the wall untouched. The wrong people might see it, and even if they couldn't interpret the meaning, they might recognize it as something new in the neighborhood. He couldn't risk it.

Dean returned to find everything as he had left it, Leah snoozing under a fuzzy pink blanket, clutching Wawas and Raggedy Ann under each arm. While she slept, he waited at the front of the house with all his weapons ready, prepared to engage anything that might have seen him and followed him home. Nothing had. Their sanctuary would hold for now.

NINETEEN

Little Emer Briggs sat on the skull-tipped throne in Saint Miguel's main chapel, the orange and yellow of sunset lighting the high stained glass with muted colors. Several panes had come crashing to the marble floor during the quake, and there was now a long, jagged crack running from the ground all the way to the top of the bell tower. Some of the windows in the parish school had fallen from their frames during the shaking, but there were no injuries. One of the dog runs had broken free at an intersection, and now a handful of men and women were out rounding up stray collared zombies.

A fire was burning in the pit in the center of the vaulted room, throwing dancing shadows on the walls. A cluster of armed men and women stood around the flames, watching the emperor hold court.

"Where did they come from?" the warlord asked. He had one leg thrown over the arm of the big chair, his head leaned back against crushed velvet. His black eyes never left the bound man kneeling at the foot of the stairs leading up to the throne.

"Answer him," Lassiter said, standing on James Garfield's left and giving the mortgage broker a shove with his rifle barrel. Russo stood to the right, filming with his digital camcorder, a crooked smile on his face.

"They didn't say," Garfield responded. He threw a glance over to where Drew stood between two bikers. His son was staring into the flames of the fire pit, unblinking.

Little Emer frowned. "Didn't say? Nothing at all?"

Garfield shook his head.

"Were they military?"

"I don't know," said Garfield. "Maybe. They had rifles like soldiers do. I don't know much about those things."

Little Emer looked over to where his father was standing, the old man wearing khakis so baggy and tightly belted they looked like a sack, and a dirty wifebeater speckled with blood drops. The man was smoking, watching the captive with prey bird eyes. Wahrman, the grower, leaned against the wall beside him, wearing his sunglasses even in the gloom of the chapel.

"You said they were looking for someone," said Little Emer.

Garfield nodded. "A man named Dean West. One of the women said she was his wife."

"That's probably Angie West, Emer," Lassiter said. "The TV chick with the gun show. That was her ranch with the bunker."

The biker lord seemed to consider the words for a moment. "So Mama's come looking for her family. Brought along a helicopter and a hunting party. That's sweet." He looked at the two bikers standing beside the little boy. "Take some people and go check out that school. From a distance, though, no shooting."

Red Hen and Stark gathered some of the people from around the fire pit and left, leaving Drew standing alone. The boy didn't move from where he stood.

"Please don't hurt us," Garfield said, his voice breaking.

Little Emer swung his leg down and leaned forward in the throne. "How the *hell* have you stayed alive this long? You are the biggest pussy I've met since the world ended."

Garfield made a choking noise and looked at the floor.

The elder Briggs climbed the steps to the throne, flicking his cigarette butt away and, stifling a series of wet coughs into a handkerchief, glanced at Garfield. In a voice soft enough that only his son would hear, he said, "What's the story with that group you sent out?" He knew his son was in touch by radio with the group hunting the missing Black Hawk.

"They checked the golf course," Little Emer replied. "They're going to check one of the ranches, bed down for the night, and check the other in the morning." He curled his lip. "Corrigan refused to go with them."

When the older man raised an eyebrow, Little Emer told him how the Army deserter had reported that this afternoon's quake had damaged the bridge, and he couldn't risk crossing it with the Bradley.

"He disobeyed me," spat the biker lord. "I should have the son of a bitch crucified."

Big Emer snorted. "Sounds like he's the only one with any sense around here. Let those morons with rifles and your asshole biker buddies smoke 'em out, if that bird is even there. Keep that armored vehicle close to home."

"Why?"

Big Emer smirked. "Because you're likely to need it. If it is that TV girl and her husband out there, they're not going to appreciate what you did to their family. What you're *still* doing." He shook his head. "They'll come for payback."

"They don't worry me," the younger Briggs said.

Big Emer nodded. "I know. And that worries *me*."

The warlord clapped his hands together loud enough to make

Garfield look up sharply. "Anything else you can tell me?" Little Emer asked.

Garfield shook his head rapidly. "I've told you everything. Please, let us go now."

"I will," the warlord said. "I promised, didn't I? But let's visit the playpen first." He hopped from the throne and walked to Garfield's son, taking him by the hand and leading him out of the room.

Garfield cried, "Drew!" before Lassiter roughly shoved him in the same direction. Russo walked behind, still filming. The elder Briggs gave his grower a look, but Wahrman just shrugged, and the two of them followed last.

The high-ceilinged room echoed over a pool that had been drained but still made the place smell of chlorine. Coleman lanterns placed around the rim threw an orange glow across the room and created a pit of shadows within the pool itself. A heavy iron bolt had been driven into one cement wall, and secured to it by a six-foot chain was Lenore Franks, more than four months dead and rotting, snarling and tugging at her leash.

"Why did you keep that?" Little Emer's father asked.

"Because she was hot for an old lady," the biker lord said, throwing a wink at Lassiter, who beamed back at him.

"You need to get rid of it," his father said, waving at the woman with a look of revulsion. "You need to clear out this whole fucking place."

The younger Briggs gave the man a handsome smile. "I like it. Maybe I'm working out some issues from my fucked-up childhood."

"You've got fucking issues, all right," Big Emer said, then gave him a crooked yellow smile. "Can you spell *sociopath*, Junior? Need me to unscramble the letters?"

The warlord glared at his father, clenching his hands. Even now the man could turn him into a frightened little boy with a word. How he despised the diseased bastard.

"Put him on the diving board," Little Emer said, and Lassiter immediately shoved Garfield out onto the textured white board. The mortgage broker stood there, hands bound behind his back, staring into the pool. A whine rose in his throat.

"He's gonna walk the plank now?" Big Emer sneered, lighting his sixty-second cigarette of the day. "I didn't know the Romans did that."

"Don't fuck with me, old man," the warlord whispered, not looking at his father as a rush of heat ran into his face.

"You're like a little boy," the elder Briggs said, "playing Let's Pretend. Grow the fuck up, will you?"

Little Emer turned and looked at his daddy under his eyebrow ridge, teeth bared. The rage boiling within him pushed away his childhood fears for a moment, revealing Big Emer Briggs to be old and sick and able to cut with words, nothing more. It was empowering, liberating. "If you speak again," Little Emer said, "you go in with him." His voice was even, his eyes flat and dark.

Wahrman the grower reached for the pistol in his shoulder holster, and Little Emer pointed at him without taking his eyes off his old man. "Lassiter!" he barked. "If this fuck draws down on me, spray the whole fucking room with that AK. No one left standing, not even me."

Lassiter snapped the bolt on his assault rifle and leveled it at the grower. "Got it."

Russo leaped across the room to stand behind the former armored-car driver, still filming, but now over the man's shoulder. The grower left his pistol in its holster.

Little Emer smiled at his daddy. "Let's have some fun."

Out on the diving board, James Garfield was shaking so hard the narrow strip wobbled beneath him. Tears streamed from his eyes as he stared, his whine rising to a wail. The warlord took Drew's hand and led him to the edge of the pool. "Want to play with your friends?" he asked, patting the boy's head. "There's toys down there too."

Drew stared at the far wall and said nothing. He took no notice of the things moving in the pool below, making the room echo with their moans and snarls. He didn't see the cloudy, dead eyes, the reaching gray hands, didn't notice short legs and small feet shuffling over the blue tile bottom, kicking plastic toys and balls out of the way. Once the clothing had been brightly colored and covered in cartoon animals and superheroes, with a few swimsuits and small hospital gowns thrown in. Now it was all stained and dark, and Drew noticed none of it. Ever since he had seen the dead come pouring into the supposedly safe area at the fairgrounds, ever since he had seen—though Daddy had missed it—his mommy pulled down and torn apart, Drew hadn't noticed much of anything. His young mind had recoiled from the ceaseless horror and taken him to a quiet inner place where none of it could touch him.

Little Emer rubbed the two-year-old's back. "Don't you want to play?"

Drew didn't respond, didn't hear his father's mad shrieking or the hungry cries of forty small figures surging against the pool wall below him, arms reaching into the air.

"Off you go," said Briggs, his hand firm against the child's back.

When Garfield saw the small figure tumble over the side and disappear into the squirming mass below, he screamed his son's name and jumped in after him.

I t was after ten o'clock that evening when Little Emer heard Corrigan's Bradley rumble back into the compound. By then his anger at the man's disobedience had evaporated, but he remained frustrated.

The group in the canyon reported finding fresh quad tracks and an area of beaten-down grass where a chopper had landed out at the raid site, but nothing else. Red Hen and Stark visited the elementary school in town that Garfield had told them of but found it overrun with the dead. There was a helicopter out there somewhere and a handful of trained, armed people loose in his city with vengeance on the mind.

Even the playpen hadn't eased his troubles. The short victory he had felt over standing up to the old man had vanished at the sight of the disappointed look on his father's face. Now he sat on his throne, alone in the chapel as the fire burned down to embers. Having an empire had been sort of fun, being able to do what you wanted, whenever you wanted. But his daddy had been right. It was all a game of Let's Pretend.

Time to get rolling? he wondered. Gather his boys and hit the road? Soon, but not yet. He wasn't quite ready to give up his throne, and he certainly wouldn't let himself be chased away by three or four people with automatic weapons. The warlord lit a joint and smoked in the darkness. He needed some leverage.

TWENTY

They had chosen the second deck of a small parking garage as their camp for the night. Dylan and Abbie were sleeping in a minivan, and parked next to them, Skye leaned against Carney in the back seat of an Escalade with tinted windows. Angie stood outside by a concrete wall, looking out at the dark city, her Galil cradled in her arms as she took watch.

Skye looked out at her friend, alone in the night. "Do you think Dean's alive?" she said.

Carney didn't move, warm and solid against her. "I'd like to think so. But this many months, on the run with a toddler? It's a long shot."

Skye sighed. She thought so too, but would never say as much to Angie. She wanted Dean to be alive, Leah too, and Angie said her husband was a combat veteran with some serious skills. Leah's presence would void most of those abilities, she suspected, preventing him from waging war if the raiders showed up, slowing him down, and attracting the dead with the innocent noise two-year-olds made.

He was probably dead, Skye thought. She believed Angie thought it too, and because of that, her friend was dying inside. She had offered to stand watch with her, but Angie had brusquely asked to be left alone, and Skye had retreated to the Escalade.

"That earthquake today," Skye said, changing the subject, "is that normal? I didn't grow up in California."

Carney shook his head. "That was good-sized, not normal at all. You saw the damage."

She had. Several buildings had sagged into the street and crushed cars, telephone poles toppled, and a lot of windows shattered. It had knocked them off their feet as they fled the elementary school, running through the neighborhood. Every drifter they encountered was standing and swaying with the tremor, all facing the same direction. When the shaking stopped, they started moving at once. It was eerie.

Skye looked up at Carney in the darkness. "You believe me about what I saw, right? The red drifter that moved out of my rifle sight?"

"I believe you."

She stared at him, looking for the lie. He saw her and laughed. "I do, I believe you. You said you saw it, so you did. It sounds dangerous."

"It is," she said. "Worse than the others. It could think."

"And if we see it again," Carney said, "we'll kill it just like the others."

They were quiet for a while. Skye watched Angie standing motionless as a stone and closed her eyes. "She's going to decide soon."

"Decide what?" Carney asked, his voice soft.

She hesitated. "Decide that Dean's dead. Then it will be time to go after the ones who burned the ranch." She felt Carney nod slowly. "We have to go with her," Skye said. "*I* have to go."

"And where do you think I'll be?" asked the ex-con.

She shrugged. "I don't know. I talk too much."

Carney's big chest shook with a laugh. "Yeah, right."

She smiled in the darkness. After a while she said, "Want to fool around?"

"Do you?"

Another sigh. "Not really."

"Me either."

Skye smiled again and shifted closer against him, burying her face in his chest, breathing him in.

Angie rolled her shoulder where TC's bullet had passed through, then rubbed at the soreness in her forearm, the fracture still healing. Both hurt. The hurt in her chest was worse.

She was out of tears. Standing at the four-foot wall of the parking garage, staring down at dark buildings and streets where there had once been life, Angie realized she had been here before. Except then it had been the rooftop of a firehouse in Alameda, looking down upon a world fast being overrun by the walking dead, alone and longing for her family. Nothing had changed but the location.

Dean would have gone down fighting, she knew, down to the last bullet and knife thrust, using his bare hands to give Leah just a few more seconds of life. For her daughter, she prayed the end had been quick, and that she hadn't been too scared.

A single tear rolled down her cheek. *Almost* out of tears, she thought, and a tiny, sad smile accompanied her sob. There was nothing left in her world, only death. The moans of earth's new conquerors floated through the night air.

The tear dried on her face, and no more followed.

Then, at five minutes past midnight, the earth began to tremble again, a mild vibration at first, then steadily building, shaking left to right and up and down at the same time. Cracks raced across concrete flooring and up pillars. Parked cars slid into one another, and Angie had to hold on to the concrete wall to keep from falling. Beyond the parking garage, the second story of a house dropped inward with a cloud of drywall and splintered beams.

Foreshock, Angie's mind screamed. The one earlier in the day had been a foreshock, a warning of things to come. The thought was only a flash from a primitive place deep inside her brain, but in that instant she knew it was true. The quake built in intensity, stretching out in length and violence.

The door to the minivan rolled open and Abbie cried, "What's happening?"

The groan of the moving parking garage drowned out the woman's cries, and Angie lunged for the Escalade, banging a fist against its hood. "We've got to get out of here!" she screamed.

Then there was a roar of broken concrete and twisted rebar as the support pillars on this level crumbled, dropping the upper deck onto Angie and her friends.

Ten point six. Four minutes long. The most massive earthquake in the recorded history of civilization. It was the great killer, the one feared for generations, the stuff of apocalypse and nightmares.

The devastating shocks felt in Chico, California, were merely ripples from the epicenter 170 miles away. That location was centered beneath the old naval air station at Alameda, and the destruction it wreaked was biblical. Cities fell, mountains and ridges shifted and collapsed, and the Pacific Ocean rushed in like a wild animal intent upon the kill.

For those in the San Francisco Bay Area who felt the full force of Mother Nature's murderous blow—Father Xavier, Rosa, Evan, and others—the quake was only the beginning of the nightmare.

TWENTY-ONE

January 13—Near the Skyway

"There," Braga said, pointing the flashlight with Titan standing beside him. In their other hands they carried shotguns. "There." He moved the flashlight beam. "And over there too."

Each time the circle of light stopped, it revealed dead people moving slowly toward them over the bare ground. Their three pickups and the burned remains of the Franks ranch were behind them, the place where the raiders had tried to settle in for the night. They had all learned of the arrival of the walking dead when one of the men from the trucks stepped away into the dark to urinate, then screamed as something caught hold of him. There was a brief flurry of gunfire as half a dozen corpses were shot down making their way toward the trucks. Now the bikers stood on the dirt road near their Harleys.

"How many you think?" Titan asked.

Braga turned and panned the flashlight left to right on the other side of the road. A dozen more dead faces snarled back at them, drawing closer.

"Shit, I dunno. Can't tell in the dark."

Back at the trucks, more flashlights clicked on. Voices rose in alarm at the sight of packs of the undead moving steadily closer.

"Doesn't matter," said Braga. "We sure as hell can't stay here."

Titan spoke into a walkie-talkie, demanding that Corrigan respond. There was nothing but silence.

"I'm gonna kill that motherfucker when we get back," Titan said.

"I'll help you, bro." Braga turned toward the trucks. "Load up," he shouted. "We're going to check that other ranch, then head home tonight."

A weak cheer went up.

Within minutes, the two motorcycles were leading the line of trucks back up the ranch road toward the Skyway. The bikes weaved around stumbling figures and the trucks simply knocked them out of the way.

The undead at the Franks ranch followed the direction the raiders had taken, hundreds strong. This was merely the vanguard, and the main body—what Halsey had dubbed the Stampede—moved through the forest on stiff legs, nearly two thousand corpses pushing through the underbrush, oblivious to the branches that tore at gray flesh or the rocks that skinned bare feet to the bone.

They were heading for the Skyway too.

The legion of ghouls from Paradise emerged from the tree line and headed toward the distant glow of a light in a cabin window, moving with jerking steps. Their feet dragged crooked trails through the thin snow at first, but soon their mass trampled the ground muddy as they crossed the fields.

At the front of the horde was a man in pale green hospital scrubs and a white doctor's coat. In its forties when it died, the thing had long claw marks down the side of its face, and much of its scalp had been stripped down to the skull. Its filmy eyes were nearly the same shade as its scrubs. The boy in swim trunks with snow dusting his shoulders and head was walking beside the decaying doctor, arms limp and swinging at his sides, and they both came to a halt in the same moment. The two corpses tipped their heads back slowly and rotated to face the same direction, then stood motionless.

Around and behind them, the thousands of corpses from Paradise followed suit.

Not far up the highway, the small column of bikes and trucks was forced to wind its way between abandoned cars and lone, wandering corpses. Up on point, the two bikers came upon a pair of stone pillars on the right topped with carriage lights, straddling a brick driveway, the gate between them standing open.

Braga used a flashlight to look at his map. "This is it. Broken Arrow Ranch."

Titan checked his pistol to be sure a round was in the chamber, then shoved it back in his shoulder holster. He was about to say something when the quake hit, dropping the bikes and sending the men scrambling. Behind them, the people in the trucks held on as the Skyway buckled. Pine trees groaned and crashed into the road, and one of the pillars with a carriage lamp shivered and collapsed to one side in a pile of bricks and concrete.

It was over quickly, lasting only a few minutes.

Braga and Titan cursed again at their banged-up Harleys and stood them upright.

"Sick of this shit," said Braga. "Twice in one day."

"Yeah, and that one was stronger," Titan said, straddling his bike.

Braga waved to the others, and the column started up the long driveway toward Pepper's Broken Arrow Ranch.

Halsey was dreaming of the Wild Mouse, a jerking, steel frame roller coaster that came to his hometown with the carnival every summer of his childhood. His mother had worried that it wasn't built well. "How can it be safe if they take it apart and put it back together every week?" she said. But his father said, "Don't sugar the boy," and let him ride. Halsey loved the sudden turns that threw him left and right, was thrilled by the rapid click of the steel tracks and the sudden plunges that sent his stomach up into his chest. He spent the entire ride with his eyes squeezed tight, laughing until tears streamed from the corners.

The sound of breaking glass was out of place. What was glass doing on a roller coaster? Then it came again and he opened his eyes, startled and unsure of where he was. Not a roller-coaster car, he realized, but in the comfortable armchair in front of his fireplace. A Coleman lantern glowed on the coffee table beside an empty glass and mostly empty bottle of Jack Daniel's. Vladimir snored on the nearby couch.

The chair was shaking. Hell, the whole cabin was shaking. He saw the drink glass vibrate to the edge of the table and fall to join its broken companion—the glass that had shattered and woken him—on the floor. The bottle fell over and broke a second later.

"Vlad," he grunted, making smacking noises with his mouth. It tasted like wet cotton, and his head still buzzed from the whiskey. How long ago had they fallen asleep? he wondered. It didn't feel like much time had passed.

"Vladimir," he said again, leaning over and slapping one of the pilot's sock feet. "Are you feeling this?"

The Russian groaned and gripped the sides of the couch, mumbling something in his native language.

Something else crashed and broke in the kitchen, and Halsey snatched the lantern off the table just before it rattled off the side. *Earthquake,* he thought, trying to clear his head. *Bigger than before.* Instead of trying to stand, he remained in the chair, holding one padded arm and keeping the lantern aloft, riding out the tremor. The shaking stopped after a few minutes, and the two men looked at one another, blinking with red eyes.

"I have decided I do not like California," Vladimir announced.

"Love it or leave it, Russkie," Halsey grumbled, heading into the kitchen. "Watch your feet on the broken glass."

Vladimir joined him, retrieving a broom and a dustpan to sweep up the glass fragments. Then he cleaned up a broken plate that had fallen from the kitchen counter.

"That was a bad one," Halsey said, eyeing the rafters and walls, looking for damage. "I think we're okay, though."

Vladimir sat at the kitchen table and rubbed his temples. "You are a bad influence, my friend."

Halsey snorted. "And you were a teetotaler before you met me." When the Russian cocked his head at the unfamiliar term, Halsey just laughed. Then he noticed the window to the left of the cabin door, its heavy shutters still open. *Careless. Showing our lights to anything that might be looking.* He moved to the window and started to close the shutters.

A face slammed against it hard enough to crack a pane, bared teeth squeaking across the glass. It had yellow eyes with pinpoint pupils, and its nose had been chewed away.

"Goddamn!" Halsey yelled, slamming and bolting the shutters.

Something thumped against the cabin door. Something else smashed against the window on the opposite side, breaking glass behind the shutters. Muffled moaning floated through the door. Without a word, Halsey and Vladimir immediately began to move through the small house, ensuring that it was tightly sealed. Then they pulled on boots and coats and headed up the ladder to Halsey's tower, the ranch hand bringing his .22 rifle with him. Out in the cold air, the men stood next to each other and peered into the dark night as a breeze dropped snowflakes on their cheeks. They could see nothing, but the growls from below were unmistakable, and they came from several sides of the cabin. The groaning of more creatures drifted up from the packed-dirt yard out front.

"I can't see to shoot them," Halsey said, rifle to his shoulder as he strained to pick out a target.

"In my helicopter," Vladimir said, looking in the direction where the Black Hawk would be, "is a box above both the pilot's and co-pilot's seats. I have night-vision goggles in them."

"They don't do us much good out there."

Vladimir climbed back down into the cabin, and when he returned minutes later he was carrying a flashlight and wearing his Browning automatic in a shoulder holster under his open coat.

"We can't tell how many there are," the ranch hand said, looking at his friend.

Vlad gave him a smile and said, "Then I will have to run very fast." He climbed over the low wall of the tower before dropping down to the cabin's sloped roof.

TWENTY-TWO

The newborn drifter opened her eyes to darkness and the smell of blood. She sensed flesh nearby, and at once her teeth clicked together. The hunger was overwhelming, and she tried to turn toward the meat, only to find that her body would not move. She tried again, unable to do more than rotate her head a few inches, still trying, still smelling the meat, jaws snapping. Then she sensed that this was not food, and let out a long moan.

The dead man in the vehicle with her was not as badly pinned by the wreckage and could move a little better. Driven by the same hunger as his companion, he reached in the darkness and found flesh, a smooth, wet length of meat. He groaned in anticipation, but the moment his hand found the leg, fractured and bent at an obscene angle, he withdrew. Though he was only minutes past turning, his primitive new instincts told him he was unable to feed upon one of his own. The male drifter struggled, trying to free himself from whatever was holding him down. He moaned. The dead girl beside him in the darkness moaned.

Neither creature had any concept of where they were, would never understand the tons of reinforced concrete that had collapsed above them and crushed their vehicle nearly flat, instantly killing their former selves and pinning their new selves hopelessly inside. It didn't matter. They would struggle endlessly in the wreckage, consumed by their hunger as long as their brains existed. Who they had been, those they had loved, the dreams they had pursued were gone now. There was only the hunger, and their inability to satisfy it.

Angie opened her eyes and for one heart-stopping moment thought she had gone blind. Then she realized it was darkness, and her brain quickly caught up: midnight, Chico, earthquake, Dean and Leah, Skye and Carney. She had been standing watch, felt the quake begin, and had tried to warn the others as the parking garage began to crumble. Then nothing.

She was alive. Was she trapped? Angie took stock of her body. Legs shifted, hands could move, there was no great weight pinning her down, but when she tried to rise, her back hit something solid. Her hands explored, touching metal and rubber, a tire. There was concrete above her, and she coughed, breathing in dust. Fingertips grazed metal and wood, her Galil assault rifle, and she gripped it, pulling. It moved. Could she reach her arms down the sides of her body? No, the space was too tight, and there was no light to see if she could move forward or back.

She tried forward, inching with the toes of her boots and pulling with her hands. She managed twelve inches of movement and her fingertips found concrete ahead of her, the way forward blocked. Still coughing up dust, she inched backward, toes scraping, palms pushing. One foot. Another foot. Angie dragged the Galil with her. More inches, and then her boots were clear of the obstruction.

Pushing and pulling herself in this manner, she backed out of the space that had nearly become her grave, climbing to her feet.

Drifters moaned behind her and she spun, bringing up the Galil. Black, unfamiliar shapes appeared around her, big shadows and strange angles. The moaning continued, but nothing reached for her. From her belt she pulled a small metal flashlight, prayed it wasn't broken, and switched it on. She was rewarded with a small circle of light, dust particles floating through the beam.

A slab of concrete had fallen onto the hood of the Escalade near where she had been standing, the impact knocking her down as the slab tipped over and created a lean-to of sorts at the grille. She had been inside that small space and was shielded from more falling debris. Random chance had saved her life.

The Escalade was crushed at the nose and flattened at the rear cargo compartment by falling concrete slabs. To the right the mini-van was hidden beneath what had been the parking deck above, hammered flat by tons of cement. Moaning came from within, and a bloody hand reached out of the jumble of metal and concrete, fingers clawing the air. Dylan's hand. The photographer's moans were joined by Abbie's, trapped deep within.

Angie looked up, seeing an overcast sky where there had once been a flat, gray ceiling. She moved to one of the Escalade's broken side windows and put the light inside. A slab had demolished the back of the SUV, pushing the rear seats forward. Two figures were wedged in there, a smaller one atop the larger. In the light, Angie could see ash-gray skin and a milky white eye staring back at her.

"Hi," Skye said, her voice soft.

Angie let out a shaky laugh. "Can you move?"

"I don't know. I haven't tried yet." The young woman looked at Angie and in that same soft voice said, "Is Carney dead?"

"No, he isn't dead," said the man beneath her. "But he will be soon. Your elbow is digging into my neck."

Angie tried to open the Escalade door, but the SUV's twisted frame had wedged it tight. Instead she used the barrel of the Galil to break out the rest of the glass and reached through the window to help her friends. It took ten minutes of wiggling and straining before both Skye and Carney were free of the wreckage. Carney had a broken finger on his left hand, and Skye's right cheek had been cut by exploding glass.

Carney looked at the flattened minivan. "I can't see them to put them out of their misery."

The women nodded. They had only known Abbie and Dylan a short time, but it wasn't a fate they would wish on decent people. There was nothing to be done, though.

"Give me those fingers," Skye said, pulling gauze and tape from the first-aid kit on her combat harness. Carney did as instructed, and Skye wrapped his broken finger to the one beside it while Angie held the light.

"This place is unstable," said Angie. "We need to get out in the open."

The others agreed, and they searched the area, collecting what they could. Skye was able to pull her pack and her silenced M4 from the Escalade wreckage. Angie located her own pack, as well as the Barrett and bandolier of fifty-caliber magazines. Carney's gear, including his M14, was hopelessly pinned within the destroyed SUV. Skye gave him her pistol belt with the silenced nine-millimeter.

None of the Hydra radios had survived, meaning any communication with Vladimir was gone.

The three of them picked their way through the remains of the parking garage using Angie's light and found a spot where crumbled concrete formed a rough ramp down from the second level. Careful climbing brought them to the street, and they stood for a moment looking up at the structure's sagging remains, well aware of how lucky they had been to escape.

Around them, Chico looked as if it had been through a war.

Houses had fallen; a three-story office building had tumbled into the street, burying cars and choking the road with steel, brick, and broken glass. Telephone poles were down with tangles of wire between them, and streetlight poles leaned at odd angles. Above, the overcast sky was breaking up, allowing moments of moonlight to illuminate the destruction below. A gentle night breeze carried the sour odor of decay.

Skye and Carney looked at Angie, waiting.

"I won't ask you to stay," Angie said, "and I can't leave."

"We're not going anywhere," Skye said. Carney nodded.

The former reality show star shook her head slowly, and when she spoke her voice cracked. "It's been so long," she began. "I thought . . . I was sure Dean could keep them alive, and he did for a while. But after what Dylan said about the bite . . ."

"Dog bite," said Carney.

Angie didn't reply.

"We're not leaving," Skye repeated. "We'll look for Dean and Leah until we find them or find their bodies. If it's time to pay those other fuckers back for what they did, so be it." She rested a hand on the back of Angie's neck. "Tell us what you want to do."

Angie took a deep breath. "My family is dead. There's only one thing left."

"Then let's get started," said Carney.

Sometime around two in the morning, Angie, Skye, and Carney came upon the high school. They had been walking through the silent city, keeping to the shadows and watching for signs of life, indications of some kind of organized defense, the lights and sounds of living people that would mark their target. They had seen only the dead, and when the creatures came near, Skye dispatched them with her machete.

At first they thought they had found what they were looking for, but the presence of so many drifters quickly changed their minds. By the looks of it, the school *had* been a defensive point, at least for a while, but not for the scum who had raided the ranch. This was clearly part of Chico's attempt to hold on during the outbreak.

"I'm surprised any of this is still here," said Carney.

Skye shrugged. "They can't have completely looted the city. They must have missed this. Look at the opposition."

A curving drive led from the street up to the school and parking lot, the pavement littered with shell casings. A pair of Chico police cars were parked nose to nose, blocking the drive, and in the lot beyond them stood a row of yellow school buses, several fire trucks, and another pair of squad cars. A box truck with the Red Cross symbol on its side was parked close to the school.

The trio walked carefully up the drive, inspecting the abandoned police cars before continuing. They were empty, and the shotguns were missing. Red plastic shotgun hulls were mixed on the pavement with the brass. Closer to the school they could see that the windows had been covered with plywood, and sandbags were piled at the front doors, leaving just enough space for one person at a time to enter or exit. Near the Red Cross trucks were stacks of blankets, cardboard boxes, and blue plastic water barrels.

"Someone's civil defense plan," said Angie. She raised her binoculars to more closely examine a shape on the football field behind the parking lot. In the scattered moonlight she could see a small news helicopter, twisted and blackened by fire.

"I wonder how long they held out," Skye said. There were dozens of rotting corpses on the pavement and sidewalks all around the building, but even more were up and walking, several moving in and out of the narrow sandbag opening at the front of the school. There were quite a few teenagers, as well as people in uniform. Two figures just up the driveway turned and walked stiffly toward the three living people, a man wearing a gas mask and a young woman in a Chico State Wildcats T-shirt.

Carney walked to them and shot both at close range with the silenced nine-millimeter.

"There's nothing here we need," Angie said, and both Skye and Carney knew she wasn't talking about Red Cross supplies. The woman turned and went back to the street, her companions following.

They passed a Harley-Davidson dealer with the double front doors propped open and the bikes missing from smashed display windows. A nearby Chevrolet dealer was untouched, rows of dirty cars lined up beneath plastic pennants, with signs on windshields declaring a *Summer Blowout!* There were no drifters in the lot, and it looked as if all one would have to do was wash the cars to be ready for business.

Angie came to an abrupt halt, and both Skye and Carney snapped their weapons up, looking for a threat. There was no movement, the street quiet and unchanged.

"This was Daddy's," Angie said softly.

Just down from the car dealer on the opposite side of the street stood a brick building with a tall pole and sign outside that read *Silhouette Arms & Loading.* The gun shop stood open, broken glass all around, the steel grilles that once covered its windows lying in the road as if ripped off by a tow truck cable. A few decaying and mostly consumed bodies lay on the sidewalk out front.

"I didn't know I was leading us here," Angie said, her voice far away. Images of her father, before and after death, made her put her hands over her mouth to stifle a sob. Why was she here in this place? Everywhere she looked were reminders of the people she had lost, and every hour in Chico was like wandering through a graveyard filled only with people she knew.

"Pull it in tight," whispered Skye, stepping in front of her friend and forcing her to make eye contact. "Make it go cold, or it's going to paralyze you. I know."

Angie looked at her young friend, eyes wet.

"Make it go cold," Skye said again. "Your family is dead. Nothing here but ghosts, and you can't change it but you can make others pay for it."

Angie wiped at her tears, nodding.

Skye grabbed Angie's combat harness and gave her a hard shake. The young woman turned and took point, M4 to her shoulder as she stalked into the night. Carney rested a hand on Angie's shoulder and looked at her silently for a moment before moving to catch up.

Angie squeezed her eyes shut. When she opened them, she was moving with her rifle raised.

TWENTY-THREE

December—Southeast Chico

Leah turned three on the second of the month. Dean gave her a Hostess cupcake with three birthday candles he had found in the convenience store in front of their little house and made a card for her with crayons and printer paper. She wasn't much interested in the card but was thrilled with the plastic pony in blister pack Dean had saved for the occasion, complete with rainbow-colored hair she could groom with the little brush inside the package.

"Thank you, Daddy!" she breathed, eyes wide and small hands grabbing as he tore the toy out of the plastic. They spent the afternoon playing in the living room, introducing the pony to Wawas and Raggedy Ann, combing the rainbow hair, and then coloring before nap time. Dean gave her a few sips from a Gatorade bottle before tucking her in and kissing her on the forehead.

While she slept, Dean sat in the living room trying to read a Larry Bond novel, finding he was unable to focus on the story. Instead he thought of Angie and how long they had been apart.

Dean stared at the floor, remembering when they had first met at a shooting competition in San Diego, and how he hadn't been able to take his eyes off her. He had asked her out that very day and she'd said yes. Their romance bloomed immediately and he knew he was hopelessly hooked. The best part was that she felt the same way.

Dean scratched at his beard. He had given up trying to shave or keep it trimmed, he didn't change his clothes as often as he should, and more and more he found he had no appetite.

The house was secure, he had seen to that, using wood from the detached garage and floorboards from a spare bedroom to cover the windows. They had food, though no way to heat it, and besides, he was concerned about the attention a fire would draw. A fifty-five-gallon drum stood in the yard just outside to catch rainwater, and he was methodical about pitching their waste as far from the house as he could. There were enough blankets to keep Leah warm, and he still had supplies of baby wipes and toothpaste to see to her hygiene, but Dean was worried about her health. What canned vegetables they had went to Leah, and he was rationing out a bottle of children's vitamins for her, one every other day. Still, she was pale and frequently had dark circles under her eyes. She had lost weight under a nutritional intake that was sketchy at best. There was no canned or powdered milk in the convenience store's stockpile.

Leah's spirits were good, though, and that was a blessing. She was learning to read, learning her numbers, and no longer seemed to miss television. Dean hadn't realized how much she had watched until it was gone. They colored and played, keeping to a structured routine of sleep and meals. But she had grown quiet, and that troubled him. Despite the benefits of her usually being silent when he needed her to, it wasn't natural for a three-year-old. How much had she been affected by all this? He couldn't tell, but it was clear she was slowly going numb. She no longer awoke in the darkness with nightmares.

She had stopped asking about her mommy.

Dean tried to keep that piece of her alive, reassuring her that they would only be waiting awhile longer, that Mommy was on her way, but it was Dean who had to bring up the topic. Leah seemed engaged when they started talking about Angie, but she quickly drifted away from the subject. He couldn't tell if that meant something, or if it was just an example of a three-year-old's short attention span.

One day Leah came to him. "Is Mommy in heaven?" she asked.

"No, honey," Dean said, putting her on his knee and brushing a strand of long blond hair behind her ear.

"Is Mommy an Icky Man?"

"No, honey, Mommy's fine. She's coming." He wondered whom he was trying to convince. Leah looked at him with those blue eyes for a long moment, then just shook her head and hopped off his knee, walking back to her coloring.

I'm failing, Dean thought now, sitting in the living room with horizontal slats of light falling through the boards and curtains. *My daughter is slipping away, and my wife is probably dead.*

Dean pressed his face into a pillow so his sleeping child wouldn't hear him cry.

Around the middle of December, Dean was outside filling water jugs from the barrel in the yard. He turned and there they were, standing in the driveway with surprised expressions on their faces, a woman in her thirties with piercings and a tattoo on her neck, and a young black man with a bald head. Both wore ski coats against the cold and were loaded down with backpacks and satchels. The woman carried an assault rifle; the man had an identical weapon slung over a shoulder and was holding a machete.

They stared at one another for a heartbeat, and then the woman turned and bolted.

These weren't wandering survivors, Dean's brain flashed. There was no question who they were scouting for. "No," Dean breathed, pulling the Glock and firing. The bullet hit her between the shoulder blades and hurled her sliding to the driveway asphalt. The gunshot echoed and carried. The bald man dropped the machete and struggled to get the rifle off his shoulder, but Dean advanced, gripping the automatic in two hands and pointing it at the man's face.

"Don't," Dean said softly.

The man froze.

Dean gestured at the rifle with his chin. "Shrug that off onto the ground."

The man complied and raised his hands slowly. "We're just looking for supplies, didn't know you were here." He glanced at the woman lying motionless a few yards away. "I won't say anything, just let me go."

Dean shot the man in the head.

He had barely hit the ground before Dean was dragging both bodies off the driveway and out of view from the street, pulling them into the yard. He imagined the echo of his second shot carrying for miles and quickly moved to the back corner of the store, peering around and down the driveway, waiting for more of them. When no companions came storming toward him, he stripped the bodies of their coats and clothing, of anything useful: packs and satchels of scavenged goods, ammunition and blades, a single walkie-talkie.

Stupid. Careless. I let them walk right up on me. Are they alone? They're going to be missed.

Dean hustled the equipment and weapons into the house, dumping it all in the living room. He was turned toward the front door when Leah's sleepy voice came from the bedroom they shared.

"Daddy? I have to go potty."

The gunshots had woken her from her nap. "Okay, honey, you're a big girl, go ahead." Then he called, "Try to go back to sleep, okay?" He knew that was a waste of breath. She would not voluntarily return to her nap. Little feet thumped across the floor toward the potty seat he had set up in the bathroom. Dean poked his head in as Leah did her business. "Not sleepy," the little girl said from the chair, rubbing her eyes with small fists.

"Okay, when you're done, just play in our room."

She gave a noncommittal shrug.

Dean returned to the front of the house and looked outside. No one else had come down the driveway, and the bodies were still—

One of them was missing.

"Shit," he hissed, snatching up the newly acquired machete and rushing outside. He saw her at once. The woman with the neck tattoo and a fresh bullet wound in her back was standing with her arms limp at her sides, swaying slightly as she stared with glassy eyes. Upon seeing Dean she bared her teeth and galloped at him with reaching arms.

Dean ran at her and buried the machete in the top of her head, jerking it free as she crumpled. He cursed himself. *Stupid! Sloppy! She could have turned when you were taking her gear, bitten you without warning.*

Another check of the empty driveway and a quick examination of the looted store told him that perhaps they had been alone after all, but he knew he was right in thinking they would be missed, and he knew on whose behalf they were out scavenging. Dean recognized the bald black man as one of the people looting the Target, the raiders he had seen during his rooftop observation just before the dog bit him. The same killers who had slaughtered Lenore and Ed.

What would he do with the bodies? The fresh meat would draw the dead. If he dragged them out into the street, it would keep the dead out of his yard but would risk discovery by others in their group.

The front door creaked open. "Daddy, can I come outside?"

Dean hurried to the door, slipping in and moving his daughter back into the living room. "Not now, honey."

She crossed her arms. "I never get to go outside."

He tried to guide her back to the bedroom. "Daddy needs you to play with Wawas for a while."

Leah didn't allow herself to be moved. "Don't wanna."

Dean didn't want to raise his voice. She was only being three and had no idea of the position her father had just put them in. He could hear the two pistol shots still in his head and closed his eyes, wishing there had been a faster, quieter way.

"Will you draw me a picture?" he asked.

"Don't wanna color," she said.

He took a deep breath. "How about if I color with you?"

She brightened. "Can we draw a horse?"

"I'll try. I'm not too good at horses."

"I'll show you, Daddy." She tugged at his pants leg.

Dean rubbed her back. "Will you take your crayons and paper into the bedroom? Daddy has to do something really quick, and then we'll draw a horse."

Leah looked at him, raising a suspicious eyebrow the same way her mother did when she thought she wasn't getting the complete story. "Okay," she said finally, collecting her crayons and running down the hall. Dean went back outside, convinced he would be walking into a pack of ghouls sniffing out the fresh meat. The yard was as he had left it.

Dean worked fast, stretching the two bodies out spread-eagle and then using the machete to turn them into more manageable pieces. It was brutal, bloody work, and he kept glancing at the front door of the house, expecting to see his daughter standing there with a horrified expression on her face as she saw what her daddy was doing. The door remained closed, however, and Dean gave thanks for small mercies.

Using a ladder from the garage, he moved the pieces up to the flat roof of the convenience store and scattered them across the tar surface, including the heads. Let the crows have them. There were still plenty of them left alive. Dean prayed he wouldn't look out in a few hours to see the store surrounded by the reaching dead, drawn by the scent.

Back in the house, he locked up and then went to the bathroom, using a liberal amount of their water and a dozen baby wipes to wash off the double murder. *Not murder,* he thought as he washed. *In war it isn't murder.* When he was done, he colored with Leah as promised, all the while waiting for the PTSD to kick in. Other than the occasional hand tremble, however, it remained at bay.

Throughout the evening he made repeated checks through gaps in the board-covered windows, looking for the dead or for anyone come looking for their missing scavengers. There was only the raucous cry of crows, and he saw them winging in to land on the convenience store roof. When he began to worry that the crows themselves might attract attention, he told himself in his inner sergeant's voice to cut the shit and trust in his plan, since things couldn't be changed anyway.

Once Leah was down for the night, Dean sat in the living room and listened to the dead man's walkie-talkie, the volume turned low. He heard some chatter and started taking notes. Saint Miguel was mentioned several times, and the context gave him a good idea that it might be the raiders' base. He also learned that there were probably more of them than he had originally thought.

The two he had just killed weren't missed until almost ten o'clock, when someone named Titan began calling for them. The woman was Kelly, the man Jared. Titan called them for only thirty minutes, his voice growing increasingly annoyed. After that, no one called for them at all.

Dean stayed up all night with one of the assault rifles across his knees and the radio on the table in front of him, wondering if and when anyone would come looking for the two dead people. He feared he had irrevocably compromised their little sanctuary.

No one came; the walking dead seemed unable to pick up the location of the dismembered meat on the rooftop and did not congregate outside. It wasn't until morning that Dean was finally able to close his eyes.

Leah was sick. She didn't want to sleep but didn't want to play either. A fever had turned her round cheeks to cherry-colored circles, and her eyes were glassy. Dean got her to drink water as often as he could and kept a cool, damp washrag on her forehead, the fever drying it out quickly. She didn't whine or complain, simply lay on the bed, lethargic. Wawas was tucked in beside her, but she showed little interest in her favorite stuffed animal.

According to the Omega watch on his wrist—an extravagant gift from Angie to celebrate their contract renewal for a second season—it was December 26. Leah's inquiries about Santa and whether he could find her in this new place had stopped the day before Christmas when she began to act out of sorts. Instead of chattering, she sat quietly on the couch or lay on the floor beside her untouched crayons, staring at nothing. Her appetite had vanished as well.

Dean gave her baby aspirin, wishing for some Children's Tylenol, and spent hours sitting with her head in his lap, stroking her hair. Sometimes she drifted off, and her daddy remained motionless so as not to disturb her.

She had been sick before, of course, but not like this, or so Dean remembered. Angie had usually been the one to keep Leah home from daycare when Dean was working. Still, he couldn't remember a fever hanging on this long. In the old world, she would have already been seen by her pediatrician and, by now, most likely an emergency room. Now there was only Dean, and he cursed himself for not taking the time to learn more about childhood illnesses, for leaving it all to Angie. Google and WebMD were no longer options.

Rest and liquids, his mother had always said, but Dean couldn't remember the old saying. Was he supposed to starve or feed a fever? His medical training had been focused on battlefield trauma.

As he sat in the living room of the small house, Leah was once more in his lap. She always wanted to cuddle more when she wasn't feeling well. Dean's hand slowly smoothed her long, damp hair.

"Daddy?" she said.

"Yes, sweetie. Are you thirsty?" He uncapped a bottle of water, but she pushed it away.

"Daddy, Santa has a deer."

"That's right, a reindeer."

She was quiet for a while, then asked, "Did Santa come yet?"

Dean smiled. It was the first time she had mentioned the subject in days. "He sure did, and he brought you a present. Would you like to see it?"

She shook her head and closed her eyes. Dean soaked the washrag from the water bottle and folded it over her head, half expecting it to sizzle when it touched her skin. He glanced at the front door, where one of the assault rifles stood on its stock, leaning against the frame. He found he looked at the door often.

It was two weeks since their discovery by the scavengers. A few drifters did finally show up to paw at the walls of the convenience store but soon moved on. Even the crows no longer came and went. He imagined by now there wouldn't be much left up there.

Once a day he switched on the walkie-talkie and listened for ten minutes, taking notes when he could, then switching it off to conserve the battery. Over the past two days the signal had seemed weaker, the voices harder to make out. Soon it would be as dead and silent as the city around them.

After that first day, however, no one mentioned the two missing people again. That told him something about the nature of the opposition. The raid on the ranch had given a clear demonstration about their regard for life, of course, but it was now obvious they cared little for their own as well. This was not only good news, but expected. Dean knew from his urban warfare training that outlaw bands tended to implode as they turned on one another. They were different from the insurgents he had fought, a people united by faith and culture, family and political ideology. The band in control of Chico was nothing like that; they were dangerous parasites feeding off a dead world and its survivors. Eventually they would begin to prey upon each other until they disappeared completely.

Dean didn't think he had that sort of time, though.

Leah needed more care than Dean could provide alone. She needed safer shelter, a community, other children. He did not doubt that there were groups of decent people still out there, communities where people relied on and trusted one another, protected each other from the horrors of this frightening new world. Dean had the kind of combat and field skills that would be welcome in such a community, and he could trade those abilities in exchange for sanctuary for Leah and himself.

Angie wasn't coming. He was beginning to accept it, forcing himself to believe it. The idea hurt, and it was difficult to even think the unspoken words, but how long could he continue to expose Leah to the dangers in Chico? Sooner or later they would be discovered, by chance or during a move to a new location once supplies ran out. This fearful Gypsy existence had to end.

Leah's eyes remained closed as in a sleepy voice she said, "Daddy, the sun is made of fire."

"Shh," he crooned, still stroking her hair.

After a moment she whispered, "And the moon is made of light."

Dean smiled and breathed deeply, resting his hand on her too-hot head. It all had to be about Leah now. His heart broke for his lost wife as he accepted what needed to be done, and he turned all his thoughts to his daughter in an attempt to push the grief away. They would be leaving, starting a new life together, and he would find them someplace truly safe.

His left hand trembled, the PTSD putting him on notice that the Fear Animal might very well decide not to cooperate.

Leah's fever broke that evening and stayed away. By morning she was hungry and wanting to play a little, and Dean breathed a sigh of shaky relief. He asked her if she was feeling okay so many times that the little girl finally said, "Daddy, stop."

By December 28 she was asking about Santa and expressed a joy unique to three-year-olds when Dean showed her the gift the jolly old elf had left for her, another small pony with hair she could comb.

"Santa loves me," she said, marching her two ponies side by side across the living room carpet.

"Yes, he does," said Dean.

He began planning immediately, as he would take the time necessary to find a vehicle, outfit and stock it properly, and calculate a route and destination. He was thinking north, possibly Eureka. There was no way he would leave Leah home alone while he prepared, so he would have to risk bringing her along on his preparation missions, but not until she was a little stronger.

Dean gave himself a two-week window. After that, he and Leah would leave Chico forever.

TWENTY-FOUR

January 13—Halsey's Place

Vladimir hit the ground beside the cabin and at once was surrounded by snarls and grabbing hands. He snapped on the flashlight and ran from Halsey's tower, intent on retrieving his night-vision goggles, shadowy shapes lurching at him from the front and sides. A hand caught at the sleeve of his coat and he jerked away, running into a rotting woman who clawed at him, ragged fingernails tearing the nylon of his jacket. He shouldered her aside as more hands tore at his back, a middle-aged man galloping in from the right, a teenage boy with yellowing skin snapping and charging him from the front.

The pilot shrugged out of his coat, freeing himself from the creatures to his rear, dodged the teenager, and straight-armed the middle-aged man, knocking him down but nearly losing fingers to gnashing teeth. The dead wailed all around him.

The jittering flashlight lit the ground before him, lumpy turf coated in snow and marred by dragging footprints. His boots pounded the earth as he broke free from the knot of drifters gathering around the cabin, a chorus of hungry growls now to his left. A pass of the light in that direction revealed a line of corpses, four or five deep, marching toward him. His heart hammering, Vlad moved in the direction of the Black Hawk, out there somewhere in the darkness.

He could smell them, a moist odor of decay curdling the air, and within several minutes the scent was joined by the acrid bite of quicklime. Halsey's mass grave. He was heading in the right direction, the Black Hawk waiting midway between the cabin and the lime pit.

Suddenly something was underfoot and he tripped, falling forward, losing the flashlight as he hit the snowy ground. In an instant there was a weight on his legs and he twisted, trying to break free. The flashlight had fallen at such an angle that the beam pointed back toward him, and in the light he saw a dead woman—a torso with arms and gnashing teeth, spinal column trailing behind her—lying across his lower legs and gripping his right boot with both hands. Teeth sank into the leather.

Vlad grunted and kicked with his other boot, kicked again, aiming for the creature's head but hitting ribs and shoulder. The dead woman seemed to realize her teeth could not penetrate the boot, so she scrabbled up his leg and gripped his shin, jaws wide.

The crack of Vladimir's Browning split the night and he screamed, pain racing up his leg. He dragged himself clear of the corpse's weight, the limp body rolling off and landing on its back. The bullet had entered just above its ear on one side and blown out a chunk of skull and corrupted gray matter on the other.

Vlad tried to swallow the pain as he crawled to his feet, retrieving the flashlight and shining it back toward the cabin. The line of corpses had turned to follow him, and now stretched out as a barrier between him and his friend. The pilot turned and got going again, limping badly, searching with the flashlight. The Black Hawk was still nowhere in sight.

Behind him, Vladimir was leaving a blood trail.

Titan and Braga throttled up the stone-paved driveway, now buckled in places and sagging in others from the quake. Their headlights illuminated a gentle rise as they drove along a curved drive through lawns once immaculately landscaped, now gone shaggy and brown with clusters of dead hedges. A rich man's place, they thought. Behind them, the three pickups added their headlights as they followed the Harleys.

The driveway curved back to the right, passing a dirt road that cut away over a hill, coming to a halt at a large paved circle in front of a burned mansion and charred garages. The pickups spread out behind them as the two bikers sat on their hogs, headlights shining on collapsed stone and a skeleton of blackened timbers. The quake had collapsed the structure further, creating a maze of debris. Engines switched off.

"What's up with this?" Braga said. "Zombies don't set fires."

Titan lit a joint. "We've seen burned shit before." He shrugged. "Gas leak, lightning maybe."

"Maybe," said Braga. He climbed off his bike and stretched, then yelled back at the people in the trucks. "Spread out and look around." A dozen men and women jumped down and started into the ruins, flashlights and weapons raised.

Braga looked around at the destruction. "No place to land a helicopter up here. The map said it was a ranch."

Titan passed the joint. "Don't know what to tell you."

Braga watched Little Emer's militia move slowly through the ruins, kicking up clouds of ash, lights jumping through fallen beams.

He doubted anyone would be hiding in there, but their leader would want him to be thorough. He held the smoke and passed the joint back to his friend. The goddamned helicopter was probably hundreds of miles away by now. Why would anyone want to land out here in the sticks?

"You see that dirt road we passed?" Braga said. "Just off the driveway?"

Titan nodded. "So what?"

"I think we should see where it goes."

The red tip of the joint flared. "Brother, we're wasting our time. Let's just tell him we didn't find anything."

Braga snorted. "Sure, let's do that, and when the fucking chopper *does* show up because we didn't find it, you can tell the man why."

The other biker made a disgusted sound and crushed the butt of the joint under a boot. "Fine, we'll check the road. But I'm telling you—"

A single, distant gunshot came from beyond the burned mansion. Titan and Braga looked at one another, then grinned and started yelling for the others to get back in the trucks.

Halsey's Stampede followed through the woods and out onto the Skyway, tracking on the distant rumble of engines. Stiff legs marched across the pavement, bodies bumping against one another as two thousand corpses trudged in the same direction. A river of rot flowing around abandoned vehicles.

The creatures at the head of the Stampede had drawn even with the driveway entrance to Pepper's Broken Arrow Ranch when a pistol shot echoed in the distance. Heads lifted, turning toward the sound. A moment later there was a new rumbling of engines.

The dead began to moan, and flowed up the driveway.

. . .

Fuck *me*!" Braga said, bringing his hog to a sliding stop, Titan doing the same, the brake lights of the trucks following an instant later. A tattered, hobbling corpse wearing scrubs and a doctor's coat stumbled into the road not twenty feet away.

Both bikers pulled their shotguns and blasted off a trio of shells each, cutting the creature down. Then they motored forward to inspect their kill.

"Damn, it stinks!" said Titan.

"That scare you, bro?" Braga said, grinning as he reloaded his shotgun.

"Hell yes," said Titan, feeding shells into his own weapon.

Braga laughed. "C'mon," he said, throttling his Harley, "let's go put in some work." Behind them, the pickups followed.

Halsey stared into the black, trying to ignore the hammering fists and snarling coming from below as the dead began stacking up against the walls of the cabin. Though he couldn't see them in the dark, he could hear more feet dragging across the yard, bumping against his pickup. He couldn't tell how many were out there and wasn't sure he wanted to know.

Where was Vlad? The man had vanished into the night as soon as he jumped off the roof. Had he run in the right direction? Was he even still alive? Halsey gripped the tower wall and leaned out, unable to see a thing.

A white flash and the crack of a pistol came from the darkness, followed immediately by a man's scream. Halsey stared at that point, thinking he saw a light, wondering if it was his imagination. No, it was a flashlight. It moved and then was gone.

Glass broke below as the dead shattered the cabin's windows and began hammering at the wooden shutters.

"Come on, buddy," Halsey said.

Vladimir's flashlight swept across the black fuselage of the helicopter just as the cloud cover parted, the landscape suddenly lit with moonlight. A corpse with one arm missing was pawing at the cockpit's windscreen, and it turned as the pilot approached, yellow eyes shining in the flashlight beam. It lurched away from the aircraft and came toward him, and Vlad raised his pistol and shot it in the face.

Moans chorused from the field behind, and the Russian turned to see the wall of decay trudging toward him. His pilot's brain calculated the math: their distance, speed of approach, the time he would need for his new task. The numbers weren't in his favor.

He climbed up into the troop compartment, wincing at the pain and leaving a blood trail across snow and metal, then ducked into the cockpit. He took the night-vision goggles from their compartment above the pilot's seat and hung them around his neck. Even without them, the newly arrived moonlight gave him a panoramic view of the approaching dead, confirming that his original plan, to return to the cabin with the goggles, was now impossible. The cabin and outbuildings, as well as the landscape around it, teemed with the walking dead. There were several hundred, maybe more, and Vladimir saw that he would not make it back to Halsey, especially limping with this wound.

Wasn't that ironic? He had survived the opening act of the apocalypse, escaped death countless times both on the ground and in the air, all without a scratch. Now this, a self-inflicted gunshot wound that had almost certainly blown off one of his toes. He had been practically touching the side of the torso-zombie's skull with the Browning when he fired, and the high-powered bullet had punched completely through the creature's head, then right through his boot just inches beyond.

It hurt like a bastard. He had crippled himself and was now leaving a bloody trail as an invitation to the undead.

A line of headlights appeared on the road above Halsey's ranch, winding down from the burned-out mansion. Vladimir didn't have to guess who they were. He threw another glance at the wall of corpses plodding toward the Black Hawk, muttered a curse in Russian, and started firing up the turbines.

The clouds were breaking up, and below them the small ranch was revealed in the moonlight. In a field beyond the cabin sat the dark shape of a military helicopter.

Braga stopped and jumped off his motorcycle, waving to the trucks. "There it is! Go kick some ass!"

The pickups raced past the Harleys and down toward the ranch, men and women in the truck beds holding on to the sides.

"Yeah, get some!" Titan shouted after them. Then he produced another joint and fired it up. Braga stood nearby with his hands in his pockets. They would have a great view of the action, safe up here on the hillside.

Halsey looked down from the tower in every direction, seeing the dead in the new moonlight. He could also see the Black Hawk now, and with his binoculars he spotted Vlad in the cockpit, illuminated in the red glow of instruments. A mob of at least fifty corpses was closing in on the chopper.

He wanted to shoot them, increase his friend's chance of getting

airborne—for that was surely what he was attempting—but didn't
dare. The dead were between Halsey's rifle and the Black Hawk. A
miss would risk hitting Vlad. It didn't occur to him that the Russian
was trying to escape while Halsey was still trapped in the tower.
Even if it had, the ranch hand had always been a practical man and
would not blame people for protecting their own lives.

Halsey dropped back down the ladder into the cabin and filled a
canvas pack with ammunition from the gun rack, including a box
of shells for the big pistol on his hip. When he climbed back up, he
was also carrying the scoped deer rifle and a Winchester lever-
action. Halsey kicked the roof hatch shut and started loading the
weapons.

The echoing blasts of shotguns pulled his attention to the hillside, where a line of headlights was snaking down from the main
house. After a moment, three pairs of lights left two others behind,
engines racing as they closed on the ranch.

"Couldn't do much when you came to the Franks place," Halsey
said, raising the deer rifle and working the bolt. "This here's a different story. You ain't got your tank, and I ain't a grandpa." He sighted
and fired, blowing out the windshield of the first pickup. It swerved
but kept on. Halsey ejected the spent casing, sending it spinning
into the night. He led the truck a bit and fired again, hitting the left
front tire. Damn! He had been aiming for the windshield. Still,
there was a loud bang and the pickup ground to a halt on the side of
the road.

Moonlight flashed on brass as a new round entered the breech.
"Ain't too smart, are you?" The rifle cracked and the stock slammed
back into his shoulder. One of the men in the bed of the stopped
truck flew out of it backward. The others scrambled after him, taking cover. He began firing faster, the darkness and partial moonlight working against his aim, causing him to miss more often than
he hit. Halsey focused simply on hitting the truck, hoping for the

best. The left rear tire blew. A hole appeared harmlessly in the side
of the truck bed. More misses, and then he was quickly reloading.
Moments later he was up and firing again. A bullet punched a hole
midway up the driver's door. Good. Anyone still inside the cab
would be trying to hold their intestines in with their hands by now.

Muzzle flashes appeared around the disabled pickup as its occupants started returning fire. A few bullets thudded into the cabin;
others chipped at the wood of the observation tower. Halsey
dropped to one knee to finish loading.

The remaining two trucks roared off the hill and up the road
toward Halsey's compound, crossing the point where he would have
had a gate and a moat if there had been enough time. Dead bodies
banged against grilles and hoods and were flung away as the trucks
full of raiders drove into the hard-packed yard. Weapons fired from
the truck bed in all directions, hitting the walking dead that turned
toward the new arrivals.

Halsey stood, saw the trucks below, and raised his rifle. A volley
of fire from the disabled pickup filled the air with snaps and whis-
tles, chewing wood off the tower and forcing the ranch hand to drop
back down. He swapped the deer rifle for the quicker lever-action
with its open sights. To his right, out across the open ground, came
the whine of aircraft turbines spooling up. A moment later he heard
the engine of one of the trucks in the yard revving as the driver
gunned away from the buildings and out into the field toward the
Black Hawk.

"Hell no," Halsey said, standing and sighting on the bed of the
departing pickup, trying to aim at the two bouncing figures within,
a woman and a chubby man, both with rifles and each hanging on
to keep from being thrown out. The .30-30 Winchester kicked, and
the bullet missed. The ranch hand worked the lever and sighted
again. This bullet passed between both passengers in the bed, but
the rear window of the pickup exploded, and the truck swerved

hard right, its nose dropping as it suddenly stopped with a crunching impact. Both passengers were hurled from the truck bed.

More bullets tore into the tower from the disabled pickup, and now also from the raiders in the yard below. Splinters flew about him as a bullet kissed Halsey's chin, laying it open to the bone. Another grazed his elbow and a third slashed across his ribs in a red line. He dropped to the floor as a bullet punched through the boards and buried itself in his right calf.

Halsey cried out, braced himself against a beam, and struggled to reload his Winchester.

Two men and a woman were standing behind the disabled pickup, pouring fire onto the little tower rising above the cabin. All three had participated on the bunker ranch raid and had been under fire before. Still, one of their number had been shot out of the bed of the truck, and the driver hadn't escaped the cab. They were rattled.

Then a pair of hands gripped the window frame on the passenger side and the driver hauled himself out. He landed hard on the road and left a red smear down the door.

"He's gut-shot," one of the men yelled, ejecting a spent magazine and reaching for another. "Barry, just stay low. Don't try to move."

The gut-shot driver looked up with milky eyes and growled, scuttling on all fours, catching hold of the man's leg and sinking his teeth into the soft tissue at the back of the knee. The man shrieked and fell, and the driver scrambled up his body, ripping his throat out.

The second raider hiding behind the truck swore and lifted his weapon, but then he was hit from the side by a snarling weight, the man who had been shot out of the pickup bed. Teeth ripped into a jugular vein, spraying the side of the truck red as the drifter bore the dying man to the ground.

The remaining woman bolted from behind the truck, running

back up the hill toward the two motorcycle lights. Winchester bullets from the tower chased her unsuccessfully but didn't prevent her from running straight into the outstretched arms of a snapping ghoul.

Halsey saw the running woman go down and swung the Winchester back toward the yard, levering a fresh round into the chamber. He didn't fire, though. It was unnecessary. The ranch hand leaned against the wall then, taking weight off his calf, blood running from his chin, his shirt and coat turning red at the elbow and ribs. He looked on in grim fascination.

The raiders who had driven into the yard, shooting at zombies and firing on his tower, had been swarmed and overrun. Dozens of DTs were clawing their way into the truck bed and through the cab's open windows, tearing into fresh meat. It was over quickly and then the feeding began.

Halsey turned his attention to the moonlit field on his right. He could see where the last pickup had come to rest, nose down in a depression in the terrain, taillights pointed up at a sharp angle. "Found yourself that little ditch, didn't you?" He pulled the can of chewing tobacco from his hip pocket, tucking a wad into his lip. He knew this land and knew exactly what had happened to the truck. There was a deep crease in the ground where a bit of a stream had once flowed, carving a furrow in the earth. It was deep enough that he stayed mindful of it when he was running the backhoe.

His binoculars revealed blood-slicked metal and glass, and the vehicle crawled with the undead. Halsey fired four quick shots into the rear of the cab just to make sure it was out of action. Then he leaned against the tower wall, wiping blood off his chin and wincing at his bullet wounds, watching the Black Hawk lift off in a cloud of blowing snow.

. . .

N ot looking too good down there," Titan said, sitting astride his
motorcycle. The moonlight had showed them everything.

"Fucking Corrigan," Braga spat, shaking the long hair out of his
face. "We could have taken this down easy if he hadn't been such a
pussy."

"He's a dead man," Titan said.

"Bet your ass."

A boy in swim trunks galloped out of the darkness behind Braga
and hit the biker in the lower back, taking him to the ground.

He bit through Braga's long hair and deep into the biker's scalp.

Titan was too shocked to react at first, even when his friend
started screaming and thrashing. The swim trunks boy nuzzled into
the biker's neck with a moan, and a bright gout of arterial blood
shot across Titan's Harley and then his leg and boot.

"Mother*fucker!*" he cried, aiming his shotgun and firing two
quick blasts at close range, both to the head, one into the dead boy
and the other into Braga. "Fuck this," he said, firing up the Harley
and kicking up stone and dirt as he spun in a U-turn and shot back
up the road toward the burned mansion.

As Titan crested the hill, his eyes widened as his headlight gave
him a quick, final glimpse of the horde, what Halsey called the Stampede, spread out ahead of him. Before the biker could even touch the
brakes, the motorcycle drove into the thick of the pack and was
instantly swallowed. Brief screams were cut short a moment later, the
outlaw biker torn apart before his Harley stopped moving.

V lad's right foot was numb, the ragged leather at the tip of his
boot slick with blood, making the control pedals slippery. He
tried to ignore it, to focus on flying, but it was like a pulsing red

shriek at the end of his leg. He was wearing the NVGs now, the world around him transformed to a bright green.

The Black Hawk thudded toward the surrounded cabin.

He didn't feel any ground fire slamming against the combat chopper's armored belly, didn't have time to worry about it anyway, and was shocked he had lifted off ahead of the horde. They had gotten close, though, and the hollow, metallic slapping of their hands along the length of the tail boom and fuselage was a noise he knew he would hear in nightmares for years to come. If he had years. It might only be minutes.

Another narrow liftoff, another human life depending on his skill as a pilot. "I have been to this dance before," he said through gritted teeth, aiming the chopper for the bullet-scarred tower atop the cabin. He hoped Halsey was smarter than he portrayed himself, for the Russian had no way to communicate with the man.

As the Black Hawk slid in beside the tower, rotor blades pounding dangerously close to the peaked roof, Halsey appeared at the wooden wall with a canvas pack and a rifle slung across his chest. The rotor wash blew the man's John Deere cap into the night as the ranch hand leaped, scrambling into the troop compartment. In an instant Vladimir was banking and climbing.

Halsey watched his home fall away beneath them. It was swarming with the walking dead, and in that moment he knew it was home no longer.

Blue January skies greeted them in the morning, the sun rising to melt away the thin layer of snow. Groundhog-7 sat quietly just off a shaggy green patch with a flag poking out of the ground. The flag read 9 and the golf course was quiet and empty around them.

"Hurt much?" Halsey said, sitting beside his friend on the lip of the troop compartment, legs dangling over the side. His calf and chin were bound in gauze, the bandage wrapping around the top of his head, making him speak through clenched teeth. Adhesive pads were taped to his elbow and ribs.

The Russian's boot was off, his foot a lump under white wrapping. Between the two of them they had exhausted the helicopter's first-aid kit.

"*Da*," said the pilot. He had managed to blow off not one toe, but two. The aspirin from the kit did little to ease the pain. "I believe if I had not done this to myself, the pain would not be so great."

"Pride can hurt worse than the wound."

"You are very wise," Vladimir said, "for a man with farm animal shit on his boots."

Halsey wiggled his feet. "*Two* boots. Did you notice that?"

A sigh. "It did not escape my attention." The Russian looked at his friend. "You are a mess."

The ranch hand spat tobacco through his teeth, staining the bandage on his chin. "Been better."

The handheld Hydra radio sat between them, a silent black brick. Vlad had tried to call Angie, Skye, and Carney repeatedly. No one had answered, and the pilot was visibly unsettled.

"You cannot go home," the Russian said quietly. "I am sorry."

"I know. I am too. Nothing to be done about it."

Vladimir nodded. "I am in need of a gunner."

"Got nothing better to do."

The Russian nodded and patted the M240 machine gun mounted in the door. "Then let me introduce you to my friend."

RENDER
UNTO CAESAR

TWENTY-FIVE

January 13—Southeast Chico

Lassiter stood in front of a small statue of a Chinese dragon, urinating into its open mouth with an exaggerated "Ahhh . . ." Russo was one shop down, looking at books in a broken display window. He selected a paperback from an author he liked and tucked it into his backpack.

The shops were set up in a small semicircle around a brick-paved plaza with little metal chairs and tables, an almond tree growing out of the center. In addition to the Chinese restaurant and bookstore, there was a candle store, a small gallery, and a boutique coffee shop. An empty bicycle rack stood to one side. Russo used to like coming here before the plague, sitting alone at a table beneath the almond tree with a latte, surfing on his tablet computer.

The film student looked around and shook his head at the random violence of earthquakes. On his side of the street there was only broken glass and overturned chairs. The opposite side of Wisconsin Street was a line of rubble and shattered timbers, barely recognizable as a row of houses. An eight-foot-wide fissure had opened up just down the block, swallowing part of a two-story house. Lassiter's truck was parked well away from the crack, just in front of the little plaza.

"There isn't shit here we need," said Lassiter, zipping up and walking to join Russo in front of the bookstore. He didn't even glance at the books in the window.

"I like it here," said Russo.

"Whoopee. Let's get back to work." The former armored-car driver walked toward the truck. "There's a little outdoor sports place not far from here. I saw a crossbow on display in there, back before all this shit. I want to check, see if maybe it's still there."

Russo looked at the books a bit longer. There would be no one writing new ones anymore, and he found that sad. He looked up at the blue early-morning sky and then followed Lassiter to the truck. They had been at it since first light, just another day of scavenging, and already the bed contained several cases of canned vegetables, a twenty-four-pack of bottled water, and three cases of motor oil.

"Bits and pieces," he muttered.

"What?" Lassiter demanded. "What did you say?"

"I said bits and pieces. That's what we do," Russo said, "collect scraps from the old world."

"You're such a whiner," Lassiter said, leaning on the hood of his truck and staring at his partner, "and you think you're so much better than everyone else because you had some college. There is no *old world*, there's only this one, it's just changed. But everything has to have some big meaning for you, doesn't it?" He hawked and spit to the side. "This is nothing more than survival. It's simple. No deep meaning. If we want things to keep running, and if we want to keep eating, we go out and take whatever we can find, 'cause sure as shit no one's making any more."

Russo shrugged. Maybe that was right, maybe it was as simple as survival, but what kind of life was that? Not much of a life at all, at least not for him. He watched his partner kneel in front of the pickup to tie his boot and decided this would be their last run together. Russo wouldn't kill him, not because he didn't want to or think he could, but because it just didn't matter anymore. This was Lassiter's world, and the man was perfectly suited to it. Hell, he'd probably been wishing for something like this his whole life. But not Russo. He wanted to be away from all this, to be alone. Maybe he could find a little house in the mountains where no one would bother him. It would be hard living, and frightening at first, but he didn't think it would be as frightening as life in Chico, under the rule of a madman and rubbing elbows with murderous scum.

The young man decided that he would pack up what he could and leave tonight, find a car that still ran and head north. A fresh start. That sounded nice.

Angie, Skye, and Carney caught a few hours of sleep in an upscale furniture store, crashed on couches and in recliners while sharing the watch. At daybreak they were moving again, walking in a line down East 8th Street. On point, Carney startled a deer that was grazing in the front yard of an animal hospital, nibbling at a row of hedges. The ex-con watched the creature bound up the street and out of sight between two buildings.

Behind him, Angie walked without looking around, eyes on the pavement and her boots. Skye caught up to her. "You okay?"

Angie shook her head, and Skye walked beside her in silence.

Carney led them around a blockage where the quake had shaken light and telephone poles into the street, dropping them on parked cars. One of the crucifixes they had seen throughout the city had toppled as well, and whatever had been hung upon it had managed to tear itself free and wander off. Part of a gray hand was still spiked to the crossbar.

After a few minutes Skye said, "We don't have to stay. We can just go back to the ship."

"Go if you want to," Angie said, not looking up.

"That's not what I'm saying and you know it," Skye said. "But if we're going to stay and do this, we need a better plan than just wandering around until someone shoots at us."

Angie kept her eyes on the pavement, her voice flat. "Carney is looking for signs of their activity. Then we'll find them and kill them."

"Oh, I see," Skye said, "simple like that."

"Simple like that."

Skye grabbed the woman's shoulder and spun her, moving her face in close. "Then get your head in the game, lady."

Angie bared her teeth. "Get your hand off me."

Skye did, giving her a hard shove. "You're walking around feeling sorry for yourself, not paying attention, and it's going to get us killed." The younger woman pointed at Angie. "I told you to go cold. Fucking do it. Carney and I aren't going to waste our lives for someone who's already given up on her own."

When Angie simply glared at her, Skye pointed at her again. "You think you're the first one to lose somebody? They might even still be alive out there, and you could live on that hope your whole life. I *watched* my family die."

Angie bristled, wanting to scream that Skye was a kid, she didn't know what it was like to lose a child, a man she loved. A child! It was something Skye couldn't possibly understand. What did she really know about loss?

Then Angie looked at the hard, unyielding face, the gray, scarred skin and patch hiding a blind eye, souvenirs of horror. This was a girl who should be concerned with dating and grades, not field-stripping rifles and chopping up corpses with a machete. The anger blew out of her like a sudden wind.

"I'm sorry," Angie said softly.

"Fuck your *sorry*," Skye growled. "Fuck sympathy and pity"—she waved an arm at the dead city—"because *they* did. Remember the ranch? Your mom and dad?" She stepped close to Angie once more, and in a low voice said, "No more pity, Ang. Not for yourself, not for them. They're worse than zombies. At least the dead don't kill for sport."

Angie met that single cold eye and nodded slowly. Skye gripped the woman's shoulder briefly and joined Carney.

The ex-con had been watching outward during the exchange, as was his habit, but now he turned and walked back to Angie, cradling his rifle in his arms in that easy way of his, like he was involved in nothing more pressing than a hunting trip with old friends. He cocked his head. "It's okay," he said.

"What's okay?" The woman had a deep weariness about her.

"To hurt. To miss people. And it never goes away."

Angie let out a small sigh. "Is that supposed to make things better?"

The corner of the ex-con's mouth lifted just the slightest. "No. And that's not the point. We're still here, and we have to keep on."

"So tell me what's the point in *that*."

Carney's mouth lifted a bit higher. "Most people would give you a load about living for their memory, that it's what they would want." He shook his head.

"Then why?" Angie asked.

"To be spiteful." He turned and walked back toward Skye, calling over his shoulder, "Death hates it when we live just to spite him. It's enough."

When Carney led off once more, Angie was following with her head up.

After only a few minutes, however, Carney held up his hand and snapped his fingers. The two women stopped at once, rifles moving to shoulders as they looked and listened. An engine, a heavy diesel like those used in construction equipment. It was coming this way.

"Cover," Angie whispered, and the three of them fled up a short driveway, ducking out of sight behind a two-story Victorian with a wraparound porch.

They were almost ready. It had taken weeks of planning and small trips out together, Leah in the carrier on Dean's back as he made his runs with a two-wheeled hand truck from the convenience store. Most of the time he carried it to avoid the extra noise, only setting it on its wheels when he was ready to load up.

Each day he would go out with a list and return with all the items he could find, rolling the hand truck through the streets, piled with boxes and plastic totes. He placed the pilfered goods in stacked rows inside the garage beside their house, a precise plan for how it would all eventually be loaded. It wasn't nearly as much as he wanted—Chico was good-sized, but there had been plenty of scavenging, and his range was limited—but it would have to be enough.

There was some canned food, water in an assortment of odd-sized containers, clothing, coats and shoes in both their sizes, or at least close enough. He had a few tools and tarps, a couple of packages of batteries, and some camping equipment. One tote held toys, books, and crayons, and some larger kids' clothing Leah could grow into. Their meager first-aid supplies and medicine were packed in a small red tote, while maps, a compass, some road flares, and a hatchet were nestled in a green one. Six full jerry cans of gasoline were lined up at the back of the load.

Dean stood now amid the shadows inside a small sporting-goods store, his latest plunder strapped to the hand truck with bungee cords: a sleeping bag, half a case of Sterno cans, and some small bottles of propane for camp stoves. Atop it all was a compound bow and bundles of arrows he had found high on a shelf in the store's small stockroom.

"Last trip, Daddy?" Leah said over his shoulder.

"That's right, honey," Dean replied, checking the street. He saw only one figure moving, a corpse in the middle of the road, half a block away.

The little girl clapped her hands. "We're going bye-bye."

Dean smiled. "Yes we are, after it gets dark."

"I can stay up late?"

"Just tonight."

"Wawas is coming with me," she confirmed.

"Yes, Wawas is coming." He reached back and squeezed her hand. "Ready to run?"

"Ready."

Dean opened the door and trotted into the street, pulling the hand truck behind him and gripping his Glock in the other hand. He ran in the direction opposite the lone corpse and turned at an intersection.

Telling Leah this was their last trip wasn't exactly true. This was their last trip for supplies, but there would be one more right at sunset. That was when the two of them would travel five blocks to where Dean had a red Chevy Silverado crew-cab pickup stashed in a garage, fueled and waiting. His plan was to retrieve the truck, drive back to their little house, and load the supplies he had staged so carefully. He had allotted himself one hour for all of this. Then they would leave under the cover of night, when he figured it was least likely for the raiders to be out, and head north.

Dean jogged down the street, his hand truck bumping behind him. He stopped to check an intersection and jogged through. The convenience store in front of their little house was just up on the left, and he crossed the distance as quickly as he could. When they reached the garage, he rolled the door up and then quickly back down once they were inside.

"Can I go color?" Leah asked as he set her down.

"Sure, but go potty first, okay?"

"I will, Daddy."

Dean held her hand as he walked her to the house, unlocking the door and then locking it behind her. Then he unpacked the latest supplies and placed them in the loading arrangement.

S hit, you see that?" Lassiter whispered, about to climb into the cab of his F-250. He snatched a pair of binoculars off the seat and looked up the street that intersected at their trendy little plaza.

"See what?" Russo asked, coming around to his partner's side.

"I'll be damned," Lassiter breathed, and then started to grin. About two blocks away, a man in dark clothing was crossing the street pulling a loaded cart of some kind behind him. A little girl was riding on his back in a carrier. Lassiter watched them duck out of sight between a house and a little convenience store.

"Remember what Little Emer told us to look for when we were out?" Lassiter asked, checking street names and addresses.

Russo nodded. He had seen the running shape but at this distance couldn't make out the details with his naked eye. "You think you saw them?"

"I know I saw them," Lassiter said, "and I found their fucking nest." He shouldered Russo aside and reached into the truck cab for his walkie-talkie.

"Rome, this is Salvage-Four, come in."

There was a long pause, and then, "Go ahead, Salvage-Four."

"I need to talk to the man."

Another pause. "What do you want him for?" asked the voice on the radio.

"I said I need to talk to Little Emer. Now go get him, goddammit!"

The radio was silent for a long while, and Lassiter simply stared at it, saying nothing to his partner. Beside him, Russo wished he had left yesterday.

The warlord's voice came over the speaker. "What do you have, Lassiter?"

The former armored-car driver told him what he had seen and gave the location. Little Emer asked a few questions, then told Lassiter to sit tight and wait.

Back at Saint Miguel's, Little Emer looked at the man operating the base radio. "Find Red Hen and Stark, then tell Corrigan to get Baby ready." It might be overkill, but then he had managed to survive the end of the world thus far without taking unnecessary chances. Besides, it would be a hell of a show. The warlord left the room to collect his weapons, unable to suppress a smile.

The rumbling of motorcycles could barely be heard over the armored vehicle's engine as three Harleys preceded the Bradley down East 8th Street. Angie and Skye peered around the corner of the big Victorian home and caught a quick glimpse of the little convoy as it rolled by. When it was gone, Angie turned to her two friends. "Let's see where they're going. Maybe they'll split up and we can take them apart a piece at a time."

The others nodded, and the three of them took off at a run, following the sound of engines.

TWENTY-SIX

January 13—Southeast Chico

Leah was lying on her tummy on the living room carpet, Wawas close by her side as she gripped a yellow crayon, tongue stuck out the corner of her mouth. She was coloring a chicken, trying hard to stay in the lines. Light from the late-morning sun threw bars of muted yellow on the floor. Dean sat on the sofa across from her with a Northern California road map spread out on the coffee table, using a highlighter—also yellow—to trace alternate routes from Chico to the small coastal town of Eureka. His secondary destination took them northeast into lower Oregon, above Klamath Falls to some tiny, remote towns near the Winema and Fremont National Forests. Remote was good. He was eager for sundown to arrive so they could be on their way.

Father and daughter looked up from their projects as a rumbling came from outside. This was not the sound of an earthquake. It was man-made, and Dean knew at once it was far more dangerous. He recognized the thrum of that engine. It was the Bradley, and it was close.

"Come here, baby," he said, opening one arm and reaching for the assault rifle propped against the end of the sofa. Leah snatched Wawas off the floor and ran to her daddy. Dean snapped on the radio the dead scavengers had carried in time to hear a single command.

"Tear it up," said the voice.

Then the world exploded.

The twenty-five-millimeter auto-cannon roared as explosive rounds ripped from its barrel, tracking left to right. The Bradley sat in the street and panned its turret across the convenience store, blowing apart brick and timber before sending its rounds crashing into the small board house out back, followed by the adjacent garage. A small explosion erupted everywhere a shell landed, splintering walls and roofs, shredding the garage door, fragmenting window frames.

On the street beside the armored vehicle, Little Emer and his two biker brothers, Stark and Red Hen, stood covering their ears with their hands. To the rear of the Bradley, Lassiter and Russo stood behind the pickup, the former armored-car driver grinning and nodding vigorously at the sound and destruction.

Russo's video recorder was in his hand but hanging limp at one side, not even switched on. He winced at the ripping sound of the main gun, looking at the bikers, then at his partner. His eyes fell on the large, empty crucifix strapped to the back deck of the armored vehicle.

The turret started back again, tearing down walls, fire and black smoke erupting deep within the structures.

All this for a man and his little girl, Russo thought, knowing their fate should they survive the Bradley's onslaught. He looked at the camcorder in his hand, thought about the horrors it contained, the hours of nightmares he had eagerly filmed. The world he had loved was dead, and *this* was to be his eulogy? Russo shook his head slowly, suddenly repelled by the sight of the small metal and plastic box, sickened at what he had allowed himself to become for the sake of survival.

Closer to the Bradley, Little Emer laughed, the sound swallowed by the auto-cannon.

A moment later, standing in his commander's hatch, Corrigan opened up with the machine gun mounted beside him, brass tinkling to the pavement as he raked the three buildings with 7.62-millimeter automatic fire. The deserter shook with his weapon, a savage grin on his scarred face as he hunted with the bullets, searching for any place a person could hide.

After a minute, the convenience store was a pile of rubble, the garage was burning from a gasoline fire, and the house was near collapse, the roof sagging and soaking up most of the machine gun rounds. Little Emer gave the signal to cease fire, and as soon as Corrigan stopped, the warlord waved to the men on the ground around him.

"Let's go," he shouted, gripping his Uzi and charging in, the other men close behind. This was one attack Little Emer would lead personally.

Russo remained in the street. After a final look at the camcorder, he turned and hurled it as far as he could down the street behind him, watching it explode in shards of plastic and glass.

Up in the turret, Corrigan tracked the charging men with the barrel of his machine gun, finger caressing the trigger. *Accidents happen,* he thought, but he did not fire. *Maybe later.* He failed to notice that Russo did not follow the men into the ruins.

Ahead, the bikers and Lassiter spread out through the destruction, searching for fresh blood.

D ean was facedown, wounded, cheek pressed against the hot grit of Iraqi sand. His body throbbed and his head was heavy. Where were his men? He heard the running boots and cries of insurgents and prayed he wouldn't live long enough for them to decapitate him on television. He missed Angie. He wished they'd had a baby.

But Angie came after the war, and they did have a baby.

He blinked his eyes and saw carpet littered with pieces of brick and timber debris. Not sand. The desert wasn't real, but the wounds were. A chunk of two-by-four not far from his face was bright with blood.

There was something beneath him, something that moved.

"Daddy?" Leah said, her voice groggy, like when she awoke in the night with a bad dream.

Dean tried to answer, couldn't. It was hard to breathe, and when he tried to move it felt like he was being stabbed by a dozen knives at the same time. Leah crawled from under the shield he had made of his body. He wanted to tell her to be careful, not to cut her hands and knees on the glass and sharp pieces of wood.

She rested a small hand on his cheek. "Daddy, wake up."

He blinked at her, tried to smile.

"Daddy, get up." She tugged at his arm.

"Leah," he croaked.

"Get up, get up." When he didn't move, she hugged him, and he felt her little body shake as a tear landed on his cheek. Dean fought to rise, biting back a scream of pain as he got his palms under him and pushed up, hissing.

Boots crunched through the ruins of the house, and Dean heard his daughter gasp as hands gripped his ankles and dragged him through the wreckage and outside. Then Leah's voice began screaming inside the house.

L ooks like he had a nice little stockpile in there," Stark said, standing in front of the burning garage and looking at the scattered supplies from Dean's preload. "Shame it's wasted."

Red Hen picked up the melted remains of a fiberglass compound bow. "This looks like it would have been fun," the biker said, sling-ing the bow back into the ashes of the garage.

Lassiter backed out of the house dragging a man facedown by his ankles. Blood soaked the man's sweater in a dozen places, and the hair at the back of his head was matted and wet. The scavenger stripped a custom leather shoulder holster from the groaning figure and slipped it on, admiring the MAC-10 machine pistol with its tubelike flash suppressor. He also took the holstered Glock from the man's hip and clipped it to his own belt.

Little Emer emerged last, carrying a struggling little girl in his arms. Her fists beat at his neck and shoulder, but he didn't appear to notice either her blows or her cries. The warlord looked down at the man on the ground and signaled for the others to flip him onto his back. Dean's face was bruised and covered in blood. His chest had a few shrapnel wounds, not as bad as his back.

Dean tried to speak, but it came out as a wheeze, and he reached for the image of his daughter in the biker's arms in slow motion. Little Emer looked down at him without expression.

"Crucify this," he told Lassiter, kicking Dean in the ribs. "We'll see you at the church." Then he grinned at Lassiter. "I think you'd look good in Skinners colors."

"Damn right," said Stark, and Red Hen clapped Lassiter on the back. Lassiter smiled so broadly he felt his face might split. He fol-lowed the bikers back to the street, dragging Dean.

Little Emer made a twirling motion in the air to Corrigan, who was still standing in his turret. The deserter gave commands to his men. As Lassiter unstrapped the heavy wooden cross from the rear deck of the armored vehicle, the biker warlord straddled his Harley and pinned Leah against his lap. The little girl struggled and wailed, crying, "Daddy!"

"Shh," said Little Emer. "I'm your daddy and we're gonna let you play with your new brothers and sisters."

Little Emer Briggs throttled up the street, his biker brothers following and the rumbling Bradley trailing last. Lassiter watched them go, then leaned the heavy wooden cross against the broken wall of the convenience store.

Russo stood nearby, his eyes moving between Lassiter and the departing shapes of the Bradley and the bikers. There was nothing he could do to save that little girl. *It's not your problem,* he told himself. And now he would witness yet another crucifixion. *He's not your problem either. Be smart. Now is not the time. The smartest thing to do is keep going along and slip away at a time of your choosing.* Russo knew he was no hero. After all that he had seen and done, he wondered if he even qualified as human anymore.

Lassiter dragged Dean over and propped him into a sitting position against the base of the cross, then produced a hammer and heavy nails from his backpack. Dean was still trying to get up, but his chin was on his chest, his head pounded, and he had to grit his teeth against the stabbing of a dozen sharp wounds.

Lassiter crouched beside him, setting his AK-47 on the ground and showing him the hammer. "This," he said, "is going to hurt."

Angie, Skye, and Carney ran through the streets dodging drifters, the creatures emerging from between houses and staggering into the road. The trio shoved them aside and kept moving. They had already lost sight of the small convoy and before long could no longer hear the engines. Still they ran. When the crash of the auto-cannon began, followed soon by the rattle of a machine gun, they altered course and picked up the pace. When the firing stopped after only a minute, they had a pretty good idea of the direction and distance.

They ran past a vacant lot with a four-foot pile of charred bodies, the remains of Chico's attempt at containment. Not far beyond was a motel with an abandoned ambulance parked outside the office. All of the doors to the rooms stood open, and a fat black crow perched upon an overturned maid's cart. Drifters wandered through the parking lot, and within the fenced swimming pool out front, a pair of water-bloated corpses stood floundering in the shallows, unable to pull themselves out.

A dead man in the uniform of a cola delivery driver lunged at Carney from between a pair of parked cars. The ex-con pistol-whipped the creature on the run, then put a silenced bullet in its head with Skye's handgun.

Angie abruptly stopped running. "Do you hear that?"

Skye and Carney listened. It was distant, a child screaming.

Then Angie was running again, her two companions trying to keep up. They traveled two more blocks and made a turn. The grumble of an armored vehicle's engine echoed over the rooftops to their left.

"We went too far," Angie shouted, running up a new street. They could smell burned wood and the cordite stink of spent gunpowder.

Angie slid to a stop in the next intersection. On the corner stood the shattered remains of a building, a black Ford pickup parked on the road out front. A young man in a knit cap was holding a shotgun, watching another man who was standing a third up against a big wooden cross.

The one about to be crucified rolled his head to the right, exposing his bloody face.

"*Dean!*" Angie screamed, raising her Galil.

That's enough," Russo said softly, pulling the shotgun's trigger. A blast of double-aught buckshot hit Lassiter in the side, pitching him away from the man about to be crucified, throwing the former armored-car driver onto a sidewalk bright with his own blood. Then Russo dropped the weapon and raised his hands, facing the people in the street and closing his eyes to the expected hail of bullets about to cut him down.

Angie, Skye, and Carney all screamed at the young man in the knit cap, conflicting commands to lie down, not to move, to get on his knees. The man simply stood with his arms raised, eyes closed.

The body armor hadn't done a thing to protect him, Lassiter thought, not at a range of three feet. He struggled to breathe, to lift his head, hands pawing at the ground. *God, it hurt. Who had done this to him? Why wasn't Russo shooting back at whoever had done this?* He was cold, and he blinked at the gray starting to close in on his vision.

One blood-slicked hand found the pistol grip of his AK-47 on the ground nearby, and with a groan he lifted it, triggering a short, unaimed burst off to his right.

Angie cried out at the sudden gunfire, dropping into a crouch and returning fire on instinct at the man on the ground. A three-round burst hit the body, making it jump, and the Russian assault rifle fell from a twitching hand.

Skye crouched too, ready to cut down the man in the knit cap, but he remained standing, arms raised, his shoulders jumping at the gunfire. She kept her finger on the trigger, the M4's sights on the man's chest, but she didn't fire.

Dean!" Angie cried again, running to her husband. She dropped to her knees on the ground beside him, taking his face in her hands. "Oh, God, Dean," she sobbed.

He looked at her, blinking for a moment. "Ang?"

She cried and held him.

Skye put a safety shot into Lassiter's head, then ordered the man in the knit cap to his knees, telling him to lace his fingers behind his neck as she had seen them do on reality cop shows. The man complied. Rifle still pointed at her prisoner's chest, Skye called back over her shoulder, "Carney, bring up some zip ties." He didn't reply.

Angie looked into her husband's eyes, still holding him. "Where's Leah?" she whispered, dreading the answer. "Is she . . . ?"

Dean stared back, his voice barely audible. "They took her."

A mother's cry was cut short by Skye's flat voice behind her. "Angie."

Angie turned to see Skye kneeling on the pavement beside Carney, the man stretched out flat, his head cradled in the young woman's lap, eyes closed. His throat had a bullet hole in it just beneath the Adam's apple, and a second black hole had been punched just above his left eyebrow, the result of the short burst Lassiter had been able to fire before going down himself.

"He's gone," Skye choked.

TWENTY-SEVEN

January 13—Southeast Chico

He won't turn, Skye thought, stroking Carney's head in her lap. *I won't have to hurt him.* She looked at the strong face, the shape she had come to know. Here was the face that made her heart race when he entered a room. Now it caused an ache so deep and terrible she wondered if she was having a heart attack. Tears welled in her good eye and dropped to Carney's forehead, where she brushed them away with her fingertips.

A hand came gently to rest on her back, and Angie's soft voice said, "The dead are coming."

Of course they are, Skye thought. *Coming to devour life, to consume every trace of what life meant.* She looked at Carney's closed eyes, wishing the lids would open so she could see that blue. Those eyes had looked at her and seen past the wounds and bleached skin, beyond the hardness. They had seen a woman.

He had loved her.

Skye had loved him too, and wished she had said the words to him just once.

"We have to go," Angie said. "I need cover so I can move Dean."

Skye nodded, taking Carney's face in her hands, leaning down to touch their foreheads together, to softly kiss his lips. She knew what he would say. *Don't waste time with my body. I won't feel anything, anyway.* Skye could hear his voice speaking the words and she smiled even as the tears fell, gently lowering his head to the pavement.

Together, the two women helped Dean into the cab of Lassiter's Ford, Skye pausing twice to fire the M4 in both directions, eliminating those drifters that were closest. The noise from the assault had stimulated the dead, and stiff-moving corpses were appearing at both ends of the street.

Dean said something to Angie about the house, then closed his eyes and leaned back against the seat while his wife ran into the ruins. On the street, Skye stripped Lassiter of his pack and weapons: the AK-47, spare magazines, Dean's Glock and MAC-10. Then she recovered her silenced pistol from Carney and pocketed a big folding knife he always carried.

Russo didn't speak or resist as Skye stripped him of his pack and weapons, then pushed him facedown on the asphalt, planting a boot between his shoulder blades as she secured his wrists with zip ties. Then she used the M4 to clear out more drifters that had drawn close while she was loading. Many more followed these advance stragglers, and she knew they wouldn't be able to stay long. An open street was no place to make a stand.

Angie emerged from the shattered house with an extra M4 and magazine bandolier in one hand, and a very dusty Wawas in the other. "What about him?" Angie asked, pointing to the prone and trussed film student.

"He's coming too," Skye said, pulling the young man to his feet, marching him around to the tailgate and shoving him up and in.

Angie drove and used the big bumper to push the dead aside until they broke clear onto another street, then followed Dean's directions to where he had concealed the truck for his and Leah's intended escape.

In the back, Skye did not watch Carney's body as it fell behind.

She looked at the young man who sat in the truck bed with her, his head down.

Dean had hidden the red Chevy Tahoe in a three-bay auto body garage, and they were able to park Lassiter's truck in the farthest bay, leaving space between the two vehicles. The closed roll-up doors shielded them from view. Working in the front seat of the Ford, Angie stripped Dean bare-chested so she could tend to his wounds. He hadn't been hit by any bullets, and it was all fragment injuries, none of the pieces so deep she couldn't grab them with long tweezers. The timbers and collapsing roof of the little house, combined with Dean's lifetime of fitness-hardened muscles, had slowed the penetration.

Still, it was painful, bloody work to remove them, and in no time the truck cab looked like a trauma room floor, wet with blood and littered with red-soaked gauze. As Angie worked, Dean closed his eyes and clenched his teeth, refusing to cry out but unable to keep from gasping when she had to dig deep.

Angie tried to keep her mind on her work, tried not to think about Leah and the man who had her. Tried not to think about what he might do. She needed Dean whole—as whole as she could get him, anyway. The man had wanted to go looking for their daughter at once, even shouted it at Angie, but she had prevailed upon him that she needed to bind his wounds at a minimum before they went anywhere.

And they needed time to gather information.

Angie removed a fragment, then packed the wound with anti-septic cream and gauze, taping down a bandage. "You're going to look like a mummy," she said, keeping her eyes on her work. She had cleaned the blood from Dean's face with alcohol wipes, revealing gaunt cheeks and dark circles beneath his eyes.

"I thought you were dead," he said.

"I thought you both . . ." She wouldn't look at him, didn't want him to see the tears. They fell anyway.

Dean reached up and touched her face with his fingertips, and she closed her eyes, leaning into his hand. "We're going to get her back," he said.

She looked at him then. "Yes, we will." Angie told him she had a Black Hawk waiting for them up the canyon, and that there was a safe place for them to go, people who would help protect their little girl.

He laughed, wincing at the pain. "Of course you brought a helicopter. I'd expect nothing less. Did you bring an army too?"

Angie looked out the side window, at the quiet young woman in the garage, dressed in black and armed for war. "As a matter of fact, I did."

Skye sat in a metal folding chair, three feet from her bound captive. She had found a chair for Russo as well, and now the man sat staring back at her with a mixture of wariness and resignation.

"You're going to talk to me, now," Skye said. "You're going to tell me everything you know, and answer any questions I have. Understand that the only reason I didn't kill you immediately was that you shot that other man. The only reason you're *still* alive is that I have a use for you."

Russo nodded, looking into a face devoid of emotion.

"I don't care about you," Skye said, pulling Carney's folding knife from a pocket and opening the blade. "So it won't bother me to hurt you if I have to."

Russo took a deep breath. "You won't need that." Then he started talking.

. . .

B y the time Russo was five minutes into his tale, Skye had folded up Carney's unused knife and put it back in her pocket. The man had no love for the bikers who were in control of the town and gave up whatever information he could: the location of the church, the wall of shipping containers, places where he knew sentries were posted and how they were armed (as best he could describe), information about the Bradley and its crew, even a description of the dog runs made of living corpses. He told her what he knew of the bikers and specifically Little Emer, and he talked about the playpen.

Russo looked down when he spoke of that horror.

Skye let him talk, only interrupting him on occasion when she needed something clarified. It was quickly clear to her that although Russo was something of an asshole, he seemed to have a conscience, and he was ashamed. She could see that he was trying in his own way to make amends, and although she couldn't quite bring herself to console him, she also couldn't make herself hate him. They were nearly the same age, but there were vast differences in their experiences. Russo had sold his soul in order to take refuge with a group. Skye had sold hers for solitude and the single-minded pursuit of destruction.

When he was finished, Russo looked up, speaking hesitantly. "I'm sorry about your friend."

Skye stood abruptly, making Russo flinch, and Carney's knife appeared in her hand, the blade snapping open.

"No, wait!" Russo shouted.

Skye stepped to him and he jerked away. She moved behind him and he tensed, waiting for the cold steel against his throat. Instead, the blade parted the plastic zip ties binding his wrists.

"Get up," Skye said, her voice cracking. She turned away so he could not see her good eye. "Get out of here."

Russo stood there dumbly.

When Skye turned to face him, her single eye was moist, but her face had a hard set to it. "I'm not giving you a gun, and you can scavenge your own supplies. You're getting your life."

Russo nodded rapidly, staring.

She took a step toward him, and he backed away. "They better not find out we're coming," Skye said, "or I'll know where they got their information. Then I'll be hunting *you* instead."

The man nodded once more.

"If I see you again," she said, giving him a push toward the garage's side door, "you won't have time to regret it."

Russo didn't say a word, just hurried out the door, the metal banging closed behind him. Skye sat again in the folding chair, put her head down, and allowed herself to cry.

An hour later, freshly bandaged, Dean told Angie and Skye what he knew about the raiders, both from his encounters and from what he had intercepted over the radio. Skye filled in the rest from her conversation with Russo and finally told them about the playpen. As she spoke, her voice was flat, hollow, her eyes dark and without depth. Husband and wife caught their breath, tears in their eyes.

"We've been sitting here!" Angie shouted. "She could already be in there!"

Skye looked at the other woman. "You need a clear head," she said in that dead tone. Skye showed them the location of Saint Miguel on the Chico map, and they quickly planned a daylight assault. With the Hydras broken, they had no way to call Vladimir in for an evacuation, so once they had Leah they would drive up the canyon and find him.

When Dean pointed at the map and began to speak about Skye's position during the attack, the young woman shook her head.

"I'm not going."

Angie blinked. "What do you mean? You said you were in no matter what, and we need you. Skye, this is my daughter."

"I know," said Skye, "and I am in, but you and Dean will hit the compound alone."

"Where will you be?" Dean asked.

Skye rested her index finger on Saint Miguel, shown on the map with a red circle drawn around it. "You've seen what that Bradley can do. It will stop your assault before you even get close."

Dean nodded slowly.

"So I'm going to take it out," Skye said in her dead voice.

"That's crazy!" Angie looked from Skye to Dean and back again. "By yourself? That's suicide."

Skye stared back with one eye. "I'm still going to do it. I'll keep it away from the compound so you two can get Leah."

"Carney was a good man," Angie said, "and he wouldn't want you to throw your life away like this."

"Carney isn't here."

Angie blinked as she realized she was seeing the Skye Dennison she had first met back in Alameda, a young woman with an icy hand cradling her heart. "Dying won't bring him back," said Angie. "How can you hope to even hurt that thing?"

Skye pointed at the fifty-caliber Barrett resting on its bipod on the garage floor, and Dean nodded. "I can tell you where to hit it," he said quietly. "It has weak points, but not many."

Angie shook her head. "Tell her not to do this, Dean."

Skye collected the heavy sniper rifle, closed the bipod, and slung the weapon across her back. Angie looked at her friend. "So that's it? You're done?"

The younger woman picked up the bandolier of fifty-caliber magazines. "Not yet."

. . .

Two garage bays rolled open, and a pair of pickups rolled into the street, one black, one red. The trucks stopped at an intersection, Skye pulling up alongside in the black Ford. In the other truck's passenger seat, Dean was slouched low and he nodded at her. The two women shared a long look before Skye turned right and drove away. Angie watched until she turned again and moved out of sight.

Angie's eyes began to harden along with her heart as she envisioned destroying those who had taken her daughter. In that moment, a cold mask slipped into place over her features, a mask without expression and devoid of mercy. She looked at her husband wearing Lassiter's damaged body armor and holding the man's AK-47, his own Glock and MAC-10 back where they belonged. He gave her a grimace of pain and encouragement, then squeezed her hand. Angie turned left.

They were going to get their little girl back, and the hunt was on.

Hours later, to the west of Chico, a rusting Jeep Cherokee climbed an on-ramp to northbound Interstate 5. In the back were a spare can of gasoline, a few canvas bags of food and water bottles, and a sleeping bag. On the passenger seat was a fire axe.

The Jeep's grill was mangled and the hood streaked with gore from the zombies it had slammed into on its way out of town, but the engine ran well. A gas station map rested on the seat beside the axe, depicting Northern California and the Oregon border.

Russo's racing heart began to slow as he reached the highway and headed north, weaving between abandoned vehicles and steadily leaving Chico behind. He didn't know what sort of future awaited him, out here on his own. Probably a short one. He decided it would at least be a future of his choosing, and that was enough.

TWENTY-EIGHT

Little Emer sat on his throne in the silent chapel, shafts of sunlight piercing the gloom through shattered stained-glass windows and a hole in the roof up where the bell tower had been. That structure, weakened by the first tremor, had completely collapsed when the much larger quake struck, taking one of the lookouts with it.

The man's moans of hunger could be heard from deep within the rubble.

Stark and Red Hen, Wahrman the Grower, and Little Emer's daddy waited in silence on the steps leading up to the throne. Corrigan and his two Bradley crewmen stood to one side. None of them spoke.

"They'll be coming," Little Emer said. "I don't know how many."

There had been no radio contact with the group he had sent up the canyon to look for the Black Hawk. Lassiter and Russo had not checked in. Little Emer was assuming they were all dead. He also assumed that Garfield, who had jumped to his death after Little Emer pushed his son into the playpen, had been wrong. There was more opposition out there than three people looking for a man and a kid.

The little girl's father was dead by now, he was sure, nailed to a cross. The kid belonged to Little Emer. At first that seemed like leverage; his enemies wouldn't dare try anything as long as he was holding the girl. Now, however, that reasoning felt hollow, untrue. Now the girl's presence felt more like provocation, an invitation to attack. He just couldn't be sure.

"Assume they'll hit us in strength," the warlord told the men gathered around him. "Put everyone we have on the walls." He looked at the three men in the shadows. "Corrigan, what's the best thing to do with Baby?"

"Get me outside," the deserter said. "I'll circle the block. Have your people on the walls radio me if they make contact."

"Make it happen," Little Emer said, waving his hand.

Dismissed by the great lord, Corrigan thought. *If he survives this, he won't survive me.* The deserter knew that he and his Bradley had been doing all the heavy lifting: taking out the helicopter, blowing apart survivor strongholds, creating the fear that kept everyone in line. When this was over, Corrigan decided, he would take his rightful place on that throne. *He* would be the warlord, and this biker scum would be food for his armored vehicle's tracks. The man left with his two crewmen. Minutes later, the Bradley engine grumbled to life in the parking lot outside.

Stark and Red Hen gathered ammunition from a pile against the wall, then left to give orders to the men and women patrolling the shipping containers. The grower stood with his hands in his pockets, still wearing sunglasses and staring at his toes as he wiggled them in his sandals. Little Emer's father suppressed a series of coughs with a blood-speckled handkerchief and climbed the stairs, standing next to his son.

"It's turning to shit," the elder Briggs said.

"No, it isn't. I've got it under control."

The older man sneered. "The hell you do." He pointed to a side door that led from the sanctuary behind the throne, a small room where the priest had once dressed and prepared for mass. The little girl his son had kidnapped was locked inside. "Why in God's name did you bring her here? *She's* what's going to draw them, you know."

"She's a hostage," Little Emer replied.

"She's a death magnet."

"So she draws them into our guns," the warlord said. "That just makes it easier."

The old man began coughing again, a long, violent stretch that bent him over with his handkerchief pressed to his lips. Eventually it trailed off to a rattle. The son watched his father in disgust. After the coughing stopped and the older man took a few moments to breathe, he said, "Those guns you're talking about? I think you're putting an awful lot of faith in those people on the wall."

"They've fought before. They're loyal."

Big Emer snorted. "They're not. They're scared of you, and that's not the same thing. And who exactly have they fought? Frightened, starving people hiding behind barricaded doors. Old men and women."

"They'll do what I tell them," said Little Emer. He was getting tired of the old man constantly telling him he was wrong.

The elder Briggs shook his head. "They fought everyday people, and when they did, there were more of them. That was before their friends started going out on your orders and not coming back." The man wiped his mouth with the handkerchief. "Those are professional shooters coming this way, Junior. That militia of yours is going to die fast, and those who don't will jump that wall and run."

The biker laughed. "Some advisor you are, nothing but bad news."

"I'm telling you the truth, son."

"*Don't* call me that." Little Emer stood abruptly, and his father took a step back. At the base of the stairs, Wahrman watched with eyes unreadable behind his shades, but his hands were no longer in his pockets.

"I've still got the Bradley," the biker said.

"And I told you not to trust Corrigan," said his father. "He takes care of himself."

"I have the kid," Little Emer said, continuing as if he hadn't heard the old man. "Everything I need."

"Except brains." The old man stifled another cough and looked at his son with runny yellow eyes. "Even if you stay, even if you win, what do you think will be left of your stupid little empire?"

"What do you mean, 'even if I stay'? Who says I'm leaving?"

"I'm saying you should." The old man's voice was a wheeze. "We all should," he said, gesturing at the two of them and the grower. "Just pack up and head out the back while everyone's watching the front."

"Run out on my brothers?"

Big Emer made a sour face. "So bring those morons along if you have to. Let your gunmen create a diversion and we'll split, find a place to start over."

Little Emer looked at his father. There had been a time not so very long ago when he had been considering that very thing. But it had been *his* idea then. Now here was his daddy, treating him like a kid who couldn't make his own decisions.

"It's gone too far for that," the biker said.

The elder Briggs's normally waxy face bloomed. "Oh, bullshit! You're being a child." He poked the biker hard in the chest. "Listen up, *boy*. You killed their family and turned their parents into those things."

The warlord looked down at the yellow-stained finger. "Don't do that," he said softly.

The old man poked him again. "You stole their kid."

"I told you to stop."

Another hard jab. "They *will* come and take your head for it!"

Little Emer grabbed his father's finger and in a quick, brutal wrench bent it back across the old man's hand with a snap. His father screamed and went to his knees. At the base of the steps, Wahrman made a move for his shoulder holster.

The warlord's pistol was already in his hand. Eight blasts echoed through the chapel, driving the grower back with hits to the chest, neck, and face. The body hit the marble floor with a dull thud.

Little Emer was still holding his daddy's finger as the old man knelt before him. He pressed the hot barrel of the automatic against the old man's face in a hot kiss, and Big Emer cried out again. The warlord released the finger.

"Go find a rifle, old man. Then find yourself a place on the wall."

The elder Briggs cradled his hand and walked slowly out of the chapel, bent over and coughing, not looking at the body of his dead friend. The warlord watched him go, then keyed his way into the small room off the sanctuary. Leah was sitting on the edge of a chair, her round cheeks wet with tears.

"I want my daddy," she said.

"I told you who your new daddy was. But right now, let's go see Grandma."

The pungent ripeness of the dead had finally erased all trace of chlorine. It hung in the air like a brown cloud, clinging to everything. From the pool rose the shuffle of dozens of little feet, accompanied by hungry snarls. Against the far wall, Lenore Franks growled and tugged at her chains.

Little Emer tugged Leah along by one arm, jerking sharply when she dragged her feet. She was crying. "Look, it's Grandma," the biker said, holding the little girl's face and forcing her to look at the rotten thing struggling against the wall.

"*Not* Gramma!" she said, pulling away.

He pulled her to the edge of the pool. "And here's your brothers and sisters."

Leah saw the agitated corpses, all about her age. "Icky," she said. "Bad boys."

The biker laughed, the sound echoing through the high-ceilinged room. "Don't you want to go down and play? There's toys down there."

Leah tried to run, but he held firm. Little Emer stood her back at the edge. "They want to play with *you*."

"Bad boys. *Bad* boys!" Leah shook a finger at the mass of small, reaching bodies.

Little Emer placed a hand against her back. *Perhaps she could be a shield. Or maybe just one last push, for old times' sake.*

B ig Emer Briggs did not find himself a place on the wall, but he did find a rifle, an M16 with a handful of loaded magazines. He made his way to the greenhouse, glancing at the empty lawn chair outside the door. Andrew Wahrman had been his friend since before his son was born, and now he was gone.

A cough rumbled in his chest, and Briggs bit it back with difficulty, pushing into the greenhouse. The humidity and sweet aroma of weed hit him, but it failed to put the usual smile on his face. The grow meant nothing now. None of this shit did.

He moved down the leafy rows and into the small tool room where he kept a cot. Within ten minutes he had packed a pair of canvas gym bags with clothes, weapons, and food. These he carried to the flatbed truck parked beside the greenhouse and dropped them in the cab along with the M16. Then he took the time to fill half a dozen plastic jugs with water.

Son or not, Little Emer was dead to him now. Let him go down fighting if that was what he wanted. Big Emer was dying, the number of his remaining days counted in weeks now probably, but he wasn't suicidal. Any fear or worry he might have had for his son's life had evaporated, replaced by the agony of a broken finger, a murdered friend, and the madness seething behind a warlord's flat, dead eyes.

He took three trips to load the water jugs into the cab of the truck, then reentered the greenhouse one last time to collect his plastic tub of handpicked, fragrant buds. When he came out, tub tucked under one arm, he found his son standing at the truck, leaning back against the cab door and holding an Uzi low at his side.

"Time to bail, Daddy?"

His father stopped and stared. Little Emer stood between him and the assault rifle inside the truck.

"What are you going to do, Daddy, crash the back gate? Leave it wide open while you drive away, so the dead come inside to keep us busy?"

Big Emer swallowed hard. That was *exactly* what he had intended to do.

"My daddy is running out on me again," the warlord said. "I may cry."

The elder Briggs dropped the plastic tub of weed, heavy buds scattering across the ground. There was only one way to survive this. "Who do you think you're talking to, boy?"

Little Emer said nothing, and the old man took a step forward. "You think you've got balls?" the old man said. "You think you can scare me? Why don't you piss yourself like you always did, little boy? Show everyone that you're really a scared little girl." Big Emer advanced another step, huffing small, wet coughs. "I'll beat the ears off the sides of your goddamned head!"

Little Emer smiled. *"Daddy,"* he hissed. His father saw the barrel of the Uzi rise a half second before a long burst cut him down.

B ig Emer strained against the leash, the leather dog collar cutting into the cold skin of his throat, a pain he could not feel. The chain gave him about four feet of slack from where it was anchored to the front bumper of the flatbed truck.

On the ground just out of reach was meat, a man in sunglasses and sandals, covered in sweet-smelling blood. Big Emer's milky eyes widened and he let out a long moan, reaching, reaching, reaching.

TWENTY-NINE

January 13—East of Chico

Halsey and Vladimir watched a girl of about nineteen limp up the fairway toward where Groundhog-7 sat near the ninth hole. She had been Hispanic, her skin now a mottled black and gray, and she wore a belly shirt and great hoop earrings that swung when she moved. Much of the flesh had been bitten away from her left arm, exposing bone, and several fingers were missing from the hand on the same side.

A dozen or more drifters shambled after her.

Halsey had the Winchester resting back over his shoulder. He had left the .22 and the scoped rifle in the tower. "Don't think I can make a head shot at this range," he said, "not with these open sights, anyway. The thirty-thirty ain't much for distance."

Vladimir walked to the helicopter's troop compartment. Angie and the others had not been able to take all the gear when they left for Chico; there hadn't been enough room in the Polaris. Still lashed to the metal deck was a case of MREs, a pair of M4s, and a five-hundred-count can of 5.56-millimeter. He loaded the M4's maga-zine and handed it to his friend.

Halsey examined the rifle, not so very different from the M16 he had trained with during his time in the service, seemingly a lifetime ago. But as was often the case, time could not completely erase training, and what he had learned about military rifles so long ago came back quickly. He immediately saw and felt that this weapon was better than the M16 of his youth: more durable, higher-quality manufacturing, and the sight optics were first rate.

His first round hit the Hispanic girl just below the neck and to the left, shattering her collarbone. She stumbled and her left shoulder sagged, but otherwise her slow, relentless pace was unchanged.

"That felt pretty good," Halsey remarked, adjusting the lumines-cent green chevrons within the sight and firing again. This bullet hit her square on the chin, knocking her down. She stood up a moment later, her lower jaw obliterated and looking like ground beef sprin-kled with bone bits.

"Gonna take some getting used to," the ranch hand said. Halsey was right-handed, and that elbow, grazed the night before by a bullet, ached when he held it elevated for any period of time, as he did while shooting. The bullet in his calf forced him to adjust his stance, but it was his chin, torn to the bone, that filled his head with red-tinted pain every time it was jolted, which meant movement of any kind.

His daddy would have looked over the top of his glasses and simply told him to be a man.

Halsey's next shot hit the mark and put the girl down for good.

"Unfortunately," said the pilot, watching from nearby, "there are no spare magazines other than what is in the other rifle."

"Load that one as a backup, just in case," Halsey said.

"That is bold talk for a man who used three rounds to make a single kill."

The ranch hand shrugged, closing his eyes briefly at the stab in his chin, and gestured with the rifle barrel down the fairway toward the crowd of drifters. "By the time I sort them out, I should be okay." He looked back at the Russian. "And I'm not boasting about not needing the second magazine. I just don't believe in wasting ammo."

Vladimir retrieved the ammunition can and the second rifle, loading the magazine slowly while his friend shot. It turned out that the cowboy didn't need the second magazine. He had cleared the field with three rounds to spare.

"I suppose it'll do," he said, gingerly spitting tobacco so as not to disturb his wounded chin too much. "Far from proficient. I'd say comfortable." He set to reloading the magazine.

The Russian was holding the Winchester. "This is a cowboy rifle," he said, running his hands over the smooth, dark wood, "from the movies, yes?"

"Winchesters were around long before there were such things as movies," Halsey said. "It's a thirty-thirty lever-action, shit on long range but a good close-to-medium brush gun."

Vladimir frowned, trying to follow.

"It'll bring down a deer and do plenty of damage to a man, I'm here to tell you."

The Russian raised it to his shoulder, enjoying the smooth, warm feel of the wood stock against his cheek. "I like this weapon. You will teach me to use it when there is time?"

"Sure. But don't think you'll be twirling that lever like *True Grit*."

Vlad confessed he did not know what *True Grit* was.

Halsey looked at him incredulously. "You're not kidding, are you?" When the Russian shook his head, he asked, "How about *Unforgiven*?"

"*Nyet*."

"*The Long Riders*? *Silverado*? Hell, what cowboy movies *have* you seen?"

"*Tombstone*," Vladimir said. "With Kirk Russet."

Halsey laughed and winced. "Kurt Russell. Yeah, that one was pretty good. Well, you're in for a treat, my friend. I imagine we'll be able to pick up a whole pile of westerns with no one to tell us otherwise. I assume this aircraft carrier of yours has a DVD player?"

The Russian assured him it did. "You have reconciled yourself to returning with us, then?"

"Yep. Unless you're planning on dropping me back at the cabin, but I don't think it's too hospitable anymore." He spat. "That window has closed."

Vladimir smiled. "As I said, *tovarich*, you will be most welcome." When Halsey shook his head slowly, Vlad explained that the word meant *friend*, and then it was Halsey's turn to smile.

The two men waited throughout the morning, Halsey explaining the workings of a ranch, and Vladimir talking about life back in Russia, and what it meant to him to be an aviator. The ranch hand heard about Sophia and Ben, his adopted family waiting for the pilot back on the ship, and he couldn't help but notice the way the homely Russian beamed when he spoke about them.

They complained about their wounds in the casual way of men, pretending they didn't hurt all *that* much, and shared a canteen when it was time for more aspirin. Every so often Halsey would make a tour around the Black Hawk to ensure that no drifters were stalking up behind them.

The Hydra radio rested between them, still silent. Vladimir attempted to reach his companions twice every hour, without response.

"You said all three of them had radios?" Halsey asked.

Vlad nodded, frowning deeply.

"Don't want to sound obvious or morbid," said Halsey, "but it doesn't seem likely they'd all crap out at once."

"No, it does not." Vladimir had been nervous about calling them at first, fearing they might be hiding quietly someplace and trying to avoid detection. His transmission could put them in jeopardy, and Angie had said she would call him when it was time for an extraction. It had been quite some time since last contact, though, and his worry had overruled his fear of exposing them at a crucial moment. "I fear the worst," the pilot said.

Halsey just nodded and looked out at the golf course.

The Russian began to pace, head down and hands in his pockets, limping a circle around the helicopter. After fifteen minutes and four circles, he stopped and clapped his hands together sharply. "Time to go."

"Figured as much," Halsey said. He patted the barrel of the M240 door gun. "You still want me behind one of these things?" The training Vlad had provided was limited to reloading, clearing weapon jams, and the basics of aiming. Halsey had yet to fire any live rounds.

"Yes," said the Russian. "Clip into your safety harness and keep your headset on. I will give firing directions at first."

"I reckon in short order I'll have to pick my own targets."

"*Da*. By then you will know what to shoot at, and this is a complicated aircraft, requiring my full attention. I cannot be distracted by a farmer who needs me to explain the difference between mud and pig shit."

"I'll do my best not to disturb Your Majesty."

"I like that," said the Russian. "Feel free to address me with that title whenever you please."

"Got a few more names for you, Ivan."

"Your Majesty will do quite nicely."

Five minutes later they were airborne.

Vladimir flew them back over Halsey's ranch. It took only a few minutes to cover the distance by air, and they settled into a slow rotation, both men looking down at the place that had been Halsey's home for so many years. The Stampede, grown to over three thousand strong, had lost its direction and now not only swarmed among the buildings and vehicles, thick as maggots on roadkill, but also wandered across the fields in all directions.

"They got into the cabin," Halsey said into the intercom. "Damn, I thought that door would hold."

"Enough constant pressure," the Russian said, remembering the fence line around NAS Lemoore, "and any barrier will fall. Better that you were in the air."

The raiders' pickups and motorcycles remained where they had been when the two men flew out in the predawn darkness. None of them had survived; they only served to strengthen the ranks of the dead. Vladimir pointed out a corpse wearing biker leathers with the image of crossed knives on its back. The sheer numbers of the walking dead below ensured there would be no landing to recover supplies or anything else Halsey might want from the cabin.

"I've seen enough," the ranch hand said.

"I did not bring you here to reminisce," the Russian said, "but to practice. Lean out as far as you dare and fire down onto their heads. It will increase your mathematical probability of achieving kills."

Halsey tipped the M240 almost straight down and put his faith in the safety harness, body extended over his weapon and open space. He fired short, hesitant bursts until he got used to the machine gun's vibration and kickback, then triggered it steadily, sweeping the M240 back and forth. Vlad had been right. Raining lead straight down on them, though far from surgical, resulted in plenty of head shots. He decided that if the fuel and bullets held out, they could clear the entire area in this manner. Both, however, were in finite supply.

The pilot let Halsey run through half a belt of ammunition before he began calling out specific targets. "Man in the red shirt" and "The big woman near your truck" and "Those two men in the cabin doorway." Vlad would swing the Black Hawk around to expose the targets to the door gun, and Halsey would have only seconds to identify, then gun down the target before Vlad jerked the aircraft away. He quickly learned that hitting individuals, especially with head shots from a jumping automatic weapon, was much more difficult than hovering above them and chopping them down with indiscriminate fire. The vibration was making his wounds throb as well, especially his elbow and chin.

Once the box of ammo was exhausted, Vladimir ordered Halsey to reload. The ranch hand would have to scramble on his butt to retrieve a can of belted ammunition from a storage space at the rear of the troop compartment, detach the empty can, secure the full can to the side of the M240, and then successfully feed the belt and arm the weapon. The Russian had instructed and drilled him on the process several times while the Black Hawk was safe and steady on the ground, but Halsey found it was another matter entirely on the move in the air. To make it more challenging, the pilot took the Black Hawk into high-speed turns, dropping low and buzzing over the heads of the reaching dead, then banking and climbing sharply.

In the back, Halsey fought to keep from sliding out the side door and almost dumped an entire can of ammunition out into space.

"Son of a bitch," he growled.

"Gunner, are you having difficulty?"

Halsey cursed. "Goddamned right." A thump and a hiss as his bullet-grazed elbow slammed into the steel deck. "Son of a bitch."

Vladimir snapped the Black Hawk left, and Halsey slid toward the opening but quickly stopped himself by bracing a boot against the weapon mount. The pilot had been watching over his shoulder and allowed himself a small smile.

"Perhaps I should fly level and slow," the Russian said over the intercom. "That way you might perform your tasks in ease and comfort."

Halsey unhooked the empty ammo can and pitched it out the door.

"And that would make us a big, slow-moving target for our enemies," Vlad continued.

"Dead things don't shoot back," Halsey muttered, attaching the fresh ammo can to the side of the weapon mount and snapping open the top of the M240. He braced himself as the Russian dove at the ground, then climbed again in a steep bank.

"Then," the Russian went on, "you will have the privilege to die in aerial combat, instead of being trampled to death by a milk cow."

Halsey fed the belt, closed the weapon, and hauled back on the arming handle with a loud click. "Right door gun is armed," he announced over the intercom.

"*Right?*" bellowed Vladimir. "There is no *right* on an aircraft! Port and starboard. Port and starboard!"

"Hey, buddy," Halsey said, "I've noticed there's some sort of metal stop built into this weapon mount that keeps me from pointing it into the cockpit."

Vlad leveled the chopper and began a long turn to bring them around to a westerly heading. "*Da*, and there is a very good reason for that."

"When we land, I'm gonna take that part off," said Halsey.

"You are assuming we will live long enough to stand on Mother Earth once again." Vlad lined up the nose of the bird with the gray ribbon of the Skyway below. "You are ready, *tovarich*?"

"Good to go, partner."

The Russian nodded. "Our friends are dead, or in need of assistance," the pilot said. "Either way, we are going to war."

The Black Hawk dipped low and accelerated toward Chico.

THIRTY

Skye lit the fuse, made sure the ropes were tight on the steering wheel, and dropped the transmission into drive. She ran across a yard and down a shadowy space between two houses, the fifty-caliber sniper rifle bouncing on her back.

Lassiter's jacked Ford F-250 rolled slowly toward one of the four intersections around Saint Miguel. In its bed, a tied-together line of rags soaked in gasoline led to a pair of open jerry cans lashed to the back of the cab and down into the truck's open fuel tank. As the fire leaped along the length of rags, the truck's grille closed on a line of decaying corpses leashed to a cable crossing the street.

Just as the bumper connected with a slumping body and pulled it under the front end, the pickup exploded.

Standing in the commander's hatch of the Bradley, Corrigan's head snapped to the right at the sudden explosion. He saw a black mushroom of smoke rising above and beyond Saint Miguel, just as the radio on his hip burst to life with a cry of "We're under attack!" A moment later, the rolling echo of a single heavy-caliber shot carried over the rooftops. Another voice on the radio shouted, "They're shooting! Jesus Christ, it took his fucking head off!"

Corrigan dropped into the Bradley and pulled the hatch closed above him. He wasn't about to let *his* head be next.

"Driver, take us to the next intersection and turn left. Gunner, stand by on the coaxial, and select HE for the main tube."

Low in the front left of the Bradley, Marx, the driver, gunned the diesel and moved swiftly to the intersection at the church's northwest corner. He rotated the tracks left, advancing toward a point a block away where a pickup was engulfed in flames, leashed and burning corpses bumping against its sides. Through the armored glass viewports set into the frame of his hatch, so thick they were blue, Corrigan could see armed figures running along the shipping container walls. They were headed toward where the fire was burning.

"Boss, we've only got a dozen HE left," the gunner reported. "The rest is all armor-piercing."

A dozen rounds of high-explosive? Corrigan thought. The twenty-five-millimeter would burn through that in seconds. Still, the high-explosive incendiary would tear apart vehicles and ground troops alike. There was just no way to replace the shells, unless he found an armory that hadn't been looted, and that was a fantasy.

What made him more anxious than running out of shells for the main gun was the idea of running into another Bradley, rolling at the head of a regular Army column here to retake Chico and punish Corrigan for his treason. Or perhaps a recon element probing their defenses. Was that what the single gunshot had been? The opening act of a full military assault? Little Emer said no, there were only a few well-armed shooters out there, but that was small comfort for Corrigan. The biker didn't know shit about war.

"Driver, take us into that intersection," Corrigan ordered. "Push that truck to the side."

Marx did as he was told, banging the sloped, armored face of the Bradley into the burning pickup and shoving it onto a lawn, where it flipped on its side, flaming tires belching black smoke. The armored vehicle drove over a trio of leashed corpses and broke the cable holding the others. The newly freed dead, most of them on fire, beat at the sides of the Bradley with their fists.

"Where are you?" Corrigan murmured, watching out his viewports.

Skye sighted on a woman lying prone atop the container wall, an assault rifle thrust out before her as she looked around frantically for something to shoot. Skye eased the trigger back, and the fifty-caliber slug hit the target at almost the same moment the heavy *crack* sounded from the rifle.

The bullet hit the woman under the armpit, as intended, nearly blowing her in half.

Time to relocate. Skye swung the rifle across her back and jumped down from the roof of a motor home where she too had been lying prone, more than a block away from the church. The moment she hit the ground, the machete cleared its scabbard so she could deal with the drifters in the street. Skye kept the blade especially sharp, and the damage caused when a full swing connected with a rotten head was startling.

She darted across the street and tucked in behind a Subaru wagon backed up close to a garage, laying the Barrett's long barrel and bipod along the rear bumper and sighting through the narrow gap. From this angle she could no longer see the church or its wall, but the intersection with the burning truck was right there at the other end of the block, and the Bradley revealed itself in all its armored glory as it shoved the truck out of the way.

"Let's see what you're made of," whispered Skye. Dean West had explained its armor: where it was thickest (most places), thinnest (not many), and where it might be most vulnerable. Skye's only job was to hit them and get the damned thing out of the area.

She squeezed the trigger.

She had been aiming for the barrel of the vehicle's 7.62-millimeter coaxial machine gun, mounted alongside the much bigger main gun tube. A fifty-caliber bullet would take out the machine gun, pulling one of the Bradley's teeth.

She missed, and the round whined off the thick front-slope armor. It did nothing more than leave a bright aluminum scratch in the paint.

Relocate! a voice screamed in her head, and she couldn't tell if it was her own or Postman's, maybe Taylor's, the dead National Guardsmen who had saved her life in Berkeley. Skye ran left, around the corner of the house, gripping the Barrett in both hands. A second later a rattle of explosive shells disintegrated the Subaru and half the garage.

Skye's boots slid to a stop on the grass, and she darted back behind the shredded remains of the Subaru, hoisting the Barrett and firing from the shoulder without bracing against anything, the weight making the cords in her arms jump out. The shot wasn't aimed beyond simply hitting the vehicle, which it did, glancing off turret armor.

As soon as she fired, she hauled ass back behind the house and kept running.

The Bradley's auto-cannon, now firing only high-explosive incendiary, tore apart what remained of the garage.

Skye bolted across the street to her left, hearing the big diesel thrum to life and send the Bradley up the block in pursuit. She bared her teeth savagely and ran for her next position.

Sergeant Scott Corrigan was not all he appeared to be, and nothing close to what he claimed. That he was Army and trained to command an M2 Bradley was accurate. That he was a murderous and hateful individual was also true, but it was here that fact and fiction parted.

The horrific scar that split his face was not a combat wound obtained overseas as he boasted, but the result of an industrial accident at a sheet metal plant where he had worked one summer. A combination of drinking and moving machinery not only maimed him but cost him his job.

Corrigan had never been active duty. He was a reservist; his unit was never deployed overseas and had in fact not been activated for anything serious until the outbreak of the Omega Virus. Before all this, Corrigan had never seen combat and thus lacked the experience earned by so many others who had faced clever, battle-hardened insurgents.

Despite his training, he failed to recognize that he was being led away from Saint Miguel.

This duel had now become a personal matter, and he kept up his pursuit, feeling invulnerable inside what was, for all practical purposes, a tank.

From her prone position behind a green curbside power company box, Skye watched the Bradley roar past the shattered garage and Subaru, stopping in the intersection. She put the Barrett's sight on the broad, flat flank of the vehicle and fired.

The round failed to penetrate.

She stood up in full view then, waiting until the turret began to swing in her direction, then sprinted up a side street as automatic weapon fire tore apart the power box, part of a lawn, and the front half of the house on the corner. Skye ducked into a backyard, then began vaulting fences, one after the other, just as she had done during her days in Oakland, but now without so much caution. If a drifter was waiting in the next yard, she wouldn't know it until she was in its arms. The roar of the Bradley's accelerating diesel floated over the rooftops.

Skye went over another fence, where a dead housewife stood swaying on a patio, bumping against a glass slider door. The corpse had barely started to turn when the young woman was through the yard and over the next fence.

She could have lost herself in the residential neighborhood, evaded the armored vehicle completely, but instead she measured her distance, wanting to only stay one block ahead. The Bradley had to stay in the game.

D river, left turn," Corrigan barked, straining to see through the thick observation blocks. He kept one hand on the commander's joystick, ready to take control of the main gun away from Lenowski if he saw his target. The Bradley turned up the new avenue, its left track crushing the rear end of a parked car.

"Boss," Lenowski said below him, "we're getting kind of far from the church."

"That's a sniper out there with a heavy-caliber rifle," Corrigan shot back. "We're not leaving her alone so she can pick at us when she pleases."

The gunner did not respond, and pressed his face back against the rubber cowling of his optics.

The Bradley prowled up the block and came to the point where the street met Chico's Esplanade, two broad, one-way streets divided by green space and trees. Several drifters stalked toward the vehicle, drawn by the noise, but nothing else moved. There was a sudden *bang* from the driver's compartment, followed by a man's scream.

"Marx, what happened?" Lenowski shouted.

"Bitch nearly blew my head off!" the driver yelled. "Blew out my viewport. Shit, my face is bleeding!"

"Where is she?" Corrigan demanded.

"Hell if I know," the driver shouted back, rising from his seat. "Fuck this, man."

"Sit back down," Corrigan snarled. "You leave your position and *I'll* take your head off. Now turn left."

"I can't see. The viewport is fucked."

"Then pop your hatch so you can see," Corrigan said.

There was silence in the Bradley then, as everyone considered what poking your head out of your hatch in sniper country would mean. Then came the soft click of the hammer easing back on Corrigan's .45. "Now," he said softly.

Marx popped his hatch a few inches, then pulled on his tanker's helmet and stuck his head up and out just enough to see what was in front of the Bradley. A drifter turned toward the sound of the opening hatch, then moaned and tried to claw its way up the sloping front armor to reach this new meal.

"Up yours," Marx muttered, driving over the corpse as he executed a left turn.

The deep crack of the Barrett arrived a quarter second after the bullet. Marx's head disintegrated in a cloud of pink, red, and white, sheared off at the bridge of his nose.

"Jesus Christ!" screamed the gunner.

Corrigan didn't make a sound and overrode the gunner's control of the turret, depressing the fire button for the twenty-five-millimeter auto-cannon. He had seen what looked like a flash of light on a scope lens, and now he poured incendiary rounds on the target.

Skye moved. She had been standing beside the front steps of a large granite building with a columned entrance, and she ran in a crouch across a lawn just as the steps and pillars disintegrated in multiple explosions. The blasts knocked her to the ground, and she lost hold of the Barrett as granite and steel fragments whined overhead. A hot piece of metal or stone slashed a red groove into the back of her neck, and a swarm of fragments buried themselves in her pack and body armor.

Alive. Move.

She scrambled to her feet, snatching the fifty-caliber off the ground and sprinting across a lawn and sidewalk, passing another large stone building. The architecture looked somehow familiar, and in an instant she realized where she was: the north end of the university. Skye had seen Chico State on the map, knew its approximate area and thus her position.

Machine gun fire tore up the turf at her heels and raked a stone wall ahead of her as she cut left, running as fast as she could between two buildings, looking for cover.

Too close. Too close.

The Bradley howled after her.

I see you, bitch!" Corrigan screamed. "Lenowski, take the driver's position. I'll handle the gun."

The gunner slipped out of his seat, moved forward, and dumped his headless friend to the side, then slid into the blood-slicked driver's chair. In a moment the Bradley was surging forward up the street, aiming for a wide space between two stately-looking stone university buildings.

Corrigan kept his face to his viewports, one hand flexing on the weapon control stick. "I see you," he growled.

Leaping over a suitcase lying on the sidewalk, Skye ducked right around the corner of the building and nearly fell over a hot-pink steamer trunk. She saw plastic totes and duffels of clothes, laptop bags and mini fridges strewn across an expanse of lawn, and came to a stop.

Chico State. It had happened on one of the moving-in days, just like at UC Berkeley. Her mouth opened silently and she stared as the memory flooded back, one of running, screaming people, sirens and gunshots, and her sister's dead eyes. She barely noticed the many drifters that turned and began moving toward her as she stood frozen as images flashed through her mind.

Something killing Dad in the parking lot.

Mom being eaten.

Crystal's eyes opening to her new *unlife*.

There was a snarl on her left and a thump as a drifter stumbled over the hot-pink trunk and fell. Another one lunged, the dried blood on its Wildcats T-shirt turned black, and it tripped over the first, banging its forehead against the trunk. They were everywhere, the walking dead in tattered clothing, flesh torn and pale, taking jerky steps and all staring at her with baleful eyes. A collective moan rose across the lawns as the creatures closed a circle about her.

The rumble of the Bradley's engine, the squeal of its tracks echoing off granite, snapped her back. It was following her between the buildings, cracking sidewalks and chewing up grass and corpses, preparing to chew her up as well. Skye ran, ripping her machete from its sheath and chopping down a dead man that came at her, burying it in the head of another and tugging the blade free, swinging again, making a hole she could dart through. She headed for the scant shelter of another stone-walled stairway, throwing the Barrett across a flat surface, raising the weapon on its tripod. The sound of the Bradley increasing speed roared off granite walls as Skye fed a fresh magazine into the sniper rifle.

As soon as the armored vehicle cleared the corner of the building and was out on the lawn, Skye braced the stock against her shoulder and fired four quick rounds, trying to keep a tight grouping. Even over the bellowing of a military diesel, the Barrett's reports echoed across the open, grassy space, bouncing off campus buildings where professors would never again speak.

Four black holes appeared in a cluster, penetrating the Bradley's side skin near the vehicle's front. Twenty-seven tons of armor bucked to a halt. At once, Skye had the rifle strap across her chest and was running again, heading for the far corner of the building while the turret whined and rotated behind her. She turned right—

—and a legless corpse rose up on its arms and hissed under her boots. Skye couldn't get her feet up high enough in time, and the tip of her right boot caught on its rib cage. She went down hard, twisting an ankle, and in a second the corpse was on her, teeth snapping at her right calf.

Skye screamed, rolling over and kicking it in the face. Its head rocked back, jaws working, cloudy eyes staring at her. Skye pulled her silenced pistol and shot it through one of those eyes, then scrambled to her feet and ran, favoring her right ankle.

Lenowski, why did we stop?" Corrigan shouted from the turret. He had rotated the main gun to the right, but the sniper was no longer in view. More than a dozen corpses were moving between the far buildings, indicating the direction she had fled, and dozens more were headed toward the Bradley, a few already arrived and beating at the armor with their fists.

The gunner-turned-driver did not respond.

Corrigan realized that something was sparking and smoking below him. The sniper had succeeded in damaging something, but he couldn't tell what. "Driver, right turn," Corrigan commanded.

The vehicle did not move.

"Lenowski!" Corrigan dropped from his seat to the lower deck, ducking his head and moving forward. To his right, several circles of daylight poked through the side armor, and an electrical box hung open where a bullet had ripped into it, fused wires giving off a curling, acrid smoke.

"Lenowski?" he repeated, grabbing the shoulder of the man in the driver's seat. The body slumped left and the head fell over at a sickening angle. There was blood everywhere, and Corrigan could see that the sniper's bullet had not only hit the man in the neck but severed his spine at the base of his skull. Lenowski's eyes stared in a perpetual state of surprise.

"Goddammit," Corrigan muttered, just as a pair of pale hands hauled the driver's hatch fully open, daylight spilling into the vehicle. A corpse began crawling down through the hole.

Corrigan fumbled for his sidearm as he backed up, smacking his head on the edge of the gunner's elevated seat. The creature scrambled over Lenowski and dropped onto the steel deck. Corrigan fired, missing, the bullet bouncing around the interior, making him cringe. A second, steadier shot from the .45 took off the top of the zombie's head.

Two more corpses fought to crawl down through the open hatch.

Corrigan cursed again and climbed back up to the commander's seat, looking through his viewports. He would have to abandon the Bradley and hunt the bitch down on foot. Fortunately, it looked like none of the dead had managed to climb as high as the turret. A short, cut-down assault rifle with a folding metal stock hung in clips beside the commander's seat, and he slung it over his shoulder as he popped the hatch above him and stood, taking a quick look around the outside of the vehicle to find his best exit route.

He saw her, a woman in black with a shaved head and an eye patch, standing on the street to the rear of his Bradley. The heavy length of a fifty-caliber Barrett was raised to her shoulder and pointed at him. Corrigan blinked at the sight. *No one tries to fire a Barrett like that!* Then he went for his assault rifle, swinging it up just as hands gripped his legs. Lenowski, head lying sideways on his shoulder, sank his teeth into the back of Corrigan's knee.

Corrigan never had a chance to scream. A fifty-caliber slug blew through his chest, taking his heart, a lung, and a length of vertebrae and exploding them out his back. The deserter's body sagged and was pulled down through the hatch by eager hands.

Skye watched the body fall, then ejected her empty magazine. As she reached for another, she caught movement out of the corner of her eye and turned to look.

A shirtless drifter with taut, shiny red skin was running at her from half a block away. Its eyes were locked on its target, teeth clicking.

Skye dropped the heavy sniper rifle and ran.

THIRTY-ONE

His name was Doug Titcombe, and before the plague he had been a greeter at a local superstore, the best job he had ever had. Until this one. At five foot five, prematurely bald, and with protruding front teeth, he looked ponylike, and the kids at the store often made neighing and snorting noises when he passed. Doug was thirty-five, looked fifty-five, and had a maturity level just shy of fifteen. Last year he'd been wearing a blue vest and a yellow name tag. Now he wore a camouflage jacket and carried a loaded .357 revolver.

"Should we tell?" Doug asked the young woman standing beside him. They were posted on the container wall that encircled Saint Miguel's property, at the farthest corner away from the church, the baseball field between them. Melanie, a twenty-year-old Chico State student, edged away from the nasty little troll with whom she had been paired for guard duty. A shotgun was slung over her shoulder.

"Mind your own business," said Melanie, her lip curling at the sight of him. The little troll never bathed, and his khakis were stained and stiff from never being washed. The two sentries watched as, half a block away, a trio of people with packs and weapons dropped to the far side of the wall and quickly vanished into the neighborhood. They had waited until the Bradley raced away and didn't look like it was coming back before they made their move.

"We should tell," Doug said, but didn't move. He looked at the girl for confirmation.

"Just shut up and keep watch." Melanie turned away to look at the intersection near their corner, two dog runs of corpses strung across the connecting streets. It was gross, and she could smell them even up here. She wished she were going with those wall jumpers. But no one had approached her to join. She was damaged goods.

In the beginning, hooking up with Little Emer's crew had seemed smart, with the promise of shelter, food, and safety. She had been given the duty of emptying shit buckets, however, and nothing could have been worse. One evening she had refused to do it, getting into an argument with another woman who told her she didn't have a choice. The angry words turned into a fight, rolling on the ground, throwing wild punches, the two women bloodying each other's nose. The bikers had appeared and watched, laughing. When Melanie came out as the winner, Little Emer had directed the beaten woman to take the shit detail, and promoted Melanie to standing watch on the wall.

Unfortunately, the beaten woman had been well liked, and now Melanie had become a pariah within the community. No one would speak to her.

Now here she was, partnered with this ugly little man, wishing she had been invited to run away with those others. That, however, would never happen.

I could go on my own, she thought. *Right now, no pack, just drop and run. I'll find food on the way, hook up with new people. They have to be out there.* Melanie found herself at the edge of the wall, staring out at the row of vacant houses across the street. Something crystal glittered briefly, maybe a sun catcher in a kitchen window. She would find a safe place and have a kitchen of her own.

Not far away, Doug stood worrying, fretting about not reporting the deserters. They had been told that bad people were coming to hurt them, to knock down their wall and let the dead into their home. The sentries had been ordered to shoot at anyone coming over the wall and raise the alarm, but what about people going *away* from the wall? No one had told him what to do if that happened.

Now here was Melanie, standing awfully close to the edge. He was afraid she would fall off and get hurt.

There was a thumping on the metal wall below where Melanie was standing, and both sentries looked down to see a corpse in a filthy Army uniform bumping repeatedly against the steel, reaching up and clutching toward Melanie's feet, sticking out over the edge. The girl looked down and let out a cry, then skittered away. She had been about to jump right down into the creature's arms. She put her face in her hands.

"Why are you crying?" Doug asked, moving toward her, wanting to put a reassuring hand on her back. He didn't, knowing she would jerk away and call him names. She didn't respond, just stood there hiding her tears, and he went back to biting his lip. What should he do about *this*? No one had told him what to do when his sentry partner started crying.

The bullet took Melanie's lower jaw off in a burst of teeth and bone, flinging her body off the wall and into the compound.

Doug stared. "Melanie?" He rushed to the edge where she had gone off, looking down at her body and all the blood around it. She was making a high squealing noise, hands fluttering weakly about her destroyed face. A bullet whipped off the steel next to Doug's feet. Neither shot made a sound, but Doug knew what a ricochet sounded like, and what it meant. He raised the .357 and looked around quickly. Should he shoot? At what? Should he run and tell?

"Melanie?" he called again. She had stopped moving down there on the grass.

He saw the truck racing toward the intersection from one of the cross streets, a flatbed type the towing companies used to pick up and carry the entire car, not just hook the front end. The deck was up, turned into a ramp. The vehicle plowed into one of the dog runs, scattering wire and corpses, and Doug saw a woman bail out the driver's door and roll just before the flatbed truck slammed into the wall where two containers met, knocking one askew.

The next bullet took Doug Titcombe just below the sternum and knocked him flat.

He couldn't breathe, felt heavy liquid in his throat and mouth, then the hot sensation as it bubbled past his lips and slid down both cheeks. His fingers clutched at the hole in his chest, getting slippery. Then he heard boots thudding up the tilted deck of the tow truck and saw two figures flash by him across the top of the container wall, a man and a woman dressed in a military style, loaded down with gear and weapons. They didn't even look at him as they passed and dropped down onto the baseball field.

Doug tried to speak, tried to breathe, could do neither as he gurgled and died. When the shooting began inside the compound, Doug Titcombe heard it with undead ears and crawled off the container in that direction, bumping briefly into Melanie, who was standing and swaying, staring at the dead pushing their way in through the gap in the containers created by the truck's impact. Both former sentries turned and joined the growing crowd of walking dead moving across the baseball field.

They moved together, husband and wife in body armor and combat harnesses, heavily laden with pouches of magazines and sidearms. Angie carried the silenced M4, handed back to her by Dean after he left his shooting position and joined her at the truck ramp. The Galil was across her back, and twin automatics hung beneath her armpits. Dean carried the AK-47, his MAC-10, and the ever-present Glock. They ran side by side, crossing the field toward the church and adjacent school.

"Hey!" yelled a voice from the right, a man with a rifle standing atop the wall fifty yards away. Angie stopped, knelt, and dropped him with a three-round silenced burst. Then they were running again.

Ahead, rising in a black line over the church's high peak, a column of smoke identified the place where Skye had sent in the gasoline-loaded truck. It was still burning and a string of blasts were going off ahead and to the left, beyond the buildings and walls, where Dean had rigged a line of cars to blow. The explosions boomed through the neighbor-hood, and Dean and Angie saw figures up ahead rushing along the wall and across the grounds toward the blasts, ready to defend against this new threat, unaware that death was already inside the perimeter.

"Greenhouse," Angie said, and they cut left, angling toward a long glass structure with a work truck parked outside. Someone had leashed a drifter to the front bumper, an old man in a bloody wife-beater, tugging against its chain. They ignored it.

Dean was puffing hard, pain flashing through his body like elec-tric shocks as the shrapnel wounds pulled against their dressings, several opening up and bleeding once more. Still, he bit it back and kept up with his wife.

Two men in baseball caps and carrying shotguns charged up the right side of the truck, yelling in surprise at the unexpected intrud-ers and bringing up their weapons. Dean sprayed them both across the chest with a three-round burst, cutting them down. The AK-47's raucous bark carried across the compound.

Angie passed the greenhouse and led them to the back of the school, then down its length, passing between the glass structure and the church. At the corner was a shelter canopy for an RV, the church parking lot, and the front gates to the wall. On their left, half a dozen people were crouched on top of the containers, looking out at the car fires Dean had arranged. Dean decided the insurgents he had fought overseas were better soldiers than these people.

Angie looked at her husband, who nodded. Dean's moral compass was that of a soldier inside the enemy's perimeter, but even more, the father of an abducted child. There would be no mercy. He stepped around the corner and switched to full auto, pouring fire into the people on the wall. All went down, some falling off. Husband and wife charged across open ground, not toward the church, but aiming for the structure they knew was the pool building, based on what Skye had described.

She's not in that pool, Angie thought, imagining the playpen.

The same thought went through Dean's mind as they reached the building's back door.

They're hitting us from all sides!" a young man shouted, running into the chapel wearing a hooded sweatshirt and carrying a pistol. "I think they're inside the walls!"

Little Emer, Red Hen, and Stark were standing near a folding table covered in ammunition, loading magazines. They had heard the explosions, followed shortly by automatic weapon fire just outside the church itself.

"Then get out there and *kill them!*" Little Emer shouted. The boy disappeared.

The Bradley's crew wasn't responding to radio calls. That son of a bitch Corrigan had either deserted or died. There were reports of sentries fleeing over the walls, and those who remained couldn't find anything to shoot at. His daddy had been right, after all. At least the bastard hadn't lived to say, *I told you so.* Nope, that was one dead old man. It made him smile.

Now it was time to bail.

"We ready?" Little Emer asked Red Hen, slipping long magazines of nine-millimeter for the Uzi into the pockets of his leather jacket.

The balding biker nodded, shoving assault rifle magazines into his waistband. "The bikes are inside the greenhouse, with full saddlebags. We'll be good until we get a chance to resupply on the road."

"What about the drums?" the warlord asked.

Stark tucked a snub-nosed revolver into the small of his back. "All set. We'll light it up on the way out."

Little Emer nodded and hung a pair of Chico Police Department flash-bangs from his belt. All three men were wearing police body armor under their leathers. "Let's go," the junior Briggs—now the *only* Briggs—said.

The same kid in the hooded sweatshirt sagged back into the chapel through the same door. The color had gone out of his face, and he was clutching a red, dripping hand. He stared at the three bikers dumbly. "Bit me," he said.

A corpse stumbled through the doorway behind him, a red thumb jutting from its moving jaws, and fell upon the boy. The bikers ran from the chapel, heading for the pool building and the drums Stark had prepared, screams chasing after them.

F ires burned in the streets, and the dead pushed through the gap in the wall, spreading out across the grounds. Sporadic firing sounded from isolated points around the perimeter but tapered off. An odd silence settled over Saint Miguel for a moment.

It was broken as Angie and Dean burst into the swimming pool building the same moment the bikers entered opposite them from the door to the church. There was a second of shock and recognition. Tiny moans rose from the pool, the corpse of a woman jerked against her chains, and in the center of the room, standing between the two groups, a dozen fifty-five-gallon drums were linked by a single line of gas-soaked rags.

Angie recognized the woman chained to the wall.

Little Emer recognized the armed man who should have been nailed to a cross.

Husband and wife saw the biker who had stolen their child, and gunfire erupted.

There was no cover, only the fuel-filled drums, so Dean dropped to one knee and sent a tight three-round burst of 7.62-millimeter toward the bikers. Stark's assault rifle rattled, chipping at tile and punching a pair of holes in a gasoline barrel. Fuel gurgled out onto the floor. Angie dove left to the floor, then triggered three fast rounds as Red Hen blasted back indiscriminately at both of them. Little Emer sprayed the Uzi wildly before ducking back out the door.

Stark went down.

Dean went down.

Red Hen screamed and ran at Angie, still firing on full automatic. Bullets clipped through the air, close enough the make Angie's hair move by her ear. Angie dropped her empty M4 and pulled a nine-millimeter from a shoulder holster. Red Hen pointed his M16 at her face and pulled the trigger on a dry magazine.

Angie's pistol barked four times; crotch, belly, throat, forehead. The balding biker slid to the tiles in a pool of blood and gasoline.

"Dean?" Angie crouched beside her fallen husband, keeping an eye—and a pistol—on the door the bikers had used. The first one lay in the same position in which he had fallen after Dean cut him down, and the biggest one did not reappear. "Dean?" she repeated, lifting him into a sitting position.

"Ohh, that hurts," Dean said through gritted teeth, pressing his hands to his chest, where a pair of slugs had flattened against the Kevlar over his sternum. Angie helped him to his feet, making sure he could stand before letting go. Their nostrils flared, and they glanced at the lake of fuel as it spread across the tiles and began spilling over the edge of the pool, down onto the heads of rotten, squirming figures. More gasoline flowed between the torn, gray feet of Angie's mother.

"See if she's in there," Dean said, looking toward the pool. "We have to know."

Angie nodded and moved to the edge of the pool, not looking at her mother over by the wall, not wanting to look down when she came to the tiled edge. She did, and sucked in a breath, covering her mouth with one hand, a sudden ache in her chest. They were so little, the small moaning shapes reaching upward with small hands that would never again color or play, would never touch another person with affection. Lost to one world, condemned to another. Angie let out a sob as she forced herself to scan every face. *Not here.*

Angie returned to her husband with tears in her eyes. "She's not in there," she sobbed, throwing her arms around Dean and holding him tight. "He still has her somewhere."

Dean nodded. "End this," he said, gesturing toward the pool.

Together they went back to the door through which they had entered, checked to see if it was clear, then went out. Dean covered with his AK-47 as Angie pulled a pencil flare from a pocket, one of several taken from the *Nimitz* armory. She lit it, then tossed the red, sputtering glow back into the pool building, where it landed amid the fifty-five-gallon drums. They ran.

Angie and Dean made it to the corner of the nearby church, finding cover behind its stone and stucco construction. Fire exploded behind them, balls of red and black blowing out windows and doors, sounding like an enraged dragon. They heard a noise behind them and turned just in time to see Little Emer, fifty feet away, sweep them both with Uzi fire.

Angie and Dean crumpled, and Emer Briggs ran past them, headed for the greenhouse.

THIRTY-TWO

January 13—Chico State University

Skye ran, her lungs and legs pumping. Her ankle hadn't been twisted badly, and she couldn't feel the pain right now. The more she ran, however, the worse it would get. There was no other choice.

Buildings flashed by, university lecture halls and administrative offices on one side of the street, a row of Victorian homes on the other. A dozen of these buildings had been shaken into the street by the earthquake, creating heaps of brick and timber, broken glass and twisted plumbing. Some of the newer admin buildings had lost their windows while others were missing entire walls, office floors standing exposed to the outside. The dead shuffled through the ruins, across debris-littered lawns, and among cars abandoned in the street. They turned stiffly toward her as she passed.

An inhuman scream split the air behind her, more terrible than the cry of a mountain wildcat, a thing freshly emerged from hell. Skye ran faster.

She went left off West Sacramento and onto Warner Street, her

course taking her through the heart of Chico State. Corpses lum-
bered among the trees of small groves and stumbled over curbs,
drawn to her movement. Skye pulled her machete on the run,
swinging at those creatures too close to avoid, chopping deep into
the sides of their heads before yanking the blade free. She dared not
spend much time in the killing because bare feet were slapping the
pavement behind her, and they were getting closer.

A dead woman in an open hospital gown galloped from behind
a wrecked campus police car, tripping over a suitcase and landing
on her face before she could reach Skye. A gas station attendant covered in blackened burns howled and lunged from the left, and Skye
dodged right. A corrupted thing in the uniform of a SkyWest pilot
charged at her from the front, arms raised, and Skye leaped right
again, vaulting over an empty bicycle rack and onto a sidewalk.

Her ankle sent a hot message of agony up her leg when she landed,
but she forced herself to keep going.

The Hobgoblin let out another wildcat shriek as it closed, shoving through drifters and knocking them aside. The corpses wavered
and looked at the running red creature, unsure of its nature. There
was no shared experience, no language. It moved like food but it
was not food.

When the Hobgoblin ducked between the cars and leaped at the
bike rack, its foot caught on the top rail and it tumbled to the sidewalk, gashing its broad forehead on the cement and losing ground.
The wound did not bleed, only leaked a dark, tar-like trickle. In seconds the creature was scrambling to its feet once more.

Nettleton Stadium sat on the west side of the campus, and Skye
sprinted through its nearly vacant parking lot, racing for the left
side of the big structure. Open gates beckoned to shadowy stadium
tunnels, but Skye feared they would become death traps and aimed
for a lone groundskeeper's truck instead. When she reached it she
turned, jerking the silenced pistol from her holster and extending

her arm back across the hood, aiming at the running figure only a hundred feet away.

She squeezed the trigger fifteen times in rapid succession, the tendons of her forearm jumping beneath the skin. Bullets tapped the pavement, hissed past its body, thudded into its thighs, belly, chest, and shoulder as she walked her aim up. The Hobgoblin moved left suddenly toward one of the few vehicles in the lot, a panel van displaying a radio station logo in black and yellow. Rounds fourteen and fifteen punched through the sheet metal side. Skye ejected the spent clip, slapped in another, and started running once more.

The howl sounded again, a piercing, wild cry that made the hairs on her neck stand up. It would be coming, but she didn't dare look back.

Down the side of the stadium brought her to a six-foot chain-link fence, and she holstered both pistol and machete before throwing herself at it, the toes of her combat boots jamming into the links, digging for purchase as she climbed to the top, hauling herself up. Any second those dead, powerful hands would catch her and rip her off the fence—but then she was over, landing in a crouch and turning. The pistol flashed out and she gripped it in two hands, finger on the trigger, ready to take out the Hobgoblin as it chased her toward the fence.

Nothing.

She had expected it to be right behind her, but there was nothing there, only a trio of rotting, moaning men and woman, drawn to her movement and walking toward the fence in a broken slouch. Skye looked left and right to see if the monster was scaling the fence farther down from her. Again, nothing.

She chose left and began running again, up a slant of cinders and pebbles and onto train tracks that flowed past the stadium. Down the embankment to her left was a wandering, unpainted board fence, untended and weathered, shielding a residential area from the tracks. Up ahead, the tail end of a passenger train sat on the rails. *Cover.* She headed for it, her ankle beginning to throb.

In minutes she came upon the train and instantly realized that the car she had seen was the last in a line, and the only one still standing on the tracks. The rest was a zigzag of crumpled passenger cars, some lying on their sides, others overturned, thrust one atop the other like jumbled straws. Twisted bits of metal and carpets of broken glass glittered in the weeds beside the tracks. As she skirted to the left, she could see a spot up ahead where the engine—well beyond its rails—had plowed a furrow through a pair of houses. The ground looked as if a madman with a bulldozer had done indiscriminate digging, and even trees had been uprooted by the force and violence of the crash.

Skye could only imagine the sound it must have made, a mix of thunder and shrieking metal. There couldn't have been any survivors, she thought as she trotted around an overturned car, forced to slow down because of the debris. She was right. The gray face of a child suddenly slammed against a passenger car window, small fingers clawing at the glass. It snarled and moved out of sight, looking for a way out of its prison in order to reach the food moving beyond the window.

The massive tangle of railroad cars had the way ahead completely blocked, and Skye had no intention of trying to negotiate the maze of steel and shattered glass. She imagined the trapped corpses waiting in there, ready to snatch her into the darkness. Even if she had been brave enough to try it, there would be no place to run if the monster showed up again. She knew it would. She was under no illusion that it had given up the hunt.

Skye headed over to what was left of the board fence, moving to the point where the train had torn through it. Here she found rusty smears like old paint and she hesitated, not wanting to go on. She forced herself to move, though. Standing still was an invitation to death.

Movement is life, a voice from her past called.

Beyond was a brown yard with patches of dirt poking through, a rusty swing set, and a nineties-era Ford Bronco without tires, resting on cinder blocks. Pistol in one hand and the bared machete in the other, she crossed the yard and slipped down the side of a tract house with peeling paint and rusting window screens, through a chain-link gate, and onto a driveway with weeds growing through the cracks.

Before her were ruins.

The house she had just passed appeared to be one of only a handful that had survived the earthquake's destruction. Old and poorly built to begin with, the tract houses had been shoved off their cement foundations and crushed. To Skye, it looked like one of those shattered neighborhoods on the news, some community in Oklahoma or the Midwest ripped apart by a tornado.

The fronts and backs of buried vehicles peered from the rubble, and the street was littered with fragments of two-by-fours, roofing material, and broken porcelain. Glass sparkled across the pavement like a blanket of diamonds. A jagged fissure three feet wide wandered up the center of the street, widening as it traveled left, until it was fifteen feet across. The nose of a Peterbilt truck poked out of the crack where it was at its widest, and Skye wondered if the entire eighteen-wheeler was down there beneath the cab.

The crash of something hitting chain link came from behind her, and Skye spun, firing four quick rounds. The Hobgoblin, on the other side of the gate through which she had just passed, turned and raced back into the yard with the swing set and Bronco on blocks, leaping out of sight behind the house, fleeing the pistol. One round hit it in the back, another in the buttocks. Neither slowed the creature.

Skye leaped over the fissure where it was three feet wide and moved left, sprinting beside the widening crack, past the swallowed tractor-trailer, weaving around crushed cars and piles of wood that had once been houses. The dead moaned. Some were trapped beneath debris, others shuffled through the ruins or climbed over fallen beams, but all of them tried to reach her. A drifter kneeling in the road ahead, feasting on a rotting coyote, looked up and hissed. Skye swung the machete as she raced past, lopping its head completely off.

Suddenly, running feet were behind her again, glass fragments burying in crimson flesh. The Hobgoblin let out its hellish shriek, and Skye spun, the pistol coming up as she squeezed off shots. It was close, twenty feet away, and a bullet took it in the throat, punching through what was left of its windpipe. The creature leaped left and out of sight, into the wide crevasse in the road where the tractor-trailer had been consumed. Skye heard its body thump against metal, followed by the long scratch of scrabbling nails digging at the trailer's side.

She darted around a mound of debris where a house had collapsed onto a small car and ran down a new street. She *thought* it was a street, though it was hard to tell amid the destruction. There were corpses ahead, dozens of them already in the road or emerging from the wreckage on both sides. She reversed and ran back to the road with the fissure, pistol arm extended, sighting for the cherry-red zombie.

It wasn't there. She ran another block to the right.

Skye's lungs were beginning to burn, her thighs and calves screaming, and the twisted ankle pulsed with electric prods. She had another block left in her, she thought, maybe two, and then she would be run out. She came to a point in the road where two houses had collapsed across their seedy lawns on either side of the street, falling toward one another. They created walls of rubble to the right and left, with a narrow gap between them. It was here that Skye stopped and turned, ready to make her stand. Chest heaving, arms leaden, she raised the pistol.

The Hobgoblin was there, racing up the street at her, teeth bared. Skye fired three quick rounds, all misses. She cursed and tried to steady her aim.

A hit to the chest.

A miss.

A hit to the cheek that blew out teeth and sheared off an ear.

The Hobgoblin didn't flinch, and accelerated. It was making its stand too.

PUFFT-PUFFT-PUFFT. Skye squeezed and squeezed, bullets hissing past or slamming harmlessly into its muscled chest. *CLICK.* The hammer fell on an empty magazine. Too close to try reloading. Skye took a wide stance, raising the machete that now felt as if it weighed a hundred pounds. Her heart was a timpani drum in her ears, her muscles and lungs screaming for oxygen, and she sobbed against the pain as her ankle trembled and then gave out beneath her.

Skye collapsed to one knee just as the Hobgoblin let out a wild-cat scream and leaped, slamming into her, taking her to the ground.

THIRTY-THREE

January 13—Saint Miguel

Dean gasped, let out a long groan, and tried to rise. The best he could do was prop himself into a sitting position against the outside wall of the church. He was pale, and the clothing on his left side was a dark red. He put his hands to his chest, where the body armor had absorbed yet more rounds—breaking three ribs and making it hard to breathe—then pressed his palm to his left hip. It came away slick with blood.

"Ang?" he said, looking to the slumped form of his wife. She was groaning too, crawling to her hands and knees, vomiting into the grass.

"Vest," she choked, rising and holding her chest. The dull gray of two flattened slugs was pressed into the Kevlar fabric at her stomach and sternum. She looked at her husband, saw the blood, and went to him.

Dean tried a smile, his voice a wheeze. "Took one in the hip. Don't think I can stand." He struggled for a deep breath. "Think it's broken."

Angie reached for him, but Dean shook his head.

"Kill him," he said. "Kill him and get our girl back."

His wife nodded and climbed to her feet, the pain visible on her face. After a few faltering steps, she picked up speed and ran toward the sound of a motorcycle engine throttling behind glass. The Galil rose to her shoulder.

"Kill that fucker," Dean whispered, closing his eyes.

L eah was strapped to a chair in the dirty little greenhouse room the elder Briggs had used for sleeping quarters. Her hands and feet were bound with duct tape, and still more was wound about her to secure her to the chair. A bandana was tied around her mouth as a gag. Her eyes were red from crying, but still she struggled against the tape and chewed at the bandana.

The big, scary man strode into the office and the three-year-old squeezed her eyes shut. He used a large knife to cut the gag away, then showed her the blade.

"We're going for a ride, baby."

"*Not* a baby!" Leah yelled. "I want my daddy!"

Little Emer cut the tape away to free her from the chair, then tucked her, struggling, under one arm.

"Bad! Bad!" Leah screamed. "Daddy! *Daaddeee!*"

The warlord carried her back into the greenhouse, where a trio of Harleys, each heavily loaded with supplies, was lined up in front of the wide, open rear double doors. Beyond lay the baseball field, dotted with staggering corpses, and beyond that was the container wall and the compound's rear gate. He could have it open in seconds, and then be gone.

Little Emer straddled his hog and started the engine, throttling, pinning Leah against his thighs and stomach. "Stop fighting me, baby girl, or you'll fall off. Don't want the monsters to eat you, do we?"

Leah screamed.

Groundhog-7 roared across the rooftops of Chico, its powerful blades thumping at the air. In the cockpit, Vladimir had the aircraft's nose pointed at the only thing that might help him find his friends, black smoke rising from a residential neighborhood. It could be nothing. Or it could mean that Angie, Skye, and Carney were tangling with the scum who had burned the Franks ranch. He had no contact with them. It was his only shot.

"Door gunner," he said over the intercom, "prepare to engage."

In the troop compartment, Halsey leaned out into space with the M240 pointed below him. "Ready," was all he said.

Vladimir Yurish opened the throttle, and the Black Hawk's turbines screamed.

Angie burst through the greenhouse door, rifle to her shoulder and muzzle sweeping in an arc, ready to destroy anything in front of her. The sweet, warm smell of pot assaulted her at once.

"*Daaddeee!*" her daughter cried from the rear of the building, concealed somewhere behind a wall of tall, leafy green plants. Angie sprinted toward her daughter's voice, lips peeling back from her teeth, and hands gripping the Galil so tightly her knuckles cracked. A rising snarl came from her throat.

The motorcycle engine revved twice and then roared, echoing off the glass walls and ceiling for an instant before dropping away into the outside air.

"No!" Angie cried, bursting through the high wall of plants.

. . .

The Black Hawk exploded over the high peak of an old Victorian and dipped as Vladimir hauled on his controls, banking left and putting Halsey in view of what lay below. Several buildings, including what looked like a damaged church, were ringed by a wall made of steel shipping containers. The walking dead moved through the street on the outside, shuffling past a row of burning cars. On the top of the wall, three armed people were running toward a gate, but they stopped and stared at the sudden appearance of a military helicopter overhead.

Halsey had seen the aftermath of the ranch. He needed no command from the cockpit.

The M240 chattered in a long staccato that sent 7.62-millimeter tracer rounds down to punch holes in the containers and chop the three defenders to pieces. The ranch hand stopped firing and spit tobacco.

Vladimir was already banking right, moving the Black Hawk over the wall and across the compound. Bullets fired from somewhere below rattled off the aircraft's armored belly, but the pilot ignored the ground fire.

"Target," he called, accelerating.

Angie pushed through the tall cannabis in time to see a single motorcycle roaring across the baseball field, a plume of turf kicking up in a rooster tail from its rear tire. She snapped the Galil up and sighted on the broad back of the rider, aiming at the patch on his biker jacket.

Then she caught a glimpse of Leah's head to one side, her open mouth screaming in the wind, held tightly against the biker's lap. Angie couldn't risk the shot, couldn't risk hitting her daughter.

"No," she cried, sprinting from the greenhouse, chasing the Harley that got farther away every second.

Little Emer aimed the hog at the far gate, barely noticing the dead creatures moving across the grass all around him, still flowing in through a gap in the wall ahead and to his right. Over the roar of the Harley's engine, he heard a heavy thumping and what he imagined a tornado might sound like, somewhere behind him, now above him. No matter. His attention was on the gate, and freedom beyond.

It would only take seconds to unbolt the gate and roll it aside wide enough to get the bike through. He could do it one-handed and still hold on to the girl. She would make a good diversion if he was cornered by the dead, just drop her and escape while they fed.

"Almost there, baby!" he shouted at the screaming girl.

The Harley slid to a halt at the far gate, and Little Emer dismounted, struggling to unbolt it as Leah squirmed under one arm. He pulled at the metal slab, finding it heavier than he remembered, and he tried to use his other hand. In that moment, Leah sank her teeth into his forearm and he snarled, dropping her.

Leah West hit the ground and ran from the bad man as fast as she could.

"Bitch!" Emer shouted, turning to pursue.

Suddenly a massive black shape dropped from the sky between him and the fleeing child, a nightmare of sound and wind and whirling blades that stopped its descent to hover less than six feet off the ground. The girl was now shielded by a protective wall of destruction.

Little Emer lunged for the motorcycle as he saw what was in the helicopter's doorway.

. . .

Not today, Hoss," Halsey said, letting the M240 rip.

Biker and motorcycle were shredded in a close-range storm of lead.

Angie ignored the walking dead all around her, ignored the Black Hawk and even the spectacular death of the man who had taken her daughter. She raced across the open ground toward the small figure running toward her across the grass. She dropped to her knees when she reached the little girl, gathering her into her arms. "Leah! Oh, God, baby. Leah!"

The little girl hugged her tightly, then blinked and looked up. "Hi, Mommy. *Not* a baby."

Angie burst into tears and laughter, holding her daughter closer than she ever had.

THIRTY-FOUR

January 13—West Chico

Skye was facedown, the weight above her savaging her back with broken nails. She couldn't fight this way and refused to die in this position. Putting all her power under her, she pushed up and rolled. The Hobgoblin was thrown for an instant, but then it scrambled back onto her. It was heavier than Skye, but she was more fit, and strong. Unfortunately her energy was all but used up, and the creature seemed tireless.

Straddling her, it shrieked its wildcat noise in her face and came at her with ragged claws. Skye threw up an arm, only to have it wrenched away. The thing's smooth, crimson face was twisted into a mask of insanity as it darted in with its head, teeth snapping.

With her other hand, Skye smashed it in the side of the head with the butt of the machete. It reared back for an instant, and she drove her other palm into its chin. It snapped, barely missing her fingers, then lunged back in for a bite. The creature began slashing with the broken nails of both curled hands, ripping at her clothing and body armor, catching flesh and digging red grooves. Its milky eyes were filled with an intelligent yet inhuman fury, and viscous black spittle sprayed past its clicking teeth.

It pinned Skye's left hand to her chest, leaning in as she swung the machete blade. The last time she had done this was on a street outside an Oakland church, and the zombie had gushed vile liquid into her face, heralding the slow burn. What would this thing's fluids do?

The blade bit into its shoulder instead, cutting to the bone. The Hobgoblin appeared not to feel it, but instead twisted its body sharply. The move tore the weapon from Skye's hand and sent it clattering across the pavement. The Hobgoblin caught her other wrist and pinned it to the asphalt, both her hands immobilized now. Its jaws widened and it lunged. Skye grunted and slipped a knee up between its legs, raising it high and planting the knee hard against its chest.

The Hobgoblin's teeth snapped but came up short. It couldn't get close enough to bite with Skye's knee between them, and it howled. Skye choked on the sour reek of the thing, the tainted air from gray, rotting lungs rising and seeping from its mouth. It squeezed her wrists at the same time and she screamed, waiting to hear the bones crack.

Then suddenly the Hobgoblin released her arms and clamped its cold, powerful hands to the sides of her head. Skye's eyes widened as in an instant she remembered Mr. Sorkin's decapitated head resting on the lab box outside the medical office, twisted off by this very creature. Skye screamed again, and the thing howled with her as the muscles in its arms bulged.

P-P-POP.

A three-round burst hit the Hobgoblin in a tight cluster just above the bridge of its nose. Its howling face disintegrated in a blast of bone and black ichor, the top of its skull sheared off. In that second the pressure against the sides of Skye's head vanished. The body went limp and heavy atop her, and with a disgusted grunt she pitched it to the side.

Combat boots scooted across the pavement beside her, two pairs, and she rolled over again, coming up to her hands and knees. Two men, both in gray-green military uniforms, each with a shoulder patch depicting a coiled snake under an American flag, ran up almost on top of her. One, a young black man with a severe Mohawk, leveled the muzzle of an M4 at the dead Hobgoblin. The second man, older and with sergeant stripes pinned to his uniform blouse, advanced and with his own machete took what was left of the creature's head off at the neck.

Skye blinked. "Thanks," she muttered, noticing that the sergeant was a corpse, or at least looked like one at first glance. His skin was completely gray, mottled with irregular patches of white, and he was hairless, including his eyebrows. He looked at her for a moment with eyes that held no color other than the black pupils, a startling, reptilian stare. Then he turned without a word and jogged back up the street.

The black soldier's name patch read *MOORE*. "Let's go," he said, turning to run after his sergeant. Skye stood slowly, collected her fallen pistol and machete, then trotted after them.

The neighborhood dead were closing on all the noise, and they surged up the street past the swallowed tractor-trailer in a pack of more than a hundred, quickly flowing through the narrow space between the two houses that had fallen toward each other. Their moans echoed through the ruins. More drifters staggered from a side street and out of tangles of brick and broken wood, joining the mass.

As she ran, trying not to cry out because of her ankle, and now the new claw marks on her chest, Skye could see four more men in the same uniforms assembled in the center of the road ahead, all with packs and rifles. One of them, a man about ten years older than Skye, with captain's bars on his uniform, gave some hand signals to his men. Without a word they formed a single-file line and began running up the street, away from the surge. The pale sergeant with the machete fell in behind them.

Moore grabbed Skye by her combat harness and gave her a sharp tug. "If you can't keep up, we'll leave you behind."

"I can keep up," she said, glaring at the young black soldier.

He nodded and turned. Then there was only running.

The captain kept them moving at a steady running pace for more than half an hour. Skye thought her legs were burning before. The officer led at the point, followed immediately by the pale sergeant and then a soldier with a belt-fed machine gun hanging across his chest by a strap. They moved out of the neighborhood, avoiding a sprawling, built-up area of what looked like university dorms, then down a long two-lane road dotted with motels, gas stations, and cheap diners.

Other than a few solitary drifters, they left the dead behind.

When they reached the turn-off for the Ranchero Airport, it occurred to Skye that these men must have gotten here somehow; perhaps they had a plane or a helicopter waiting. But there was nothing on the tarmac other than a burned fuel truck next to the blackened framework of a small private plane. The soldiers ran for a hangar, checked inside before entering, and then pulled the rolling doors closed behind them.

Bedrolls, equipment, some spare weapons, and a cluster of packaged food and bottled water were collected at the near end of the hangar, maintenance equipment occupying the rest of the space. Two of the soldiers took guard positions at the front and back as the others settled in and immediately began breaking down their weapons for cleaning. The captain gestured for Skye to sit in a folding chair near the gear. She did, and the sergeant with the bleached skin knelt in front of her with a small medical pack, quickly unlacing her boot and pulling it off.

"I'm fine," Skye said, trying to pull her leg away. "I'm not bitten." The sergeant trying to tend to her glared with his pinpoint eyes.

"No, you're not," said the captain, as the wound was revealed. "I saw you limping. Hopefully it's just a sprain. Let Oscar look at it."

Skye relented, watching as the sergeant held her calf and turned her foot, inspecting the ankle. Skye hissed. "Go easy, okay?" The sergeant said nothing and produced a cold pack, crushing it in his hands and rubbing the plastic vigorously. He wrapped it around the ankle and secured it with a bandage. Skye gritted her teeth, refusing to let the man hear her cry out a second time. Then she looked up at the captain. "You're not worried I'm bitten?"

"You're a burn victim," the captain said. "Survived a fluid exposure, right?"

Skye nodded.

"Then you're immune. Just like him." He nodded at the sergeant. "But if you can't walk, you'll be just as dead as if the virus took you." The captain waited while the sergeant pressed two white pills into Skye's hand. "Advil," the officer said, and offered her a canteen. Skye washed them down.

"Captain Lee Salinger," he said, extending a hand. "U.S. Army Rangers."

Skye shook it, watching the sergeant pack his medical gear, looking at his pale, blotchy skin and those frightening eyes. He glanced up once from his work, lifted his lip in what could have been a sneer or an attempt at a smile, then moved away to join the other men.

"I'm Skye Dennison," she said. "And thanks for killing that thing. What the hell was it?"

"We've never seen anything like it before," he said.

"I saw it once, a couple of days ago. It ducked my rifle. It's smart."

Captain Salinger stood with his arms folded, looking at his guest. Then he nodded slowly, making Skye wonder why.

THIRTY-FIVE

January 13—Saint Miguel

Leah was belted into the co-pilot's seat of the Black Hawk, clutching a battered Wawas and wearing the oversized earmuffs of a radio headset. She stared at Vladimir in wide-eyed wonder as he held the aircraft in a hover thirty feet above the baseball field. Hooked into his safety harness behind them, perched behind the port door gun, Halsey tracked the M240 left and right, searching for live targets. He wasn't interested in the dead things wandering below; they couldn't shoot at the chopper. He saw no one.

"I have a little boy your age," Vladimir said, and Leah blinked when his voice came through the headset she was wearing. She patted the earpieces and smiled.

"His name is Ben," said the pilot. "You will meet him very soon."

Leah bit her lip. "Is he a bad boy?"

The Russian smiled and shook his head. "No, little one. He is a very good boy."

"I want my mommy and daddy."

Vladimir patted her knee with a big hand. "They are coming."

On the ground, Angie stalked across the open field with the Galil to her shoulder, watching left and right, moving steadily toward the church. Most of the dead had been drawn to the noise and motion of the helicopter hovering to her rear. When she neared the corner of the building where Dean would be, she slowed, suddenly afraid that she would find a drifter crouched over him, feeding.

She found three drifters.

They were dead, lying crumpled on the grass a dozen feet from her husband, each with a head wound. Dean was slumped against the wall, the Glock in his lap.

He opened one eye. "Leah."

"She's safe," Angie breathed, kneeling beside him. Dean closed his eye and nodded slowly. He was so very pale. "We're going to get you to the helicopter," Angie said, slinging one of his arms around her shoulder and lifting. Dean got to his feet with a groan, favoring his bloody hip.

They moved slowly back toward the baseball field, and then Angie lowered him gently to the ground. "Give me a minute," she said, then unslung the Galil and her bandolier of magazines. She worked for ten minutes, aiming and shooting, firing in all directions, dropping empty magazines and loading fresh. Dean lay on the grass, propped up on one elbow, watching their backs as his wife finished off every drifter within a hundred feet of the helicopter.

"You made that look easy," he said as she lifted him once more.

"I've had a lot of practice the last few months."

He chuckled, his voice soft. "I'll bet."

The Black Hawk settled in front of them, and Halsey was there to help them aboard. In the front seat, a little girl looked back and cried, "Daddy!"

Groundhog-7 flew slow circles above Chico for an hour, all eyes looking down, searching for Skye. Of their friend, there was no trace. Finally Vladimir spoke over the intercom.

"Time to leave. It is a matter of fuel."

Angie stared down at streets where only the dead moved. There were no waving figures, no signals, only a city that no longer belonged to the living. Skye had left them on a one-way trip, and because of it, Angie and Dean's little girl was safe and with them once more.

Thank you, Angie thought, her tears whipped away in the wind from the rotors. "Vlad, take us home," she said into the intercom. The Russian banked his Black Hawk to a southwest course and quickly put Chico behind them.

"Daddy," Leah said, looking back into the troop compartment from her seat up front, "we're going on a boat." Her mother had told her about the *Nimitz*, at least as much as a three-year-old could understand. Dean smiled and winked at his daughter.

"That's right, honey," Angie said. "We're going someplace safe."

THIRTY-SIX

January 13—Ranchero Airport

Skye stood with the Rangers on the tarmac outside the hangar, one boot off, leaning on the soldier Moore's shoulder. Everyone watched as the Black Hawk, already tiny, became a distant speck and disappeared completely. They had no radio, no flares. No way to make contact.

"There goes our ride," Moore said. The other soldiers nodded.

Captain Salinger had told Skye the only reason they had come across her battling the zombie hybrid was that they had heard the helicopter over the city and were trying to get close enough to signal it. He also told her he and his team had been on the outskirts of Chico for days, ever since their own helicopter had been shot down.

"Your *own* helicopter? How—where did you come from?"

"Long story," Salinger said. "We'll have time to tell you the whole thing. I'll bet you have a good story of your own." He mentally caught himself, regretting the words. The haunted look in this girl's one good eye said she had a story, but there was nothing good about it.

"In the meantime," he said, clearing his throat, "we're headed back to base, and it doesn't look like we're flying. Best make sure your boots are laced tight. It's a long walk to Reno."

Skye looked at him, confused. Moore handed her a bandolier of magazines, followed by an M4. "Ever seen one of these?"

Skye snatched the weapon from him, ejected the magazine to ensure it was full, then reinserted and armed the weapon. "We're old friends."

"That's good," the captain said, "because it looks like you're with us."

They set out within the hour, six Army Rangers walking east, a young woman with an eye patch and an assault rifle walking last in line, wearing a new backpack. Captain Salinger said they would be looking for vehicles soon, something to get them into the mountains. At least until the snow forced them to go ahead on foot.

Skye had questions, but for now she kept them to herself. Her heart was aching, for Carney, for her friends, but she used the silence of these serious young men to help wrap the pain away. In that, she found a measure of peace.

The Hobgoblin had red hair, reborn in this new form under a midnight sky outside Saint Miguel. Now she kept out of sight as she stalked the small party on foot, her hybrid mind a dark jumble of sensations, the strongest of all being hunger and a craving for violence.

She stayed half a mile back, and unerringly followed their trail.

ACKNOWLEDGMENTS

I want to thank my editor, Amanda Ng, for her critical eye and skillful collaboration, her ability to stand her ground when changes had to be made, and yield when her author wouldn't. I didn't make it easy for her, but as a result of her guidance, I came out the other end of this project a better writer (I hope) and delivered a better novel (I know).

Special appreciation goes to Jennifer for her continued support, and to all the wonderful people at Berkley for making this possible. Finally, I want to thank my family, friends, and readers for believing in the story, and the writer.